MISS CAYLEY'S ADVENTURES

Ex Libris
Mary Wildman
Fiction

"I AM GOING OUT, SIMPLY IN SEARCH OF ADVENTURE."

VALANCOURT CLASSICS

MISS CAYLEY'S ADVENTURES

BY

GRANT ALLEN

Introduction by Elizabeth Foxwell

Kansas City:
VALANCOURT BOOKS
2008

Miss Cayley's Adventures by Grant Allen
Originally published London: Grant Richards, 1899
First Valancourt Books edition 2008

Introduction © 2008 by Elizabeth Foxwell
This edition © 2008 by Valancourt Books

Library of Congress Cataloguing-in-Publication Data

Allen, Grant, 1848-1899.
Miss Cayley's adventures / by Grant Allen ; introduction by
Elizabeth Foxwell. – 1st Valancourt Books ed.
p. cm. – (Valancourt classics)
ISBN 1-934555-43-6 (alk. paper)
I. Title.
PR4004.A2M57 2008
823'.8–dc22

2008004986

Design and typography by James D. Jenkins
Published by Valancourt Books
Kansas City, Missouri
http://www.valancourtbooks.com

CONTENTS

Introduction   vii

Miss Cayley's Adventures   I

I   THE ADVENTURE OF THE CANTANKEROUS OLD LADY   3
2   THE ADVENTURE OF THE SUPERCILIOUS *ATTACHÉ*   22
3   THE ADVENTURE OF THE INQUISITIVE AMERICAN   4I
4   THE ADVENTURE OF THE AMATEUR COMMISSION AGENT   58
5   THE ADVENTURE OF THE IMPROMPTU MOUNTAINEER   76
6   THE ADVENTURE OF THE URBANE OLD GENTLEMAN   93
7   THE ADVENTURE OF THE UNOBTRUSIVE OASIS   II2
8   THE ADVENTURE OF THE PEA-GREEN PATRICIAN   130
9   THE ADVENTURE OF THE MAGNIFICENT MAHARAJAH   147
IO   THE ADVENTURE OF THE CROSS-EYED Q.C.   164
II   THE ADVENTURE OF THE ORIENTAL ATTENDANT   183
I2   THE ADVENTURE OF THE UNPROFESSIONAL DETECTIVE   198

INTRODUCTION

In Praise of "Vulgar Stories"

I dropped into romance as many men drop into drink, or opium eating, or other bad practices, not of native perversity, but by pure force of circumstances. And this is how fate (or an enterprising publisher) turned me from an innocent and impecunious naturalist into a devotee of the muse of shilling shockers.

—Grant Allen, "'Physiological Aesthetics'" 43

As can be seen above, author Grant Allen thought little of his popular fiction works, referring to fiction writing as a "downward path" and even terming his work at one point "vulgar stories" ("'Physiological Aesthetics'" 49; qtd. in Morton 128). Like his friend and neighbor Arthur Conan Doyle, who hoped to be remembered for his historical novels rather than his Sherlock Holmes stories (see Stashower), Allen regarded his scientific journalism as preeminent and his mysteries and sensation-oriented works as checks that paid the bills. Yet when he tried to inject serious commentary on marriage and motherhood into his New Woman novel *The Woman Who Did* (1895), he unleashed a firestorm of criticism that continues today,[1] casting his mysteries, science fiction, and paranormal works into an undeserved shade, including his notable contribution as the creator of early, independent female detectives.

In a career that spanned twenty-two years, Allen was a veritable dynamo of literary output, producing more than 30 books, more than 150 short stories, and hundreds of articles despite his frequently poor health. Because of his numerous pseudonyms, anonymous works, and pieces in hard-to-find periodicals, his entire oeuvre may never be known, according to his biographer Peter Morton.

Charles Grant Blairfindie Allen was born in Kingston, Ontario on February 24, 1848, the son of a former minister and grandson of the fifth Baron of Longueuil (the only Canadian barony).[2] He was the third child out of seven siblings and had a transcontinental upbringing, living in New Haven, Connecticut, for nearly a year when he was thirteen, followed by periods in England and

France. He entered Merton College, Oxford in 1867, graduating in
1871 with a first-class degree in Moderations and a second-class degree in Greats. He taught Latin and Greek to support his first wife,
Caroline Anne Bootheway, who suffered from tuberculosis and
died some three years into the marriage. He then married Ellen
Jerrard, the sister-in-law of his friend Franklin Richards, and they
eventually made their way to Jamaica, where Allen took up a post
as chair of mental and moral philosophy at Queen's College. After
three years, his position was eliminated, and the Allens returned
home. Their son, Jerrard Grant Allen, was born in July 1878. Leslie
Stephen, the father of Virginia Woolf, accepted two articles from
Allen for *Cornhill Magazine*, launching Allen's journalistic career.

His sensational stories in *Cornhill*—"The Reverend John
Creedy" (featuring a savage African missionary) and "The Curate
of Churnside" (featuring a clerical killer)—"[b]oth were so well
noticed that I began to think seriously of fiction as an alternative subject," stated Allen ("'Physiological'" 49). His first novel
was *Philistia* (1884), produced for Andrew Chatto; Allen scored
a noteworthy success with *What's Bred in the Bone* (1891), which
won a £1000 prize from George Newnes's magazine *Tit-bits* and
later became a silent film. With secret marriages, hidden identities,
a fortune in jewels, forgery, and murder, *What's Bred in the Bone*
seemed designed to appeal to Mary Elizabeth Braddon's audience.
His detective fiction credentials were further established with the
publication of *Recalled to Life* (1891), which featured a female amne-
siac as the detective; "The Great Ruby Robbery" (*The Strand*, 1892,
illustrated by famed Holmes artist Sidney Paget), in which a maid
accused of theft serves as the investigator—a rare appearance of
a working-class female detective (Willis, "New Women"); and *An
African Millionaire* (1897), a serial that first appeared in the *Strand*
and featured the con artist Colonel Clay. The first installment of
Miss Cayley's Adventures, "The Adventure of the Cantankerous Old
Lady," and the first installment of *Hilda Wade*, "The Episode of
the Patient Who Disappointed her Doctor," followed in the *Strand*
in March 1898 and March 1899 respectively. Allen died in October
1899, after he secured a promise from Conan Doyle to complete
the last installment of *Hilda Wade*. Conan Doyle described his contribution as "difficult collar work" but stated that he did it to "re-

lieve [Allen's] mind" and called Allen "an amiable and benevolent man" (254, 255).

In posthumous appreciations, Allen's friends and colleagues often mentioned his generosity of spirit. He provided funds for the respective publishing operations of his nephew, Grant Richards, and John Lane, although, Richards noted, "he was very far indeed from being a rich man" (4-5). H. G. Wells, who had savaged *The Woman Who Did* in the *Saturday Review*, was nonplussed to be invited to Allen's house, noting later, "He behaved charmingly ... I was a new and aggressive beginner in that world and I was being welcomed very generously" (*Experiment* 466).[3]

Yet the mild-mannered Allen was often passionate. He wrote in response to a request for a piece for the 1898 *Canadian Year Book*:

> I hate war, and everything that leads to it, as I hate murder, rapine, or the ill-treatment of women. . . . I contribute gladly to works designed to strengthen the bonds of amity between nations and to render war impossible, but I cannot contribute to one which aims at making peaceable Canadian citizens throw themselves into the devouring whirlpool of militarism. (qtd. in Clodd 201)

His poet friend Richard Le Gallienne, father of actress Eva Le Gallienne, observed, "Grant Allen had a really enviable faculty of provoking the world to throw stones" (190). He seems to have had the fiction writer's desire to be regarded as a legitimate agent for social comment, as seen in "The Worm Turns," a letter published by *Athenæum* in which he stated that "the English author, unless rich enough actually to defy his public, must work under painfully soul-killing restrictions." He was responding to a trusted publisher's advice to leave unpublished his slaved-over novel manuscript with a social theme because it would ruin him. For this outburst, he was roundly criticized; for one, Allen's waspish colleague Andrew Lang rejected Allen's notion of the novel as social commentary, observing in *Longman's* that "a novel is not a treatise. Many things that need to be said should be said simply, directly, with all authorities and evidence. They ought not to be mixed up with flirtations, love affairs, and fanciful episodes" (545; see also Stead).

Continuing the stone throwing, reviewers sniped when the book version of *Miss Cayley's Adventures* was published, often conveying irritation that they had enjoyed Allen's effort. "They [the installments in the serial] are good enough in their way," sniffed the reviewer in *Literature*, "and there is only a small dose of improbability in each of them. Improbability, however, is a literary medicine with cumulative effects; and twelve doses of it taken in rapid succession are calculated to leave the patient's nerves rather shattered." *Athenæum*, although calling Miss Cayley "enterprising," wrote, "[Allen's] lively entertainment is only marred here and there by such conventionally silly and vulgar touches as the sketch of youthful aristocratic scoundrel who talks the forgotten language of the ducal villain on the Surrey side of the river." Summed up William Morton Payne in *Dial*, "a pot-boiler unabashed ... pleasant, unprofitable reading, and holds the attention throughout."

In general, criticism of *Miss Cayley's Adventures*, with few exceptions—Michele Slung does see the character clearly and describes her affectionately—echoes its original reviewers. The bulk of Allen criticism focuses on *The Woman Who Did*; little analysis exists of his detective fiction, and most of the few mentions of *Miss Cayley's Adventures* tend to be dismissive. An essay by the late Chris Willis focuses on *What's Bred in the Bone*, *Recalled to Life*, and *Hilda Wade*, with only one mention of *Miss Cayley's Adventures*, although Willis's Web site contains a fuller depiction of Allen's protagonist ("Doppelganger"; "New Women"). Morton's biography of Allen includes just two passing references to *Miss Cayley's Adventures*, and Allen is not mentioned at all in Kathleen Gregory Klein's *The Woman Detective: Gender and Genre*. The sole Allen work covered in Karin Kay Jacobson's dissertation on the woman detective in Victorian fiction is *Hilda Wade*. Patricia Craig and Mary Cadogan cover *Miss Cayley's Adventures* in just over a page, asserting that Allen is "actually reinforcing traditional ideas of feminine inferiority" in *The Woman Who Did*, and Miss Cayley and Hilda Wade are the main character's "sisters under the skin"; they also misspell Miss Cayley's surname throughout (26). Paul Stuewe devotes five pages to *Miss Cayley's Adventures*, but his focus is race relations, with a few sentences on the roles of the sexes (100-105). Only Joseph Kestner has examined *Miss Cayley's Adventures* at length, and even he, like Craig and Cadogan, dubs the book "a profound fantasy of female empowerment," based on the fact that women were not permitted to join the British Metropolitan Police's Criminal Investigation Department until the 1920s ("New Woman" 150).[4]

Yet Allen did not invent the clever female investigator; her prior appearances include Wilkie Collins's "The Diary of Anne Rodway" (1856), *The Woman in White* (1860), and *The Law and the Lady* (1875); *Revelations of a Lady Detective* (attributed to W. S. Hayward, 1864); Andrew Forrester's *The Female Detective* (1864); Catherine Louisa Pirkis's *The Experiences of Loveday Brooke, Lady Detective* (1894); Anna Katharine Green's *That Affair Next Door* (1897); and George R. Sims's *Dorcas Dene, Detective: Her Adventures* (1897).[5] The nineteenth-century woman's lack of widespread opportunities in law enforcement does not seem to have precluded authors from envisioning effective female detectives, the public from accepting and enjoying narratives featuring their successful exploits, or individual women from serving in such a capacity.

The critical neglect of *Miss Cayley's Adventures* is unfortunate, for in Allen's Girton-educated heroine, there is an extension of his thought[7] on the intelligent, physically fit, and resourceful New Woman (as Kestner notes), but presented in an entertaining package—the marriage of social critique and good storytelling that Allen hoped to achieve in the work described in "The Worm Turns." Willis points out ("New Women") that Miss Cayley's origins lie in an earlier Allen heroine, Juliet Appleton, who appears in *The Type-Writer Girl* (1897) under the Olive Pratt Rayner pseudonym. Also evident is the prototype for Allen's later nurse-detective Hilda Wade, whose cool, Holmes-like abilities for observation and deduction are dismissed by the male physician characters as "intuition." *Miss Cayley's Adventures* also reflects Allen's liberal views on race that stem from his experiences in Jamaica, as seen in Lord Southminster's application of the word *nigger* to a maharajah. Miss Cayley—who has shown her contempt for the aristocrat by dubbing him with her own color-based epithet, "the pea-green patrician"—retaliates: "[The maharajah's] ancestors were princes while ours were dressed in woad and oak-leaves. But you were right about one thing; *he* behaves—like a gentleman" (152; emphasis in original).[6] Lady Georgina Fawley, aka the Cantankerous Old

Lady, reinforces this view of the maharajah by calling him, in the highest words of British praise, "a regular brick" (167).

In *Miss Cayley's Adventures*, Kestner has noted Allen's combination of the detective story, the New Woman novel, and the travel narrative (*Sherlock's* 134). When the story begins, Miss (Georgina) Lois Cayley, who has "suppressed the Georgina" (11), has been left penniless by the death of her wastrel stepfather. Instead of displaying panic or even a mild consternation, Miss Cayley views her situation as an opportunity: "I am going out, simply in search of adventure" (5). She rejects the typical female occupations of teacher or shopkeeper and is unrelentingly honest: "What I say, that I mean" (10). Further underscoring her status as outsider are her school nickname of Brownie, with its fairytale connotations of elves and their fey behavior (4), and her prowess at cycling, climbing, and rowing (51). She signs on as a traveling companion to Lady Georgina in the first adventure and thwarts an attempt to steal the elderly lady's jewelry by figuring out a fellow passenger's nefarious intentions. In subsequent adventures, Miss Cayley wins a cycling race in Germany; sells bicycles in Europe for an appreciative American manufacturer; operates a typing agency in Italy; writes articles as a foreign correspondent for the delightfully named *Daily Telephone*; rescues an Englishwoman from white slavery in Egypt with the help of an Irish doctor; and, with some trepidation, kills an attacking tiger in India, scandalizing her aunt with her "unladylike" behavior (78) and displaying remarkable flexibility and adaptability in her efforts. "If he [the American bicycle manufacturer] wished to cut my throat, I was well within reach of the resources of civilisation," she muses pragmatically (46).

A significant interlude is her rescue of the man she loves, Harold Tillington, from a precarious mountainside; she brushes aside her friend Elsie's suggestion that they obtain male assistance and accomplishes the task on her own. In the 1899 Putnam edition, British children's book illustrator Gordon Browne provides evocative illustrations of Miss Cayley deciding her next move at "the edge of the precipice" and ably conquering the mountain. In the course of her adventures, Miss Cayley rejects several proposals of marriage, most notably the wealthy Harold's because of her position as a penniless "adventuress"—she refuses to be viewed by the world as a conniving opportunist and will only consider an offer from a man of equal economic and intellectual standing. She says to Elsie, "[... I]f you think I could sell myself for a coronet to a pasty-faced young man with a pea-green complexion and glassy blue eyes—I can only say, my child, that you have misread my character. He isn't a man; he's a lump of putty!" (138). Her superior reasoning abilities are again victorious when she unmasks a reputed faith healer through her knowledge of chemistry and uncovers fraud involving the will of Harold's uncle after a bout with a condescending barrister, thus exonerating the innocent and nabbing the guilty.

Despite Miss Cayley's initial resistance, her adventures do end in marriage, a predictable end for most female detectives of the period. "A little muscle and a little mind are no doubt advisable adjuncts for a housewife," she observes (34). With his declaration (via Harold) in Miss Cayley's Adventures that "a man ought to wish the woman he loves to be a free agent, his equal in point of action, even as she is nobler and better than he in all spiritual matters" (35) and his presentation of a smart, independent female detective who turns into a conventional wife, Allen sends mixed messages but ones that are not inconsistent with the period or with the state of detective fiction at the time. Overall, Allen's heroine is a progressive one. The straightforward Miss Cayley exercises her considerable wits in times of crisis and is admired for her powerful combination of intelligence and athleticism; she helps all those who appeal to her; she triumphs over the evildoer, the arrogant, and the complacent—surely a positive message for readers from any era.

Until now, Miss Cayley has been out of mass circulation since 1902. Read her adventures and partake of the enjoyment and innovative thought that Allen's "vulgar stories" provide.

ELIZABETH FOXWELL
Alexandria, Virginia

December 7, 2007

WORKS CITED

Allen, Grant. *Miss Cayley's Adventures.* New York: Putnam, 1899.

———. *Miss Cayley's Adventures.* Kansas City: Valancourt Books, 2008.

———. "Pallinghurst Barrow." *Illustrated London News* [Christmas No.] 1892: 12-18.

———. "'Physiological Aesthetics' and 'Philistia.'" *My First Book.* Introduction by Jerome K. Jerome. 1894. London: Chatto, 1897. 43-52.

———. "Plain Words on the Woman Question." *Fortnightly Review,* Oct. 1, 1889: 448-458.

———. *The Woman Who Did.* London: Lane, 1895.

———. "The Worm Turns." *Athenæum* (30 July 1892): 160.

Allen, Grant [and Arthur Conan Doyle]. *Hilda Wade: A Woman with Tenacity of Purpose.* 1899. New York: Putnam, 1900.

Ardis, Ann L. *New Women, New Novels: Feminism and Early Modernism.* New Brunswick: Rutgers University Press, 1990.

Brown, Dee. *The Gentle Tamers: Women of the Old Wild West.* 1958. Lincoln: University of Nebraska Press, 1981.

Clarke, George Herbert. "Grant Allen." *Queen's Quarterly* 45 (1938): 487-496.

Clodd, Edward. *Grant Allen: A Memoir.* London: Grant Richards, 1900. 15 Aug. 2007 <http://www.canadiana.org/ECO/PageView/03011/0007?id=03e40a963f302690>.

Craig, Patricia, and Mary Cadogan. *The Lady Investigates: Women Detectives and Spies in Fiction.* New York: St. Martin's, 1981.

Doyle, Arthur Conan. *Memories and Adventures.* Boston: Little, 1924.

Fawcett, Millicent Garrett. Rev. of *The Woman Who Did*, by Grant Allen. *Contemporary Review* 67 (May 1895): 625-631.

Greenslade, William, and Terence Rodgers, eds. *Grant Allen: Literature and Politics at the Fin de Siècle.* Burlington: Ashgate, 2005.

Hughes, David Y. "H. G. Wells and the Charge of Plagiarism." *Nineteenth-Century Fiction* 21 (June 1966): 85-90.

———. "A Queer Notion of Grant Allen's." *Science Fiction Studies* 25.2 (July 1998): 271-284.

Jacobson, Karin Kay. *Unsettling Questions, Hysterical Answers: The Woman Detective in Victorian Fiction.* Dissertation, Ohio State University, 1997.

Kestner, Joseph A. "The New Woman and the Female Detective: Grant Allen's *Miss Cayley's Adventures* (1899)." *Redefining the Modern: Essays on Literature and Society in Honor of Joseph Wiesenfarth*. Ed. William Baker and Ira B. Nadel. Madison: Fairleigh Dickinson University Press, 2004. 148-164.

———. *Sherlock's Sisters: The British Female Detective, 1864-1913*. Aldershot: Ashgate, 2003.

Klein, Kathleen Gregory. *The Woman Detective: Gender and Genre*. 1988. 2nd ed. Urbana: University of Illinois Press, 1995.

Lang, Andrew. "At the Sign of the Ship." *Longman's* Sept. 1892: 543-548.

Ledger, Sally. *The New Woman: Fiction and Feminism at the fin de siècle*. Manchester: Manchester University Press, 1997.

Le Gallienne, Richard. *Attitudes and Avowals, with Some Retrospective Reviews*. London: Lane, 1910.

Miller, Jane Eldridge. *Rebel Women: Feminism, Modernism, and the Edwardian Novel*. London: Virago, 1994.

Morton, Peter. *"The Busiest Man in England": Grant Allen and the Writing Trade, 1875-1900*. New York: Palgrave, 2005.

Payne, William Morton. Review of *Miss Cayley's Adventures*, by Grant Allen. *Dial* 16 Sept. 1899: 176.

Pinkerton, Allan. *The Spy of the Rebellion: Being a True History of the Spy System of the United States Army*. New York: Carleton, 1883.

Rayner, Olive Pratt [Grant Allen]. *The Type-writer Girl*. London: Pearson, 1897.

Review of *Miss Cayley's Adventures*, by Grant Allen. *Athenæum* 17 June 1899: 749.

———. *Literature* 20 May 1899: 527.

Richards, Grant. *Author Hunting by an Old Literary Sports Man: Memories of Years Spent Mainly in Publishing, 1897-1925*. New York: Coward-McCann, 1934.

Roth, Mitchel P. *Historical Dictionary of Law Enforcement*. Westport: Greenwood, 2001.

Rubinstein, David. *Before the Suffragettes: Women's Emancipation in the 1890s*. Brighton: Harvester, 1986.

Sanders, Matthew J. "An Introduction to Phoebe Wilson Couzins." *Women's Legal History Biography Project*. Robert Crown Law Lib., Stanford University, 13 Aug. 2007 <http://womenslegalhistory.stanford.edu/papers/CouzinsP-Sander­soo.pdf>.

Shumaker, Jeanette. "Fallen Madonnas in Late-Victorian Fiction: Kate Chopin's and Grant Allen's Ambivalence about Sacrifice." *South Carolina Review* 36.1 (2003): 40-50.

Slung, Michele, ed. *Crime on Her Mind*. New York: Pantheon, 1975.

Stashower, Daniel. *Teller of Tales: The Life of Arthur Conan Doyle*. New York: Holt, 1999.

Stead, W. T. "Mr. Grant Allen: His Work and His Critics." *Review of Reviews* 6 (Sept. 1892): 266.

Stuewe, Paul. *Britishers at Home and Overseas: Imperial and Colonial Identity in the Work of Grant Allen, Robert Barr and Sir Gilbert Parker*. Dissertation, University of Waterloo, 2000. ProQuest Digital Dissertations, University of Maryland, 20 Aug. 2007.

Warne, Vanessa and Colette Colligan. "The Man Who Wrote a New Woman Novel: Grant Allen's *The Woman Who Did* and the Gendering of New Woman Authorship." *Victorian Literature and Culture* 33.1 (2005): 21-46.

Weeks, Jeffrey. *Sex, Politics, and Society: The Regulation of Sexuality Since 1800*. 2nd ed. London: Longman, 1989.

Wells, H. G. *Experiment in Autobiography*. 1934. Boston: Little, 1962.

———. *The Time Machine*. 1895. *The Time Machine and the Invisible Man*. New York: Barnes & Noble Classics, 2003.

Willis, Chris. "The Detective's Doppelganger: Conflicting States of Female Consciousness in Grant Allen's Detective Fiction." Greenslade and Rodgers 143-153.

———. "New Women – New Crimes: A Survey of Grant Allen's Detective-Heroines." 13 Aug. 2007 <http://www.chriswillis.freeserve.co.uk/allen1.htm>.

"Women Police." *Metropolitan Police Service*. 13 Aug. 2007 <http://www.met.police.uk/history/women_police.htm>.

NOTES

1   See, for example, Ardis; Fawcett; Ledger 15; Miller; Rubenstein; Shumaker; Warne and Colligan; and Weeks.

2   For further details on Allen's lineage, see Clarke and Morton.

3   Allen's effect on Wells is marked; there is a reference to "a queer notion of Grant Allen's" in *The Time Machine* (1895, 46), and David Y. Hughes ("Queer Notion") has noted the influence of Allen's ghost story "Pallinghurst Barrow" (1892) on both *The Time Machine* and *The Croquet Player* (1936). Hughes also refuted the notion that Wells plagiarized Allen's *British Barbarians* (1895) in *The Wonderful Visit*, his novel published in the same year ("Charge").

4   Actually, the volunteer Women Police Service dates from 1914. In addition, the United States had a better record than Britain of employing women in the nineteenth-century criminal justice system, including Esther Hobart Morris, the first female judge (1870); and Phoebe Wilson Couzins, the second female law school graduate and the first female marshal in the United States (1887). Allan Pinkerton hired women as private detectives, including Kate Warne in 1856. Warne was a key figure in the protection detail for President Abraham Lincoln as he traveled to his first inauguration. Thus, in this context, the idea of a female detective is hardly outrageous. See Brown; Pinkerton; Roth; Sanders; and "Women Police."

5   Braddon's Eleanor Vane in *Eleanor's Victory* (1863) is not included in this list, as she often discovers clues by chance rather than active detection or deduction.

6   Page references in this introduction are to the 2008 Valancourt Books edition.

7   In Allen's "Plain Words on the Woman Question," he affirms the right of women to be educated and casts marriage as slavery, yet asserts the maternal role is the predominant one for women. He states that although not all women are suited to become wives and mothers, those who are should bear "at least four children apiece" and that "[a] woman ought to be ashamed to say she has no desire to be a wife and mother" (449, 452). This article is a curious mixture of progressive and traditional ideas about the role of women and, in combination with *The Woman Who Did*, suggests that there may have been limitations on Allen's conception of the New Woman.

NOTE ON THE TEXT

The Valancourt Books edition of *Miss Cayley's Adventures* follows the first edition of the novel, published by Grant Richards in London in 1899. The cover illustration for this edition is taken from the front cover of the first American edition, published by Putnam in 1899. The original editions were profusely illustrated by Gordon Browne; one of these illustrations appears as the frontispiece to this new edition.

Miss Cayley's Adventures

CHAPTER I

THE ADVENTURE OF THE CANTANKEROUS OLD LADY

On the day when I found myself with twopence in my pocket, I naturally made up my mind to go round the world.

It was my stepfather's death that drove me to it. I had never seen my stepfather. Indeed, I never even thought of him as anything more than Colonel Watts-Morgan. I owed him nothing, except my poverty. He married my dear mother when I was a girl at school in Switzerland; and he proceeded to spend her little fortune, left at her sole disposal by my father's will, in paying his gambling debts. After that, he carried my dear mother off to Burma; and when he and the climate between them had succeeded in killing her, he made up for his appropriations at the cheapest rate by allowing me just enough to send me to Girton. So, when the Colonel died, in the year I was leaving college, I did not think it necessary to go into mourning for him, especially as he chose the precise moment when my allowance was due, and bequeathed me nothing but his consolidated liabilities.

'Of course you will teach,' said Elsie Petheridge, when I explained my affairs to her. 'There is a good demand just now for high-school teachers.'

I looked at her, aghast. '*Teach!* Elsie,' I cried. (I had come up to town to settle her in at her unfurnished lodgings.) 'Did you say *teach?* That's just like you dear good schoolmistresses! You go to Cambridge, and get examined till the heart and life have been examined out of you; then you say to yourselves at the end of it all, "Let me see; what am I good for now? I'm just about fit to go away and examine other people!" That's what our Principal would call "a vicious circle"—if one could ever admit there was anything vicious at all about *you*, dear. No, Elsie, I do *not* propose to teach. Nature did not cut me out for a high-school teacher. I couldn't swallow a poker if I tried for weeks. Pokers don't agree with me. Between ourselves, I am a bit of a rebel.'

'You are, Brownie,' she answered, pausing in her papering, with

3

her sleeves rolled up—they called me 'Brownie,' partly because of my dark complexion, but partly because they could never understand me. 'We all knew that long ago.'

I laid down the paste-brush and mused.

'Do you remember, Elsie,' I said, staring hard at the paperboard, 'when I first went to Girton, how all you girls wore your hair quite straight, in neat smooth coils, plaited up at the back about the size of a pancake; and how of a sudden I burst in upon you, like a tropical hurricane, and demoralised you; and how, after three days of me, some of the dear innocents began with awe to cut themselves artless fringes, while others went out in fear and trembling and surreptitiously purchased a pair of curling-tongs? I was a bomb-shell in your midst in those days; why, you yourself were almost afraid at first to speak to me.'

'You see, you had a bicycle,' Elsie put in, smoothing the half-papered wall; 'and in those days, of course, ladies didn't bicycle. You must admit, Brownie, dear, it *was* a startling innovation. You terrified us so. And yet, after all, there isn't much harm in you.'

'I hope not,' I said devoutly. 'I was before my time, that was all; at present, even a curate's wife may blamelessly bicycle.'

'But if you don't teach,' Elsie went on, gazing at me with those wondering big blue eyes of hers, 'whatever will you do, Brownie?' Her horizon was bounded by the scholastic circle.

'I haven't the faintest idea,' I answered, continuing to paste. 'Only, as I can't trespass upon your elegant hospitality for life, whatever I mean to do, I must begin doing this morning, when we've finished the papering. I couldn't teach' (teaching, like mauve, is the refuge of the incompetent); 'and I don't, if possible, want to sell bonnets.'

'As a milliner's girl?' Elsie asked, with a face of red horror.

'As a milliner's girl; why not? 'Tis an honest calling. Earls' daughters do it now. But you needn't look so shocked. I tell you, just at present, I am not contemplating it.'

'Then what *do* you contemplate?'

I paused and reflected. 'I am here in London,' I answered, gazing rapt at the ceiling; 'London, whose streets are paved with gold—though it *looks* at first sight like muddy flagstones; London, the greatest and richest city in the world, where an adventurous soul ought surely to find some loophole for an adventure. (That piece is hung crooked, dear; we shall have to take it down again.) I devise a Plan, therefore. I submit myself to fate; or, if you prefer it, I leave my future in the hands of Providence. I shall stroll out this morning, as soon as I've "cleaned myself," and embrace the first stray enterprise that offers. Our Bagdad teems with enchanted carpets. Let one but float my way, and, hi, presto, I seize it. I go where glory or a modest competence waits me. I snatch at the first offer, the first hint of an opening.'

Elsie stared at me, more aghast and more puzzled than ever. 'But, how?' she asked. 'Where? When? You *are* so strange! What will you do to find one?'

'Put on my hat and walk out,' I answered. 'Nothing could be simpler. This city bursts with enterprises and surprises. Strangers from east and west hurry through it in all directions. Omnibuses traverse it from end to end—even, I am told, to Islington and Putney; within, folk sit face to face who never saw one another before in their lives, and who may never see one another again, or, on the contrary, may pass the rest of their days together.'

I had a lovely harangue all pat in my head, in much the same strain, on the infinite possibilities of entertaining angels unawares, in cabs, on the Underground, in the aërated bread shops; but Elsie's widening eyes of horror pulled me up short, like a hansom in Piccadilly when the inexorable upturned hand of the policeman checks it. 'Oh, Brownie,' she cried, drawing back, 'you *don't* mean to tell me you're going to ask the first young man you meet in an omnibus to marry you?'

I shrieked with laughter. 'Elsie,' I cried, kissing her dear yellow little head, 'you are *impayable*. You never will learn what I mean. You don't understand the language. No, no; I am going out, simply in search of adventure. What adventure may come, I have not at this moment the faintest conception. The fun lies in the search, the uncertainty, the toss-up of it. What is the good of being penniless—with the trifling exception of twopence—unless you are prepared to accept your position in the spirit of a masked ball at Covent Garden?'

'I have never been to one,' Elsie put in.

'Gracious heavens, neither have I! What on earth do you take me for? But I mean to see where fate will lead me.'

'I may go with you?' Elsie pleaded.

'Certainly *not*, my child,' I answered—she was three years older than I, so I had the right to patronise her. 'That would spoil all. Your dear little face would be quite enough to scare away a timid adventure.' She knew what I meant. It was gentle and pensive, but it lacked initiative.

So, when we had finished that wall, I popped on my best hat, and popped out by myself into Kensington Gardens.

I am told I ought to have been terribly alarmed at the straits in which I found myself—a girl of twenty-one, alone in the world, and only twopence short of penniless, without a friend to protect, a relation to counsel her. (I don't count Aunt Susan, who lurked in ladylike indigence at Blackheath, and whose counsel, like her tracts, was given away too profusely to everybody to allow of one's placing any very high value upon it.) But, as a matter of fact, I must admit I was not in the least alarmed. Nature had endowed me with a profusion of crisp black hair, and plenty of high spirits. If my eyes had been like Elsie's—that liquid blue which looks out upon life with mingled pity and amazement—I might have felt as a girl ought to feel under such conditions; but having large dark eyes, with a bit of a twinkle in them, and being as well able to pilot a bicycle as any girl of my acquaintance, I have inherited or acquired an outlook on the world which distinctly leans rather towards cheeriness than despondency. I croak with difficulty. So I accepted my plight as an amusing experience, affording full scope for the congenial exercise of courage and ingenuity.

How boundless are the opportunities of Kensington Gardens—the Round Pond, the winding Serpentine, the mysterious seclusion of the Dutch brick Palace! Genii swarm there. One jostles possibilities. It is a land of romance, bounded on the north by the Abyss of Bayswater, and on the south by the Amphitheatre of the Albert Hall. But for a centre of adventure I choose the Long Walk; it beckoned me somewhat as the North-West Passage beckoned my seafaring ancestors—the buccaneering mariners of Elizabethan Devon. I sat down on a chair at the foot of an old elm with a poetic hollow, prosaically filled by a utilitarian plate of galvanised iron. Two ancient ladies were seated on the other side already—very grand-looking dames, with the haughty and exclusive ugliness of the English aristocracy in its later stages. For frank hideousness, commend me to the noble dowager. They were talking confidentially as I sat down; the trifling episode of my approach did not suffice to stem the full stream of their conversation. The great ignore the intrusion of their inferiors.

'Yes, it's a terrible nuisance,' the eldest and ugliest of the two observed—she was a high-born lady, with a distinctly cantankerous cast of countenance. She had a Roman nose, and her skin was wrinkled like a wilted apple; she wore coffee-coloured point-lace in her bonnet, with a complexion to match. 'But what could I do, my dear? I simply *couldn't* put up with such insolence. So I looked her straight back in the face—oh, she quailed, I can tell you—and I said to her in my iciest voice—you know how icy I can be when occasion demands it'—the second old lady nodded an ungrudging assent, as if perfectly prepared to admit her friend's rare gift of iciness—'I said to her, "Célestine, you can take your month's wages, and half an hour to get out of this house." And she dropped me a deep reverence, and she answered: "*Oui, madame; merci beaucoup, madame; je ne désire pas mieux, madame.*" And out she flounced. So there was the end of it.'

'Still, you go to Schlangenbad on Monday?'

'That's the point. On Monday. If it weren't for the journey, I should have been glad enough to be rid of the minx. I'm glad as it is, indeed; for a more insolent, upstanding, independent, answer-you-back-again young woman, with a sneer of her own, I never saw, Amelia—but I *must* get to Schlangenbad. Now, there the difficulty comes in. On the one hand, if I engage a maid in London, I have the choice of two evils. Either I must take a trapesing English girl—and I know by experience that an English girl on the Continent is a vast deal worse than no maid at all: *you* have to wait upon *her*, instead of her waiting upon you; she gets seasick on the crossing, and when she reaches France or Germany, she hates the meals, and she detests the hotel servants, and she can't speak the language, so that she's always calling you to interpret for her in her private differences with the *fille-de-chambre* and the landlord; or else I must pick up a French maid in London, and I know equally by experience that the French maids one engages in London are invariably dishonest—more dishonest than the rest

even; they've come here because they have no character to speak
of elsewhere, and they think you aren't likely to write and enquire
of their last mistress in Toulouse or St. Petersburg. Then, again, on
the other hand, I can't wait to get a Gretchen, an unsophisticated
little Gretchen of the Taunus at Schlangenbad—I suppose there *are*
unsophisticated girls in Germany still—made in Germany—they
don't make 'em any longer in England, I'm sure—like everything
else, the trade in rustic innocence has been driven from the country. I can't wait to get a Gretchen, as I should like to do, of course,
because I simply *daren't* undertake to cross the Channel alone and
go all that long journey by Ostend or Calais, Brussels and Cologne,
to Schlangenbad.'

'You could get a temporary maid,' her friend suggested, in a lull
of the tornado.

The Cantankerous Old Lady flared up. 'Yes, and have my jewel-
case stolen! Or find she was an English girl without one word
of German. Or nurse her on the boat when I want to give my
undivided attention to my own misfortunes. No, Amelia, I call it
positively unkind of you to suggest such a thing. You're *so* unsympathetic! I put my foot down there. I will *not* take any temporary
person.'

I saw my chance. This was a delightful idea. Why not start for
Schlangenbad with the Cantankerous Old Lady?

Of course, I had not the slightest intention of taking a lady's-
maid's place for a permanency. Nor even, if it comes to that, as
a passing expedient. But *if* I wanted to go round the world, how
could I do better than set out by the Rhine country? The Rhine
leads you on to the Danube, the Danube to the Black Sea, the Black
Sea to Asia; and so by way of India, China, and Japan, you reach
the Pacific and San Francisco; whence one returns quite easily by
New York and the White Star Liners. I began to feel like a globe-
trotter already; the Cantankerous Old Lady was the thin end of
the wedge—the first rung of the ladder! I proceeded to put my
foot on it.

I leaned around the corner of the tree and spoke. 'Excuse me,'
I said, in my suavest voice, 'but I think I see a way out of your
difficulty.'

My first impression was that the Cantankerous Old Lady

would go off in a fit of apoplexy. She grew purple in the face with indignation and astonishment, that a casual outsider should venture to address her; so much so, indeed, that for a second I almost regretted my well-meant interposition. Then she scanned me up and down, as if I were a girl in a mantle shop, and she contemplated buying either me or the mantle. At last, catching my eye, she thought better of it, and burst out laughing.

'What do you mean by this eavesdropping?' she asked.

I flushed up in turn. 'This is a public place,' I replied, with dignity; 'and you spoke in a tone which was hardly designed for the strictest privacy. If you don't wish to be overheard, you oughtn't to shout. Besides, I desired to do you a service.'

The Cantankerous Old Lady regarded me once more from head to foot. I did not quail. Then she turned to her companion. 'The girl has spirit,' she remarked, in an encouraging tone, as if she were discussing some absent person. 'Upon my word, Amelia, I rather like the look of her. Well, my good woman, what do you want to suggest to me?'

'Merely this,' I replied, bridling up and crushing her. 'I am a Girton girl, an officer's daughter, no more a good woman than most others of my class; and I have nothing in particular to do for the moment. I don't object to going to Schlangenbad. I would convoy you over, as companion, or lady-help, or anything else you choose to call it; I would remain with you there for a week, till you could arrange with your Gretchen, presumably unsophisticated; and then I would leave you. Salary is unimportant; my fare suffices. I accept the chance as a cheap opportunity of attaining Schlangenbad.'

The yellow-faced old lady put up her long-handled tortoiseshell eyeglasses and inspected me all over again. 'Well, I declare,' she murmured. 'What are girls coming to, I wonder? Girton, you say; Girton! That place at Cambridge! You speak Greek, of course; but how about German?'

'Like a native,' I answered, with cheerful promptitude. 'I was at school in Canton Berne; it is a mother tongue to me.'

'No, no,' the old lady went on, fixing her keen small eyes on my mouth. 'Those little lips could never frame themselves to "schlecht" or "wunderschön"; they were not cut out for it.'

'Pardon me,' I answered, in German. 'What I say, that I mean. The never-to-be-forgotten music of the Fatherland's-speech has on my infant ear from the first-beginning impressed itself.'

The old lady laughed aloud.

'Don't jabber it to me, child,' she cried. 'I hate the lingo. It's the one tongue on earth that even a pretty girl's lips fail to render attractive. You yourself make faces over it. What's your name, young woman?'

'Lois Cayley.'

'Lois! *What* a name! I never heard of any Lois in my life before, except Timothy's grandmother. *You're* not anybody's grandmother, are you?'

'Not to my knowledge,' I answered, gravely.

She burst out laughing again.

'Well, you'll do, I think,' she said, catching my arm. 'That big mill down yonder hasn't ground the originality altogether out of you. I adore originality. It was clever of you to catch at the suggestion of this arrangement. Lois Cayley, you say; any relation of a madcap Captain Cayley whom I used once to know, in the Forty-second Highlanders?'

'His daughter,' I answered, flushing. For I was proud of my father.

'Ha! I remember; he died, poor fellow; he was a good soldier—and his'—I felt she was going to say 'his fool of a widow,' but a glance from me quelled her; 'his widow went and married that good-looking scapegrace, Jack Watts-Morgan. Never marry a man, my dear, with a double-barrelled name and no visible means of subsistence; above all, if he's generally known by a nickname. So you're poor Tom Cayley's daughter, are you? Well, well, we can settle this little matter between us. Mind, I'm a person who always expects to have my own way. If you come with *me* to Schlangenbad, you must do as I tell you.'

'I *think* I could manage it—for a week,' I answered, demurely.

She smiled at my audacity. We passed on to terms. They were quite satisfactory. She wanted no references. 'Do I look like a woman who cares about a reference? What are called *characters* are usually essays in how not to say it. You take my fancy; that's the point! And poor Tom Cayley! But, mind, I will *not* be contradicted.'

'I will not contradict your wildest misstatement,' I answered, smiling.

'*And* your name and address?' I asked, after we had settled preliminaries.

A faint red spot rose quaintly in the centre of the Cantankerous Old Lady's sallow cheek. 'My dear,' she murmured, 'my name is the one thing on earth I'm really ashamed of. My parents chose to inflict upon me the most odious label that human ingenuity ever devised for a Christian soul; and I've not had courage enough to burst out and change it.'

A gleam of intuition flashed across me, 'You don't mean to say,' I exclaimed, 'that you're called Georgina?'

The Cantankerous Old Lady gripped my arm hard. 'What an unusually intelligent girl!' she broke in. 'How on earth did you guess? It *is* Georgina.'

'Fellow-feeling,' I answered. 'So is mine, Georgina Lois. But as I quite agree with you as to the atrocity of such conduct, I have suppressed the Georgina. It ought to be made penal to send innocent girls into the world so burdened.'

'My opinion to a T! You are really an exceptionally sensible young woman. There's my name and address; I start on Monday.'

I glanced at her card. The very copperplate was noisy. 'Lady Georgina Fawley, 49 Fortescue Crescent, W.'

It had taken us twenty minutes to arrange our protocols. As I walked off, well pleased, Lady Georgina's friend ran after me quickly.

'You must take care,' she said, in a warning voice. 'You've caught a Tartar.'

'So I suspect,' I answered. 'But a week in Tartary will be at least an experience.'

'She has an awful temper.'

'That's nothing. So have I. Appalling, I assure you. And if it comes to blows, I'm bigger and younger and stronger than she is.'

'Well, I wish you well out of it.'

'Thank you. It is kind of you to give me this warning. But I think I can take care of myself. I come, you see, of a military family.'

I nodded my thanks, and strolled back to Elsie's. Dear little Elsie was in transports of surprise when I related my adventure.

'Will you really go? And what will you do, my dear, when you get there?'

'I haven't a notion,' I answered; 'that's where the fun comes in. But, anyhow, I shall have got there.'

'Oh, Brownie, you might starve!'

'And I might starve in London. In either place, I have only two hands and one head to help me.'

'But, then, here you are among friends. You might stop with me for ever.'

I kissed her fluffy forehead. 'You good, generous little Elsie!' I cried; 'I won't stop here one moment after I have finished the painting and papering. I came here to help you. I couldn't go on eating your hard-earned bread and doing nothing. I know how sweet you are; but the last thing I want is to add to your burdens. Now let us roll up our sleeves again and hurry on with the dado.'

'But, Brownie, you'll want to be getting your own things ready. Remember, you're off to Germany on Monday.'

I shrugged my shoulders. 'Tis a foreign trick I picked up in Switzerland. 'What have I got to get ready?' I asked. 'I can't go out and buy a complete summer outfit in Bond Street for twopence. Now, don't look at me like that: be practical, Elsie, and let me help you paint the dado.' For unless I helped her, poor Elsie could never have finished it herself. I cut out half her clothes for her; her own ideas were almost entirely limited to differential calculus. And cutting out a blouse by differential calculus is weary, uphill work for a high-school teacher.

By Monday I had papered and furnished the rooms, and was ready to start on my voyage of exploration. I met the Cantankerous Old Lady at Charing Cross, by appointment, and proceeded to take charge of her luggage and tickets.

Oh my, how fussy she was! 'You will drop that basket! I hope you have got through tickets, *viâ* Malines, *not* by Brussels—I won't go by Brussels. You have to change there. Now, mind you notice how much the luggage weighs in English pounds, and make the man at the office give you a note of it to check those horrid Belgian porters. They'll charge you for double the weight, unless you reduce it at once to kilogrammes. *I* know their ways. Foreigners have no consciences. They just go to the priest and confess, you know, and wipe it all out, and start fresh again on a career of crime next morning. I'm sure I don't know why I *ever* go abroad. The only country in the world fit to live in is England. No mosquitoes, no passports, no—goodness gracious, child, don't let that odious man bang about my hat-box! Have you no immortal soul, porter, that you crush other people's property as if it was blackbeetles? No, I will *not* let you take this, Lois; this is my jewel-box—it contains all that remains of the Fawley family jewels. I positively decline to appear at Schlangenbad without a diamond to my back. This never leaves my hands. It's hard enough nowadays to keep body and skirt together. *Have* you secured that *coupé* at Ostend?'

We got into our first-class carriage. It was clean and comfortable; but the Cantankerous Old Lady made the porter mop the floor, and fidgeted and worried till we slid out of the station. Fortunately, the only other occupant of the compartment was a most urbane and obliging Continental gentleman—I say Continental, because I couldn't quite make out whether he was French, German, or Austrian—who was anxious in every way to meet Lady Georgina's wishes. Did madame desire to have the window open? Oh, certainly, with pleasure; the day was so sultry. Closed a little more? *Parfaitement*, there *was* a current of air, *il faut l'admettre*. Madame would prefer the corner? No? Then perhaps she would like this valise for a footstool? *Permettez*—just thus. A cold draught runs so often along the floor in railway carriages. This is Kent that we traverse; ah, the garden of England! As a diplomat, he knew every nook of Europe, and he echoed the *mot* he had accidentally heard drop from madame's lips on the platform: no country in the world so delightful as England!

'Monsieur is attached to the Embassy in London?' Lady Georgina inquired, growing affable.

He twirled his grey moustache: a waxed moustache of great distinction. 'No, madame; I have quitted the diplomatic service; I inhabit London now *pour mon agrément*. Some of my compatriots call it *triste;* for me, I find it the most fascinating capital in Europe. What gaiety! What movement! What poetry! What mystery!'

'If mystery means fog, it challenges the world,' I interposed.

He gazed at me with fixed eyes. 'Yes, mademoiselle,' he answered, in quite a different and markedly chilly voice. 'Whatever your great country attempts—were it only a fog—it achieves consummately.'

I have quick intuitions. I felt the foreign gentleman took an instinctive dislike to me.

To make up for it, he talked much, and with animation, to Lady Georgina. They ferreted out friends in common, and were as much surprised at it as people always are at that inevitable experience.

'Ah yes, madame, I recollect him well in Vienna. I was there at the time, attached to our Legation. He was a charming man; you read his masterly paper on the Central Problem of the Dual Empire?'

'You were in Vienna then!' the Cantankerous Old Lady mused back. 'Lois, my child, don't stare'—she had covenanted from the first to call me Lois, as my father's daughter, and I confess I preferred it to being Miss Cayley'd. 'We must surely have met. Dare I ask your name, monsieur?'

I could see the foreign gentleman was delighted at this turn. He had played for it, and carried his point. He meant her to ask him. He had a card in his pocket, conveniently close; and he handed it across to her. She read it, and passed it on: 'M. le Comte de Laroche-sur-Loiret.'

'Oh, I remember your name well,' the Cantankerous Old Lady broke in. 'I think you knew my husband, Sir Evelyn Fawley, and my father, Lord Kynaston.'

The Count looked profoundly surprised and delighted. 'What! you are then Lady Georgina Fawley!' he cried, striking an attitude. 'Indeed, miladi, your admirable husband was one of the very first to exert his influence in my favour at Vienna. Do I recall him, *ce cher* Sir Evelyn? If I recall him! What a fortunate rencounter! I must have seen you some years ago at Vienna, miladi, though I had not then the great pleasure of making your acquaintance. But your face had impressed itself on my sub-conscious self!' (I did not learn till later that the esoteric doctrine of the sub-conscious self was Lady Georgina's favourite hobby.) 'The moment chance led me to this carriage this morning, I said to myself, "That face, those features: so vivid, so striking: I have seen them somewhere. With what do I connect them in the recesses of my memory? A high-born family; genius; rank; the diplomatic service; some unnameable charm; some faint touch of eccentricity. Ha! I have it. Vienna, a carriage with footmen in red livery, a noble presence, a crowd of wits—poets, artists, politicians—pressing eagerly round the landau." That was my mental picture as I sat and confronted you: I understand it all now; this is Lady Georgina Fawley!'

I thought the Cantankerous Old Lady, who was a shrewd person in her way, must surely see through this obvious patter; but I had under-estimated the average human capacity for swallowing flattery. Instead of dismissing his fulsome nonsense with a contemptuous smile, Lady Georgina perked herself up with a conscious air of coquetry, and asked for more. 'Yes, they were delightful days in Vienna,' she said, simpering; 'I was young then, Count; I enjoyed life with a zest.'

'Persons of miladi's temperament are always young,' the Count retorted, glibly, leaning forward and gazing at her. 'Growing old is a foolish habit of the stupid and the vacant. Men and women of *esprit* are never older. One learns as one goes on in life to admire, not the obvious beauty of mere youth and health'—he glanced across at me disdainfully—'but the profounder beauty of deep character in a face—that calm and serene beauty which is imprinted on the brow by experience of the emotions.'

'I have had my moments,' Lady Georgina murmured, with her head on one side.

'I believe it, miladi,' the Count answered, and ogled her.

Thenceforward to Dover, they talked together with ceaseless animation. The Cantankerous Old Lady was capital company. She had a tang in her tongue, and in the course of ninety minutes she had flayed alive the greater part of London society, with keen wit and sprightliness. I laughed against my will at her ill-tempered sallies; they were too funny not to amuse, in spite of their vitriol. As for the Count, he was charmed. He talked well himself, too, and between them, I almost forgot the time till we arrived at Dover.

It was a very rough passage. The Count helped us to carry our nineteen hand-packages and four rugs on board; but I noticed that, fascinated as she was with him, Lady Georgina resisted his ingenious efforts to gain possession of her precious jewel-case as she descended the gangway. She clung to it like grim death, even in the chops of the Channel. Fortunately I am a good sailor, and when

Lady Georgina's sallow cheeks began to grow pale, I was steady enough to supply her with her shawl and her smelling-bottle. She fidgeted and worried the whole way over. She *would* be treated like a vertebrate animal. Those horrid Belgians had no right to stick their deck-chairs just in front of her. The impertinence of the hussies with the bright red hair—a grocer's daughters, she felt sure—in venturing to come and sit on the same bench with *her*—the bench 'for ladies only,' under the lee of the funnel!' Ladies only,' indeed! Did the baggages pretend they considered themselves ladies? Oh, that placid old gentleman in the episcopal gaiters was their father, was he? Well, a bishop should bring up his daughters better, having his children in subjection with all gravity. Instead of which— 'Lois, my smelling-salts!' This was a beastly boat; such an odour of machinery; they had no decent boats nowadays; with all our boasted improvements, she could remember well when the cross-Channel service was much better conducted than it was at present. But *that* was before we had compulsory education. The working classes were driving trade out of the country, and the consequence was, we couldn't build a boat which didn't reek like an oil-shop. Even the sailors on board were French—jabbering idiots; not an honest British Jack-tar among the lot of them; though the stewards were English, and very inferior Cockney English at that, with their offhand ways, and their School Board airs and graces. *She'd* School Board them if they were her servants; *she'd* show them the sort of respect that was due to people of birth and education. But the children of the lower classes never learnt their catechism nowadays; they were too much occupied with literatoor, jography, and free-'and drawrin'. Happily for my nerves, a good lurch to leeward put a stop for a while to the course of her thoughts on the present distresses.

At Ostend the Count made a second gallant attempt to capture the jewel-case, which Lady Georgina automatically repulsed. She had a fixed habit, I believe, of sticking fast to that jewel-case; for she was too overpowered by the Count's urbanity, I feel sure, to suspect for a moment his honesty of purpose. But whenever she travelled, I fancy, she clung to her case as if her life depended upon it; it contained the whole of her valuable diamonds.

We had twenty minutes for refreshments at Ostend, during

which interval my old lady declared with warmth that I *must* look
after her registered luggage; though, as it was booked through to
Cologne, I could not even see it till we crossed the German frontier; for the Belgian *douaniers* seal up the van as soon as the through
baggage for Germany is unloaded. To satisfy her, however, I went
through the formality of pretending to inspect it, and rendered
myself hateful to the head of the *douane* by asking various foolish
and inept questions, on which Lady Georgina insisted. When I had
finished this silly and uncongenial task—for I am not by nature
fussy, and it is hard to assume fussiness as another person's proxy—
I returned to our *coupé* which I had arranged for in London. To
my great amazement, I found the Cantankerous Old Lady and the
egregious Count comfortably seated there. 'Monsieur has been
good enough to accept a place in our carriage,' she observed, as I
entered.

He bowed and smiled. 'Or, rather, madame has been so kind as
to offer me one,' he corrected.

'Would you like some lunch, Lady Georgina?' I asked, in my
chilliest voice. 'There are ten minutes to spare, and the *buffet* is
excellent.'

'An admirable inspiration,' the Count murmured. 'Permit me
to escort you, miladi.'

'You will come, Lois?' Lady Georgina asked.

'No, thank you,' I answered, for I had an idea. 'I am a capital
sailor, but the sea takes away my appetite.'

'Then you'll keep our places,' she said, turning to me. 'I hope
you won't allow them to stick in any horrid foreigners! They will
try to force them on you unless you insist. *I* know their tricky ways.
You have the tickets, I trust? And the *bulletin* for the *coupé*? Well,
mind you don't lose the paper for the registered luggage. Don't let
those dreadful porters touch my cloaks. And if anybody attempts
to get in, be sure you stand in front of the door as they mount to
prevent them.'

The Count handed her out; he was all high courtly politeness. As Lady Georgina descended, he made yet another dexterous effort to relieve her of the jewel-case. I don't think she noticed
it, but automatically once more she waved him aside. Then she
turned to me. 'Here, my dear,' she said, handing it to me, 'you'd

better take care of it. If I lay it down in the *buffet* while I am eating my soup, some rogue may run away with it. But mind, don't let it out of your hands on any account. Hold it so, on your knee; and, for Heaven's sake, don't part with it.'

By this time my suspicions of the Count were profound. From the first I had doubted him; he was so blandly plausible. But as we landed at Ostend I had accidentally overheard a low whispered conversation when he passed a shabby-looking man, who had travelled in a second-class carriage from London. 'That succeeds?' the shabby-looking man had muttered under his breath in French, as the haughty nobleman with the waxed moustache brushed by him.

'That succeeds admirably,' the Count had answered, in the same soft undertone. '*Ça réussit à merveille.*'

I understood him to mean that he had prospered in his attempt to impose on Lady Georgina.

They had been gone five minutes at the *buffet*, when the Count came back hurriedly to the door of the *coupé* with a *nonchalant* air. 'Oh, mademoiselle,' he said, in an off-hand tone, 'Lady Georgina has sent me to fetch her jewel-case.'

I gripped it hard with both hands. '*Pardon*, M. le Comte,' I answered; 'Lady Georgina intrusted it to *my* safe keeping, and, without her leave, I cannot give it up to any one.'

'You mistrust me?' he cried, looking black. 'You doubt my honour? You doubt my word when I say that miladi has sent me?'

'*Du tout*,' I answered, calmly. 'But I have Lady Georgina's orders to stick to this case; and till Lady Georgina returns I stick to it.'

He murmured some indignant remark below his breath, and walked off. The shabby-looking passenger was pacing up and down the platform outside in a badly made dust-coat. As they passed their lips moved. The Count's seemed to mutter, '*C'est un coup manqué.*'

However, he did not desist even so. I saw he meant to go on with his dangerous little game. He returned to the *buffet* and rejoined Lady Georgina. I felt sure it would be useless to warn her, so completely had the Count succeeded in gulling her; but I took my own steps. I examined the jewel-case closely. It had a leather outer covering; within was a strong steel box, with stout bands of metal to bind it. I took my cue at once, and acted for the best on my own responsibility.

When Lady Georgina and the Count returned, they were like old friends together. The quails in aspic and the sparkling hock had evidently opened their hearts to one another. As far as Malines they laughed and talked without ceasing. Lady Georgina was now in her finest vein of spleen; her acid wit grew sharper and more caustic each moment. Not a reputation in Europe had a rag left to cover it as we steamed in beneath the huge iron roof of the main central junction.

I had observed all the way from Ostend that the Count had been anxious lest we might have to give up our *coupé* at Malines. I assured him more than once that his fears were groundless, for I had arranged at Charing Cross that it should run right through to the German frontier. But he waved me aside with one lordly hand. I had not told Lady Georgina of his vain attempt to take possession of her jewel-case; and the bare fact of my silence made him increasingly suspicious of me.

'Pardon me, mademoiselle,' he said, coldly; 'you do not understand these lines as well as I do. Nothing is more common than for those rascals of railway clerks to sell one a place in a *coupé* or a *wagon-lit*, and then never reserve it, or turn one out half way. It is very possible miladi may have to descend at Malines.'

Lady Georgina bore him out by a large variety of selected stories concerning the various atrocities of the rival companies which had stolen her luggage on her way to Italy. As for *trains de luxe*, they were dens of robbers.

So when we reached Malines, just to satisfy Lady Georgina, I put out my head and inquired of a porter. As I anticipated, he replied that there was no change; we went through to Verviers.

The Count, however, was still unsatisfied. He descended, and made some remarks a little farther down the platform to an official in the gold-banded cap of a *chef-de-gare*, or some such functionary. Then he returned to us, all fuming. 'It is as I said,' he exclaimed, flinging open the door. 'These rogues have deceived us. The *coupé* goes no farther. You must dismount at once, miladi, and take the train just opposite.'

I felt sure he was wrong, and I ventured to say so. But Lady

Georgina cried, 'Nonsense, child! The *chef-de-gare* must know. Get out at once! Bring my bag and the rugs! Mind that cloak! Don't forget the sandwich-tin! Thanks, Count; will you kindly take charge of my umbrellas? Hurry up, Lois; hurry up! the train is just starting!'

I scrambled after her, with my fourteen bundles, keeping a quiet eye meanwhile on the jewel-case.

We took our seats in the opposite train, which I noticed was marked 'Amsterdam, Bruxelles, Paris.' But I said nothing. The Count jumped in, jumped about, arranged our parcels, jumped out again. He spoke to a porter; then he rushed back excitedly. '*Mille pardons*, miladi,' he cried. 'I find the *chef-de-gare* has cruelly deceived me. You were right, after all, mademoiselle! We must return to the *coupé!*'

With singular magnanimity, I refrained from saying, 'I told you so.'

Lady Georgina, very flustered and hot by this time, tumbled out once more, and bolted back to the *coupé*. Both trains were just starting. In her hurry, at last, she let the Count take possession of her jewel-case. I rather fancy that as he passed one window he handed it in to the shabby-looking passenger; but I am not certain. At any rate, when we were comfortably seated in our own compartment once more, and he stood on the footboard just about to enter, of a sudden he made an unexpected dash back, and flung himself wildly into a Paris carriage. At the self-same moment, with a piercing shriek, both trains started.

Lady Georgina threw up her hands in a frenzy of horror. 'My diamonds!' she cried aloud. 'Oh, Lois, my diamonds!'

'Don't distress yourself,' I answered, holding her back, or I verily believe she would have leapt from the train. 'He has only taken the outer shell, with the sandwich-case inside it. *Here* is the steel box!' And I produced it, triumphantly.

She seized it, overjoyed. 'How did this happen?' she cried, hugging it, for she loved those diamonds.

'Very simply,' I answered. 'I saw the man was a rogue, and that he had a confederate with him in another carriage. So, while you were gone to the *buffet* at Ostend, I slipped the box out of the case, and put in the sandwich-tin, that he might carry it off, and we might have proofs against him. All you will have to do now is to inform the conductor, who will telegraph to stop the train to Paris. I spoke to him about that at Ostend, so that everything is ready.'

She positively hugged me. 'My dear,' she cried, 'you are the cleverest little woman I ever met in my life! Who on earth could have suspected such a polished gentleman! Why, you're worth your weight in gold. What the dickens shall I do without you at Schlangenbad?'

CHAPTER II

THE ADVENTURE OF THE SUPERCILIOUS *ATTACHÉ*

THE Count must have been an adept in the gentle art of quick-change disguise; for though we telegraphed full particulars of his appearance from Louvain, the next station, nobody in the least resembling either him or his accomplice, the shabby-looking man, could be unearthed in the Paris train when it drew up at Brussels, its first stopping-place. They must have transformed themselves meanwhile into two different persons. Indeed, from the outset, I had suspected his moustache—'twas so *very* distinguished.

When we reached Cologne, the Cantankerous Old Lady over-whelmed me with the warmth of her thanks and praises. Nay, more; after breakfast next morning, before we set out by slow train for Schlangenbad, she burst like a tornado into my bedroom at the Cologne hotel with a cheque for twenty guineas, drawn in my favour. 'That's for you, my dear,' she said, handing it to me, and looking really quite gracious.

I glanced at the piece of paper and felt my face glow crimson. 'Oh, Lady Georgina,' I cried; 'you misunderstand. You forget that I am a lady.'

'Nonsense, child, nonsense! Your courage and promptitude were worth ten times that sum,' she exclaimed, positively slip-ping her arm round my neck. 'It was your courage I particularly admired, Lois; because you faced the risk of my happening to look inside the outer case, and finding you had abstracted the blessed box; in which case I might quite naturally have concluded you meant to steal it.'

'I thought of that,' I answered. 'But I decided to risk it. I felt it was worth while. For I was sure the man meant to take the case as soon as ever you gave him the opportunity.'

'Then you deserve to be rewarded,' she insisted, pressing the cheque upon me.

I put her hand back firmly. 'Lady Georgina,' I said, 'it is very amiable of you. I think you do right in offering me the money; but

I think I should do altogether wrong in accepting it. A lady is not honest from the hope of gain; she is not brave because she expects to be paid for her bravery. You were my employer, and I was bound to serve my employer's interests. I did so as well as I could, and there is the end of it.'

She looked absolutely disappointed; we all hate to crush a benevolent impulse; but she tore the cheque up into very small pieces. 'As you will, my dear,' she said, with her hands on her hips; 'I see you are poor Tom Cayley's daughter. He was always a bit Quixotic.' Though I believe she liked me all the better for my refusal.

On the way from Cologne to Eltville, however, and on the drive up to Schlangenbad, I found her just as fussy and as worrying as ever. 'Let me see, how many of these horrid pfennigs make an English penny? I never *can* remember. Oh, those silly little nickel things are ten pfennigs each, are they? Well, eight would be a penny, I suppose. A mark's a shilling; ridiculous of them to divide it into ten pence instead of twelve; one never really knows how much one's paying for anything. Why these Continental people can't be content to use pounds, shillings, and pence, all over alike, the same as we do, passes *my* comprehension. They're glad enough to get English sovereigns when they can; why, then, don't they use them as such, instead of reckoning them each at twenty-five francs, and then trying to cheat you out of the proper exchange, which is *always* ten centimes more than the brokers give you? What, *we* use their beastly decimal system? Lois, I'm ashamed of you. An English girl to turn and rend her native country like that! Francs and centimes, indeed! Fancy proposing it at Peter Robinson's! No, I will *not* go by the boat, my dear. I hate the Rhine boats, crowded with nasty selfish pigs of Germans. What *I* like is a first-class compartment all to myself, and no horrid foreigners. Especially Germans. They're bursting with self-satisfaction—have such an exaggerated belief in their "land" and their "folk." And when they come to England, they do nothing but find fault with us. If people aren't satisfied with the countries they travel in, they'd better stop at home—that's *my* opinion. Nasty pigs of Germans! The very sight of them sickens me. Oh, I don't mind if they *do* understand me, child. They all learn English nowadays; it helps them in trade—

that's why they're driving us out of all the markets. But it *must*
be good for them to learn once in a way what other people really
think of them—civilised people, I mean; not Germans. They're a
set of barbarians.'

We reached Schlangenbad alive, though I sometimes doubted
it, for my old lady did her boisterous best to rouse some peppery
German officer into cutting our throats incontinently by the way;
and when we got there, we took up our abode in the nicest hotel in
the village. Lady Georgina had engaged the best front room on the
first floor, with a charming view across the pine-clad valley; but I
must do her the justice to say that she took the second best for me,
and that she treated me in every way like the guest she delighted
to honour. My refusal to accept her twenty guineas made her anxious to pay it back to me within the terms of our agreement. She
described me to everybody as a young friend who was travelling
with her, and never gave any one the slightest hint of my being
a paid companion. Our arrangement was that I was to have two
guineas for the week, besides my travelling expenses, board, and
lodging.

On our first morning at Schlangenbad, Lady Georgina sallied
forth, very much overdressed, and in a youthful hat, to use the
waters. They are valued chiefly for the complexion, I learned; I
wondered then why Lady Georgina came there—for she hadn't
any; but they are also recommended for nervous irritability, and as
Lady Georgina had visited the place almost every summer for fifteen years, it opened before one's mind an appalling vista of what
her temper might have been if she had *not* gone to Schlangenbad.
The hot springs are used in the form of a bath. 'You don't need
them, my dear,' Lady Georgina said to me, with a good-humoured
smile; and I will own that I did not, for nature had gifted me with
a tolerable cuticle. But I like when at Rome to do as Rome does; so
I tried the baths once. I found them unpleasantly smooth and oily.
I do not freckle, but if I did, I think I should prefer freckles.

We walked much on the terrace—the inevitable dawdling
promenade of all German watering-places—it reeked of Serene
Highness. We also drove out among the low wooded hills which
bound the Rhine valley. The majority of the visitors, I found, were
ladies—Court ladies, most of them; all there for their complexions,

but all anxious to assure me privately they had come for what they described as 'nervous debility.' I divided them at once into two classes: half of them never had and never would have a complexion at all; the other half had exceptionally smooth and beautiful skins, of which they were obviously proud, and whose pink-and-white peach-blossom they thought to preserve by assiduous bathing. It was vanity working on two opposite bases. There was a sprinkling of men, however, who were really there for a sufficient reason— wounds or serious complaints; while a few good old sticks, porty and whisty, were in attendance on invalid wives or sisters.

From the beginning I noticed that Lady Georgina went peering about all over the place, as if she were hunting for something she had lost, with her long-handled tortoise-shell glasses perpetually in evidence—the 'aristocratic outrage' I called them—and that she eyed all the men with peculiar attention. But I took no open notice of her little weakness. On our second day at the Spa, I was sauntering with her down the chief street—'a beastly little hole, my dear; not a decent shop where one can buy a reel of thread or a yard of tape in the place!'—when I observed a tall and handsome young man on the opposite side of the road cast a hasty glance at us, and then sneak around the corner hurriedly. He was a loose-limbed, languid-looking young man, with large, dreamy eyes, and a peculiarly beautiful and gentle expression; but what I noted about him most was an odd superficial air of superciliousness. He seemed always to be looking down with scorn on that foolish jumble, the universe. He darted away so rapidly, however, that I hardly discovered all this just then. I piece it out from subsequent observations.

Later in the day, we chanced to pass a *café*, where three young exquisites sat sipping Rhine wines after the fashion of the country. One of them, with a gold-tipped cigarette held gracefully between two slender fingers, was my languid-looking young aristocrat. He was blowing out smoke in a lazy blue stream. The moment he saw me, however, he turned away as if he desired to escape observation, and ducked down so as to hide his face behind his companions. I wondered why on earth he should want to avoid me. Could this be the Count? No, the young man with the halo of cigarette smoke stood three inches taller. Who, then, at Schlangenbad could wish to avoid my notice? It was a singular mystery; for I was quite certain the supercilious young man was trying his best to prevent my seeing him.

That evening, after dinner, the Cantankerous Old Lady burst out suddenly: 'Well, I can't for the life of me imagine why Harold hasn't turned up here. The wretch knew I was coming; and I heard from our Ambassador at Rome last week that he was going to be at Schlangenbad.'

'Who is Harold?' I asked.

'My nephew,' Lady Georgina snapped back, beating a devil's tattoo with her fan on the table. 'The only member of my family, except myself, who isn't a born idiot. Harold's not an idiot; he's an *attaché* at Rome.'

I saw it at a glance. 'Then he *is* in Schlangenbad,' I answered. 'I noticed him this morning.'

The old lady turned towards me sharply. She peered right through me, as if she were a Röntgen ray. I could see she was asking herself whether this was a conspiracy, and whether I had come there on purpose to meet 'Harold.' But I flatter myself I am tolerably mistress of my own countenance. I did not blench. 'How do you know?' she asked quickly, with an acid intonation.

If I had answered the truth, I should have said, 'I know he is here, because I saw a good-looking young man evidently trying to avoid you this morning; and if a young man has the misfortune to be born your nephew, and also to have expectations from you, it is easy to understand that he would prefer to keep out of your way as long as possible.' But that would have been neither polite nor politic. Moreover, I reflected that I had no particular reason for wishing to do Mr. Harold a bad turn; and that it would be kinder to him, as well as to her, to conceal the reasons on which I based my instinctive inference. So I took up a strong strategic position. 'I have an intuition that I saw him in the village this morning,' I said. 'Family likeness, perhaps. I merely jumped at it as you spoke. A tall, languid young man; large, poetical eyes; an artistic moustache—just a trifle Oriental-looking.'

'That's Harold!' the Cantankerous Old Lady rapped out sharply, with clear conviction. 'The miserable boy! Why on earth hasn't he been round to see me?'

I reflected that I knew why; but I did not say so. Silence is golden. I also remarked mentally on that curious human blindness which had made me conclude at first that the supercilious young man was trying to avoid *me*, when I might have guessed it was far more likely he was trying to avoid my companion. I was a nobody; Lady Georgina Fawley was a woman of European reputation.

'Perhaps he didn't know which hotel you were stopping at,' I put in. 'Or even that you were here.' I felt a sudden desire to shield poor Harold.

'Not know which hotel? Nonsense, child; he knows I come here on this precise date regularly every summer; and if he didn't know, is it likely I should try any other inn, when this is the only moderately decent house to stop at in Schlangenbad? And the morning coffee undrinkable at that; while the hash—*such* hash! But that's the way in Germany. He's an ungrateful monster; if he comes now, I shall refuse to see him.'

Next morning after breakfast, however, in spite of these threats, she hauled me forth with her on the Harold hunt. She had sent the *concierge* to inquire at all the hotels already, it seemed, and found her truant at none of them; now she ransacked the *pensions*. At last she hunted him down in a house on the hill. I could see she was really hurt. 'Harold, you viper, what do you mean by trying to avoid me?'

'My dear aunt, *you* here in Schlangenbad! Why, when did you arrive? And what a colour you've got! You're looking *so* well!' That clever thrust saved him.

He cast me an appealing glance. 'You will not betray me?' it said. I answered, mutely, 'Not for worlds,' with a faltering pair of downcast eyelids.

'Oh, I'm *well* enough, thank you,' Lady Georgina replied, somewhat mollified by his astute allusion to her personal appearance. He had hit her weak point dexterously. 'As well, that is, as one can expect to be nowadays. Hereditary gout—the sins of the fathers visited as usual. But why didn't you come to see me?'

'How can I come to see you if you don't tell me where you are? "Lady Georgina Fawley, Europe," was the only address I knew. It strikes me as insufficient.'

His gentle drawl was a capital foil to Lady Georgina's acidulous soprano. It seemed to disarm her. She turned to me with a benig-

nant wave of her hand. 'Miss Cayley,' she said, introducing me;
'my nephew, Mr. Harold Tillington. You've heard me talk of poor
Tom Cayley, Harold? This is poor Tom Cayley's daughter.'

'Indeed?' the supercilious *attaché* put in, looking hard at me.
'Delighted to make Miss Cayley's acquaintance.'

'Now, Harold, I can tell from your voice at once you haven't
remembered one word about Captain Cayley.'

Harold stood on the defensive. 'My dear aunt,' he observed,
expanding both palms, 'I have heard you talk of so *very* many
people, that even *my* diplomatic memory fails at times to recollect
them all. But I do better: I dissemble. I will plead forgetfulness
now of Captain Cayley, since you force it on me. It is not likely I
shall have to plead it of Captain Cayley's daughter.' And he bowed
toward me gallantly.

The Cantankerous Old Lady darted a lightning glance at him.
It was a glance of quick suspicion. Then she turned her Röntgen
rays upon my face once more. I fear I burned crimson.

'A friend?' he asked. 'Or a fellow-guest?'

'A companion.' It was the first nasty thing she had said of me.

'Ha! more than a friend, then. A comrade.' He turned the edge
neatly.

We walked out on the terrace and a little way up the zigzag
path. The day was superb. I found Mr. Tillington, in spite of his studiously languid and supercilious air, a most agreeable companion.
He knew Europe. He was full of talk of Rome and the Romans.
He had epigrammatic wit, curt, keen, and pointed. We sat down
on a bench; he kept Lady Georgina and myself amused for an hour
by his crisp sallies. Besides, he had been everywhere and seen everybody. Culture and agriculture seemed all one to him.

When we rose to go in, Lady Georgina remarked, with emphasis, 'Of course, Harold, you'll come and take up your diggings at
our hotel?'

'Of course, my dear aunt. How can you ask? Free quarters.
Nothing would give me greater pleasure.'

She glanced at him keenly again. I saw she had expected him to
fake up some lame excuse for not joining us; and I fancied she was
annoyed at his prompt acquiescence, which had done her out of

the chance for a family disagreement. 'Oh, you'll come then?' she said, grudgingly.

'Certainly, most respected aunt. I shall much prefer it.'

She let her piercing eye descend upon me once more. I was aware that I had been talking with frank ease of manner to Mr. Tillington, and that I had said several things which clearly amused him. Then I remembered all at once our relative positions. A companion, I felt, should know her place: it is not her *rôle* to be smart and amusing. 'Perhaps,' I said, drawing back, 'Mr. Tillington would like to remain in his present quarters till the end of the week, while I am with you, Lady Georgina; after that, he could have my room; it might be more convenient.'

His eye caught mine quickly. 'Oh, you're only going to stop a week, then, Miss Cayley?' he put in, with an air of disappointment.

'Only a week,' I nodded.

'My dear child,' the Cantankerous Old Lady broke out, 'what nonsense you do talk! Only going to stop a week? How can I exist without you?'

'That was the arrangement,' I said, mischievously. 'You were going to look about, you recollect, for an unsophisticated Gretchen. You don't happen to know of any warehouse where a supply of unsophisticated Gretchens is kept constantly in stock, do you, Mr. Tillington?'

'No, I don't,' he answered, laughing. 'I believe there are dodos' and auks' eggs, in very small numbers, still to be procured in the proper quarters; but the unsophisticated Gretchen, I am credibly informed, is an extinct animal. Why, the cap of one fetches high prices nowadays among collectors.'

'But you will come to the hotel at once, Harold?' Lady Georgina interposed.

'Certainly, aunt. I will move in without delay. If Miss Cayley is going to stay for a single week only, that adds one extra inducement for joining you immediately.'

His aunt's stony eye was cold as marble.

So when we got back to our hotel after the baths that afternoon, the *concierge* greeted us with: 'Well, your noble nephew has arrived, high-well-born countess! He came with his boxes just now, and has taken a room near your honourable ladyship's.'

Lady Georgina's face was a study of mingled emotions. I don't know whether she looked more pleased or jealous.

Later in the day, I chanced on Mr. Tillington, sunning himself on a bench in the hotel garden. He rose, and came up to me, as fast as his languid nature permitted. 'Oh, Miss Cayley,' he said, abruptly, 'I do want to thank you so much for not betraying me. I know you spotted me twice in the town yesterday; and I also know you were good enough to say nothing to my revered aunt about it.'

'I had no reason for wishing to hurt Lady Georgina's feelings,' I answered, with a permissible evasion.

His countenance fell. 'I never thought of that,' he interposed, with one hand on his moustache. 'I—I fancied you did it out of fellow-feeling.'

'We all think of things mainly from our own point of view first,' I answered. 'The difference is that some of us think of them from other people's afterwards. Motives are mixed.'

He smiled. 'I didn't know my deeply venerated relative was coming here so soon,' he went on. 'I thought she wasn't expected till next week; my brother wrote me that she had quarrelled with her French maid, and 'twould take her full ten days to get another. I meant to clear out before she arrived. To tell you the truth, I was going to-morrow.'

'And now you are stopping on?'

He caught my eye again.

'Circumstances alter cases,' he murmured, with meaning.

'It is hardly polite to describe one as a circumstance,' I objected.

'I meant,' he said, quickly, 'my aunt alone is one thing; my aunt with a friend is quite another.'

'I see,' I answered. 'There is safety in numbers.'

He eyed me hard.

'Are you mediæval or modern?' he asked.

'Modern, I hope,' I replied. Then I looked at him again. 'Oxford?'

He nodded. 'And you?' half joking.

'Cambridge,' I said, glad to catch him out. 'What college?'

'Merton. Yours?'

'Girton.'

The odd rhyme amused him. Thenceforth we were friends—
'two 'Varsity men,' he said. And indeed it does make a queer sort
of link—a freemasonry to which even women are now admitted.

At dinner and through the evening he talked a great deal to
me, Lady Georgina putting in from time to time a characteristic
growl about the *table-d'hôte* chicken—'a special breed, my dear,
with eight drumsticks apiece'—or about the inadequate lighting
of the heavy German *salon*. She was worse than ever: pungent as a
rule, that evening she was grumpy. When we retired for the night,
to my great surprise, she walked into my bedroom. She seated
herself on my bed: I saw she had come to talk over Harold.

'He will be very rich, my dear, you know. A great catch in time.
He will inherit all my brother's money.'

'Lord Kynaston's?'

'Bless the child, no. Kynaston's as poor as a church mouse
with the tithes unpaid; he has three sons of his own, and not a
blessed stiver to leave between them. How could he, poor dear
idiot? Agricultural depression; a splendid pauper. He has only
the estate, and that's in Essex; land going begging; worth nothing a year, encumbered up to the eyes, and loaded with first rent-
charges, jointures, settlements. Money, indeed! poor Kynaston! It's
my brother Marmaduke's I mean; lucky dog, *he* went in for specu-
lation—began life as a guinea-pig, and rose with the rise of soap
and cocoa. He's worth his half-million.'

'Oh, Mr. Marmaduke Ashurst.'

Lady Georgina nodded. 'Marmy's a fool,' she said, briefly; 'but
he knows which side of his bread is buttered.'

'And Mr. Tillington is—his nephew?'

'Bless the child, yes; have you never read your British Bible, the
peerage? Astonishing, the ignorance of these Girton girls! They
don't even know the Leger's run at Doncaster. The family name's
Ashurst. Kynaston's an earl—I was Lady Georgina Ashurst before
I took it into my head to marry and do for poor Evelyn Fawley. My
younger brother's the Honourable Marmaduke Ashurst—women
get the best of it there—it's about the only place where they do get

the best of it: an earl's daughter is Lady Betty; his son's nothing
more than the Honourable Tom. So one scores off one's broth-
ers. My younger sister, Lady Guinevere Ashurst, married Stanley
Tillington of the Foreign Office. Harold's their eldest son. Now,
child, do you grasp it?'

'Perfectly,' I answered. 'You speak like Debrett. Has issue,
Harold.'

'And Harold will inherit all Marmaduke's money. What I'm
always afraid of is that some fascinating adventuress will try to
marry him out of hand. A pretty face, and over goes Harold! My
business in life is to stand in the way and prevent it.'

She looked me through and through again with her X-ray
scrutiny.

'I don't think Mr. Tillington is quite the sort that falls a prey to
adventuresses,' I answered, boldly.

'Ah, but there are faggots and faggots,' the old lady said, wag-
ging her head with profound meaning. 'Never mind, though; I'd
like to see an adventuress marry off Harold without my leave! I'd
lead her a life! I'd turn her black hair grey for her!'

'I should think,' I assented, 'you could do it, Lady Georgina, if
you gave your attention seriously to it.'

From that moment forth, I was aware that my Cantankerous
Old Lady's malign eye was inexorably fixed upon me every time
I went within speaking distance of Mr. Tillington. She watched
him like a lynx. She watched *me* like a dozen lynxes. Wherever we
went, Lady Georgina was sure to turn up in the neighbourhood.
She was perfectly ubiquitous: she seemed to possess a world-wide
circulation. I don't know whether it was this constant suggestion
of hers that I was stalking her nephew which roused my latent
human feeling of opposition; but in the end, I began to be aware
that I rather liked the supercilious attaché than otherwise. He evidently liked me, and he tried to meet me. Whenever he spoke to
me, indeed, it was without the superciliousness which marked his
manner toward others; in point of fact, it was with graceful deference. He watched for me on the stairs, in the garden, by the terrace; whenever he got a chance, he sidled over and talked to me.
Sometimes he stopped in to read me Heine: he also introduced
me to select portions of Gabriele d'Annunzio. It is feminine to be

touched by such obvious attention; I confess, before long, I grew to like Mr. Harold Tillington.

The closer he followed me up, the more did I perceive that Lady Georgina threw out acrid hints with increasing spleen about the ways of adventuresses. They were hints of that acrimonious generalised kind, too, which one cannot answer back without seeming to admit that the cap has fitted. It was atrocious how middle-class young women nowadays ran after young men of birth and fortune. A girl would stoop to anything in order to catch five hundred thousand. Guileless youths should be thrown among their natural equals. It was a mistake to let them see too much of people of a lower rank who consider themselves good-looking. And the clever ones were the worst: they pretended to go in for intellectual companionship.

I also noticed that though at first Lady Georgina had expressed the strongest disinclination to my leaving her after the time originally proposed, she now began to take for granted that I would go at the end of my week, as arranged in London, and she even went on to some overt steps towards securing the help of the blameless Gretchen.

We had arrived at Schlangenbad on Tuesday. I was to stop with the Cantankerous Old Lady till the corresponding day of the following week. On the Sunday, I wandered out on the wooded hillside behind the village; and as I mounted the path I was dimly aware by a sort of instinct that Harold Tillington was following me.

He came up with me at last near a ledge of rock. 'How fast you walk!' he exclaimed. 'I gave you only a few minutes' start, and yet even my long legs have had hard work to overtake you.'

'I am a fairly good climber,' I answered, sitting down on a little wooden bench. 'You see, at Cambridge, I went on the river a great deal—I canoed and sculled: and then, besides, I've done a lot of bicycling.'

'What a splendid birthright it is,' he cried, 'to be a wholesome athletic English girl! You can't think how one admires English girls after living a year or two in Italy—where women are dolls, except for a brief period of intrigue, before they settle down to be contented frumps with an outline like a barrel.'

'A little muscle and a little mind are no doubt advisable adjuncts for a housewife,' I admitted.

'You shall not say that word,' he cried, seating himself at my side. 'It is a word for Germans, "housewife." Our English ideal is something immeasurably higher and better. A companion, a complement! Do you know, Miss Cayley, it always sickens me when I hear German students sentimentalising over their *mädchen:* their beautiful, pure, insipid, yellow-haired, blue-eyed *mädchen;* her, so fair, so innocent, so unapproachably vacuous—so like a wax doll—and then think of how they design her in days to come to cook sausages for their dinner, and knit them endless stockings through a placid middle age, till the needles drop from her paralysed fingers, and she retires into frilled caps and Teutonic senility.'

'You seem to have almost as low an opinion of foreigners as your respected aunt!' I exclaimed, looking quizzically at him.

He drew back, surprised. 'Oh, no; I'm not narrow-minded, like my aunt, I hope,' he answered. 'I am a good cosmopolitan. I allow Continental nations all their own good points, and each has many. But their women, Miss Cayley—and their point of view of their women—you will admit that there they can't hold a candle to English women.'

I drew a circle in the dust with the tip of my parasol.

'On that issue, I may not be a wholly unprejudiced observer,' I answered. 'The fact of my being myself an Englishwoman may possibly to some extent influence my judgment.'

'You are sarcastic,' he cried, drawing away.

'Not at all,' I answered, making a wider circle. 'I spoke a simple fact. But what is *your* ideal, then, as opposed to the German one?'

He gazed at me and hesitated. His lips half parted. 'My ideal?' he said, after a pause. 'Well, *my* ideal—do you happen to have such a thing as a pocket-mirror about you?'

I laughed in spite of myself. 'Now, Mr. Tillington,' I said severely, 'if you're going to pay compliments, I shall have to return. If you want to stop here with me, you must remember that I am only Lady Georgina Fawley's temporary lady's-maid. Besides, I didn't mean that. I meant, what is your ideal of a man's right relation to his *mädchen?*'

'Don't say *mädchen*,' he cried, petulantly. 'It sounds as if you thought me one of those sentimental Germans. I hate sentiment.'

'Then, towards the woman of his choice.'

He glanced up through the trees at the light overhead, and spoke more slowly than ever. 'I think,' he said, fumbling his watch-chain nervously, 'a man ought to wish the woman he loves to be a free agent, his equal in point of action, even as she is nobler and better than he in all spiritual matters. I think he ought to desire for her a life as high as she is capable of leading, with full scope for every faculty of her intellect or her emotional nature. She should be beautiful, with a vigorous, wholesome, many-sided beauty, moral, intellectual, physical; yet with soul in her, too; and with the soul and the mind lighting up her eyes, as it lights up—well, that is immaterial. And if a man can discover such a woman as that, and can induce her to believe in him, to love him, to accept him—though how such a woman can be satisfied with any man at all is to me unfathomable—well, then, I think he should be happy in devoting his whole life to her, and should give himself up to repay her condescension in taking him.'

'And you hate sentiment!' I put in, smiling.

He brought his eyes back from the sky suddenly. 'Miss Cayley,' he said, 'this is cruel. I was in earnest. You are playing with me.'

'I believe the chief characteristic of the English girl is supposed to be common sense,' I answered, calmly, 'and I trust I possess it.' But indeed, as he spoke, my heart was beginning to make its beat felt; for he was a charming young man; he had a soft voice and lustrous eyes; it was a summer's day; and alone in the woods with one other person, where the sunlight falls mellow in spots like a leopard's skin, one is apt to remember that we are all human.

That evening Lady Georgina managed to blurt out more malicious things than ever about the ways of adventuresses, and the duty of relations in saving young men from the clever clutches of designing creatures. She was ruthless in her rancour; her gibes stung me.

On Monday at breakfast I asked her casually if she had yet found a Gretchen.

'No,' she answered, in a gloomy voice. 'All slatterns, my dear;

all slatterns! Brought up in pig-sties. I wouldn't let one of them touch my hair for thousands.'

'That's unfortunate,' I said, drily, 'for you know I'm going to-morrow.'

If I had dropped a bomb in their midst they couldn't have looked more astonished. 'To-morrow?' Lady Georgina gasped, clutching my arm. 'You don't mean it, child; you don't mean it?'

I asserted my Ego. 'Certainly,' I answered, with my coolest air. 'I said I thought I could manage you for a week; and I have managed you.'

She almost burst into tears. 'But, my child, my child, what shall I do without you?'

'The unsophisticated Gretchen,' I answered, trying not to look concerned; for in my heart of hearts, in spite of her innuendoes, I had really grown rather to like the Cantankerous Old Lady.

She rose hastily from the table, and darted up to her own room. 'Lois,' she said, as she rose, in a curious voice of mingled regret and suspicion, 'I will talk to you about this later.' I could see she was not quite satisfied in her own mind whether Harold Tillington and I had not arranged this *coup* together.

I put on my hat and strolled off into the garden, and then along the mossy hill path. In a minute more, Harold Tillington was beside me.

He seated me, half against my will, on a rustic bench. 'Look here, Miss Cayley,' he said, with a very earnest face; 'is this really true? Are you going to-morrow?'

My voice trembled a little. 'Yes,' I answered, biting my lip, 'I am going. I see several reasons why I should go, Mr. Tillington.'

'But so soon?'

'Yes, I think so; the sooner the better.' My heart was racing now, and his eyes pleaded mutely.

'Then where are you going?'

I shrugged my shoulders, and pouted my lips a little. 'I don't know,' I replied. 'The world is all before me where to choose. I am an adventuress,' I said it boldly, 'and I am in quest of adventures. I really have not yet given a thought to my next place of sojourn.'

'But you will let me know when you have decided?'

It was time to speak out. 'No, Mr. Tillington,' I said, with decision. 'I will *not* let you know. One of my reasons for going is, that I think I had better see no more of you.'

He flung himself on the bench at my side, and folded his hands in a helpless attitude. 'But, Miss Cayley,' he cried, 'this is so short a notice; you give a fellow no chance; I hoped I might have seen more of you—might have had some opportunity of—of letting you realise how deeply I admired and respected you—some opportunity of showing myself as I really am to you—before—before——' he paused, and looked hard at me.

I did not know what to say. I really liked him so much; and when he spoke in that voice, I could not bear to seem cruel to him. Indeed, I was aware at the moment how much I had grown to care for him in those six short days. But I knew it was impossible. 'Don't say it, Mr. Tillington,' I murmured, turning my face away. 'The less said, the sooner mended.'

'But I must,' he cried. 'I must tell you now, if I am to have no chance afterwards. I wanted you to see more of me before I ventured to ask you if you could ever love me, if you could ever suffer me to go through life with you, to share my all with you.' He seized my trembling hand. 'Lois,' he cried, in a pleading voice, 'I *must* ask you; I can't expect you to answer me now, but *do* say you will give me at least some other chance of seeing you, and then, in time, of pressing my suit upon you.'

Tears stood in my eyes. He was so earnest, so charming. But I remembered Lady Georgina, and his prospective half-million. I moved his hand away gently. 'I cannot,' I said. 'I cannot—I am a penniless girl—an adventuress. Your family, your uncle, would never forgive you if you married me. I will not stand in your way. I—I like you very much, though I have seen so little of you. But I feel it is impossible—and I am going to-morrow.'

Then I rose of a sudden, and ran down the hill with all my might, lest I should break my resolve, never stopping once till I reached my own bedroom.

An hour later, Lady Georgina burst in upon me in high dudgeon. 'Why, Lois, my child!' she cried. 'What's this? What on earth does it mean? Harold tells me he has proposed to you—proposed to you—and you've rejected him!'

I dried my eyes and tried to look steadily at her. 'Yes, Lady

Georgina,' I faltered. 'You need not be afraid. I have refused him; and I mean it.'

She looked at me, all aghast. '*And* you mean it!' she repeated. 'You mean to refuse him. Then, all I can say is, Lois Cayley, I call it pure cheek of you!'

'What?' I cried, drawing back.

'Yes, cheek,' she answered, volubly. 'Forty thousand a year, and a good old family! Harold Tillington is my nephew; he's an earl's grandson; he's an attaché at Rome; and he's bound to be one of the richest commoners in England. Who are you, I'd like to know, miss, that you dare to reject him?'

I stared at her, amazed. 'But, Lady Georgina,' I cried, 'you said you wished to protect your nephew against barefaced adventuresses who were setting their caps at him.'

She fixed her eyes on me, half angry, half tremulous.

'Of course,' she answered, with withering scorn. 'But, *then,* I thought you were trying to catch him. He tells me now you won't have him, and you won't tell him where you are going. I call it sheer insolence. Where do you hail from, girl, that you should refuse my nephew? A man that any woman in England would be proud to marry! Forty thousand a year, and an earl's grandson! That's what comes, I suppose, of going to Girton!'

I drew myself up. 'Lady Georgina,' I said, coldly, 'I cannot allow you to use such language to me. I promised to accompany you to Germany for a week; and I have kept my word. I like your nephew; I respect your nephew; he has behaved like a gentleman. But I will *not* marry him. Your own conduct showed me in the plainest way that you did not judge such a match desirable for him; and I have common sense enough to see that you were quite right. I am a lady by birth and education; I am an officer's daughter; but I am not what society calls a "good match" for Mr. Tillington. He had better marry into a rich stock-broker's family.'

It was an unworthy taunt; the moment it escaped my lips I regretted it.

To my intense surprise, however, Lady Georgina flung herself on my bed, and burst into tears. 'My dear,' she sobbed out, covering her face with her hands, 'I thought you would be sure to set your cap at Harold; and after I had seen you for twenty-four hours,

I said to myself, 'That's just the sort of girl Harold ought to fall in love with.' I felt sure he would fall in love with you. I brought you here on purpose. I saw you had all the qualities that would strike Harold's fancy. So I had made up my mind for a delightful regulation family quarrel. I was going to oppose you and Harold, tooth and nail; I was going to threaten that Marmy would leave his money to Kynaston's eldest son; I was going to kick up, oh, a dickens of a row about it! Then, of course, in the end, we should all have been reconciled; we should have kissed and made friends: for you're just the one girl in the world for Harold; indeed, I never met anybody so capable and so intelligent. And now you spoil all my sport by going and refusing him! It's really most ill-timed of you. And Harold has sent me here—he's trembling with anxiety—to see whether I can't induce you to think better of your decision.'

I made up my mind at once. 'No, Lady Georgina,' I said, in my gentlest voice—positively stooping down and kissing her. 'I like Mr. Tillington very much. I dare not tell you how much I like him. He is a dear, good, kind fellow. But I cannot rest under the cruel imputation of being moved by his wealth and having tried to capture him. Even if *you* didn't think so, his family would. I am sorry to go; for in a way I like you. But it is best to adhere to our original plan. If *I* changed my mind, *you* might change yours again. Let us say no more. I will go to-morrow.'

'But you will see Harold again?'

'Not alone. Only at dinner.' For I feared lest, if he spoke to me alone, he might over-persuade me.

'Then at least you will tell him where you are going?'

'No, Lady Georgina; I do not know myself. And besides, it is best that this should now be final.'

She flung herself upon me. 'But, my dear child, a lady can't go out into the world with only two pounds in pocket. You *must* let me lend you something.'

I unwound her clasping hands. 'No, dear Lady Georgina,' I said, though I was loth to say it. 'You are very sweet and good, but I must work out my life in my own way. I have started to work it out, and I won't be turned aside just here on the threshold.'

'And you won't stop with me?' she cried, opening her arms. 'You think me too cantankerous?'

'I think you have a dear, kind old heart,' I said, 'under the quaintest and crustiest outside such a heart ever wore; you're a truculent old darling; so that's the plain truth of it.'

She kissed me. I kissed her in return with fervour, though I am but a poor hand at kissing, for a woman. 'So now this episode is concluded,' I murmured.

'I don't know about that,' she said, drying her eyes. 'I have set my heart upon you now; and Harold has set his heart upon you; and considering that your own heart goes much the same way, I daresay, my dear, we shall find in the end some convenient road out of it.'

Nevertheless, next morning I set out by myself in the coach from Schlangenbad. I went forth into the world to live my own life, partly because it was just then so fashionable, but mainly because fate had denied me the chance of living anybody else's.

MISS CAYLEY'S ADVENTURES 41

CHAPTER III

THE ADVENTURE OF THE INQUISITIVE AMERICAN

IN one week I had multiplied my capital two-hundred-and-forty-fold! I left London with twopence in the world; I quitted Schlangenbad with two pounds in pocket. 'There's a splendid turn-over!' I thought to myself. 'If this luck holds, at the same rate, I shall have made four hundred and eighty pounds by Tuesday next, and I may look forward to being a Barney Barnato by Christmas.' For I had taken high mathematical honours at Cambridge, and if there is anything on earth on which I pride myself, it is my firm grasp of the principle of ratios.

Still, in spite of this brilliant financial prospect, a budding Klondike, I went away from the little Spa on the flanks of the Taunus with a heavy heart. I had grown quite to like dear, virulent, fidgety old Lady Georgina; and I felt that it had cost me a distinct wrench to part with Harold Tillington. The wrench left a scar which was long in healing; but as I am not a professional sentimentalist, I will not trouble you here with details of the symptoms.

My livelihood, however, was now assured me. With two pounds in pocket, a sensible girl can read her title clear to six days' board and lodging, at six marks a day, with a glorious margin of four marks over for pocket-money. And if at the end of six days my fairy godmother had not pointed me out some other means of earning my bread honestly—well, I should feel myself unworthy to be ranked in the noble army of adventuresses. I thank thee, Lady Georgina, for teaching me that word. An adventuress I would be; for I loved adventure.

Meanwhile, it occurred to me that I might fill up the interval by going to study art at Frankfort. Elsie Petheridge had been there, and had impressed upon me the fact that I must on no account omit to see the Städel Gallery. She was strong on culture. Besides, the study of art should be most useful to an adventuress; for she must need all the arts that human skill has developed.

So to Frankfort I betook myself, and found there a nice little *pension*—'for ladies only,' Frau Bockenheimer assured me—at very moderate rates, in a pleasant part of the Lindenstrasse. It had dimity curtains. I will not deny that as I entered the house I was conscious of feeling lonely; my heart sank once or twice as I glanced round the luncheon-table at the domestically-unsympathetic German old maids who formed the rank-and-file of my fellow-boarders. There they sat—eight comfortable Fraus who had missed their vocation; plentiful ladies, bulging and surging in tightly-stretched black silk bodices. They had been cut out for such housewives as Harold Tillington had described, but found themselves deprived of their natural sphere in life by the unaccountable caprice of the men of their nation. Each was a model Teutonic matron *manquée*. Each looked capable of frying Frankfort sausages to a turn, and knitting woollen socks to a remote eternity. But I sought in vain for one kindred soul among them. How horrified they would have been, with their fat pudding-faces and big saucer-eyes, had I boldly announced myself as an English adventuress!

I spent my first morning in laborious self-education at the Ariadneum and the Städel Gallery. I borrowed a catalogue. I wrestled with Van der Weyden; I toiled like a galley-slave at Meister Wilhelm and Meister Stephan. I have a confused recollection that I saw a number of stiff mediæval pictures, and an alabaster statue of the lady who smiled as she rode on a tiger, taken at the beginning of that interesting episode. But the remainder of the Institute has faded from my memory.

In the afternoon I consoled myself for my herculean efforts in the direction of culture by going out for a bicycle ride on a hired machine, to which end I decided to devote my pocket-money. You will, perhaps, object here that my conduct was imprudent. To raise that objection is to misunderstand the spirit of these artless adventures. I told you that I set out to go round the world; but to go round the world does not necessarily mean to circumnavigate it. My idea was to go round by easy stages, seeing the world as I went as far as I got, and taking as little heed as possible of the morrow. Most of my readers, no doubt, accept that philosophy of life on Sundays only; on week-days they swallow the usual contradictory economic platitudes about prudential forethought and the horrid improvidence of the lower classes. For myself, I am not built that way. I prefer to take life in a spirit of pure inquiry. I put on my hat; I saunter where I choose, so far as circumstances permit; and I wait to see what chance will bring me. My ideal is breeziness.

The hired bicycle was not a bad machine, as hired bicycles go; it jolted one as little as you can expect from a common hack; it never stopped at a Bier-Garten; and it showed very few signs of having been ridden by beginners with an unconquerable desire to tilt at the hedgerow. So off I soared at once, heedless of the jeers of Teutonic youth who found the sight of a lady in skirts riding a cycle a strange one—for in South Germany the 'rational' costume is so universal among women cyclists that 'tis the skirt that provokes unfavourable comment from those jealous guardians of female propriety, the street boys. I hurried on at a brisk pace past the Palm-Garden and the suburbs, with my loose hair straying on the breeze behind, till I found myself pedalling at a good round pace on a broad, level road, which led towards a village, by name Fraunheim.

As I scurried across the plain, with the wind in my face, not unpleasantly, I had some dim consciousness of somebody unknown flying after me headlong. My first idea was that Harold Tillington had hunted me down and tracked me to my lair; but gazing back, I saw my pursuer was a tall and ungainly man, with a straw-coloured moustache, apparently American, and that he was following me on his machine, closely watching my action. He had such a cunning expression on his face, and seemed so strangely inquisitive, with eyes riveted on my treadles, that I didn't quite like the look of him. I put on the pace, to see if I could outstrip him, for I am a swift cyclist. But his long legs were too much for me. He did not gain on me, it is true; but neither did I outpace him. Pedalling my very hardest—and I can make good time when necessary—I still kept pretty much at the same distance in front of him all the way to Fraunheim.

Gradually I began to feel sure that the weedy-looking man with the alert face was really pursuing me. When I went faster, he went faster too; when I gave him a chance to pass me, he kept close at my heels, and appeared to be keenly watching the style of my ankle-action. I gathered that he was a connoisseur; but why on earth he should persecute me I could not imagine. My spirit was roused now—I pedalled with a will; if I rode all day I would not let him go past me.

Beyond the cobble-paved chief street of Fraunheim the road took a sharp bend, and began to mount the slopes of the Taunus suddenly. It was an abrupt, steep climb; but I flatter myself I am a tolerable mountain cyclist. I rode sturdily on; my pursuer darted after me. But on this stiff upward grade my light weight and agile ankle-action told; I began to distance him. He seemed afraid that I would give him the slip, and called out suddenly, with a whoop, in English, 'Stop, miss!' I looked back with dignity, but answered nothing. He put on the pace, panting; I pedalled away and got clear from him.

At a turn of the corner, however, as luck would have it, I was pulled up short by a mounted policeman. He blocked the road with his horse, like an ogre, and asked me, in a very gruff Swabian voice, if this was a licensed bicycle. I had no idea, till he spoke, that any license was required; though to be sure I might have guessed it; for modern Germany is studded with notices at all the street corners, to inform you in minute detail that everything is forbidden. I stammered out that I did not know. The mounted policeman drew near and inspected me rudely. 'It is strongly undersaid,' he began, but just at that moment my pursuer came up, and, with American quickness, took in the situation. He accosted the policeman in choice bad German. 'I have two licenses,' he said, producing a handful. 'The Fräulein rides with me.'

I was too much taken aback at so providential an interposition to contradict this highly imaginative statement. My highwayman had turned into a protecting knight-errant of injured innocence. I let the policeman go his way; then I glanced at my preserver. A very ordinary modern St. George he looked, with no lance to speak of, and no steed but a bicycle. Yet his mien was reassuring.

'Good-morning, miss,' he began—he called me 'Miss' every time he addressed me, as though he took me for a barmaid. 'Excuse *me*, but why did you want to speed her?'

'I thought you were pursuing me,' I answered, a little tremulous, I will confess, but avid of incident.

'And if I was,' he went on, 'you might have con-jectured, miss, it was for our mutual advantage. A business man don't go out of

his way unless he expects to turn an honest dollar; and he don't
reckon on other folks going out of theirs, unless he knows he can
put them in the way of turning an honest dollar with him.'

'That's reasonable,' I answered: for I am a political economist.
'The benefit should be mutual.' But I wondered if he were going
to propose at sight to me.

He looked me all up and down. 'You're a lady of considerable
personal attractions,' he said, musingly, as if he were criticising a
horse; 'and I want one that sort. That's jest why I trailed you, see?
Besides which, there's some style about you.'

'Style!' I repeated.

'Yes,' he went on; 'you know how to use your feet; and you
have good understandings.'

I gathered from his glance that he referred to my nether limbs.
We are all vertebrate animals; why seek to conceal the fact?

'I fail to follow you,' I answered frigidly; for I really didn't know
what the man might say next.

'That's so!' he replied. 'It was I that followed you; seems I didn't
make much of a job of it, either, anyway.'

I mounted my machine again. 'Well, good-morning,' I said,
coldly. 'I am much obliged for your kind assistance; but your
remark was fictitious, and I desire to go on unaccompanied.'

He held up his hand in warning. 'You ain't going!' he cried, horrified. 'You ain't going without hearing me! I mean business, say!
Don't chuck away good money like that. I tell you, there's dollars
in it.'

'In what?' I asked, still moving on, but curious. On the slope, if
need were, I could easily distance him.

'Why, in this cycling of yours,' he replied. 'You're jest about the
very woman I'm looking for, miss. Lithe—that's what I call you. I
kin put you in the way of making your pile, I kin. This is a bonâ-
fide offer. No flies on my business! You decline it? Prejudice! Injures
you; injures me! Be reasonable anyway!'

I looked around and laughed. 'Formulate yourself,' I said,
briefly.

He rose to it like a man. 'Meet me at Fraunheim; corner by
the Post Office; ten o'clock to-morrow morning,' he shouted, as I

rode off, 'and ef I don't convince you there's money in this job, my name's not Cyrus W. Hitchcock.'

Something about his keen, unlovely face impressed me with a sense of his underlying honesty. 'Very well,' I answered, 'I'll come, if you follow me no farther.' I reflected that Fraunheim was a populous village, and that only beyond it did the mountain road over the Taunus begin to grow lonely. If he wished to cut my throat, I was well within reach of the resources of civilisation.

When I got home to the Abode of Blighted Fraus that evening, I debated seriously with myself whether or not I should accept Mr. Cyrus W. Hitchcock's mysterious invitation. Prudence said *no;* curiosity said *yes;* I put the question to a meeting of one; and, since I am a daughter of Eve, curiosity had it. Carried unanimously. I think I might have hesitated, indeed, had it not been for the Blighted Fraus. Their talk was of dinner and of the digestive process; they were critics of digestion. They each of them sat so complacently through the evening—solid and stolid, stodgy and podgy, stuffed comatose images, knitting white woollen shawls, to throw over their capacious shoulders at *table d'hôte*—and they purred in such content in their middle-aged rotundity that I made up my mind I must take warning betimes, and avoid their temptations to adipose deposit. I prefer to grow upwards; the frau grows sideways. Better get my throat cut by an American desperado, in my pursuit of romance, than settle down on a rock like a placid fat oyster. I am not by nature sessile.

Adventures are to the adventurous. They abound on every side; but only the chosen few have the courage to embrace them. And they will not come to you: you must go out to seek them. Then they meet you half-way, and rush into your arms, for they know their true lovers. There were eight Blighted Fraus at the Home for Lost Ideals, and I could tell by simple inspection that they had not had an average of half an adventure per lifetime between them. They sat and knitted still, like Awful Examples.

If I had declined to meet Mr. Hitchcock at Fraunheim, I know not what changes it might have induced in my life. I might now be knitting. But I went boldly forth, on a voyage of exploration, prepared to accept aught that fate held in store for me.

As Mr. Hitchcock had assured me there was money in his offer,

I felt justified in speculating. I expended another three marks on the hire of a bicycle, though I ran the risk thereby of going, perhaps, without Monday's dinner. That showed my vocation. The Blighted Fraus, I felt sure, would have clung to their dinner at all hazards.

When I arrived at Fraunheim, I found my alert American punctually there before me. He raised his crush hat with awkward politeness. I could see he was little accustomed to ladies' society. Then he pointed to a close cab in which he had reached the village.

'I've got it inside,' he whispered, in a confidential tone. 'I couldn't let 'em ketch sight of it. You see, there's dollars in it.'

'What have you got inside?' I asked, suspiciously, drawing back. I don't know why, but the word 'it' somehow suggested a corpse; I began to grow frightened.

'Why, the wheel, of course,' he answered. 'Ain't you come here to ride it?'

'Oh, the wheel?' I echoed, vaguely, pretending to look wise; but unaware, as yet, that that word was the accepted Americanism for a bicycle. 'And I have come to ride it?'

'Why, certainly,' he replied, jerking his hand towards the cab. 'But we mustn't start right here. This thing has got to be kept dark, don't you see, till the last day.'

Till the last day! That was ominous. It sounded like monomania. So ghostly and elusive! I began to suspect my American ally of being a dangerous madman.

'Jest you wheel away a bit up the hill,' he went on, 'out o' sight of the folks, and I'll fetch her along to you.'

'Her?' I cried. 'Who?' For the man bewildered me.

'Why, the wheel, miss! *You* understand! This is business, you bet! And you're jest the right woman!'

He motioned me on. Urged by a sort of spell, I remounted my machine and rode out of the village. He followed, on the box-seat of his cab. Then, when we had left the world well behind, and stood among the sun-smitten boles of the pine-trees, he opened the door mysteriously, and produced from the vehicle a very odd-looking bicycle.

It was clumsy to look at. It differed immensely, in many particulars, from any machine I had yet seen or ridden.

The strenuous American fondled it for a moment with his hand, as if it were a pet child. Then he mounted nimbly. Pride shone in his eye. I saw in a second he was a fond inventor.

He rode a few yards on. Next he turned to me eagerly. 'This ma-chine,' he said, in an impressive voice, 'is pro-pelled *by* an eccentric.' Like all his countrymen, he laid most stress on unaccented syllables.

'Oh, I knew you were an eccentric,' I said, 'the moment I set eyes upon you.'

He surveyed me gravely. 'You misunderstand me, miss,' he corrected. '*When* I say an eccentric, I mean a crank.'

'They are much the same thing,' I answered, briskly. 'Though I confess I would hardly have applied so rude a word as *crank* to you.'

He looked me over suspiciously, as if I were trying to make game of him, but my face was sphinx-like. So he brought the machine a yard or two nearer, and explained its construction to me. He was quite right: it *was* driven by a crank. It had no chain, but was moved by a pedal, working narrowly up and down, and attached to a rigid bar, which impelled the wheels by means of an eccentric.

Besides this, it had a curious device for altering the gearing automatically while one rode, so as to enable one to adapt it to the varying slope in mounting hills. This part of the mechanism he explained to me elaborately. There was a gauge in front which allowed one to sight the steepness of the slope by mere inspection; and according as the gauge marked one, two, three, or four, as its gradient on the scale, the rider pressed a button on the handle-bar with his left hand once, twice, thrice, or four times, so that the gearing adapted itself without an effort to the rise in the surface. Besides, there were devices for rigidity and compensation. Altogether, it was a most apt and ingenious piece of mechanism. I did not wonder he was proud of it.

'Get up and ride, miss,' he said in a persuasive voice.

I did as I was bid. To my immense surprise, I ran up the steep hill as smoothly and easily as if it were a perfectly-laid level.

'Goes nicely, doesn't she?' Mr. Hitchcock murmured, rubbing his hands.

'Beautifully,' I answered. 'One could ride such a machine up Mont Blanc, I should fancy.'

He stroked his chin with nervous fingers. 'It ought to knock 'em,' he said, in an eager voice. 'It's geared to run up most anything in creation.'

'How steep?'

'One foot in three.'

'That's good.'

'Yes. It'll climb Mount Washington.'

'What do you call it?' I asked.

He looked me over with close scrutiny.

'In Amurrica,' he said, slowly, 'we call it the Great Manitou, because it kin do pretty well what it chooses; but in Europe, I am thinking of calling it the Martin Conway or the Whymper, or something like that.'

'Why so?'

'Well, because it's a famous mountain climber.'

'I see,' I said. 'With such a machine you'll put a notice on the Matterhorn, "This hill is dangerous to cyclists."'

He laughed low to himself, and rubbed his hands again. 'You'll do, miss,' he said. 'You're the right sort, you are. The moment I seen you, I thought we two could do a trade together. Benefits me; benefits you. A mutual advantage. Reciprocity is the soul of business. You hev some go in you, you hev. There's money in your feet. You'll give these Meinherrs fits. You'll take the clear-starch out of them.'

'I fail to catch on,' I answered, speaking his own dialect to humour him.

'Oh, you'll get there all the same,' he replied, stroking his machine meanwhile. 'It was a squirrel, it was!' (He pronounced it *squirl*.) 'It 'ud run up a tree ef it wanted, wouldn't it?' He was talking to it now as if it were a dog or a baby. 'There, there, it mustn't kick; it was a frisky little thing! Jest you step up on it, miss, and have a go at that there mountain.'

I stepped up and had a 'go.' The machine bounded forward like an agile greyhound. You had but to touch it, and it ran of itself. Never had I ridden so vivacious, so animated a cycle. I returned to him, sailing, with the gradient reversed. The Manitou glided smoothly, as on a gentle slope, without the need for back-pedalling.

'It soars!' he remarked, with enthusiasm.

'Balloons are at a discount beside it,' I answered.

'Now you want to know about this business, I guess,' he went on. 'You want to know jest where the reciprocity comes in, anyhow?'

'I am ready to hear you expound,' I admitted, smiling.

'Oh, it ain't all on one side,' he continued, eyeing his machine at an angle with parental affection. 'I'm a-going to make your fortune right here. You shall ride her for me on the last day; and ef you pull this thing off, don't you be scared that I won't treat you handsome.'

'If you were a little more succinct,' I said, gravely, 'we should get forrader faster.'

'Perhaps you wonder,' he put in, 'that with money on it like this, I should intrust the job *into* the hands of a female.' I winced, but was silent. 'Well, it's like this, don't you see; ef a female wins, it makes success all the more striking and con-spicuous. The world to-day *is* ruled *by* advertizement.'

I could stand it no longer. 'Mr. Hitchcock,' I said, with dignity, 'I haven't the remotest idea what on earth you are talking about.'

He gazed at me with surprise. 'What?' he exclaimed, at last. 'And you kin cycle like that! Not know what all the cycling world is mad about? Why, you don't mean to tell me you're not a pro-fessional?'

I enlightened him at once as to my position in society, which was respectable if not lucrative. His face fell somewhat. 'High-toned, eh? Still, you'd run all the same, wouldn't you?' he inquired.

'Run for what?' I asked, innocently. 'Parliament? The Presidency? The Frankfort Town Council?'

He had difficulty in fathoming the depths of my ignorance. But by degrees I understood him. It seemed that the German Imperial and Prussian Royal Governments had offered a Kaiserly and Kingly prize for the best military bicycle; the course to be run over the Taunus, from Frankfort to Limburg; the winning machine to get the equivalent of a thousand pounds; each firm to supply its own make and rider. The 'last day' was Saturday next; and the Great Manitou was the dark horse of the contest.

Then all was clear as day to me. Mr. Cyrus W. Hitchcock was keeping his machine a profound secret; he wanted a woman to ride it, so that his triumph might be the more complete; and the moment he saw me pedal up the hill, in trying to avoid him, he recognised at once that I was that woman.

I recognised it too. 'Twas a pre-ordained harmony. After two or three trials I felt that the Manitou was built for me, and I was built for the Manitou. We ran together like parts of one mechanism. I was always famed for my circular ankle-action; and in this new machine, ankle-action was everything. Strength of limb counted for naught; what told was the power of 'clawing up again' promptly. I possess that power; I have prehistoric feet; my remote progenitors must certainly have been tree-haunting monkeys.

We arranged terms then and there.

'You accept?'

'Implicitly.'

If I 'pulled off' the race, I was to have fifty pounds. If I didn't, I was to have five. 'It ain't only your skill, you see,' Mr. Hitchcock said, with frank commercialism. 'It's your personal attractiveness as well that I go upon. That's an element to consider in business relations.'

'My face is my fortune,' I answered, gravely. He nodded acquiescence.

Till Saturday, then, I was free. Meanwhile, I trained, and practised quietly with the Manitou, in sequestered parts of the hills. I also took spells, turn about, at the Städel Institute. I like to intersperse culture and athletics. I know something about athletics, and hope in time to acquire a taste for culture. 'Tis expected of a Girton girl, though my own accomplishments run rather towards rowing, punting, and bicycling.

On Saturday, I confess, I rose with great misgivings. I was not a professional; and to find oneself practically backed for a thousand pounds in a race against men is a trifle disquieting. Still, having once put my hand to the plough, I felt I was bound to pull it through somehow. I dressed my hair neatly, in a very tight coil. I ate a light breakfast, eschewing the fried sausages which the Blighted Fraus pressed upon my notice, and satisfying myself with a gently boiled egg and some toast and coffee. I always found I rowed best at Cambridge on the lightest diet; in my opinion, the raw-beef *régime* is a serious error in training.

At a minute or two before eleven I turned up at the Schiller Platz in my short serge dress and cycling jacket. The great square was thronged with spectators to see the start; the police made a lane through their midst for the riders. My backer had advised me to come to the post as late as possible, 'For I have entered your name,' he said, 'simply as Lois Cayley. These Deutschers don't think but what you're a man and a brother. But I am apprehensive of contingencies. When you put in a show they'll try to raise objections to you on account of your being a female. There won't be much time, though, and I shall rush the objections. Once they let you run and win, it don't matter to me whether I get the twenty thousand marks or not. It's the advertizement that tells. Jest you mark my words, miss, and don't you make no mistake about it—the world is governed to-day by advertizement.'

So I turned up at the last moment, and cast a timid glance at my competitors. They were all men, of course, and two of them were German officers in a sort of undress cycling uniform. They eyed me superciliously. One of them went up and spoke to the Herr Over-Superintendent who had charge of the contest. I understood him to be lodging an objection against a mere woman taking part in the race. The Herr Over-Superintendent, a bulky official, came up beside me and perpended visibly. He bent his big brows to it. 'Twas appalling to observe the measurable amount of Teutonic cerebration going on under cover of his round, green glasses. He was perpending for some minutes. Time was almost up. Then he turned to Mr. Hitchcock, having finally made up his colossal mind, and murmured rudely, 'The woman cannot compete.'

'Why not?' I inquired, in my very sweetest German, with an angelic smile, though my heart trembled.

'Warum nicht? Because the word "rider" in the Kaiserly and Kingly for-this-contest-provided decree is distinctly in the masculine gender stated.'

'Pardon me, Herr Over-Superintendent,' I replied, pulling out a copy of Law 97 on this subject, with which I had duly provided myself, 'if you will to Section 45 of the Bicycles-Circulation-Regulation-Act your attention turn, you will find it therein expressly enacted that unless any clause be anywhere to the contrary inserted, the word "rider," in the masculine gender put, shall here the word "rideress" in the feminine to embrace be considered.'

For, anticipating this objection, I had taken the precaution to look the legal question up beforehand.

'That is true,' the Herr Over-Superintendent observed, in a musing voice, gazing down at me with relenting eyes. 'The masculine habitually embraces the feminine.' And he brought his massive intellect to bear upon the problem once more with prodigious concentration.

I seized my opportunity. 'Let me start, at least,' I urged, holding out the Act. 'If I win, you can the matter more fully with the Kaiserly and Kingly Governments hereafter argue out.'

'I guess this will be an international affair,' Mr. Hitchcock remarked, well pleased. 'It would be a first-rate advertizement for the Great Manitou ef England and Germany were to make the question into a *casus belli*. The United States could look on, and pocket the chestnuts.'

'Two minutes to go!' the official starter with the watch called out.

'Fall in, then, Fräulein Englanderin,' the Herr Over-Superintendent observed, without prejudice, waving me into line. He pinned a badge with a large number, 7, on my dress. 'The Kaiserly and Kingly Governments shall on the affair of the starting's legality hereafter on my report more at leisure pass judgment.'

The lieutenant in undress uniform drew back a little.

'Oh, if this is to be woman's play,' he muttered, 'then can a Prussian officer himself by competing not into contempt bring.'

I dropped a little curtsy. 'If the Herr Lieutenant is afraid even to *enter* against an Englishwoman——' I said, smiling.

He came up to the scratch sullenly. 'One minute to go!' called out the starter.

We were all on the alert. There was a pause; a deep breath. I was horribly frightened, but I tried to look calm. Then sharp and quick came the word 'Go!' And like arrows from a bow, off we all started.

I had ridden over the whole course the day but one before, on a mountain pony, with an observant eye and my sedulous American—rising at five o'clock, so as not to excite undue attention; and I therefore knew beforehand the exact route we were to follow; but I confess when I saw the Prussian lieutenant and one of my other competitors dash forward at a pace that simply astonished me, that fifty pounds seemed to melt away in the dim abyss of the *Ewigkeit*. I gave up all for lost. I could never make the running against such practised cyclists.

However, we all turned out into the open road which leads across the plain and down the Main Valley, in the direction of Mayence. For the first ten miles or so, it is a dusty level. The surface is perfect; but 'twas a blinding white thread. As I toiled along it, that broiling June day, I could hear the voice of my backer, who followed on horseback, exhorting me in loud tones, 'Don't scorch, miss; don't scorch; never mind ef you lose sight of 'em. Keep your wind; that's the point. The wind, the wind's everything. Let 'em beat you on the level; you'll catch 'em up fast enough when you get on the Taunus!'

But in spite of his encouragement, I almost lost heart as I saw one after another of my opponents' backs disappear in the distance, till at last I was left toiling along the bare white road alone, in a shower-bath of sunlight, with just a dense cloud of dust rising grey far ahead of me. My head swam. It repented me of my boldness.

Then the riders on horseback began to grumble; for by police regulation they were not allowed to pass the hindmost of the cyclists; and they were kept back by my presence from following up their special champions. 'Give it up! Fräulein, give it up!' they cried. 'You're beaten. You're beaten! Let us pass and get forward!' But at the selfsame moment, I heard the shrill voice of my American friend whooping aloud across the din, 'Don't you do nothing of the sort, miss! You stick to it, and keep your wind! It's the wind that wins! Them Germans won't be worth a cent on the high slopes, anyway!'

Encouraged by his voice, I worked steadily on, neither scorching nor relaxing, but maintaining an even pace at my natural pitch under the broiling sunshine. Heat rose in waves on my face from the road below; in the thin white dust the accusing tracks of six wheels confronted me. Still I kept on following them, till I reached the town of Höchst—nine miles from Frankfort. Soldiers along the route were timing us at intervals with chronometers, and noting our numbers. As I rattled over the paved High Street, I called aloud to one of them. 'How far ahead the last man?'

He shouted back, good-humouredly: 'Four minutes, Fräulein.'

Again I lost heart. Then I mounted a slight slope, and felt how easily the Manitou moved up the gradient. From its summit I could note a long grey cloud of dust rolling steadily onward down the hill towards Hattersheim.

I coasted down, with my feet up, and a slight breeze just cooling me. Mr. Hitchcock, behind, called out, full-throated, from his seat: 'No hurry! No flurry! Take your time! Take—your—time, miss!'

Over the bridge at Hattersheim you turn to the right abruptly, and begin to mount by the side of a pretty little stream, the Schwarzbach, which runs brawling over rocks down the Taunus from Eppstein. By this time the excitement had somewhat cooled down for the moment; I was getting reconciled to be beaten on the level, and began to realise that my chances would be best as we approached the steepest bits of the mountain road about Niederhausen. So I positively plucked up heart to look about me and enjoy the scenery. With hair flying behind—that coil had played me false—I swept through Hofheim, a pleasant little village at the mouth of a grassy valley inclosed by wooded slopes, the Schwarzbach making cool music in the glen below as I mounted beside it. Clambering larches, like huge candelabra, stood out on the ridge, silhouetted against the skyline.

'How far ahead the last man?' I cried to the recording soldier. He answered me back, 'Two minutes, Fräulein.'

I was gaining on them; I was gaining! I thundered across the Schwarzbach, by half-a-dozen clamorous little iron bridges, making easy time now, and with my feet working as if they were themselves an integral part of the machinery. Up, up, up; it looked a vertical ascent; the Manitou glided well in its oil-bath at its half-way gearing. I rode for dear life. At sixteen miles, Lorsbach; at eighteen, Eppstein; the road still rising. 'How far ahead the last man?' 'Just round the corner, Fräulein!'

I put on a little steam. Sure enough, round the corner I caught sight of his back. With a spurt, I passed him—a dust-covered soul, very hot and uncomfortable. He had not kept his wind; I flew past him like a whirlwind. But, oh, how sultry hot in that sweltering, close valley! A pretty little town, Eppstein, with its mediæval castle perched high on a craggy rock. I owed it some gratitude, I felt, as I left it behind, for 'twas here that I came up with the tail-end of my opponents.

That one victory cheered me. So far, our route had lain along the well-made but dusty high road in the steaming valley; at Nieder-Josbach, two miles on, we quitted the road abruptly, by the course marked out for us, and turned up a mountain path, only wide enough for two cycles abreast—a path that clambered towards the higher slopes of the Taunus. That was arranged on purpose—for this was no fair-weather show—but a practical trial for military bicycles, under the conditions they might meet with in actual warfare. It was rugged riding: black walls of pine rose steep on either hand; the ground was uncertain. Our path mounted sharply from the first; the steeper the better. By the time I had reached Ober-Josbach, nestling high among larch-woods, I had distanced all but two of my opponents. It was cooler now too. As I passed the hamlet my cry altered.

'How far ahead the first man?'

'Two minutes, Fräulein.'

'A civilian?'

'No, no; a Prussian officer.'

The Herr Lieutenant led, then. For Old England's sake, I felt I must beat him.

The steepest slope of all lay in the next two miles. If I were going to win I must pass these two there, for my advantage lay all in the climb; if it came to coasting, the men's mere weight scored a point in their favour. Bump, crash, jolt! I pedalled away like a machine; the Manitou sobbed; my ankles flew round so that I scarcely felt them. But the road was rough and scarred with water-ways—ruts turned by rain to runnels. At half a mile, after a desperate struggle among sand and pebbles, I passed the second man; just ahead, the Prussian officer looked round and saw me. 'Thunder-weather! you there, Engländerin?' he cried, darting me a look of unchivalrous dislike, such as only your sentimental German can cast at a woman.

'Yes, I am here, behind you, Herr Lieutenant,' I answered, putting on a spurt; 'and I hope next to be before you.'

He answered not a word, but worked his hardest. So did I. He bent forward: I sat erect on my Manitou, pulling hard at my handles. Now, my front wheel was upon him. It reached his pedal. We were abreast. He had a narrow thread of solid path, and he forced me into a runnel. Still I gained. He swerved; I think he tried to foul me. But the slope was too steep; his attempt recoiled on himself; he ran against the rock at the side and almost overbalanced. That second lost him. I waved my hand as I sailed ahead. 'Good morning,' I cried, gaily. 'See you again at Limburg!'

From the top of the slope I put my feet up and flew down into Idstein. A thunder-shower burst: I was glad of the cool of it. It laid the dust. I regained the high road. From that moment, save for the risk of sideslips, 'twas easy running—just an undulating line with occasional ups and downs; but I saw no more of my pursuers till, twenty-two kilomètres farther on, I rattled on the cobble-paved causeway into Limburg. I had covered the forty-six miles in quick time for a mountain climb. As I crossed the bridge over the Lahn, to my immense surprise, Mr. Hitchcock waved his arms, all excitement, to greet me. He had taken the train on from Eppstein, it seemed, and got there before me. As I dismounted at the cathedral, which was our appointed end, and gave my badge to the soldier, he rushed up and shook my hand. 'Fifty pounds!' he cried. 'Fifty pounds! How's that for the great Anglo-Saxon race! And hooray for the Manitou!'

The second man, the civilian, rode in, wet and draggled, forty seconds later. As for the Herr Lieutenant, a disappointed man, he fell out by the way, alleging a puncture. I believe he was ashamed to admit the fact that he had been beaten in open fight by the objurgated Englanderin.

So the end of it was, I was now a woman of means, with fifty pounds of my own to my credit.

I lunched with my backer royally at the best inn in Limburg.

CHAPTER IV

THE ADVENTURE OF THE AMATEUR COMMISSION AGENT

MY eccentric American had assured me that if I won the great race for him I need not be 'skeert' lest he should fail to treat me well; and, to do him justice, I must admit that he kept his word magnanimously. While we sat at lunch in the cosy hotel at Limburg he counted out and paid me in hand the fifty good gold pieces he had promised me. 'Whether these Deutschers fork out my twenty thousand marks or not,' he said, in his brisk way, 'it don't much matter. I shall get the contract, and I shall hev gotten the advertizement!'

'Why do you start your bicycles in Germany, though?' I asked, innocently. 'I should have thought myself there was a much better chance of selling them in England.'

He closed one eye, and looked abstractedly at the light through his glass of pale yellow Brauneberger with the other. 'England? Yes, England! Well, you see, miss, you hev not been raised in business. Business is business. The way to do it in Germany is—to manufacture for yourself—and I've got my works started right here in Frankfort. The way to do it in England—where capital's dirt-cheap—is, to sell your patent for every cent it's worth to an English company, and let them boom or bust on it.'

'I see,' I said, catching at it. 'The principle's as clear as mud, the moment you point it out to one. An English company will pay you well for the concession, and work for a smaller return on its investment than you Americans are content to receive on your capital!'

'That's so! You hit it in one, miss! Which will you take, a cigar or a cocoa-nut?'

I smiled. 'And what do you think you will call the machine in Europe?'

He gazed hard at me, and stroked his straw-coloured moustache. 'Well, what do *you* think of the *Lois Cayley*?'

'For Heaven's sake, no!' I cried, fervently. 'Mr. Hitchcock, I implore you!'

He smiled pity for my weakness. 'Ah, high-toned again?' he repeated, as if it were some natural malformation under which I laboured. 'Oh, ef you don't like it, miss, we'll say no more about it. I am a gentleman, I am. What's the matter with the *Excelsior*?' 'Nothing, except that it's very bad Latin,' I objected. 'That may be so; but it's very good business.' He paused and mused, then he murmured low to himself, '"When through an Alpine village passed." That's where the idea of the *Excelsior* comes in; see? "It goes up Mont Blanc," you said yourself. "Through snow and ice, A cycle with the strange device, Excelsior!"'

'If I were you,' I said, 'I would stick to the name *Manitou*. It's original, and it's distinctive.'

'Think so? Then chalk it up; the thing's done. You may not be aware of it, miss, but you are a lady for whose opinion in such matters I hev a high regard. *And* you understand Europe. I do not. I admit it. Everything seems to be *verboten* in Germany; and everything else to be *bad form* in England.'

We walked down the steps together. 'What a picturesque old town!' I said, looking round me, well pleased. Its beauty appealed to me, for I had fifty pounds in pocket, and I had lunched sumptuously.

'*Old* town?' he repeated, gazing with a blank stare. 'You call this town *old*, do you?'

'Why, of course! Just look at the cathedral! Eight hundred years old, at least!'

He ran his eye down the streets, dissatisfied.

'Well, ef this town is old,' he said at last, with a snap of his fingers, 'it's precious little for its age.' And he strode away towards the railway station.

'What about the bicycle?' I asked; for it lay, a silent victor, against the railing of the steps, surrounded by a crowd of inquiring Teutons.

He glanced at it carelessly. 'Oh, the wheel?' he said. 'You may keep it.'

He said it so exactly in the tone in which one tells a waiter he may keep the change that I resented the impertinence. 'No, thank you,' I answered. 'I do not require it.'

He gazed at me open-mouthed. 'What? Put my foot in it again?' he interposed. 'Not high-toned enough, eh? Now, I do regret it. No offence meant, miss, nor none need be taken. What I meant to in-sinuate was this: you hev won the big race for me. Folks will notice you and talk about you at Frankfort. Ef you ride a Manitou, that'll make 'em talk the more. A mutual advantage. Benefits you; benefits me. You get the wheel; I get the advertizement.'

I saw that reciprocity was the lodestar of his life. 'Very well, Mr. Hitchcock,' I said, pocketing my pride, 'I'll accept the machine, and I'll ride it.'

Then a light dawned upon me. I saw eventualities. 'Look here,' I went on, innocently—recollect, I was a girl just fresh from Girton—'I am thinking of going on very soon to Switzerland. Now, why shouldn't I do this—try to sell your machines, or, rather, take orders for them, from anybody that admires them? A mutual advantage. Benefits you; benefits me. You sell your wheels; I get——'

He stared at me. 'The commission?'

'I don't know what commission means,' I answered, somewhat at sea as to the term; 'but I thought it might be worth your while, till the Manitou becomes better known, to pay me, say, ten per cent, on all orders I brought you.'

His face was one broad smile. 'I do admire you, miss,' he cried, standing still to inspect me. 'You may not know the meaning of the *word* commission; but durned ef you haven't got a hang of the *thing* itself that would do honour to a Wall Street operator, anyway.'

'Then that's business?' I asked, eagerly; for I beheld vistas.

'Business?' he repeated. 'Yes, that's jest about the size of it—business. Advertizement, miss, may be the soul of commerce, but commission's its body. You go in and win. Ten per cent, on every order you send me!'

He insisted on taking my ticket back to Frankfort. 'My affair, miss; my affair!' There was no gainsaying him. He was immensely elated. 'The biggest thing in cycles since Dunlop tires,' he repeated. 'And to-morrow, they'll give me advertizements gratis in every newspaper!'

Next morning, he came round to call on me at the Abode of

Unclaimed Domestic Angels. He was explicit and generous. 'Look
here, miss,' he began; 'I didn't do fair by you when you interviewed
me about your agency last evening. I took advantage, *at the time*,
of *your* youth and inexperience. You suggested ten per cent, *as* the
amount of your commission on sales you might effect; and I jumped
at it. That was conduct unworthy *of* a gentleman. Now, I will not
deceive you. The ordinary commission on transactions in wheels
is 25 per cent. I am going to sell the Manitou at twenty English
pounds apiece. You shall hev your 25 per cent, on all orders.'

'Five pounds for every machine I sell?' I exclaimed, overjoyed.
He nodded. 'That's so.'

I was simply amazed at this magnificent prospect. 'The cycle
trade must be honeycombed with middlemen's profits!' I cried; for
I had my misgivings.

'That's so,' he replied again. 'Then jest you take and be a
middlewoman.'

'But, as a consistent socialist——'

'It is your duty to fleece the capitalist and the consumer. A
mutual benefit—triangular this time. I get the order, the public
gets the machine, and you get the commission. I am richer, you are
richer, and the public is mounted on much the best wheel ever yet
invented.'

'That sounds plausible,' I admitted. 'I shall try it on in
Switzerland. I shall run up steep hills whenever I see any likely
customers looking on; then I shall stop and ask them the time, as
if quite accidentally.'

He rubbed his hands. 'You take to business like a young duck
to the water,' he exclaimed, admiringly. 'That's the way to rake
'em in! You go up and say to them, "Why not investigate? We defy
competition. Leave the drudgery of walking up-hill beside your
cycle! Progress is the order of the day. Use modern methods! This
is the age of the telegraph, the telephone, *and* the typewriter. You
kin no longer afford to go on with an antiquated, antediluvian,
armour-plated wheel. Invest in a Hill-Climber, the last and lightest product of evvolootion. *Is* it common-sense to buy an old-
style, unautomatic, single-geared, inconvertible ten-ton machine,
when for the same money or less you can purchase the self-acting
Manitou, a priceless gem, as light as a feather, with all the most

recent additions and improvements? Be reasonable! Get the best!"
That's the style to fetch 'em!'

I laughed, in spite of myself. 'Oh, Mr. Hitchcock,' I burst out,
'that's not *my* style at all. I shall say simply, "This is a lovely new
bicycle. You can see for yourself how it climbs hills. Try it, if you
wish. It skims like a swallow. And I get what they call five pounds
commission on every one I can sell of them!" I think that way of
dealing is much more likely to bring you in orders.'

His admiration was undisguised. 'Well, I *do* call you a woman
of business, miss,' he cried. 'You see it at a glance. That's so. That's
the right kind of thing to rope in the Europeans. Some originality about you. You take 'em on their own ground. You've got the
draw on them, you hev. I like your system. You'll jest haul in the
dollars!'

'I hope so,' I said, fervently; for I had evolved in my own mind,
oh, such a *lovely* scheme for Elsie Petheridge's holidays!

He gazed at me once more. 'Ef only I could get hold of a woman
of business like you to soar through life with me,' he murmured.

I grew interested in my shoes. His open admiration was getting
quite embarrassing.

He paused a minute. Then he went on: 'Well, what do you say
to it?'

'To what?' I asked, amazed.

'To my proposition—my offer.'

'I—I don't understand,' I stammered out bewildered. 'The 25
per cent, you mean?'

'No, the de-votion of a lifetime,' he answered, looking sideways
at me. 'Miss Cayley, when a business man advances a proposition,
commercial or otherwise, he advances it because he means it. He
asks a prompt reply. Your time is valuable. So is mine. *Are* you prepared to consider it?'

'Mr. Hitchcock,' I said, drawing back, 'I think you misunderstand. I think you do not realise——'

'All right, miss,' he answered promptly, though with a disappointed air. 'Ef it kin not be managed, it kin not be managed. I
understand your European exclusiveness. I know your prejudices.
But this little episode need not antagonise with the normal course
of ordinary business. I respect you, Miss Cayley. You are a lady *of*

intelligence, *of* initiative, and *of* high-toned culture. I will wish you good day for the present, without further words; and I shall be happy at any time to receive your orders on the usual commission.'

He backed out and was gone. He was so honestly blunt that I really quite liked him.

Next day I bade a tearless farewell to the Blighted Fraus. When I told those eight phlegmatic souls I was going, they all said 'So!' much as they had said 'So!' to every previous remark I had been moved to make to them. 'So' is capital garnishing; but viewed as a staple of conversation, I find it a trifle vapid, not to say monotonous.

I set out on my wanderings, therefore, to go round the world on my own account and my own Manitou, which last I grew to love in time with a love passing the love of Mr. Cyrus Hitchcock. I carried the strictly necessary before me in a small waterproof bicycling valise; but I sent on the portmanteau containing my whole estate, real and personal, to some point in advance which I hoped to reach from time to time in a day or two. My first day's journey was along a pleasant road from Frankfort to Heidelberg, some fifty-four miles in all, skirting the mountains the greater part of the way; the Manitou took the ups and downs so easily that I diverged at intervals, to choose side-paths over the wooded hills. I arrived at Heidelberg as fresh as a daisy, my mount not having turned a hair meanwhile—a favourite expression of cyclists which carries all the more conviction to an impartial mind because of the machine being obviously hairless. Thence I journeyed on by easy stages to Karlsruhe, Baden, Appenweier, and Offenburg, where I set my front wheel resolutely for the Black Forest. It is the prettiest and most picturesque route to Switzerland; and, being also the hilliest, it would afford me, I thought, the best opportunity for showing off the Manitou's paces, and trying my prentice hand as an amateur cycle-agent.

From the quaint little Black Eagle at Offenburg, however, before I dashed into the Forest, I sent off a letter to Elsie Petheridge, setting forth my lovely scheme for her summer holidays. She was delicate, poor child, and the London winters sorely tried her; I was now a millionaire, with the better part of fifty pounds in my pocket, so I felt I could afford to be royal in my hospitality. As I

was leaving Frankfort, I had called at a tourist agency and bought
a second-class circular ticket from London to Lucerne and back—I
made it second-class because I am opposed on principle to exces-
sive luxury, and also because it was three guineas cheaper. Even
fifty pounds will not last forever, though I could scarcely believe it.
(You see, I am not wholly free, after all, from the besetting British
vice of prudence.) It was a mighty joy to me to be able to send this
ticket to Elsie, at her lodgings in Bayswater, pointing out to her
that now the whole mischief was done, and that if she would not
come out as soon as her summer vacation began—'twas a point of
honour with Elsie to say *vacation*, instead of *holidays*—to join me
at Lucerne, and stop with me as my guest at a mountain *pension*,
the ticket would be wasted. I love burning my boats; 'tis the only
safe way for securing prompt action.

Then I turned my flying wheels up into the Black Forest, growing weary of my loneliness—for it is not all jam to ride by oneself
in Germany—and longing for Elsie to come out and join me. I
loved to think how her dear, pale cheeks would gain colour and
tone on the hills about the Brünig, where, for business reasons (so I
said to myself with the conscious pride of the commission agent),
I proposed to pass the greater part of the summer.

From Offenburg to Hornberg the road makes a good stiff climb
of twenty-seven miles, and some 1200 English feet in altitude, with
a fair number of minor undulations on the way to diversify it. I
will not describe the route, though it is one of the most beautiful I have ever travelled—rocky hills, ruined castles, huge, straight-
stemmed pines that clamber up green slopes, or halt in sombre
line against steeps of broken crag; the reality surpasses my poor
powers of description. And the people I passed on the road were
almost as quaint and picturesque in their way as the hills and the
villages—the men in red-lined jackets; the women in black petti-
coats, short-waisted green bodices, and broad-brimmed straw hats
with black-and-crimson pompons. But on the steepest gradient,
just before reaching Hornberg, I got my first nibble—strange to
say, from two German students; they wore Heidelberg caps, and
were toiling up the incline with short, broken wind; I put on a
spurt with the Manitou, and passed them easily. I did it just at first
in pure wantonness of health and strength; but the moment I was

clear of them, it occurred to the business half of me that here was a good chance of taking an order. Filled with this bright idea, I dismounted near the summit, and pretended to be engaged in lubricating my bearings; though as a matter of fact the Manitou runs in a bath of oil, self-feeding, and needs no looking after. Presently, my two Heidelbergers straggled up—hot, dusty, panting. Woman-like, I pretended to take no notice. One of them drew near and cast an eye on the Manitou.

'That's a new machine, Fräulein,' he said, at last, with more politeness than I expected.

'It is,' I answered, casually; 'the latest model. Climbs hills like no other.' And I feigned to mount and glide off towards Hornberg.

'Stop a moment, pray, Fräulein,' my prospective buyer called out. 'Here, Heinrich, I wish you this new so excellent mountain-climbing machine, without chain propelled, more fully to investigate.'

'I am going on to Hornberg,' I said, with mixed feminine guile and commercial strategy; 'still, if your friend wishes to look——'

They both jostled round it, with *achs* innumerable, and, after minute inspection, pronounced its principle *wunderschön*. 'Might I essay it?' Heinrich asked.

'Oh, by all means,' I answered. He paced it down hill a few yards; then skimmed up again.

'It is a bird!' he cried to his friend, with many guttural interjections. 'Like the eagle's flight, so soars it. Come, try the thing, Ludwig!'

'You permit, Fräulein?'

I nodded. They both mounted it several times. It behaved like a beauty. Then one of them asked, 'And where can man of this new so remarkable machine nearest by purchase himself make possessor?'

'I am the Sole Agent,' I burst out, with swelling dignity. 'If you will give me your orders, with cash in hand for the amount, I will send the cycle, carriage paid, to any address you desire in Germany.'

'You!' they exclaimed, incredulously. 'The Fräulein is pleased to be humorous!'

'Oh, very well,' I answered, vaulting into the saddle; 'if you choose to doubt my word——' I waved one careless hand and coasted off. 'Good-morning, meine Herren.'

They lumbered after me on their ramshackle traction-engines. 'Pardon, Fräulein! Do not thus go away! Oblige us at least with the name and address of the maker.'

I perpended—like the Herr Over-Superintendent at Frankfort. 'Look here,' I said at last, telling the truth with frankness, 'I get 25 per cent on all bicycles I sell. I am, as I say, the maker's Sole Agent. If you order through me, I touch my profit; if otherwise, I do not. Still, since you seem to be gentlemen,'—they bowed and swelled visibly,—'I will give you the address of the firm, trusting to your honour to mention my name'—I handed them a card—'if you decide on ordering. The price of the palfrey is four hundred marks. It is worth every pfennig of it.' And, before they could say more, I had spurred my steed and swept off at full speed round a curve of the highway.

I pencilled a note to my American that night from Hornberg, detailing the circumstance; but I am sorry to say, for the discredit of humanity, that when those two students wrote the same evening from their inn in the village to order Manitous, they did *not* mention my name, doubtless under the misconception that by suppressing it they would save my commission. However, it gives me pleasure to add *per contra* (as we say in business) that when I arrived at Lucerne a week or so later I found a letter, *poste restante*, from Mr. Cyrus Hitchcock, inclosing an English ten-pound note. He wrote that he had received two orders for Manitous from Hornberg; and 'feeling considerable confidence that these must necessarily originate' from my German students, he had the pleasure of forwarding me what he hoped would be the first of many similar commissions.

I will not describe my further adventures on the still steeper mountain road from Hornberg to Triberg and St. Georgen—how I got bites on the way from an English curate, an Austrian hussar, and two unprotected American ladies; nor how I angled for them all by riding my machine up impossible hills, and then reclining gracefully to eat my lunch (three times in one day) on mossy banks at the summit. I felt a perfect little hypocrite. But Mr. Hitchcock had remarked that business is business; and I will only add (in con-

firmation of his view) that by the time I reached Lucerne I had
sown the good seed in fifteen separate human souls, no less than
four of which brought forth fruit in orders for Manitous before the
end of the season.

I had now so little fear what the morrow might bring forth that
I settled down in a comfortable hotel at Lucerne till Elsie's holidays
began; and amused myself meanwhile by picking out the hilliest
roads I could find in the neighbourhood, in order to display my
steel steed's possibilities to the best advantage.

By the end of July, little Elsie joined me. She was half-angry at
first that I should have forced the ticket and my hospitality upon
her. 'Nonsense, dear,' I said, smoothing her hair, for her pale face
quite frightened me. 'What is the good of a friend if she will not
allow you to do her little favours?'

'But, Brownie, you said you wouldn't stop and be dependent
upon *me* one day longer than was necessary in London.'

'That was different,' I cried. 'That was Me! This is You! I am a
great, strong, healthy thing, fit to fight the battle of life and take
care of myself; you, Elsie, are one of those fragile little flowers
which 'tis everybody's duty to protect and to care for.'

She would have protested more; but I stifled her mouth with
kisses. Indeed, for nothing did I rejoice in my prosperity so much
as for the chance it gave me of helping poor dear, overworked,
overwrought Elsie.

We took up our quarters thenceforth at a high-perched little
guest-house near the top of the Brünig. It was bracing for Elsie;
and it lay close to a tourist track where I could spread my snares
and exhibit the Manitou in its true colours to many passing visitors. Elsie tried it, and found she could ride on it with ease. She
wished she had one of her own. A bright idea struck me. In fear
and trembling, I wrote, suggesting to Mr. Hitchcock that I had a
girl friend from England stopping with me in Switzerland, and
that two Manitous would surely be better than one as an advertizement. I confess I stood aghast at my own cheek; but my hand, I
fear, was rapidly growing 'subdued to that it worked in.' Anyhow
I sent the letter off, and waited developments.

By return of post came an answer from my American:

'DEAR MISS—By rail herewith please receive one lady's No. 4 automatic quadruple-geared self-feeding Manitou, as per your esteemed favour of July 27th, for which I desire to thank you. The more I see of your way of doing business, the more I do admire you. This is an elegant poster! Two high-toned English ladies, mounted on Manitous, careering up the Alps, represent to both of us quite a mint of money. The mutual benefit to me, to you, and to the other lady, ought to be simply incalculable. I shall be pleased at any time to hear of any further developments of your very remarkable advertising skill, and I am obliged to you for this brilliant suggestion you have been good enough to make to me.—Respectfully,
                                        'CYRUS W. HITCHCOCK.'

'What? Am I to have it for nothing, Brownie?' Elsie exclaimed, bewildered, when I read the letter to her.

I assumed the airs of a woman of the world. 'Why, certainly, my dear,' I answered, as if I always expected to find bicycles showered upon me. 'It's a mutual arrangement. Benefits him; benefits you. Reciprocity is the groundwork of business. *He* gets the advertisement; *you* get the amusement. It's a form of handbill. Like the ladies who exhibit their back hair, don't you know, in that window in Regent Street.'

Thus inexpensively mounted, we scoured the country together, up the steepest hills between Stanzstadt and Meiringen. We had lots of nibbles. One lady in particular often stopped to look on and admire the Manitou. She was a nice-looking widow of forty-five, very fresh and round-faced; a Mrs. Evelegh, we soon found out, who owned a charming *chalet* on the hills above Lungern. She spoke to us more than once: 'What a perfect dear of a machine!' she cried. 'I wonder if I dare try it!'

'Can you cycle?' I asked.

'I could once,' she answered. 'I was awfully fond of it. But Dr. Fortescue-Langley won't let me any longer.'

'Try it!' I said, dismounting. She got up and rode. 'Oh, isn't it just lovely!' she cried ecstatically.

'Buy one!' I put in. 'They're as smooth as silk; they cost only twenty pounds; and, on every machine I sell, I get five pounds commission.'

'I should love to,' she answered; 'but Dr. Fortescue-Langley——'

'Who is he?' I asked. 'I don't believe in drug-drenchers.'

She looked quite shocked. 'Oh, he's not that kind, you know,' she put in, breathlessly. 'He's the celebrated esoteric faith-healer. He won't let me move far away from Lungern, though I'm longing to be off to England again for the summer. My boy's at Portsmouth.'

'Then, why don't you disobey him?'

Her face was a study. 'I daren't,' she answered in an awe-struck voice. 'He comes here every summer; and he does me *so* much good, you know. He diagnoses my inner self. He treats me psychically. When my inner self goes wrong, my bangle turns dusky.' She held up her right hand with an Indian silver bangle on it; and sure enough it was tarnished with a very thin black deposit. 'My soul is ailing now,' she said in a comically serious voice. 'But it is seldom so in Switzerland. The moment I land in England the bangle turns black and remains black till I get back to Lucerne again.'

When she had gone, I said to Elsie: 'That *is* odd about the bangle. State of health might affect it, I suppose. Though it looks to me like a surface deposit of sulphide.' I knew nothing of chemistry, I admit; but I had sometimes messed about in the laboratory at college with some of the other girls; and I remembered now that sulphide of silver was a blackish-looking body, like the film on the bangle.

However, at the time I thought no more about it.

By dint of stopping and talking, we soon got quite intimate with Mrs. Evelegh. As always happens, I found out I had known some of her cousins in Edinburgh, where I always spent my holidays while I was at Girton. She took an interest in what she was kind enough to call my originality; and before a fortnight was out, our hotel being uncomfortably crowded, she had invited Elsie and myself to stop with her at the *chalet*. We went and found it a delightful little home. Mrs. Evelegh was charming; but we could see at every turn that Dr. Fortescue-Langley had acquired a firm hold over her. 'He's so clever, you know,' she said; 'and *so* spiritual! He exercises such strong odylic force. He binds my being together. If he misses a visit, I feel my inner self goes all to pieces.'

'Does he come often?' I asked, growing interested.

'Oh, dear, no,' she answered. 'I wish he did; it would be ever so good for me. But he's so much run after; I am but one among many. He lives at Château-d'Oex, and comes across to see patients in this district once a fortnight. It is a privilege to be attended by an intuitive seer like Dr. Fortescue-Langley.'

Mrs. Evelegh was rich—'left comfortably,' as the phrase goes, but with a clause which prevented her marrying again without losing her fortune; and I could gather from various hints that Dr. Fortescue-Langley, whoever he might be, was bleeding her to some tune, using her soul and her inner self as his financial lancet. I also noticed that what she said about the bangle was strictly true; generally bright as a new pin, on certain mornings it was completely blackened. I had been at the *chalet* ten days, however, before I began to suspect the real reason. Then it dawned upon me one morning in a flash of inspiration. The evening before had been cold, for at the height where we were perched, even in August, we often found the temperature chilly in the night, and I heard Mrs. Evelegh tell Cécile, her maid, to fill the hot-water bottle. It was a small point, but it somehow went home to me. Next day the bangle was black, and Mrs. Evelegh lamented that her inner self must be suffering from an attack of evil vapours.

I held my peace at the time, but I asked Cécile a little later to bring me that hot-water bottle. As I more than half suspected, it was made of india-rubber, wrapped carefully up in the usual red flannel bag. 'Lend me your brooch, Elsie,' I said. 'I want to try a little experiment.'

'Won't a franc do as well?' Elsie asked, tendering one. 'That's equally silver.'

'I think not,' I answered. 'A franc is most likely too hard; it has base metal to alloy it. But I will vary the experiment by trying both together. Your brooch is Indian, and therefore soft silver. The native jewellers never use alloy. Hand it over; it will clean with a little plate-powder, if necessary. I'm going to see what blackens Mrs. Evelegh's bangle.'

I laid the franc and the brooch on the bottle, filled with hot water, and placed them for warmth in the fold of a blanket. After *déjeûner*, we inspected them. As I anticipated, the brooch had grown black on the surface with a thin iridescent layer of silver sulphide, while the franc had hardly suffered at all from the exposure.

I called in Mrs. Evelegh, and explained what I had done. She was astonished and half incredulous. 'How could you ever think of it?' she cried, admiringly.

'Why, I was reading an article yesterday about india-rubber in one of your magazines,' I answered; 'and the person who wrote it said the raw gum was hardened for vulcanising by mixing it with sulphur. When I heard you ask Cécile for the hot-water bottle, I thought at once: "The sulphur and the heat account for the tarnishing of Mrs. Evelegh's bangle."'

'And the franc doesn't tarnish! Then that must be why my other silver bracelet, which is English make, and harder, never changes colour! And Dr. Fortescue-Langley assured me it was because the soft one was of Indian metal, and had mystic symbols on it—symbols that answered to the cardinal moods of my sub-conscious self, and that darkened in sympathy.'

I jumped at a clue. 'He talked about your sub-conscious self?' I broke in.

'Yes,' she answered. 'He always does. It's the keynote of his system. He heals by that alone. But, my dear, after this, how can I ever believe in him?'

'Does he know about the hot-water-bottle?' I asked.

'Oh, yes; he ordered me to use it on certain nights; and when I go to England he says I must never be without one. I see now that was why my inner self invariably went wrong in England. It was all just the sulphur blackening the bangle.'

I reflected. 'A middle-aged man?' I asked. 'Stout, diplomatic-looking, with wrinkles round his eyes, and a distinguished grey moustache, twirled up oddly at the corners?'

'That's the man, my dear! His very picture. Where on earth have you seen him?'

'And he talks of sub-conscious selves?' I went on.

'He practises on that basis. He says it's no use prescribing for the outer man; to do that is to treat mere symptoms; the sub-conscious self is the inner seat of diseases.'

'How long has he been in Switzerland?'

'Oh, he comes here every year. He arrived this season late in May, I fancy.'

'When will he visit you again, Mrs. Evelegh?'

'To-morrow morning.'

I made up my mind at once. 'Then I must see him, without being seen,' I said. 'I think I know him. He is our Count, I believe.' For I had told Mrs. Evelegh and Elsie the queer story of my journey from London.

'Impossible, my dear! Im-possible! I have implicit faith in him!'

'Wait and see, Mrs. Evelegh. You acknowledge that he duped you over the affair of the bangle.'

There are two kinds of dupes; one kind, the commonest, goes on believing in its deceiver, no matter what happens; the other, far rarer, has the sense to know it has been deceived if you make the deception as clear as day to it. Mrs. Evelegh was, fortunately, of the rarer class. Next morning, Dr. Fortescue-Langley arrived, by appointment. As he walked up the path, I glanced at him from my window. It was the Count, not a doubt of it. On his way to gull his dupes in Switzerland, he had tried to throw in an incidental trifle of a diamond robbery.

I telegraphed the facts at once to Lady Georgina, at Schlangenbad. She answered, 'I am coming. Ask the man to meet his friend on Wednesday.'

Mrs. Evelegh, now almost convinced, invited him. On Wednesday morning, with a bounce, Lady Georgina burst in upon us. 'My dear, such a journey!—alone, at my age—but there, I haven't known a happy day since you left me! Oh, yes, I got my Gretchen—unsophisticated?—well—h'm—that's not the word for it: I declare to you, Lois, there isn't a trick of the trade, in Paris or London—not a perquisite or a tip—that that girl isn't up to. Comes straight from the remotest recesses of the Black Forest, and hadn't been with me a week, I assure you, honour bright, before she was bandolining her yellow hair, and rouging her cheeks, and wearing my brooches, and wagering gloves with the hotel waiters upon the Baden races. *And* her language: *and* her manners! Why weren't you born in that station of life, I wonder, child, so that I might offer you five hundred a year, and all found, to come and live with me for ever? But this Gretchen—her fringe, her shoes, her ribbons—upon my soul, my dear, I don't know what girls are coming to nowadays.'

'Ask Mrs. Lynn-Linton,' I suggested, as she paused. 'She is a recognised authority on the subject.'

The Cantankerous Old Lady stared at me. 'And this Count?' she went on. 'So you have really tracked him? You're a wonderful girl, my dear. I wish you were a lady's-maid. You'd be worth me any money.'

I explained how I had come to hear of Dr. Fortescue-Langley.

Lady Georgina waxed warm. 'Dr. Fortescue-Langley!' she exclaimed. 'The wicked wretch! But he didn't get my diamonds! I've carried them here in my hands, all the way from Wiesbaden: I wasn't going to leave them for a single day to the tender mercies of that unspeakable Gretchen. The fool would lose them. Well, we'll catch him this time, Lois: and we'll give him ten years for it!'

'Ten years!' Mrs. Evelegh cried, clasping her hands in horror. 'Oh, Lady Georgina!'

We waited in Mrs. Evelegh's dining-room, the old lady and I, behind the folding-doors. At three precisely, Dr. Fortescue-Langley walked in. I had difficulty in restraining Lady Georgina from falling upon him prematurely. He talked a lot of high-flown nonsense to Mrs. Evelegh and Elsie about the influences of the planets, and the seventy-five emanations, and the eternal wisdom of the East, and the medical efficacy of sub-conscious suggestion. Excellent patter, all of it—quite as good in its way as the diplomatic patter he had poured forth in the train to Lady Georgina. It was rich in spheres, in elements, in cosmic forces. At last, as he was discussing the reciprocal action of the inner self upon the exhalations of the lungs, we pushed back the door and walked calmly in upon him.

His breath came and went. The exhalations of the lungs showed visible perturbation. He rose and stared at us. For a second he lost his composure. Then, as bold as brass, he turned, with a cunning smile, to Mrs. Evelegh. 'Where on earth did you pick up such acquaintances?' he inquired, in a well-simulated tone of surprise. 'Yes, Lady Georgina, I have met you before, I admit; but—it can hardly be agreeable to you to reflect under what circumstances.'

Lady Georgina was beside herself. 'You dare?' she cried, confronting him. 'You dare to brazen it out? You miserable sneak! But

you can't bluff me now. I have the police outside.' Which I regret
to confess was a light-hearted fiction.

'The police?' he echoed, drawing back. I could see he was
frightened.

I had an inspiration again. 'Take off that moustache!' I said,
calmly, in my most commanding voice.

He clapped his hand to it in horror. In his agitation, he managed to pull it a little bit awry. It looked so absurd, hanging there,
all crooked, that I thought it kinder to him to remove it altogether.
The thing peeled off with difficulty; for it was a work of art, very
firmly and gracefully fastened with sticking-plaster. But it peeled
off at last—and with it the whole of the Count's and Dr. Fortescue-
Langley's distinction. The man stood revealed, a very palpable
man-servant.

Lady Georgina stared hard at him. 'Where have I seen you
before?' she murmured slowly. 'That face is familiar to me. Why,
yes; you went once to Italy as Mr. Marmaduke Ashurst's courier! I
know you now. Your name is Higginson.'

It was a come-down for the Comte de Laroche-sur-Loiret, but
he swallowed it like a man at a single gulp.

'Yes, my lady,' he said, fingering his hat nervously, now all was
up. 'You are quite right, my lady. But what would you have me do?
Times are hard on us couriers. Nobody wants us now. I must take
to what I can.' He assumed once more the tone of the Vienna diplomat. '*Que voulez-vous*, madame? These are revolutionary days. A
man of intelligence must move with the zeitgeist!'

Lady Georgina burst into a loud laugh. 'And to think,' she cried,
'that I talked to this lackey from London to Malines without ever
suspecting him! Higginson, you're a fraud—but you're a precious
clever one.'

He bowed. 'I am happy to have merited Lady Georgina Fawley's
commendation,' he answered, with his palm on his heart, in his
grandiose manner.

'But I shall hand you over to the police, all the same! You are a
thief and a swindler!'

He assumed a comic expression. 'Unhappily, not a thief,' he
objected. 'This young lady prevented me from appropriating your
diamonds. *Convey*, the wise call it. I wanted to take your jewel-

case—and she put me off with a sandwich-tin. I wanted to make an honest penny out of Mrs. Evelegh; and—she confronts me with your ladyship and tears my moustache off.'

Lady Georgina regarded him with a hesitating expression. 'But I shall call the police,' she said, wavering visibly.

'*De grace*, my lady, *de grace!* Is it worth while, *pour si peu de chose?* Consider, I have really effected nothing. Will you charge me with having taken—in error—a small tin sandwich-case—value, elevenpence? An affair of a week's imprisonment. That is positively all you can bring up against me. And,' brightening up visibly, 'I have the case still; I will return it to-morrow with pleasure to your ladyship!'

'But the india-rubber water-bottle?' I put in. 'You have been deceiving Mrs. Evelegh. It blackens silver. And you told her lies in order to extort money under false pretences.'

He shrugged his shoulders. 'You are too clever for me, young lady,' he broke out. 'I have nothing to say to you. But Lady Georgina, Mrs. Evelegh—you are human—let me go! Reflect; I have things I could tell that would make both of you look ridiculous. That journey to Malines, Lady Georgina! Those Indian charms, Mrs. Evelegh! Besides, you have spoiled my game. Let that suffice you! I can practise in Switzerland no longer. Allow me to go in peace, and I will try once more to be indifferent honest!'

He backed slowly towards the door, with his eyes fixed on them. I stood by and waited. Inch by inch he retreated. Lady Georgina looked down abstractedly at the carpet. Mrs. Evelegh looked up abstractedly at the ceiling. Neither spoke another word. The rogue backed out by degrees. Then he sprang down-stairs, and before they could decide was well out into the open.

Lady Georgina was the first to break the silence. 'After all, my dear,' she murmured, turning to me, 'there was a deal of sound English common-sense about Dogberry!'

I remembered then his charge to the watch to apprehend a rogue. 'How if 'a will not stand?'

'Why, then, take no note of him, but let him go; and presently call the rest of the watch together, and thank God you are rid of a knave.' When I remembered how Lady Georgina had hob-nobbed with the Count from Ostend to Malines, I agreed to a great extent both with her and with Dogberry.

CHAPTER V

THE ADVENTURE OF THE IMPROMPTU MOUNTAINEER

THE explosion and evaporation of Dr. Fortescue-Langley (with whom were amalgamated the Comte de Laroche-sur-Loiret, Mr. Higginson the courier, and whatever else that versatile gentleman chose to call himself) entailed many results of varying magnitudes.

In the first place, Mrs. Evelegh ordered a Great Manitou. That, however, mattered little to 'the firm,' as I loved to call us (because it shocked dear Elsie so); for, of course, after all her kindness we couldn't accept our commission on her purchase, so that she got her machine cheap for £15 from the maker. But, in the second place—I declare I am beginning to write like a woman of business—she decided to run over to England for the summer to see her boy at Portsmouth, being certain now that the discoloration of her bangle depended more on the presence of sulphur in the india-rubber bottle than on the passing state of her astral body. 'Tis an abrupt descent from the inner self to a hot-water bottle, I admit; but Mrs. Evelegh took the plunge with grace, like a sensible woman. Dr. Fortescue-Langley had been annihilated for her at one blow: she returned forthwith to common-sense and England.

'What will you do with the *chalet* while you're away?' Lady Georgina asked, when she announced her intention. 'You can't shut it up to take care of itself. Every blessed thing in the place will go to rack and ruin. Shutting up a house means spoiling it for ever. Why, I've got a cottage of my own in the best part of Surrey that I let for the summer—a pretty little place, now vacant, for which, by the way, I want a tenant, if you happen to know of one—and when it's left empty for a month or two——'

'Perhaps it would do for me?' Mrs. Evelegh suggested, jumping at it. 'I'm looking out for a furnished house for the summer, within easy reach of Portsmouth and London, for myself and Oliver.'

Lady Georgina seized her arm, with a face of blank horror. 'My dear!' she cried. 'For you! I wouldn't dream of letting it to you.

A nasty, damp, cold, unwholesome house, on stiff clay soil, with detestable drains, in the deadliest part of the Weald of Surrey,—why, you and your boy would catch your deaths of rheumatism.'

'Is it the one I saw advertised in the *Times* this morning, I wonder?' Mrs. Evelegh inquired in a placid voice. '"Charmingly furnished house on Holmesdale Common; six bedrooms, four reception-rooms; splendid views; pure air; picturesque surroundings; exceptionally situated." I thought of writing about it.'

'That's it!' Lady Georgina exclaimed, with a demonstrative wave of her hand. 'I drew up the advertisement myself. Exceptionally situated! I should just think it was! Why, my dear, I wouldn't let you rent the place for worlds; a horrid, poky little hole, stuck down in the bottom of a boggy hollow, as damp as Devonshire, with the paper peeling off the walls, so that I had to take my choice between giving it up myself ten years ago or removing to the cemetery; and I've let it ever since to City men with large families. Nothing would induce me to allow you and your boy to expose yourself to such risks.' For Lady Georgina had taken quite a fancy to Mrs. Evelegh. 'But what I was just going to say was this: you can't shut your house up; it'll all go mouldy. Houses always go mouldy, shut up in summer. And you can't leave it to your servants; *I* know the baggages; no conscience—no conscience; they'll ask their entire families to come up and stop with them *en bloc*, and turn your place into a perfect piggery. Why, when I went away from my house in town one autumn, didn't I leave a policeman and his wife in charge—a most respectable man—only he happened to be an Irishman? And what was the consequence? My dear, I assure you, I came back unexpectedly from poor dear Kynaston's one day—at a moment's notice—having quarrelled with him over Home Rule or Education or something—poor dear Kynaston's what they call a Liberal, I believe—got at by that man Rosebery—and there didn't I find all the O'Flanagans, and O'Flahertys, and O'Flynns in the neighbourhood camping out in my drawing-room; with a strong detachment of O'Donohues, and O'Dohertys, and O'Driscolls lying around loose in possession of the library? Never leave a house to the servants, my dear! It's positively suicidal. Put in a responsible caretaker of whom you know something—like Lois here, for instance.'

'Lois!' Mrs. Evelegh echoed. 'Dear me, that's just the very thing. What a capital idea! I never thought of Lois! She and Elsie might stop on here, with Ursula and the gardener.'

I protested that if we did it was our clear duty to pay a small rent; but Mrs. Evelegh brushed that aside. 'You've robbed yourselves about the bicycle,' she insisted, 'and I'm delighted to let you have it. It's I who ought to pay, for you'll keep the house dry for me.'

I remembered Mr. Hitchcock—'Mutual advantage: benefits you, benefits me'—and made no bones about it. So in the end Mrs. Evelegh set off for England with Cécile, leaving Elsie and me in charge of Ursula, the gardener, and the *chalet*.

As for Lady Georgina, having by this time completed her 'cure' at Schlangenbad (complexion as usual; no guinea yellower), she telegraphed for Gretchen—'I can't do without the idiot'—and hung round Lucerne, apparently for no other purpose but to send people up the Brünig on the hunt for our wonderful new machines, and so put money in our pockets. She was much amused when I told her that Aunt Susan (who lived, you will remember, in respectable indigence at Blackheath) had written to expostulate with me on my 'unladylike' conduct in becoming a bicycle commission agent. 'Unladylike!' the Cantankerous Old Lady exclaimed, with warmth. 'What does the woman mean? Has she got no gumption? It's "ladylike," I suppose, to be a companion, or a governess, or a music-teacher, or something else in the black-thread-glove way, in London; but not to sell bicycles for a good round commission. My dear, between you and me, I don't see it. If you had a brother, now, *he* might sell bicycles, or corner wheat, or rig the share market, or do anything else he pleased, in these days, and nobody'd think the worse of him—as long as he made money; and it's my opinion that what is sauce for the goose can't be far out for the gander—and *vice-versâ*. Besides which, what's the use of *trying* to be ladylike? You *are* a lady, child, and you couldn't help being one; why trouble to be *like* what nature made you? Tell Aunt Susan from me to put *that* in her pipe and smoke it!'

I *did* tell Aunt Susan by letter, giving Lady Georgina as authority for the statement; and I really believe it had a consoling effect upon her; for Aunt Susan is one of those innocent-minded people who cherish a profound respect for the opinions and ideas of a Lady of Title. Especially where questions of delicacy are concerned. It calmed her to think that though I, an officer's daughter, had declined upon trade, I was mixing at least with the Best People!

We had a lovely time at the *chalet*—two girls alone, messing just as we pleased in the kitchen, and learning from Ursula how to concoct *pot-au-feu* in the most approved Swiss fashion. We pottered, as we women love to potter, half the day long; the other half we spent in riding our cycles about the eternal hills, and ensnaring the flies whom Lady Georgina dutifully sent up to us. She was our decoy duck: and, in virtue of her handle, she decoyed to a marvel. Indeed, I sold so many Manitous that I began to entertain a deep respect for my own commercial faculties. As for Mr. Cyrus W. Hitchcock, he wrote to me from Frankfort: 'The world continues to revolve on its axis, the Manitou, and the machine is booming. Orders romp in daily. When you ventilated the suggestion of an agency at Limburg, I concluded at a glance you had the material of a first-class business woman about you; but I reckon I did not know what a traveller meant till you started on the road. I am now enlarging and altering this factory, to meet increased demands. Branch offices at Berlin, Hamburg, Crefeld, and Düsseldorf. Inspect our stock before dealing elsewhere. A liberal discount allowed to the trade. Two hundred agents wanted in all towns of Germany. If they were every one of them like *you*, miss,—well, I guess I would hire the town of Frankfort for my business premises.'

One morning, after we had spent about a week at the *chalet* by ourselves, I was surprised to see a young man with a knapsack on his back walking up the garden path towards our cottage. 'Quick, quick, Elsie!' I cried, being in a mischievous mood. 'Come here with the opera-glass! There's a Man in the offing!'

'A *what?*' Elsie exclaimed, shocked as usual at my levity.

'A Man,' I answered, squeezing her arm. 'A Man! A real live Man! A specimen of the masculine gender in the human being! Man, ahoy! He has come at last—the lodestar of our existence!'

Next minute, I was sorry I spoke; for as the man drew nearer, I perceived that he was endowed with very long legs and a languidly poetical bearing. That supercilious smile—that enticing moustache! Could it be?—yes, it was—not a doubt of it—Harold Tillington!

I grew grave at once; Harold Tillington and the situation were serious. 'What can he want here?' I exclaimed, drawing back.

'Who is it?' Elsie asked; for, being a woman, she read at once in my altered demeanour the fact that the Man was not unknown to me.

'Lady Georgina's nephew,' I answered, with a tell-tale cheek, I fear. 'You remember I mentioned to you that I had met him at Schlangenbad. But this is really too bad of that wicked old Lady Georgina. She has told him where we lived and sent him up to see us.'

'Perhaps,' Elsie put in, 'he wants to charter a bicycle.'

I glanced at Elsie sideways. I had an uncomfortable suspicion that she said it slyly, like one who knew he wanted nothing of the sort. But at any rate, I brushed the suggestion aside frankly. 'Nonsense,' I answered. 'He wants *me*, not a bicycle.'

He came up to us, waving his hat. He *did* look handsome! 'Well, Miss Cayley,' he cried from afar, 'I have tracked you to your lair! I have found out where you abide! What a beautiful spot! And how well you're looking!'

'This is an unexpected——' I paused. He thought I was going to say, 'pleasure,' but I finished it, 'intrusion.' His face fell. 'How did you know we were at Lungern, Mr. Tillington?'

'My respected relative,' he answered, laughing. 'She mentioned—casually—' his eyes met mine—'that you were stopping in a *chalet*. And, as I was on my way back to the diplomatic mill, I thought I might just as well walk over the Grimsel and the Furca, and then on to the Gotthard. The Court is at Monza. So it occurred to me . . . . that in passing . . . . I might venture to drop in and say how-do-you-do to you.'

'Thank you,' I answered, severely—but my heart spoke otherwise—'I do very well. And you, Mr. Tillington?'

'Badly,' he echoed. 'Badly, since *you* went away from Schlangenbad.'

I gazed at his dusty feet. 'You are tramping,' I said, cruelly. 'I suppose you will get forward for lunch to Meiringen?'

'I—I did not contemplate it.'

'Indeed?'

He grew bolder. 'No; to say the truth, I half hoped I might stop and spend the day here with you.'

'Elsie,' I remarked firmly, 'if Mr. Tillington persists in planting himself upon us like this, one of us must go and investigate the kitchen department.'

Elsie rose like a lamb. I have an impression that she gathered we wanted to be left alone.

He turned to me imploringly. 'Lois,' he cried, stretching out his arms, with an appealing air, 'I *may* stay, mayn't I?'

I tried to be stern; but I fear 'twas a feeble pretence. 'We are two girls, alone in a house,' I answered. 'Lady Georgina, as a matron of experience, ought to have protected us. Merely to give you lunch is almost irregular.' (Good diplomatic word, irregular.) 'Still, in these days, I suppose you *may* stay, if you leave early in the afternoon. That's the utmost I can do for you.'

'You are not gracious,' he cried, gazing at me with a wistful look.

I did not dare to be gracious. 'Uninvited guests must not quarrel with their welcome,' I answered severely. Then the woman in me broke forth. 'But, indeed, Mr. Tillington, I am glad to see you.'

He leaned forward eagerly. 'So you are not angry with me, Lois? I may call you *Lois*?'

I trembled and hesitated. 'I am not angry with you. I—I like you too much to be ever angry with you. And I am glad you came— just this once—to see me. . . . Yes—when we are alone—you may call me Lois.'

He tried to seize my hand. I withdrew it. 'Then I may perhaps hope,' he began, 'that some day——'

I shook my head. 'No, no,' I said regretfully. 'You misunderstand me. I like you very much; and I like to see you. But as long as you are rich and have prospects like yours, I could never marry you. My pride wouldn't let me. Take that as final.'

I looked away. He bent forward again. 'But if I were poor?' he put in eagerly.

I hesitated. Then my heart rose, and I gave way. 'If ever you are poor,' I faltered,—'penniless, hunted, friendless—come to me,

Harold, and I will help and comfort you. But not till then. Not till then, I implore you.'

He leaned back and clasped his hands. 'You have given me something to live for, dear Lois,' he murmured. 'I will try to be poor—penniless, hunted, friendless. To win you I will try. And when that day arrives, I shall come to claim you.'

We sat for an hour and had a delicious talk—about nothing. But we understood each other. Only that artificial barrier divided us. At the end of the hour, I heard Elsie coming back by judiciously slow stages from the kitchen to the living-room, through six feet of passage, discoursing audibly to Ursula all the way, with a tardiness that did honour to her heart and her understanding. Dear, kind little Elsie! I believe she had never a tiny romance of her own; yet her sympathy for others was sweet to look upon.

We lunched at a small deal table on the veranda. Around us rose the pinnacles. The scent of pines and moist moss was in the air. Elsie had arranged the flowers, and got ready the omelette, and cooked the cutlets, and prepared the junket. 'I never thought I could do it alone without you, Brownie; but I tried, and it all came right by magic, somehow.' We laughed and talked incessantly. Harold was in excellent cue; and Elsie took to him. A livelier or merrier table there wasn't in the twenty-two Cantons that day than ours, under the sapphire sky, looking out on the sun-smitten snows of the Jungfrau.

After lunch, Harold begged hard to be allowed to stop for tea. I had misgivings, but I gave way—he *was* such good company. One may as well be hanged for a sheep as a lamb, says the wisdom of our ancestors: and, after all, Mrs. Grundy was only represented here by Elsie, the gentlest and least censorious of her daughters. So he stopped and chatted till four; when I made tea and insisted on dismissing him. He meant to take the rough mountain path over the screes from Lungern to Meiringen, which ran right behind the *chalet*. I feared lest he might be belated, and urged him to hurry.

'Thanks, I'm happier here,' he answered.

I was sternness itself. 'You *promised* me!' I said, in a reproachful voice.

He rose instantly, and bowed. 'Your will is law—even when it pronounces sentence of exile.'

Would we walk a little way with him? No, I faltered; we would not. We would follow him with the opera-glasses and wave him farewell when he reached the Kulm. He shook our hands unwillingly, and turned up the little path, looking handsomer than ever. It led ascending through a fir-wood to the rock-strewn hillside.

Once, a quarter of an hour later, we caught a glimpse of him near a sharp turn in the road; after that we waited in vain, with our eyes fixed on the Kulm; not a sign could we discern of him. At last I grew anxious. 'He ought to be there,' I cried, fuming.

'He ought,' Elsie answered.

I swept the slopes with the opera-glasses. Anxiety and interest in him quickened my senses, I suppose. 'Look here, Elsie,' I burst out at last. 'Just take this glass and have a glance at those birds, down the crag below the Kulm. Don't they seem to be circling and behaving most oddly?'

Elsie gazed where I bid her. 'They're wheeling round and round,' she answered, after a minute; 'and they certainly *do* look as if they were screaming.'

'They seem to be frightened,' I suggested.

'It looks like it, Brownie.'

'Then he's fallen over a precipice!' I cried, rising up; 'and he's lying there on a ledge by their nest. Elsie, we must go to him!'

She clasped her hands and looked terrified. 'Oh, Brownie, how dreadful!' she exclaimed. Her face was deadly white. Mine burned like fire.

'Not a moment to lose!' I said, holding my breath. 'Get out the rope and let us run to him!'

'Don't you think,' Elsie suggested, 'we had better hurry down on our cycles to Lungern and call some men from the village to help us? We are two girls, and alone. What can we do to aid him?'

'No,' I answered, promptly, 'that won't do. It would only lose time—and time may be precious. You and I must go; I'll send Ursula off to bring up guides from the village.'

Fortunately, we had a good long coil of new rope in the house, which Mrs. Evelegh had provided in case of accident. I slipped it on my arm, and set out on foot; for the path was by far too rough for cycles. I was sorry afterwards that I had not taken Ursula, and sent Elsie to Lungern to rouse the men; for she found the climbing hard, and I had difficulty at times in dragging her up the steep and stony pathway, almost a watercourse. However, we persisted in the direction of the Kulm, tracking Harold by his footprints; for he wore mountain boots with sharp-headed nails, which made dints in the moist soil, and scratched the smooth surface of the rock where he trod on it.

We followed him thus for a mile or two, along the regular path; then of a sudden, in an open part, the trail failed us. I turned back a few yards and looked close, with my eyes fixed on the spongy soil, as keen as a hound that sniffs his way after his quarry. 'He went off *here*, Elsie!' I said at last, pulling up short by a spindle bush on the hillside.

'How do you know, Brownie?'

'Why, see, there are the marks of his stick; he had a thick one, you remember, with a square iron spike. These are its dints; I have been watching them all the way along from the *chalet.*'

'But there are so many such marks!'

'Yes, I know; I can tell his from the older ones made by the spikes of alpenstocks because Harold's are fresher and sharper on the edge. They look so much newer. See, here, he slipped on the rock; you can know that scratch is recent by the clean way it's traced, and the little glistening crystals still left behind in it. Those other marks have been wind-swept and washed by the rain. There are no broken particles.'

'How on earth did you find that out, Brownie?'

How on earth did I find it out! I wondered myself. But the emergency seemed somehow to teach me something of the instinctive lore of hunters and savages. I did not trouble to answer her. 'At this bush, the tracks fail,' I went on; 'and, look, he must have clutched at that branch and crushed the broken leaves as the twigs slipped through his fingers. He left the path here, then, and struck off on a short cut of his own along the hillside, lower down. Elsie, we must follow him.'

She shrank from it; but I held her hand. It was a more difficult task to track him now; for we had no longer the path to guide us. However, I explored the ground on my hands and knees, and soon found marks of footsteps on the boggy patches, with scratches on the rock where he had leaped from point to point, or planted his

stick to steady himself. I tried to help Elsie along among the lit-
tered boulders and the dwarf growth of wind-swept daphne: but,
poor child, it was too much for her: she sat down after a few minutes upon the flat juniper scrub and began to cry. What was I to
do? My anxiety was breathless. I couldn't leave her there alone,
and I couldn't forsake Harold. Yet I felt every minute might now
be critical. We were making among wet whortleberry thicket and
torn rock towards the spot where I had seen the birds wheel and
circle, screaming. The only way left was to encourage Elsie and
make her feel the necessity for instant action. 'He is alive still,' I
exclaimed, looking up; 'the birds are crying! If he were dead, they
would return to their nest—Elsie, we *must* get to him!'

She rose, bewildered, and followed me. I held her hand tight,
and coaxed her to scramble over the rocks where the scratches
showed the way, or to clamber at times over fallen trunks of huge
fir-trees. Yet it was hard work climbing; even Harold's sure feet had
slipped often on the wet and slimy boulders, though, like most of
Queen Margherita's set, he was an expert mountaineer. Then, at
times, I lost the faint track, so that I had to diverge and look close
to find it. These delays fretted me. 'See, a stone loosed from its
bed—he must have passed by here. . . . That twig is newly snapped;
no doubt he caught at it. . . . Ha, the moss there has been crushed;
a foot has gone by. And the ants on that ant-hill, with their eggs in
their mouths—a man's tread has frightened them.' So, by some
instinctive sense, as if the spirit of my savage ancestors revived
within me, I managed to recover the spoor again and again by a
miracle, till at last, round a corner by a defiant cliff—with a terrible
foreboding, my heart stood still within me.

We had come to an end. A great projecting buttress of crag rose
sheer in front. Above lay loose boulders. Below was a shrub-hung
precipice. The birds we had seen from home were still circling and
screaming.

They were a pair of peregrine hawks. Their nest seemed to lie
far below the broken scar, some sixty or seventy feet beneath us.

'He is not dead!' I cried once more, with my heart in my mouth.
'If he were, they would have returned. He has fallen, and is lying,
alive, below there!'

Elsie shrank back against the wall of rock. I advanced on my hands and knees to the edge of the precipice. It was not quite sheer, but it dropped like a sea-cliff, with broken ledges.

I could see where Harold had slipped. He had tried to climb round the crag that blocked the road, and the ground at the edge of the precipice had given way with him; it showed a recent founder of a few inches. Then he clutched at a branch of broom as he fell; but it slipped through his fingers, cutting them; for there was blood on the wiry stem. I knelt by the side of the cliff and craned my head over. I scarcely dared to look. In spite of the birds, my heart misgave me.

There, on a ledge deep below, he lay in a mass, half raised on one arm. But not dead, I believed. 'Harold!' I cried. 'Harold!'

He turned his face up and saw me; his eyes lighted with joy. He shouted back something, but I could not hear it.

I turned to Elsie. 'I must go down to him!'

Her tears rose again. 'Oh, Brownie!'

I unwound the coil of rope. The first thing was to fasten it. I could not trust Elsie to hold it; she was too weak and too frightened to bear my weight: even if I wound it round her body, I feared my mere mass might drag her over. I peered about at the surroundings. No tree grew near; no rock had a pinnacle sufficiently safe to depend upon. But I found a plan soon. In the crag behind me was a cleft, narrowing wedge-shape as it descended. I tied the end of the rope round a stone, a good big water-worn stone, rudely girdled with a groove near the middle, which prevented it from slipping; then I dropped it down the fissure till it jammed; after which, I tried it to see if it would bear. It was firm as the rock itself. I let the rope down by it, and waited a moment to discover whether Harold could climb. He shook his head, and took a note-book with evident pain from his pocket. Then he scribbled a few words, and pinned them to the rope. I hauled it up. 'Can't move. Either severely bruised and sprained, or else legs broken.'

There was no help for it, then. I must go to him.

My first idea was merely to glide down the rope with my gloved hands, for I chanced to have my dog-skin bicycling gloves in my pocket. Fortunately, however, I did not carry out this crude idea too hastily; for next instant it occurred to me that I could not swarm up again. I have had no practice in rope-climbing. Here was a problem. But the moment suggested its own solution. I began making knots, or rather nooses or loops, in the rope, at intervals of about eighteen inches. 'What are they for?' Elsie asked, looking on in wonder.

'Footholds, to climb up by.'

'But the ones above will pull out with your weight.'

'I don't think so. Still, to make sure, I shall tie them with this string. I *must* get down to him.'

I threaded a sufficient number of loops, trying the length over the ledge. Then I said to Elsie, who sat cowering, propped against the crag, 'You must come and look over, and do as I wave to you. Mind, dear, you *must!* Two lives depend upon it.'

'Brownie, I daren't! I shall turn giddy and fall over!'

I smoothed her golden hair. 'Elsie, dear,' I said gently, gazing into her blue eyes, 'you are a woman. A woman can always be brave, where those she loves are concerned; and I believe you love me.' I led her, coaxingly, to the edge. 'Sit there,' I said, in my quietest voice, so as not to alarm her. 'You can lie at full length, if you like, and only just peep over. But when I wave my hand, remember, you must pull the rope up.'

She obeyed me like a child. I knew she loved me.

I gripped the rope and let myself down, not using the loops to descend, but just sliding with hands and knees, and allowing the knots to slacken my pace. Half-way down, I will confess, the eerie feeling of physical suspense was horrible. One hung so in mid-air! The hawks flapped their wings. But Harold was below; and a woman can always be brave where those she loves—well, just that moment, catching my breath, I knew I loved Harold.

I glided down swiftly. The air whizzed. At last, on a narrow shelf of rock, I leant over him. He seized my hand. 'I knew you would come!' he cried. 'I felt sure you would find out. Though *how* you found out, Heaven only knows, you clever, brave little woman!'

'Are you terribly hurt?' I asked, bending close. His clothes were torn.

'I hardly know. I can't move. It may only be bruises.'

'Can you climb by these nooses with my help?'

He shook his head. 'Oh, no. I couldn't climb at all. I must be

lifted, somehow. You had better go back to Lungern and bring men
to help you.'

'And leave you here alone! Never, Harold; never!'

'Then what can we do?'

I reflected a moment. 'Lend me your pencil,' I said. He pulled
it out—his arms were almost unhurt, fortunately. I scribbled a line
to Elsie. 'Tie my plaid to the rope and let it down.' Then I waved
to her to pull up again.

I was half surprised to find she obeyed the signal, for she crouched
there, white-faced and open-mouthed, watching; but I have often
observed that women are almost always brave in the great emer-
gencies. She pinned on the plaid and let it down with commendable
quickness. I doubled it, and tied firm knots in the four corners, so
as to make it into a sort of basket; then I fastened it at each corner
with a piece of the rope, crossed in the middle, till it looked like one
of the cages they use in mills for letting down sacks with. As soon as
it was finished, I said, 'Now, just try to crawl into it.'

He raised himself on his arms and crawled in with difficulty.
His legs dragged after him. I could see he was in great pain. But
still, he managed it.

I planted my foot in the first noose. 'You must sit still,' I said,
breathless. 'I am going back to haul you up.'

'Are you strong enough, Lois?'

'With Elsie to help me, yes. I often stroked a four at Girton.'

'I can trust you,' he answered. It thrilled me that he said so.

I began my hazardous journey; I mounted the rope by the
nooses—one, two, three, four, counting them as I mounted. I did
not dare to look up or down as I did so, lest I should grow giddy
and fall, but kept my eyes fixed firmly always on the one noose
in front of me. My brain swam: the rope swayed and creaked.
Twenty, thirty, forty! Foot after foot, I slipped them in mechanically, taking up with me the longer coil whose ends were attached
to the cage and Harold. My hands trembled; it was ghastly, swinging there between earth and heaven. Forty-five, forty-six, forty-
seven—I knew there were forty-eight of them. At last, after some
weeks, as it seemed, I reached the summit. Tremulous and half
dead, I prised myself over the edge with my hands, and knelt once
more on the hill beside Elsie.

She was white, but attentive. 'What next, Brownie?' Her voice quivered.

I looked about me. I was too faint and shaky after my perilous ascent to be fit for work, but there was no help for it. What could I use as a pulley? Not a tree grew near; but the stone jammed in the fissure might once more serve my purpose. I tried it again. It had borne my weight; was it strong enough to bear the precious weight of Harold? I tugged at it, and thought so. I passed the rope round it like a pulley, and then tied it about my own waist. I had a happy thought: I could use myself as a windlass. I turned on my feet for a pivot. Elsie helped me to pull. 'Up you go!' I cried, cheerily. We wound slowly, for fear of shaking him. Bit by bit, I could feel the cage rise gradually from the ground; its weight, taken so, with living capstan and stone axle, was less than I should have expected. But the pulley helped us, and Elsie, spurred by need, put forth more reserve of nervous strength than I could easily have believed lay in that tiny body. I twisted myself round and round, close to the edge, so as to look over from time to time, but not at all quickly, for fear of dizziness. The rope strained and gave. It was a deadly ten minutes of suspense and anxiety. Twice or thrice as I looked down I saw a spasm of pain break over Harold's face; but when I paused and glanced inquiringly, he motioned me to go on with my venturesome task. There was no turning back now. We had almost got him up when the rope at the edge began to creak ominously.

It was straining at the point where it grated against the brink of the precipice. My heart gave a leap. If the rope broke, all was over.

With a sudden dart forward, I seized it with my hands, below the part that gave; then—one fierce little run back—and I brought him level with the edge. He clutched at Elsie's hand. I turned thrice round, to wind the slack about my body. The taut rope cut deep into my flesh; but nothing mattered now, except to save him. 'Catch the cloak, Elsie!' I cried; 'catch it: pull him gently in!' Elsie caught it and pulled him in, with wonderful pluck and calmness. We hauled him over the edge. He lay safe on the bank. Then we all three broke down and cried like children together. I took his hand in mine and held it in silence.

When we found words again I drew a deep breath, and said, simply, 'How did you manage to do it?'

'I tried to clamber past the wall that barred the way there by sheer force of stride—you know, my legs are long—and I somehow overbalanced myself. But I didn't exactly fall—if I had fallen I must have been killed; I rolled and slid down, clutching at the weeds in the crannies as I slipped, and stumbling over the projections, without quite losing my foothold on the ledges, till I found myself brought up short with a bump at the end of it.'

'And you think no bones are broken?'

'I can't feel sure. It hurts me horribly to move. I fancy just at first I must have fainted. But I'm inclined to guess I'm only sprained and bruised and sore all over. Why, you're as bad as me, I believe. See, your dear hands are all torn and bleeding!'

'How are we ever to get him back again, Brownie?' Elsie put in. She was paler than ever now, and prostrate with the after-effects of her unwonted effort.

'You are a practical woman, Elsie,' I answered. 'Stop with him here a minute or two. I'll climb up the hillside and halloo for Ursula and the men from Lungern.'

I climbed and hallooed. In a few minutes, worn out as I was, I had reached the path above and attracted their attention. They hurried down to where Harold lay, and, using my cage for a litter, slung on a young fir-trunk, carried him back between them across their shoulders to the village. He pleaded hard to be allowed to remain at the *chalet*, and Elsie joined her prayers to his; but, there, I was adamant. It was not so much what people might say that I minded, but a deeper difficulty. For if once I nursed him through his trouble, how could I or any woman in my place any longer refuse him? So I passed him ruthlessly on to Lungern (though my heart ached for it), and telegraphed at once to his nearest relative, Lady Georgina, to come up and take care of him.

He recovered rapidly. Though sore and shaken, his worst hurts, it turned out, were sprains; and in three or four days he was ready to go on again. I called to see him before he left. I dreaded the interview; for one's own heart is a hard enemy to fight so long; but how could I let him go without one word of farewell to him?

'After this, Lois,' he said, taking my hand in his—and I was weak enough, for a moment, to let it lie there—'you *cannot* say No to me!'

Oh, how I longed to fling myself upon him and cry out, 'No, Harold, I cannot! I love you too dearly!' But his future and Marmaduke Ashurst's half million restrained me: for his sake and for my own I held myself in courageously. Though, indeed, it needed some courage and self-control. I withdrew my hand slowly. 'Do you remember,' I said, 'you asked me that first day at Schlangenbad'—it was an epoch to me, now, that first day—'whether I was mediæval or modern? And I answered, "Modern, I hope." And you said, "That's well!"'—You see, I don't forget the least things you say to me. Well, because I am modern'—my lips trembled and belied me—'I can answer you No. I can even now refuse you. The old-fashioned girl, the mediæval girl, would have held that because she saved your life (if I *did* save your life, which is a matter of opinion) she was bound to marry you. But *I* am modern, and I see things differently. If there were reasons at Schlangenbad which made it impracticable for me to accept you—though my heart pleaded hard—I do not deny it—those reasons cannot have disappeared merely because you have chosen to fall over a precipice, and I have pulled you up again. My decision was founded, you see, not on passing accidents of situation, but on permanent considerations. Nothing has happened in the last three days to affect those considerations. We are still ourselves: you rich; I, a penniless adventuress. I could not accept you when you asked me at Schlangenbad. On just the same grounds, I cannot accept you now. I do not see how the unessential fact that I made myself into a winch to pull you up the cliff, and that I am still smarting for it——'

He looked me all over comically. 'How severe we are!' he cried, in a bantering tone. 'And how extremely Girtony! A System of Logic, Ratiocinative and Inductive, by Lois Cayley! What a pity we didn't take a professor's chair. My child that isn't *you*! It's not yourself at all! It's an attempt to be unnaturally and unfemininely reasonable.'

Logic fled. I broke down utterly. 'Harold,' I cried, rising, 'I love you! I admit I love you! But I will never marry you—while you have those thousands.'

'I haven't got them yet!'

'Or the chance of inheriting them.'

He smothered my hand with kisses—for I withdrew my face. 'If you admit you love me,' he cried, quite joyously, 'then all is well. When once a woman admits that, the rest is but a matter of time—and, Lois, I can wait a thousand years for you.'

'Not in my case,' I answered through my tears. 'Not in my case, Harold! I am a modern woman, and what I say I mean. I will renew my promise. If ever you are poor and friendless, come to me; I am yours. Till then, don't harrow me by asking me the impossible!'

I tore myself away. At the hall door, Lady Georgina intercepted me. She glanced at my red eyes. 'Then you have taken him?' she cried, seizing my hand.

I shook my head firmly. I could hardly speak. 'No, Lady Georgina,' I answered, in a choking voice. 'I have refused him again. I will not stand in his way. I will not ruin his prospects.'

She drew back and let her chin drop. 'Well, of all the hard-hearted, cruel, obdurate young women I ever saw in my born days, if you're not the very hardest——'

I half ran from the house. I hurried home to the *chalet*. There, I dashed into my own room, locked the door behind me, flung myself wildly on my bed, and, burying my face in my hands, had a good, long, hard-hearted, cruel, obdurate cry—exactly like any mediæval woman. It's all very well being modern; but my experience is that, when it comes to a man one loves—well, the Middle Ages are still horribly strong within us.

CHAPTER VI

THE ADVENTURE OF THE URBANE OLD GENTLEMAN

WHEN Elsie's holidays—I beg pardon, vacation—came to an end, she proposed to return to her High School in London. Zeal for the higher mathematics devoured her. But she still looked so frail, and coughed so often—a perfect *Campo Santo* of a cough—in spite of her summer of open-air exercise, that I positively worried her into consulting a doctor—not one of the Fortescue-Langley order. The report he gave was mildly unfavourable. He spoke disrespectfully of the apex of her right lung. It was not exactly tubercular, he remarked, but he 'feared tuberculosis'—excuse the long words; the phrase was his, not mine; I repeat *verbatim*. He vetoed her exposing herself to a winter in London in her present unstable condition. Davos? Well, no. *Not* Davos: with deliberative thumb and finger on close-shaven chin. He judged her too delicate for such drastic remedies. Those high mountain stations suited best the robust invalid, who had dropped by accident into casual phthisis. For Miss Petheridge's case—looking wise—he would not recommend the Riviera, either: too stimulating, too exciting. What this young lady needed most was rest: rest in some agreeable southern town, some city of the soul—say Rome or Florence—where she might find much to interest her, and might forget the apex of her right lung in the new world of art that opened around her.

'Very well,' I said promptly; 'that's settled, Elsie. The apex and you shall winter in Florence.'

'But, Brownie, can we afford it?'

'Afford it?' I echoed. 'Goodness gracious, my dear child, what a bourgeois sentiment! Your medical attendant says to you, "Go to Florence": and to Florence you must go; there's no getting out of it. Why, even the swallows fly south when their medical attendant tells them England is turning a trifle too cold for them.'

'But what will Miss Latimer say? She depends upon me to come back at the beginning of term. She *must* have *somebody* to undertake the higher mathematics.'

'And she will get somebody, dear,' I answered, calmly. 'Don't trouble your sweet little head about that. An eminent statistician has calculated that five hundred and thirty duly qualified young women are now standing four-square in a solid phalanx in the streets of London, all agog to teach the higher mathematics to anyone who wants them at a moment's notice. Let Miss Latimer take her pick of the five hundred and thirty. I'll wire to her at once: "Elsie Petheridge unable through ill health to resume her duties. Ordered to Florence. Resigns post. Engage substitute." *That's* the way to do it.'

Elsie clasped her small white hands in the despair of the woman who considers herself indispensable—as if we were any of us indispensable! 'But, dearest, the girls! They'll be *so* disappointed!'

'They'll get over it,' I answered, grimly. 'There are worse disappointments in store for them in life—which is a fine old crusted platitude worthy of Aunt Susan. Anyhow, I've decided. Look here, Elsie: I stand to you *in loco parentis.*' I have already remarked, I think, that she was three years my senior; but I was so pleased with this phrase that I repeated it lovingly. 'I stand to you, dear, *in loco parentis.* Now, I can't let you endanger your precious health by returning to town and Miss Latimer this winter. Let us be categorical. I go to Florence; you go with me.'

'What shall we live upon?' Elsie suggested, piteously.

'Our fellow-creatures, as usual,' I answered, with prompt callousness. 'I object to these base utilitarian considerations being imported into the discussion of a serious question. Florence is the city of art; as a woman of culture, it behoves you to revel in it. Your medical attendant sends you there; as a patient and an invalid, you can revel with a clear conscience. Money? Well, money is a secondary matter. All philosophies and all religions agree that money is mere dross, filthy lucre. Rise superior to it. We have a fair sum in hand to the credit of the firm; we can pick up some more, I suppose, in Florence.'

'How?'

I reflected. 'Elsie,' I said, 'you are deficient in faith—which is one of the leading Christian graces. My mission in life is to correct that want in your spiritual nature. Now, observe how beautifully all these events work in together! The winter comes, when

no man can bicycle, especially in Switzerland. Therefore, what is
the use of my stopping on here after October? Again, in pursuance
of my general plan of going round the world, I must get forward
to Italy. Your medical attendant considerately orders you at the
same time to Florence. In Florence we shall still have chances of
selling Manitous, though possibly, I admit, in diminished numbers.
I confess at once that people come to Switzerland to tour, and are
therefore liable to need our machines; while they go to Florence
to look at pictures, and a bicycle would doubtless prove inconve-
nient in the Uffizi or the Pitti. Still, we *may* sell a few. But I descry
another opening. You write shorthand, don't you?'

'A little, dear; only ninety words a minute.'

'*That's* not business. Advertise yourself, à la Cyrus Hitchcock!
Say boldly, "I write shorthand." Leave the world to ask, "How fast?"
It will ask it quick enough without your suggesting it. Well, my
idea is this. Florence is a town teeming with English tourists of the
cultivated classes—men of letters, painters, antiquaries, art-critics.
I suppose even art-critics may be classed as cultivated. Such people
are sure to need literary aid. We exist to supply it. We will set up
the Florentine School of Stenography and Typewriting. We'll buy
a couple of typewriters.'

'How can we pay for them, Brownie?'

I gazed at her in despair. 'Elsie,' I cried, clapping my hand to
my head, 'you are not practical. Did I ever suggest we should pay
for them? I said merely, buy them. 'Base is the slave that pays.'
That's Shakespeare. And we all know Shakespeare is the mirror of
nature. Argal, it would be unnatural to pay for a typewriter. We
will hire a room in Florence (on tick, of course), and begin operations. Clients will flock in; and we tide over the winter. *There's*
enterprise for you!' And I struck an attitude.

Elsie's face looked her doubts. I walked across to Mrs. Evelegh's
desk, and began writing a letter. It occurred to me that Mr.
Hitchcock, who was a man of business, might be able to help a
woman of business in this delicate matter. I put the point to him
fairly and squarely, without circumlocution; we were going to start
an English typewriting office in Florence; what was the ordinary
way for people to become possessed of a typewriting machine,
without the odious and mercenary preliminary of paying for it?

The answer came back with commendable promptitude:

'DEAR MISS,—Your spirit of enterprise is really remarkable! I have forwarded your letter to my friends of the Spread Eagle Typewriting and Phonograph Company, Limited, of New York City, informing them of your desire to open an agency for the sale of their machines in Florence, Italy, and giving them my estimate of your business capacities. I have advised their London house to present you with two complimentary machines for your own use and your partner's, and also to supply a number of others for disposal in the city of Florence. If you would further like to undertake an agency for the development of the trade in salt codfish (large quantities of which are, of course, consumed in Catholic Europe), I could put you into communication with my respected friends, Messrs. Abel Woodward and Co., exporters of preserved provisions, St. John's, Newfoundland. But, perhaps, in this suggestion I am not sufficiently high-toned.—Respectfully, CYRUS W. HITCHCOCK.'

The moment had arrived for Elsie to be firm. 'I have no prejudice against trade, Brownie,' she observed emphatically; 'but I do draw the line at salt fish.'

'So do I, dear,' I answered.

She sighed her relief. I really believe she half expected to find me trotting about Florence with miscellaneous samples of Messrs. Abel Woodward's esteemed productions protruding from my pocket.

So to Florence we went. My first idea was to travel by the Brenner route through the Tyrol; but a queer little episode which met us at the outset on the Austrian frontier put a check to this plan. We cycled to the border, sending our trunks by rail. When we went to claim them at the Austrian Custom-house, we were told that they were detained 'for political reasons.'

'Political reasons?' I exclaimed, nonplussed.

'Even so, Fräulein. Your boxes contain revolutionary literature.'

'Some mistake!' I cried, warmly. I am but a drawing-room Socialist.

'Not at all; look here.' And he drew a small book out of Elsie's portmanteau.

What? Elsie a conspirator? Elsie in league with Nihilists? So mild and so meek! I could never have believed it. I took the book in my hands and read the title, 'Revolution of the Heavenly Bodies.'

'But this is astronomy,' I burst out. 'Don't you see? Sun-and-star circling. The revolution of the planets.'

'It matters not, Fräulein. Our instructions are strict. We have orders to intercept *all* revolutionary literature without distinction.'

'Come, Elsie,' I said, firmly, 'this is *too* ridiculous. Let us give them a clear berth, these Kaiserly-Kingly blockheads!' So we registered our luggage right back to Lucerne, and cycled over the Gotthard.

When at last, by leisurely stages, we arrived at Florence, I felt there was no use in doing things by halves. If you are going to start the Florentine School of Stenography and Typewriting, you may as well start it on a proper basis. So I took sunny rooms at a nice hotel for myself and Elsie, and hired a ground floor in a convenient house, close under the shadow of the great marble Campanile. (Considerations of space compel me to curtail the usual gush about Arnolfo and Giotto.) This was our office. When I had got a Tuscan painter to plant our flag in the shape of a signboard, I sailed forth into the street and inspected it from outside with a swelling heart. It is true, the Tuscan painter's unaccountable predilection for the rare spellings 'Scool' without an *h*, and 'Stenografy' with an *f*, somewhat damped my exuberant pride for the moment; but I made him take the board back and correct his Italianate English. As soon as all was fitted up with desk and tables we reposed upon our laurels, and waited only for customers in shoals to pour in upon us. *I* called them 'customers'; Elsie maintained that we ought rather to say 'clients.' Being by temperament averse to sectarianism, I did not dispute the point with her.

We reposed on our laurels—in vain. Neither customers nor clients seemed in any particular hurry to disturb our leisure.

I confess I took this ill. It was a rude awakening. I had begun to regard myself as the special favourite of a fairy godmother; it surprised me to find that any undertaking of mine did not succeed

immediately. However, reflecting that my fairy godmother's name
was really Enterprise, I recalled Mr. Cyrus W. Hitchcock's advice,
and advertised.

'There's one good thing about Florence, Elsie,' I said, just to
keep up her courage. 'When the customers *do* come, they'll be
interesting people, and it will be interesting work. Artistic work,
don't you know—Fra Angelico, and Della Robbia, and all that sort
of thing; or else fresh light on Dante and Petrarch!'

'When they *do* come, no doubt,' Elsie answered, dubiously. 'But
do you know, Brownie, it strikes me there isn't quite that literary
stir and ferment one might expect in Florence. Dante and Petrarch
appear to be dead. The distinguished authors fail to stream in upon
us as one imagined with manuscripts to copy.'

I affected an air of confidence—for I had sunk capital in the concern (that's business-like—sunk capital!). 'Oh, we're a new firm,' I
assented, carelessly. 'Our enterprise is yet young. When cultivated
Florence learns we're here, cultivated Florence will invade us by
thousands.'

But we sat in our office and bit our thumbs all day; the thousands stopped at home. We had ample opportunities for making
studies of the decorative detail on the Campanile, till we knew
every square inch of it better than Mr. Ruskin. Elsie's note-book
contains, I believe, eleven hundred separate sketches of the
Campanile, from the right end, the left end, and the middle of
our window, with eight hundred and five distinct distortions of the
individual statues that adorn its niches on the side turned towards
us.

At last, after we had sat, and bitten our thumbs, and sketched
the Four Greater Prophets for a fortnight on end, an immense
excitement occurred. An old gentleman was distinctly seen to
approach and to look up at the sign-board which decorated our
office.

I instantly slipped in a sheet of foolscap, and began to type-
write with alarming speed—click, click, click; while Elsie, rising to
the occasion, set to work to transcribe imaginary shorthand as if
her life depended upon it.

The old gentleman, after a moment's hesitation, lifted the latch
of the door somewhat nervously. I affected to take no notice of

him, so breathless was the haste with which our immense business connection compelled me to finger the keyboard: but, looking up at him under my eyelashes, I could just make out he was a peculiarly bland and urbane old person, dressed with the greatest care, and some attention to fashion. His face was smooth; it tended towards portliness.

He made up his mind, and entered the office. I continued to click till I had reached the close of a sentence—'Or to take arms against a sea of troubles, and by opposing, end them.' Then I looked up sharply. 'Can I do anything for you?' I inquired, in the smartest tone of business. (I observe that politeness is not professional.)

The Urbane Old Gentleman came forward with his hat in his hand. He looked as if he had just landed from the Eighteenth Century. His figure was that of Mr. Edward Gibbon. 'Yes, madam,' he said, in a markedly deferential tone, fussing about with the rim of his hat as he spoke, and adjusting his *pince-nez*. 'I was recommended to your—ur—your establishment for shorthand and typewriting. I have some work which I wish done, if it falls within your province. But I am *rather* particular. I require a quick worker. Excuse my asking it, but how many words can you do a minute?'

'Shorthand?' I asked, sharply, for I wished to imitate official habits.

The Urbane Old Gentleman bowed. 'Yes, shorthand. Certainly.'

I waved my hand with careless grace towards Elsie—as if these things happened to us daily. 'Miss Petheridge undertakes the shorthand department,' I said, with decision. 'I am the type-writing from dictation. Miss Petheridge, forward!'

Elsie rose to it like an angel. 'A hundred,' she answered, confronting him.

The old gentleman bowed again. 'And your terms?' he inquired, in a honey-tongued voice. 'If I may venture to ask them.'

We handed him our printed tariff. He seemed satisfied.

'Could you spare me an hour this morning?' he asked, still fingering his hat nervously with his puffy hand. 'But perhaps you are engaged. I fear I intrude upon you.'

'Not at all,' I answered, consulting an imaginary engagement list. 'This work can wait. Let me see: 11.30. Elsie, I think you have

nothing to do before one, that cannot be put off? Quite so!—very
well, then; yes, we are both at your service.'

The Urbane Old Gentleman looked about him for a seat. I
pushed him our one easy-chair. He withdrew his gloves with great
deliberation, and sat down in it with an apologetic glance. I could
gather from his dress and his diamond pin that he was wealthy.
Indeed, I half guessed who he was already. There was a fussiness
about his manner which seemed strangely familiar to me.

He sat down by slow degrees, edging himself about till he
was thoroughly comfortable. I could see he was of the kind that
will have comfort. He took out his notes and a packet of letters,
which he sorted slowly. Then he looked hard at me and at Elsie. He
seemed to be making his choice between us. After a time he spoke.
'I *think*,' he said, in a most leisurely voice, 'I will not trouble your
friend to write shorthand for me, after all. Or should I say your
assistant? Excuse my change of plan. I will content myself with
dictation. You can follow on the machine?'

'As fast as you choose to dictate to me.'

He glanced at his notes and began a letter. It was a curious
communication. It seemed to be all about buying Bertha and selling Clara—a cold-blooded proceeding which almost suggested
slave-dealing. I gathered he was giving instructions to his agent:
could he have business relations with Cuba, I wondered. But there
were also hints of mysterious middies—brave British tars to the
rescue, possibly! Perhaps my bewilderment showed itself upon my
face, for at last he looked queerly at me. 'You don't quite like this,
I'm afraid,' he said, breaking off short.

I was the soul of business. 'Not at all,' I answered. 'I am an
automaton—nothing more. It is a typewriter's function to transcribe the words a client dictates as if they were absolutely mean-
ingless to her.'

'Quite right,' he answered, approvingly. 'Quite right. I see you
understand. A very proper spirit!'

Then the Woman within me got the better of the Type-writer.
'Though I confess,' I continued, 'I *do* feel it is a little unkind
to sell Clara at once for whatever she will fetch. It seems to
me—well—unchivalrous.'

He smiled, but held his peace.

'Still—the middies,' I went on: 'they will perhaps take care that these poor girls are not ill-treated.'

He leaned back, clasped his hands, and regarded me fixedly. 'Bertha,' he said, after a pause, 'is Brighton A's—to be strictly correct, London, Brighton, and South Coast First Preference Debentures. Clara is Glasgow and South-Western Deferred Stock. Middies are Midland Ordinary. But I respect your feeling. You are a young lady of principle.' And he fidgeted more than ever.

He went on dictating for just an hour. His subject-matter bewildered me. It was all about India Bills, and telegraphic transfers, and selling cotton short, and holding tight to Egyptian Unified. Markets, it seemed, were glutted. Hungarians were only to be dealt in if they hardened—hardened sinners I know, but what are hardened Hungarians? And fears were not unnaturally expressed that Turks might be 'irregular.' Consols, it appeared, were certain to give way for political reasons; but the downward tendency of Australians, I was relieved to learn, for the honour of so great a group of colonies, could only be temporary. Greeks were growing decidedly worse, though I had always understood Greeks were bad enough already; and Argentine Central were likely to be weak; but Provincials must soon become commendably firm, and if Uruguays went flat, something good ought to be made out of them. Scotch rails might shortly be quiet—I always understood they were based upon sleepers; but if South-Eastern stiffened, advantage should certainly be taken of their stiffening. He would telegraph particulars on Monday morning. And so on till my brain reeled. Oh, artistic Florence! was *this* the Filippo Lippi, the Michael Angelo I dreamed of?

At the end of the hour, the Urbane Old Gentleman rose urbanely. He drew on his gloves again with the greatest deliberation, and hunted for his stick as if his life depended upon it. 'Let me see; I had a pencil; oh, thanks; yes, that is it. This cover protects the point. My hat? Ah, certainly. And my notes; much obliged; notes *always* get mislaid. People are so careless. Then I will come again to-morrow; the same hour, if you will kindly keep yourself disengaged. Though, excuse me, you had better make an entry of it at once upon your agenda.'

'I shall remember it,' I answered, smiling.

'No; will you? But you haven't my name.'

'I know it,' I answered. 'At least, I think so. You are Mr. Marmaduke Ashurst. Lady Georgina Fawley sent you here.'

He laid down his hat and gloves again, so as to regard me more undistracted. 'You are a most remarkable young lady,' he said, in a very slow voice. 'I impressed upon Georgina that she must not mention to you that I was coming. How on earth did you recognise me?'

'Intuition, most likely.'

He stared at me with a sort of suspicion. '*Please* don't tell me that you think me like my sister,' he went on. 'For though, of course, every right-minded man feels—ur—a natural respect and affection for the members of his family—bows, if I may so say, to the inscrutable decrees of Providence—which has mysteriously burdened him with them—still, there *are* points about Lady Georgina which I cannot conscientiously assert I approve of.'

I remembered 'Marmy's a fool,' and held my tongue judiciously.

'I do not resemble her, I hope,' he persisted, with a look which I could almost describe as wistful.

'A family likeness, perhaps,' I put in. 'Family likenesses exist, you know—often with complete divergence of tastes and character.'

He looked relieved. 'That is true. Oh, how true! But the likeness in my case, I must admit, escapes me.'

I temporised. 'Strangers see these things most,' I said, airing the stock platitudes. 'It may be superficial. And, of course, one knows that profound differences of intellect and moral feeling often occur within the limits of a single family.'

'You are quite right,' he said, with decision. 'Georgina's principles are not mine. Excuse my remarking it, but you seem to be a young lady of unusual penetration.'

I saw he took my remark as a compliment. What I really meant to say was that a commonplace man might easily be the brother to so clever a woman as Lady Georgina.

He gathered up his hat, his stick, his gloves, his notes, and his typewritten letters, one by one, and backed out politely. He was a punctilious millionaire. He had risen by urbanity to his brother directors, like a model guinea-pig. He bowed to us each separately as if we had been duchesses.

As soon as he was gone, Elsie turned to me. 'Brownie, how on earth did you guess it? They're so awfully different!'

'Not at all,' I answered. 'A few surface unlikenesses only just mask an underlying identity. Their features are the same; but his are plump; hers, shrunken. Lady Georgina's expression is sharp and worldly; Mr. Ashurst's is smooth, and bland, and financial. And then their manner! Both are fussy; but Lady Georgina's is honest, open, ill-tempered fussiness; Mr. Ashurst's is concealed under an artificial mask of obsequious politeness. One's cantankerous; the other's only pernicketty. It's one tune, after all, in two different keys.'

From that day forth, the Urbane Old Gentleman was a daily visitor. He took an hour at a time at first; but after a few days, the hour lengthened out (apologetically) to an entire morning. He 'presumed to ask' my Christian name the second day, and remembered my father—'a man of excellent principles.' But he didn't care for Elsie to work for him. Fortunately for her, other work dropped in, once we had found a client, or else, poor girl, she would have felt sadly slighted. I was glad she had something to do; the sense of dependence weighed heavily upon her.

The Urbane Old Gentleman did not confine himself entirely, after the first few days, to Stock Exchange literature. He was engaged on a Work—he spoke of it always with bated breath, and a capital letter was implied in his intonation; the Work was one on the Interpretation of Prophecy. Unlike Lady Georgina, who was tart and crisp, Mr. Marmaduke Ashurst was devout and decorous; where she said 'pack of fools,' he talked with unction of 'the mental deficiencies of our poorer brethren.' But his religious opinions and his stockbroking had got strangely mixed up at the wash somehow. He was convinced that the British nation represented the Lost Ten Tribes of Israel—and in particular Ephraim—a matter on which, as a mere lay-woman, I would not presume either to agree with him or to differ from him. 'That being so, Miss Cayley, we can easily understand that the existing commercial prosperity of England depends upon the promises made to Abraham.'

I assented, without committing myself, 'It would seem to
follow.'

Mr. Ashurst, encouraged by so much assent, went on to unfold
his System of Interpretation, which was of a strictly commercial or
company-promoting character. It ran like a prospectus. 'We have
inherited the gold of Australia and the diamonds of the Cape,' he
said, growing didactic, and lifting one fat forefinger; 'we are now
inheriting Klondike and the Rand, for it is morally certain that we
shall annex the Transvaal. Again, "the chief things of the ancient
mountains, and the precious things of the everlasting hills." What
does that mean? The ancient mountains are clearly the Rockies;
can the everlasting hills be anything but the Himalayas? "For they
shall suck of the abundance of the seas"—that refers, of course,
to our world-wide commerce, due mainly to imports—"and of
the treasures hid in the sand." Which sand? Undoubtedly, I say, the
desert of Mount Sinai. What then is our obvious destiny? A lady
of your intelligence must gather at once that it is——?' He paused
and gazed at me.

'To drive the Sultan out of Syria,' I suggested tentatively, 'and
to annex Palestine to our practical province of Egypt?'

He leaned back in his chair and folded his fat hands in undisguised satisfaction. 'Now, you are a thinker of exceptional penetration,' he broke out. 'Do you know, Miss Cayley, I have tried to
make that point clear to the War Office, and the Prime Minister,
and many leading financiers in the City of London, and I can't get
them to see it. They have no heads, those people. But *you* catch
at it at a glance. Why, I endeavoured to interest Rothschild and
induce him to join me in my Palestine Development Syndicate,
and, will you believe it, the man refused point blank. Though if he
had only looked at Nahum iii. 17——'

'Mere financiers,' I said, smiling, 'will not consider these questions from a historical and prophetic point of view. They see nothing above percentages.'

'That's it,' he replied, lighting up. 'They have no higher feelings. Though, mind you, there will be dividends too; mark my
words, there will be dividends. This syndicate, besides fulfilling
the prophecies, will pay forty per cent on every penny embarked
in it.'

'Only forty per cent for Ephraim!' I murmured, half below my breath. 'Why, Judah is said to batten upon sixty.'

He caught at it eagerly, without perceiving my gentle sarcasm.

'In that case, we might even expect seventy,' he put in with a gasp of anticipation. 'Though I approached Rothschild first with my scheme on purpose, so that Israel and Judah might once more unite in sharing the promises.'

'Your combined generosity and commercial instinct does you credit,' I answered. 'It is rare to find so much love for an abstract study side by side with such conspicuous financial ability.'

His guilelessness was beyond words. He swallowed it like an infant. 'So I think,' he answered. 'I am glad to observe that you understand my character. Mere City men don't. They have no souls above shekels. Though, as I show them, there are shekels in it, too. Dividends, dividends, di-vidends. But *you* are a lady of understanding and comprehension. You have been to Girton, haven't you? Perhaps you read Greek, then?'

'Enough to get on with.'

'Could you look up things in Herodotus?'

'Certainly.'

'In the original?'

'Oh, dear, yes.'

He regarded me once more with the same astonished glance. His own classics, I soon learnt, were limited to the amount which a public school succeeds in dinning, during the intervals of cricket and football, into an English gentleman. Then he informed me that he wished me to hunt up certain facts in Herodotus 'and elsewhere' confirmatory of his view that the English were the descendants of the Ten Tribes. I promised to do so, swallowing even that comprehensive 'elsewhere.' It was none of my business to believe or disbelieve; I was paid to get up a case, and I got one up to the best of my ability. I imagine it was at least as good as most other cases in similar matters; at any rate, it pleased the old gentleman vastly.

By dint of listening, I began to like him. But Elsie couldn't bear him. She hated the fat crease at the back of his neck, she told me.

After a week or two devoted to the Interpretation of Prophecy on a strictly commercial basis of Founders' Shares, with interludes of mining engineers' reports upon the rubies of Mount Sinai and the supposed auriferous quartzites of Palestine, the Urbane Old Gentleman trotted down to the office one day, carrying a packet of notes of most voluminous magnitude. 'Can we work in a room alone this morning, Miss Cayley?' he asked, with mystery in his voice; he was always mysterious. 'I want to intrust you with a piece of work of an exceptionally private and confidential character. It concerns Property. In point of fact,' he dropped his voice to a whisper, 'I want you to draw up my will for me.'

'Certainly,' I said, opening the door into the back office.

But I trembled in my shoes. Could this mean that he was going to draw up a will, disinheriting Harold Tillington?

And suppose he did, what then? My heart was in a tumult. If Harold were rich—well and good, I could never marry him. But, if Harold were poor—I must keep my promise. Could I wish him to be rich? Could I wish him to be poor? My heart stood divided two ways within me.

The Urbane Old Gentleman began with immense deliberation, as befits a man of principle when Property is at stake. 'You will kindly take down notes from my dictation,' he said, fussing with his papers; 'and afterwards I will ask you to be so good as to copy it all out fair on your typewriter for signature.'

'Is a typewritten form legal?' I ventured to inquire.

'A most perspicacious young lady!' he interjected, well pleased. 'I have investigated that point, and find it perfectly regular. Only, if I may venture to say so, there should be no erasures.'

'There shall be none,' I answered.

The Urbane Old Gentleman leant back in his easy chair, and began dictating from his notes with tantalising deliberateness. This was the last will and testament of him, Marmaduke Courtney Ashurst. Its verbiage wearied me. I was eager for him to come to the point about Harold. Instead of that, he did what it seems is usual in such cases—set out with a number of unimportant legacies to old family servants and other hangers-on among 'our poorer brethren.' I fumed and fretted inwardly. Next came a series of quaint bequests of a quite novel character. 'I give and bequeath to James Walsh and Sons, of 720 High Holborn, London, the sum of Five Hundred Pounds, in consideration of the benefit they have conferred upon humanity by the invention of a sugar-spoon or silver sugar-sifter, by means of which it is possible to dust sugar upon a tart or pudding without letting the whole or the greater part of the material run through the apertures uselessly in transit. You must have observed, Miss Cayley—with your usual perspicacity—that most sugar-sifters allow the sugar to fall through them on to the table prematurely.'

'I have noticed it,' I answered, trembling with anxiety.

'James Walsh and Sons, acting on a hint from me, have succeeded in inventing a form of spoon which does not possess that regrettable drawback. "Run through the apertures uselessly in transit," I think I said last. Yes, thank you. Very good. We will now continue. And I give and bequeath the like sum of Five Hundred Pounds—did I say, free of legacy duty? No? Then please add it to James Walsh's clause. Five Hundred Pounds, free of legacy duty, to Thomas Webster Jones, of Wheeler Street, Soho, for his admirable invention of a pair of braces which will not slip down on the wearer's shoulders after half an hour's use. Most braces, you must have observed, Miss Cayley——'

'My acquaintance with braces is limited, not to say abstract,' I interposed, smiling.

He gazed at me, and twirled his fat thumbs.

'*Of* course,' he murmured. '*Of* course. But most braces, you may not be aware, slip down unpleasantly on the shoulder-blade, and so lead to an awkward habit of hitching them up by the sleeve-hole of the waistcoat at frequent intervals. Such a habit must be felt to be ungraceful. Thomas Webster Jones, to whom I pointed out this error of manufacture, has invented a brace the two halves of which diverge at a higher angle than usual, and fasten further towards the centre of the body in front—pardon these details—so as to obviate that difficulty. He has given me satisfaction, and he deserves to be rewarded.'

I heard through it all the voice of Lady Georgina observing, tartly, 'Why the idiots can't make braces to fit one at first passes *my* comprehension. But, there, my dear; the people who manufacture them are a set of born fools, and what can you expect from an imbecile?' Mr. Ashurst was Lady Georgina, veneered with a thin layer of ingratiating urbanity. Lady Georgina was clever, and therefore acrimonious. Mr. Ashurst was astute, and therefore obsequious.

He went on with legacies to the inventor of a sauce-bottle which did not let the last drop dribble down so as to spot the table-cloth; of a shoe-horn the handle of which did not come undone; and of a pair of sleeve-links which you could put off and on without injury to the temper. 'A real benefactor, Miss Cayley; a real benefactor to the link-wearing classes; for he has sensibly diminished the average annual output of profane swearing.'

When he left Five Hundred Pounds to his faithful servant Frederic Higginson, courier, I was tempted to interpose; but I refrained in time, and I was glad of it afterwards.

At last, after many divagations, my Urbane Old Gentleman arrived at the central point—'And I give and bequeath to my nephew, Harold Ashurst Tillington, Younger of Gledcliffe, Dumfriesshire, attaché to Her Majesty's Embassy at Rome——'

I waited, breathless.

He was annoyingly dilatory. 'My house and estate of Ashurst Court, in the County of Gloucester, and my town house at 24 Park Lane North, in London, together with the residue of all my estate, real or personal——' and so forth.

I breathed again. At least, I had not been called upon to disinherit Harold.

'Provided always——' he went on, in the same voice.

I wondered what was coming.

'Provided always that the said Harold Ashurst Tillington does not marry——leave a blank there, Miss Cayley. I will find out the name of the person I desire to exclude, and fill it in afterward. I don't recollect it at this moment, but Higginson, no doubt, will be able to supply the deficiency. In fact, I don't think I ever heard it; though Higginson has told me all about the woman.'

'Higginson?' I inquired. 'Is he here?'

'Oh, dear, yes. You heard of him, I suppose, from Georgina. Georgina is prejudiced. He has come back to me, I am glad to say. An excellent servant, Higginson, though a trifle too omniscient. All men are equal in the eyes of their Maker, of course; but we must have due subordination. A courier ought not to be better informed than his master—or ought at least to conceal the fact dexterously. Well, Higginson knows this young person's name; my sister wrote to me about her disgraceful conduct when she first went to Schlangenbad. An adventuress, it seems; an adventuress; quite a shocking creature. Foisted herself upon Lady Georgina in Kensington Gardens—unintroduced, if you can believe such a thing—with the most astonishing effrontery; and Georgina, who will forgive anything on earth, for the sake of what she calls originality—another name for impudence, as I am sure you must know—took the young woman with her as her maid to Germany. There, this minx tried to set her cap at my nephew Harold, who can be caught at once by a pretty face; and Harold was bowled over—almost got engaged to her. Georgina took a fancy to the girl later, having a taste for dubious people (I cannot say I approve of Georgina's friends), and wrote again to say her first suspicions were unfounded: the young woman was in reality a paragon of virtue. But *I* know better than that. Georgina has no judgment. I regret to be obliged to confess it, but cleverness, I fear, is the only thing in the world my excellent sister cares for. The hussy, it seems, was certainly clever. Higginson has told me about her. He says her bare appearance would suffice to condemn her—a bold, fast, shameless, brazen-faced creature. But you will forgive me, I am sure, my dear young lady; I ought not to discuss such painted Jezebels before you. We will leave this person's name blank. I will not sully your pen—I mean, your typewriter—by asking you to transcribe it.'

I made up my mind at once. 'Mr. Ashurst,' I said, looking up from my keyboard, '*I* can give you this girl's name; and then you can insert the proviso immediately.'

'*You* can? My dear young lady, what a wonderful person you are! You seem to know everybody, and everything. But perhaps she was at Schlangenbad with Lady Georgina, and you were there also?'

"She was,' I answered, deliberately. 'The name you want is— Lois Cayley!'

He let his notes drop in his astonishment.

I went on with my typewriting, unmoved. 'Provided always that the said Harold Ashurst Tillington does not marry Lois Cayley; in which case I will and desire that the said estate shall pass to—— whom shall I put in, Mr. Ashurst?'

He leant forward with his fat hands on his ample knees. 'It was really *you?*' he inquired, open-mouthed.

I nodded. 'There is no use in denying the truth. Mr. Tillington did ask me to be his wife, and I refused him.'

'But, my dear Miss Cayley——'

'The difference in station?' I said; 'the difference, still greater, in this world's goods? Yes, I know. I admit all that. So I declined his offer. I did not wish to ruin his prospects.'

The Urbane Old Gentleman eyed me with a sudden tenderness in his glance. 'Young men are lucky,' he said, slowly, after a short pause; '—and—Higginson is an idiot. I say it deliberately—an idiot! How could one dream of trusting the judgment of a flunkey about a lady? My dear, excuse the familiarity from one who may consider himself in a certain sense a contingent uncle—suppose we amend the last clause by the omission of the word *not*. It strikes me as superfluous. "Provided always the said Harold Ashurst Tillington consents to marry"—I think that sounds better!'

He looked at me with such fatherly regard that it pricked my heart ever to have poked fun at his Interpretation of Prophecy on Stock Exchange principles. I think I flushed crimson. 'No, no,' I answered, firmly. 'That will not do either, please. That's worse than the other way. You must not put it, Mr. Ashurst. I could not consent to be willed away to anybody.'

He leant forward, with real earnestness. 'My dear,' he said, 'that's not the point. Pardon my reminding you that you are here in your capacity as my amanuensis. I am drawing up my will, and if you will allow me to say so, I cannot admit that anyone has a claim to influence me in the disposition of my Property.'

'*Please!*' I cried, pleadingly.

He looked at me and paused. 'Well,' he went on at last, after a long interval; 'since *you* insist upon it, I will leave the bequest to stand without condition.'

'Thank you,' I murmured, bending low over my machine.

'If I did as I like, though,' he went on, 'I should say, Unless he marries Miss Lois Cayley (who is a deal too good for him), the estate shall revert to Kynaston's eldest son, a confounded jackass. I do not usually indulge in intemperate language; but I desire to assure you, with the utmost calmness, that Kynaston's eldest son, Lord Southminster, is a con-founded jackass.'

I rose and took his hand in my own spontaneously. 'Mr. Ashurst,' I said, 'you may interpret prophecy as long as ever you like, but you are a dear, kind old gentleman. I am truly grateful to you for your good opinion.'

'And you will marry Harold?'

'Never,' I answered; 'while he is rich. I have said as much to him.'

'That's hard,' he went on, slowly. 'For . . . I should like to be your uncle.'

I trembled all over. Elsie saved the situation by bursting in abruptly.

I will only add that when Mr. Ashurst left, I copied the will out neatly, without erasures. The rough original I threw (somewhat carelessly) into the waste-paper basket.

That afternoon, somebody called to fetch the fair copy for Mr. Ashurst. I went out into the front office to see him. To my surprise, it was Higginson—in his guise as courier.

He was as astonished as myself. 'What, *you* here!' he cried. 'You dog me!'

'I was thinking the same thing of you, M. le Comte,' I answered, curtsying.

He made no attempt at an excuse. 'Well, I have been sent for the will,' he broke out, curtly.

'And you were sent for the jewel-case,' I retorted. 'No, no, Dr. Fortescue-Langley; *I* am in charge of the will, and I will take it myself to Mr. Ashurst.'

'I will be even with you yet,' he snapped out. 'I have gone back to my old trade, and am trying to lead an honest life; but *you* won't let me.'

'On the contrary,' I answered, smiling a polite smile, 'I rejoice to hear it. If you say nothing more against me to your employer, I will not disclose to him what I know about you. But if you slander me, I will. So now we understand one another.'

And I kept the will till I could give it myself into Mr. Ashurst's own hands in his rooms that evening.

CHAPTER VII

THE ADVENTURE OF THE UNOBTRUSIVE OASIS

I WILL not attempt to describe to you the minor episodes of our next twelve months—the manuscripts we type-wrote and the Manitous we sold. 'Tis one of my aims in a world so rich in bores to avoid being tedious. I will merely say, therefore, that we spent the greater part of the year in Florence, where we were building up a connection, but rode back for the summer months to Switzerland, as being a livelier place for the trade in bicycles. The net result was not only that we covered our expenses, but that, as chancellor of the exchequer, I found myself with a surplus in hand at the end of the season.

When we returned to Florence for the winter, however, I confess I began to chafe. 'This is slow work, Elsie!' I said. 'I started out to go round the world; it has taken me eighteen months to travel no further than Italy! At this rate, I shall reach New York a grey-haired old lady, in a nice lace cap, and totter back into London a venerable crone on the verge of ninety.'

However, those invaluable doctors came to my rescue unexpectedly. I do love doctors; they are always sending you off at a moment's notice to delightful places you never dreamt of. Elsie was better, but still far from strong. I took it upon me to consult our medical attendant; and his verdict was decisive. He did just what a doctor ought to do. 'She is getting on very well in Florence,' he said; 'but if you want to restore her health completely, I should advise you to take her for a winter to Egypt. After six months of the dry, warm desert air, I don't doubt she might return to her work in London.'

That last point I used as a lever with Elsie. She positively revels in teaching mathematics. At first, to be sure, she objected that we had only just money enough to pay our way to Cairo, and that when we got there we might starve—her favourite programme. I have not this extraordinary taste for starving; my idea is, to go where you like, and find something decent to eat when you get there. However, to humour her, I began to cast about me for a source of income. There is no absolute harm in seeing your way clear before you for a twelvemonth, though of course it deprives you of the plot-interest of poverty.

'Elsie,' I said, in my best didactic style—I excel in didactics,— 'you do not learn from the lessons that life sets before you. Look at the stage, for example; the stage is universally acknowledged at the present day to be a great teacher of morals. Does not Irving say so?—and he ought to know. There is that splendid model for imitation, for instance, the Clown in the pantomime. How does Clown regulate his life? Does he take heed for the morrow? Not a bit of it! "I wish I had a goose," he says, at some critical juncture; and just as he says it—pat—a super strolls upon the stage with a property goose on a wooden tray; and Clown cries, "Oh, look here, Joey; here's a goose!" and proceeds to appropriate it. Then he puts his fingers in his mouth and observes, "I wish I had a few apples to make the sauce with"; and as the words escape him—pat again—a small boy with a very squeaky voice runs on, carrying a basket of apples. Clown trips him up, and bolts with the basket. There's a model for imitation! The stage sets these great moral lessons before you regularly every Christmas; yet you fail to profit by them. Govern your life on the principles exemplified by Clown; expect to find that whatever you want will turn up with punctuality and dispatch at the proper moment. Be adventurous and you will be happy. Take that as a new maxim to put in your copy-book!'

'I wish I could think so, dear,' Elsie answered. 'But your confidence staggers me.'

That evening at our *table-d'hôte*, however, it was amply justified. A smooth-faced young man of ample girth and most prosperous exterior happened to sit next us. He had his wife with him, so I judged it safe to launch on conversation. We soon found out that he was the millionaire editor-proprietor of a great London daily, with many more strings to his journalistic bow; his honoured name was Elworthy. I mentioned casually that we thought of going for the winter to Egypt. He pricked his ears up. But at the time he said nothing. After dinner, we adjourned to the cosy *salon*. I talked to him and his wife; and somehow, that evening, the devil entered into me. I am subject to devils. I hasten to add, they are mild ones. I

had one of my reckless moods just then, however, and I reeled off
rattling stories of our various adventures. Mr. Elworthy believed
in youth and audacity; I could see I interested him. The more he
was amused, the more reckless I became. 'That's bright,' he said at
last, when I told him the tale of our amateur exploits in the sale of
Manitous. 'That would make a good article!'

'Yes,' I answered, with bravado, determined to strike while the
iron was hot. 'What the *Daily Telephone* lacks is just one enlivening
touch of feminine brightness.'

He smiled. 'What is your forte?' he inquired.

'My forte,' I answered, 'is—to go where I choose, and write
what I like about it.'

He smiled again. 'And a very good new departure in journalism too! A roving commission! Have you ever tried your hand at
writing?'

Had I ever tried! It was the ambition of my life to see myself
in print; though, hitherto, it had been ineffectual. 'I have written a
few sketches,' I answered, with becoming modesty. As a matter of
fact, our office bulged with my unpublished manuscripts.

'Could you let me see them?' he asked.

I assented, with inner joy, but outer reluctance. 'If you wish it,'
I murmured; 'but—you must be *very* lenient!'

Though I had not told Elsie, the truth of the matter was, I had
just then conceived an idea for a novel—my *magnum opus*—the setting of which compelled Egyptian local colour; and I was therefore dying to get to Egypt, if chance so willed it. I accordingly
submitted a few of my picked manuscripts to Mr. Elworthy, in fear
and trembling. He read them, cruel man, before my very eyes; I sat
and waited, twiddling my thumbs, demure but apprehensive.

When he had finished, he laid them down.

'Racy!' he said. 'Racy! You're quite right, Miss Cayley. That's just
what we want on the *Daily Telephone*. I should like to print these
three,' selecting them out, 'at our usual rate of pay per thousand.'

'You are very kind.' But the room reeled with me.

'Not at all. I am a man of business. And these are good copy.
Now, about this Egypt. I will put the matter in the shape of a business proposition. Will you undertake, if I pay your passage, and
your friend's, with all travelling expenses, to let me have three

descriptive articles a week, on Cairo, the Nile, Syria, and India, running to about two thousand words apiece, at three guineas a thousand?'

My breath came and went. It was positive opulence. The super with the goose couldn't approach it for patness. My editor had brought me the apple sauce as well, without even giving me the trouble of cooking it.

The very next day everything was arranged. Elsie tried to protest, on the foolish ground that she had no money: but the faculty had ordered the apex of her right lung to go to Egypt, and I couldn't let her fly in the face of the faculty. We secured our berths in a P. and O. steamer from Brindisi; and within a week we were tossing upon the bosom of the blue Mediterranean.

People who haven't crossed the blue Mediterranean cherish an absurd idea that it is always calm and warm and sunny. I am sorry to take away any sea's character; but I speak of it as I find it (to borrow a phrase from my old gyp at Girton); and I am bound to admit that the Mediterranean did not treat me as a lady expects to be treated. It behaved disgracefully. People may rhapsodize as long as they choose about a life on the ocean wave; for my own part, I wouldn't give a pin for sea-sickness. We glided down the Adriatic from Brindisi to Corfu with a reckless profusion of lateral motion which suggested the idea that the ship must have been drinking.

I tried to rouse Elsie when we came abreast of the Ionian Islands, and to remind her that 'Here was the home of Nausicaa in the Odyssey.' Elsie failed to respond; she was otherwise occupied. At last, I succumbed and gave it up. I remember nothing further till a day and a half later, when we got under lee of Crete, and the ship showed a tendency to resume the perpendicular. Then I began once more to take a languid interest in the dinner question.

I may add parenthetically that the Mediterranean is a mere bit of a sea, when you look at it on the map—a pocket sea to be regarded with mingled contempt and affection; but you learn to respect it when you find that it takes four clear days and nights of abject misery merely to run across its eastern basin from Brindisi to Alexandria. I respected the Mediterranean immensely while we lay off the Peloponnesus in the trough of the waves with a north wind blowing; I only began to temper my respect with a distant liking when we passed under the welcome shelter of Crete on a calm, star-lit evening.

It was deadly cold. We had not counted upon such weather in the sunny south. I recollect now that the Greeks were wont to represent Boreas as a chilly deity, and spoke of the Thracian breeze with the same deferentially deprecating adjectives which we ourselves apply to the east wind of our fatherland; but that apt classical memory somehow failed to console or warm me. A good-natured male passenger, however, volunteered to ask us, 'Will I get ye a rug, ladies?' The form of his courteous question suggested the probability of his Irish origin.

'You are very kind,' I answered. 'If you don't want it for yourself, I'm sure my friend would be glad to have the use of it.'

'Is it meself? Sure, I've got me big ulsther, and I'm as warrum as a toast in it. But ye're not provided for this weather. Ye've thrusted too much to those rascals the po-uts. "Where breaks the blue Sicilian say," the rogues write. I'd like to set them down in it, wid a nor'-easter blowing!'

He fetched up his rug. It was ample and soft, a smooth brown camel-hair. He wrapped us both up in it. We sat late on deck that night, as warm as a toast ourselves, thanks to our genial Irishman.

We asked his name. ''Tis Dr. Macloghlen,' he answered. 'I'm from County Clare, ye see; and I'm on me way to Egypt for thravel and exploration. Me fader whisht me to see the worruld a bit before I'd settle down to practise me profession at Liscannor. Have ye ever been in County Clare? Sure, 'tis the pick of Oireland.'

'We have that pleasure still in store,' I answered, smiling. 'It spreads gold-leaf over the future, as George Meredith puts it.'

'Is it Meredith? Ah, there's the foine writer! 'Tis jaynius the man has: I can't undtherstand a word of him. But he's half Oirish, ye know. What proof have I got of it? An' would he write like that if there wasn't a dhrop of the blood of the Celt in him?'

Next day and next night, Dr. Macloghlen was our devoted slave. I had won his heart by admitting frankly that his countrywomen had the finest and liveliest eyes in Europe—eyes with a deep twinkle, half fun, half passion. He took to us at once, and talked to us incessantly. He was a red-haired, raw-boned Munster-man, but a real good fellow. We forgot the aggressive inequalities of the Mediterranean while he talked to us of 'the pizzantry.' Late the second evening he propounded a confidence. It was a lovely night; Orion overhead, and the plashing phosphorescence on the water below conspired with the hour to make him specially confidential. 'Now, Miss Cayley,' he said, leaning forward on his deck chair, and gazing earnestly into my eyes, 'there's wan question I'd like to ask ye. The ambition of me life is to get into Parlimint. And I want to know from ye, as a frind—if I accomplish me heart's wish—is there annything, in me apparence, ar in me voice, ar in me accent, ar in me manner, that would lade annybody to suppose I was an Oirishman?'

I succeeded, by good luck, in avoiding Elsie's eye. What on earth could I answer? Then a happy thought struck me. 'Dr. Macloghlen,' I said, 'it would not be the slightest use your trying to conceal it; for even if nobody ever detected a faint Irish intonation in your words or phrases—how could your eloquence fail to betray you for a countryman of Sheridan and Burke and Grattan?'

He seized my hand with such warmth that I thought it best to hurry down to my state-room at once, under cover of my compliment.

At Alexandria and Cairo we found him invaluable. He looked after our luggage, which he gallantly rescued from the lean hands of fifteen Arab porters, all eagerly struggling to gain possession of our effects; he saw us safe into the train; and he never quitted us till he had safely ensconced us in our rooms at Shepheard's. For himself, he said, with subdued melancholy, 'twas to some cheaper hotel he must go; Shepheard's wasn't for the likes of him; though if land in County Clare was wort' what it ought to be, there wasn't a finer estate in all Oireland than his fader's.

Our Mr. Elworthy was a modern proprietor, who knew how to do things on the lordly scale. Having commissioned me to write this series of articles, he intended them to be written in the first style of art, and he had instructed me accordingly to hire one of Cook's little steam dahabeeahs, where I could work at leisure. Dr. Macloghlen was in his element arranging for the trip. 'Sure the only thing I mind,' he said, 'is—that I'll not be going wid ye.' I think he was half inclined to invite himself; but there again I drew a line. I will not sell salt fish; and I will not go up the Nile, unchaperoned, with a casual man acquaintance.

He did the next best thing, however: he took a place in a sailing dahabeeah; and as we steamed up slowly, stopping often on the way, to give me time to write my articles, he managed to arrive almost always at every town or ruin exactly when we did.

I will not describe the voyage. The Nile is the Nile. Just at first, before we got used to it, we conscientiously looked up the name of every village we passed on the bank in our Murray and our Baedeker. After a couple of days' Niling, however, we found that formality quite unnecessary. They were all the same village, under a number of aliases. They did not even take the trouble to disguise themselves anew, like Dr. Fortescue-Langley, on each fresh appearance. They had every one of them a small white-washed mosque, with a couple of tall minarets; and around it spread a number of mud-built cottages, looking more like bee-hives than human habitations. They had also every one of them a group of date-palms, overhanging a cluster of mean bare houses; and they all alike had a picturesque and even imposing air from a distance, but faded away into indescribable squalor as one got abreast of them. Our progress was monotonous. At twelve, noon, we would pass Aboo-Teeg, with its mosque, its palms, its mud-huts, and its camels; then for a couple of hours we would go on through the midst of a green field on either side, studded by more mud-huts, and backed up by a range of grey desert mountains; only to come at 2 P.M., twenty miles higher up, upon Aboo-Teeg once more, with the same mosque, the same mud-huts, and the same haughty camels, placidly chewing the same aristocratic cud, but under the alias of Koos-kam. After a wild hubbub at the quay, we would leave Koos-kam behind, with its camels still serenely munching day-before-yesterday's dinner; and twenty miles further on, again, having passed through the same green plain, backed by the same grey mountains, we would stop once more at the identical Koos-kam, which this time absurdly described itself as Tahtah. But whether it was Aboo-Teeg or Koos-kam or Tahtah or anything else, only the name differed: it was always the same town, and had always the same camels at precisely the same stage of the digestive process. It seemed to us immaterial whether you saw all the Nile or only five miles of it. It was just like wall-paper. A sample sufficed; the whole was the sample infinitely repeated.

However, I had my letters to write, and I wrote them valiantly. I described the various episodes of the complicated digestive process in the camel in the minutest detail. I gloated over the date-palms, which I knew in three days as if I had been brought up upon dates. I gave word-pictures of every individual child, veiled woman, Arab sheikh, and Coptic priest whom we encountered on the voyage. And I am open to reprint those conscientious studies of mud-huts and minarets with any enterprising publisher who will make me an offer.

Another disillusion weighed upon my soul. Before I went up the Nile, I had a fancy of my own that the bank was studded with endless ruined temples, whose vast red colonnades were reflected in the water at every turn. I think Macaulay's Lays were primarily answerable for that particular misapprehension. As a matter of fact, it surprised me to find that we often went for two whole days' hard steaming without ever a temple breaking the monotony of those eternal date-palms, those calm and superciliously irresponsive camels. In my humble opinion, Egypt is a fraud; there is too much Nile—very dirty Nile at that—and not nearly enough temple. Besides, the temples, when you *do* come up with them, are just like the villages; they are the same temple over again, under a different name each time, and they have the same gods, the same kings, the same wearisome bas-reliefs, except that the gentleman in a chariot, ten feet high, who is mowing down enemies a quarter his own size, with unsportsmanlike recklessness, is called Rameses in this place, and Sethi in that, and Amen-hotep in the other. With this trifling variation, when you have seen one temple, one obelisk, one hieroglyphic table, you have seen the whole of Ancient Egypt.

At last, after many days' voyage through the same scenery daily—rising in the morning off a village with a mosque, ten palms, and two minarets, and retiring late at night off the same village once more, with mosque, palms, and minarets, as before, *da capo*—we arrived one evening at a place called Geergeh. In itself, I believe, Geergeh did not differ materially from all the other places we had passed on our voyage; it had its mosque, its ten palms, and its two minarets as usual. But I remember its name, because something mysterious went wrong there with our machinery; and the engineer informed us we must wait at least three days to mend it. Dr. Macloghlen's dahabeeah happened opportunely to arrive at the same spot on the same day; and he declared with fervour he would 'see us through our throubles.' But what on earth were we to do with ourselves through three long days and nights at Geergeh? There were the ruins of Abydus close at hand, to be sure; though I defy anybody not a professed Egyptologist to give more than one day to the ruins of Abydus. In this emergency, Dr. Macloghlen came gallantly to our aid. He discovered by inquiring from an English-speaking guide that there was an unobtrusive oasis, never visited by Europeans, one long day's journey off, across the desert. As a rule, it takes at least three days to get camels and guides together for such an expedition: for Egypt is not a land to hurry in. But the indefatigable Doctor further unearthed the fact that a sheikh had just come in, who (for a consideration) would lend us camels for a two days' trip; and we seized the chance to do our duty by Mr. Elworthy and the world-wide circulation. An unvisited oasis—and two Christian ladies to be the first to explore it: there's journalistic enterprise for you! If we happened to be killed, so much the better for the *Daily Telephone*. I pictured the excitement at Piccadilly Circus. 'Extra Special, Our Own Correspondent brutally murdered!' I rejoiced at the opportunity.

I cannot honestly say that Elsie rejoiced with me. She cherished a prejudice against camels, massacres, and the new journalism. She didn't like being murdered: though this was premature, for she had never tried it. She objected that the fanatical Mohammedans of the Senoosi sect, who were said to inhabit the oasis in question, might cut our throats for dogs of infidels. I pointed out to her at some length that it was just that chance which added zest to our expedition as a journalistic venture: fancy the glory of being the first lady journalists martyred in the cause! But she failed to grasp this aspect of the question. However, if I went, she would go too, she said, like a dear girl that she is: she would not desert me when I was getting my throat cut.

Dr. Macloghlen made the bargain for us, and insisted on accompanying us across the desert. He told us his method of negotiation with the Arabs with extreme gusto. "'Is it pay in advance ye want?" says I to the dirty beggars: "divvil a penny will ye get till ye bring these ladies safe back to Geergeh. And remimber, Mr. Sheikh," says I, fingering me pistol, so, by way of emphasis, "we take no money wid us; so if yer friends at Wadi Bou choose to cut our throats, 'tis for the pleasure of it they'll be cutting them, not for anything they'll gain by it." "Provisions, effendi?" says he, salaaming. "Provisions, is it?" says I. "Take everything ye'll want wid you; I suppose ye can buy food fit for a Crischun in the bazaar in Geergeh; and never wan penny do ye touch for it all till ye've landed us on the bank again, as safe as ye took us. So if the religious sintiments of the faithful at Wadi Bou should lade them to hack us to pieces," says I, just waving me revolver, "thin 'tis yerself that will be out of pocket by it." And the ould divvil cringed as if he took me for the Prince of Wales. Faix, 'tis the purse that's the best argumint to catch these haythen Arabs upon.'

When we set out for the desert in the early dawn next day, it looked as if we were starting for a few months' voyage. We had a company of camels that might have befitted a caravan. We had two large tents, one for ourselves, and one for Dr. Macloghlen, with a third to dine in. We had bedding, and cushions, and drinking water tied up in swollen pig-skins, which were really goat-skins, looking far from tempting. We had bread and meat, and a supply of presents to soften the hearts and weaken the religious scruples of the sheikhs at Wadi Bou. 'We thravel *en prince*,' said the Doctor. When all was ready we got under way solemnly, our camels rising and sniffing the breeze with a superior air, as who should say, 'I happen to be going where you happen to be going; but don't for a moment suppose I do it to please you. It is mere coincidence. You are bound for Wadi Bou: I have business of my own which chances to take me there.'

Over the incidents of the journey I draw a veil. Riding a camel, I find, does not greatly differ from sea-sickness. They are the same phenomenon under altered circumstances. We had been assured beforehand on excellent authority that 'much of the comfort on a desert journey depends upon having a good camel.' On this matter I am no authority. I do not set up as a judge of camel-flesh. But I did not notice *any* of the comfort; so I venture to believe my camel must have been an exceptionally bad one.

We expected trouble from the fanatical natives; I am bound to admit, we had most trouble with Elsie. She was not insubordinate, but she did not care for camel-riding. And her beast took advantage of her youth and innocence. A well-behaved camel should go almost as fast as a child can walk, and should not sit down plump on the burning sand without due reason. Elsie's brute crawled, and called halts for prayer at frequent intervals; it tried to kneel like a good Mussulman many times a day; and it showed an intolerant disposition to crush the infidel by rolling over on top of Elsie. Dr. Macloghlen admonished it with Irish eloquence, not always in language intended for publication; but it only turned up its supercilious lip and inquired in its own unspoken tongue what *he* knew about the desert.

'I feel like a wurrum before the baste,' the Doctor said, nonplussed.

If the Nile was monotonous, the road to Wadi Bou was nothing short of dreary. We crossed a great ridge of bare, grey rock, and followed a rolling valley of sand, scored by dry ravines, and baking in the sun. It was ghastly to look upon. All day long, save at the midday rest by some brackish wells, we rode on and on, the brutes stepping forward with slow, outstretched legs; though sometimes we walked by the camels' sides to vary the monotony; but ever through that dreary upland plain, sand in the centre, rocky mountain at the edge, and not a thing to look at. We were relieved towards evening to stumble against stunted tamarisks, half buried in sand, and to feel we were approaching the edge of the oasis.

When at last our arrogant beasts condescended to stop, in their patronising way, we saw by the dim light of the moon a sort of uneven basin or hollow, studded with date-palms, and in the midst of the depression a crumbling walled town, with a whitewashed mosque, two minarets by its side, and a crowd of mud-houses. It was strangely familiar. We had come all this way just to see Aboo-Teeg or Koos-kam over again!

We camped outside the fortified town that night. Next morning we essayed to make our entry.

At first, the servants of the Prophet on watch at the gate raised serious objections. No infidel might enter. But we had a pass from Cairo, exhorting the faithful in the name of the Khedive to give us food and shelter; and after much examination and many loud discussions, the gatemen passed us. We entered the town, and stood alone, three Christian Europeans, in the midst of three thousand fanatical Mohammedans.

I confess it was weird. Elsie shrank by my side. 'Suppose they were to attack us, Brownie?'

'Thin the sheikh here would never get paid,' Dr. Macloghlen put in with true Irish recklessness. 'Faix, he'll whistle for his money on the whistle I gave him.' That touch of humour saved us. We laughed; and the people about saw we could laugh. They left off scowling, and pressed around trying to sell us pottery and native brooches. In the intervals of fanaticism, the Arab has an eye to business.

We passed up the chief street of the bazaar. The inhabitants told us in pantomime the chief of the town was away at Asioot, whither he had gone two days ago on business. If he were here, our interpreter gave us to understand, things might have been different; for the chief had determined that, whatever came, no infidel dog should settle in *his* oasis.

The women with their veiled faces attracted us strangely. They were wilder than on the river. They ran when one looked at them. Suddenly, as we passed one, we saw her give a little start. She was veiled like the rest, but her agitation was evident through her thick covering.

'She is afraid of Christians,' Elsie cried, nestling towards me.

The woman passed close to us. She never looked in our direction, but in a very low voice she murmured, as she passed, 'Then you are English!'

I had presence of mind enough to conceal my surprise at this unexpected utterance. 'Don't seem to notice her, Elsie,' I said, looking away. 'Yes, we are English.'

She stopped and pretended to examine some jewellery on a stall. 'So am I,' she went on, in the same suppressed, low voice. 'For Heaven's sake, help me!'

'What are you doing here?'

'I live here—married. I was with Gordon's force at Khartoum. They carried me off. A mere girl then. Now I am thirty.'

'And you have been here ever since?'

She turned away and walked off, but kept whispering behind

her veil. We followed, unobtrusively. 'Yes; I was sold to a man at Dongola. He passed me on again to the chief of this oasis. I don't know where it is; but I have been here ever since. I hate this life. Is there any chance of a rescue?'

'Anny chance of a rescue, is it?' the Doctor broke in, a trifle too ostensibly. 'If it costs us a whole British Army, me dear lady, we'll fetch you away and save you.'

'But now—to-day? You won't go away and leave me? You are the first Europeans I have seen since Khartoum fell. They may sell me again. You will not desert me?'

'No,' I said. 'We will not.' Then I reflected for a moment.

What on earth could we do? This was a painful dilemma. If we once lost sight of her, we might not see her again. Yet if we walked with her openly, and talked like friends, we would betray ourselves, and her, to those fanatical Senoosis.

I made up my mind promptly. I may not have much of a mind; but, such as it is, I flatter myself I can make it up at a moment's notice.

'Can you come to us outside the gate at sunset?' I asked, as if speaking to Elsie.

The woman hesitated. 'I think so.'

'Then keep us in sight all day, and when evening comes, stroll out behind us.'

She turned over some embroidered slippers on a booth, and seemed to be inspecting them. 'But my children?' she murmured anxiously.

The Doctor interposed. 'Is it childern she has?' he asked. 'Thin they'll be the Mohammedan gintleman's. We mustn't interfere wid *them*. We can take away the lady—she's English, and detained against her will: but we can't deprive anny man of his own childern.'

I was firm, and categorical. 'Yes, we can,' I said, stoutly; 'if he has forced a woman to bear them to him whether she would or not. That's common justice. I have no respect for the Mohammedan gentleman's rights. Let her bring them with her. How many are there?'

'Two—a boy and a girl; not very old; the eldest is seven.' She spoke wistfully. A mother is a mother.

'Then say no more now, but keep us always in sight, and we will keep *you*. Come to us at the gate about sundown. We will carry you off with us.'

She clasped her hands and moved off with the peculiar gliding air of the veiled Mohammedan woman. Our eyes followed her. We walked on through the bazaar, thinking of nothing else now. It was strange how this episode made us forget our selfish fears for our own safety. Even dear timid Elsie remembered only that an Englishwoman's life and liberty were at stake. We kept her more or less in view all day. She glided in and out among the people in the alleys. When we went back to the camels at lunch-time, she followed us unobtrusively through the open gate, and sat watching us from a little way off, among a crowd of gazers; for all Wadi Bou was of course agog at this unwonted invasion.

We discussed the circumstance loudly, so that she might hear our plans. Dr. Macloghlen advised that we should tell our sheikh we meant to return part of the way to Geergeh that evening by moonlight. I quite agreed with him. It was the only way out. Besides, I didn't like the looks of the people. They eyed us askance. This was getting exciting now. I felt a professional journalistic interest. Whether we escaped or got killed, what splendid business for the *Daily Telephone!*

The sheikh, of course, declared it was impossible to start that evening. The men wouldn't move—the camels needed rest. But Dr. Macloghlen was inexorable. 'Very well, thin, Mr. Sheikh,' he answered, philosophically. 'Ye'll plaze yerself about whether ye come on wid us or whether ye shtop. That's yer own business. But *we* set out at sundown; and whin ye return by yerself on foot to Geergeh, ye can ask for yer camels at the British Consulate.'

All through that anxious afternoon we sat in our tents, under the shade of the mud-wall, wondering whether we could carry out our plan or not. About an hour before sunset the veiled woman strolled out of the gate with her two children. She joined the crowd of sight-seers once more, for never through the day were we left alone for a second. The excitement grew intense. Elsie and I moved up carelessly towards the group, talking as if to one another. I looked hard at Elsie, then I said, as though I were speaking about one of the children: 'Go straight along the road

to Geergeh till you are past the big clump of palms at the edge of
the oasis. Just beyond it comes a sharp ridge of rock. Wait behind
the ridge where no one can see you. When we get there,' I patted
the little girl's head, 'don't say a word, but jump on my camel. My
two friends will each take one of the children. If you understand
and consent, stroke your boy's curls. We will accept that for a
signal.'

She stroked the child's head at once without the least hesitation. Even through her veil and behind her dress, I could somehow
feel and see her trembling nerves, her beating heart. But she gave
no overt token. She merely turned and muttered something carelessly in Arabic to a woman beside her.

We waited once more, in long-drawn suspense. Would she
manage to escape them? Would they suspect her motives?

After ten minutes, when we had returned to our crouching-
place under the shadow of the wall, the woman detached herself
slowly from the group, and began strolling with almost overdone
nonchalance along the road to Geergeh. We could see the little
girl was frightened and seemed to expostulate with her mother:
fortunately, the Arabs about were too much occupied in watching
the suspicious strangers to notice this episode of their own people.
Presently, our new friend disappeared; and, with beating hearts,
we awaited the sunset.

Then came the usual scene of hubbub with the sheikh, the
camels, the porters, and the drivers. It was eagerness against
apathy. With difficulty we made them understand we meant to
get under way at all hazards. I stormed in bad Arabic. The Doctor
inveighed in very choice Irish. At last they yielded, and set out.
One by one the camels rose, bent their slow knees, and began to
stalk in their lordly way with outstretched necks along the road to
the river. We moved through the palm groves, a crowd of boys following us and shouting for backsheesh. We began to be afraid they
would accompany us too far and discover our fugitive; but fortunately they all turned back with one accord at a little whitewashed
shrine near the edge of the oasis. We reached the clump of palms;
we turned the corner of the ridge. Had we missed one another?
No! There, crouching by the rocks, with her children by her side,
sat our mysterious stranger.

The Doctor was equal to the emergency. 'Make those bastes kneel!' he cried authoritatively to the sheikh. The sheikh was taken aback. This was a new exploit burst upon him. He flung his arms up, gesticulating wildly. The Doctor, unmoved, made the drivers understand by some strange panto-mime what he wanted. They nodded, half terrified. In a second, the stranger was by my side, Elsie had taken the girl, the Doctor the boy, and the camels were passively beginning to rise again. That is the best of your camel. Once set him on his road, and he goes mechanically.

The sheikh broke out with several loud remarks in Arabic, which we did not understand, but whose hostile character could not easily escape us. He was beside himself with anger. Then I was suddenly aware of the splendid advantage of having an Irishman on our side. Dr. Macloghlen drew his revolver, like one well used to such episodes, and pointed it full at the angry Arab. 'Look here, Mr. Sheikh,' he said, calmly, yet with a fine touch of bravado; 'do ye see this revolver? Well, unless ye make yer camels thravel shtraight to Geergeh widout wan other wurrud, 'tis yer own brains will be spattered, sor, on the sand of this desert! And if ye touch wan hair of our heads, ye'll answer for it wid yer life to the British Government.'

I do not feel sure that the sheikh comprehended the exact nature of each word in this comprehensive threat, but I am certain he took in its general meaning, punctuated as it was with some flourishes of the revolver. He turned to the drivers and made a gesture of despair. It meant, apparently, that this infidel was too much for him. Then he called out a few sharp directions in Arabic. Next minute, our camels' legs were stepping out briskly along the road to Geergeh with a promptitude which I'm sure must have astonished their owners. We rode on and on through the gloom in a fever of suspense. Had any of the Senoosis noticed our presence? Would they miss the chief's wife before long, and follow us under arms? Would our own sheikh betray us? I am no coward, as women go, but I confess, if it had not been for our fiery Irishman, I should have felt my heart sink. We were grateful to him for the reckless and good-humoured courage of the untamed Celt. It kept us from giving way. 'Ye'll take notice, Mr. Sheikh,' he said, as we threaded

our way among the moon-lit rocks, 'that I have twinty-wan car-
tridges in me case for me revolver; and that if there's throuble to-
night, 'tis twinty of them there'll be for your frinds the Senoosis,
and wan for yerself; but for fear of disappointing a gintleman, 'tis
yer own special bullet I'll distribute first, if it comes to fighting.'

The sheikh's English was a vanishing quantity, but to judge by
the way he nodded and salaamed at this playful remark, I am convinced he understood the Doctor's Irish quite as well as I did.

We spoke little by the way; we were all far too frightened, except
the Doctor, who kept our hearts up by a running fire of wild Celtic
humour. But I found time meanwhile to learn by a few questions
from our veiled friend something of her captivity. She had seen
her father massacred before her eyes at Khartoum, and had then
been sold away to a merchant, who conveyed her by degrees and
by various exchanges across the desert through lonely spots to the
Senoosi oasis. There she had lived all those years with the chief to
whom her last purchaser had trafficked her. She did not even know
that her husband's village was an integral part of the Khedive's ter-
ritory; far less that the English were now in practical occupation of
Egypt. She had heard nothing and learnt nothing since that fateful
day; she had waited in vain for the off-chance of a deliverer.

'But did you never try to run away to the Nile?' I cried,
astonished.

'Run away? How could I? I did not even know which way the
river lay; and was it possible for me to cross the desert on foot, or
find the chance of a camel? The Senoosis would have killed me.
Even with you to help me, see what dangers surround me; alone,
I should have perished, like Hagar in the wilderness, with no angel
to save me.'

'An' ye've got the angel now,' Dr. Macloghlen exclaimed, glancing at me. 'Steady, there, Mr. Sheikh. What's this that's coming?'

It was another caravan, going the opposite way, on its road to
the oasis! A voice halloaed from it.

Our new friend clung tightly to me. 'My husband!' she whispered, gasping.

They were still far off on the desert, and the moon shone
bright. A few hurried words to the Doctor, and with a wild resolve
we faced the emergency. He made the camels halt, and all of us,

springing off, crouched down behind their shadows in such a way that the coming caravan must pass on the far side of us. At the same moment the Doctor turned resolutely to the sheikh. 'Look here, Mr. Arab,' he said in a quiet voice, with one more appeal to the simple Volapuk of the pointed revolver; 'I cover ye wid this. Let these frinds of yours go by. If there's anny unnecessary talking betwixt ye, or anny throuble of anny kind, remimber, the first bullet goes sthraight as an arrow t'rough that haythen head of yours!'

The sheikh salaamed more submissively than ever.

The caravan drew abreast of us. We could hear them cry aloud on either side the customary salutes: 'In Allah's name, peace!' answered by 'Allah is great; there is no god but Allah.'

Would anything more happen? Would our sheikh play us false? It was a moment of breathlessness. We crouched and cowered in the shade, holding our hearts with fear, while the Arab drivers pretended to be unsaddling the camels. A minute or two of anxious suspense; then, peering over our beasts' backs, we saw their long line filing off towards the oasis. We watched their turbaned heads, silhouetted against the sky, disappear slowly. One by one they faded away. The danger was past. With beating hearts we rose up again.

The Doctor sprang into his place and seated himself on his camel. 'Now ride on, Mr. Sheikh,' he said, 'wid all yer men, as if grim death was afther ye. Camels or no camels, ye've got to march all night, for ye'll never draw rein till we're safe back at Geergeh!'

And sure enough we never halted, under the persuasive influence of that loaded revolver, till we dismounted once more in the early dawn upon the Nile bank, under British protection.

Then Elsie and I and our rescued country-woman broke down together in an orgy of relief. We hugged one another and cried like so many children.

CHAPTER VIII

THE ADVENTURE OF THE PEA-GREEN PATRICIAN

Away to India! A life on the ocean wave once more; and—may it prove less wavy!

In plain prose, my arrangement with 'my proprietor,' Mr. Elworthy (thus we speak in the newspaper trade), included a trip to Bombay for myself and Elsie. So, as soon as we had drained Upper Egypt journalistically dry, we returned to Cairo on our road to Suez. I am glad to say, my letters to the *Daily Telephone* gave satisfaction. My employer wrote, 'You are a born journalist.' I confess this surprised me; for I have always considered myself a truthful person. Still, as he evidently meant it for praise, I took the doubtful compliment in good part, and offered no remonstrance.

I have a mercurial temperament. My spirits rise and fall as if they were Consols. Monotonous Egypt depressed me, as it depressed the Israelites; but the passage of the Red Sea set me sounding my timbrel. I love fresh air; I love the sea, if the sea will but behave itself; and I positively revelled in the change from Egypt.

Unfortunately, we had taken our passages by a P. and O. steamer from Suez to Bombay many weeks beforehand, so as to secure good berths; and still more unfortunately, in a letter to Lady Georgina, I had chanced to mention the name of our ship and the date of the voyage. I kept up a spasmodic correspondence with Lady Georgina nowadays—tuppence-ha'penny a fortnight; the dear, cantankerous, racy old lady had been the foundation of my fortunes, and I was genuinely grateful to her; or, rather, I ought to say, she had been their second foundress, for I will do myself the justice to admit that the first was my own initiative and enterprise. I flatter myself I have the knack of taking the tide on the turn, and I am justly proud of it. But, being a grateful animal, I wrote once a fortnight to report progress to Lady Georgina. Besides—let me whisper—strictly between ourselves—'twas an indirect way of hearing about Harold.

This time, however, as events turned out, I recognised that

I had made a grave mistake in confiding my movements to my shrewd old lady. She did not betray me on purpose, of course; but I gathered later that casually in conversation she must have mentioned the fact and date of my sailing before somebody who ought to have had no concern in it; and the somebody, I found, had governed himself accordingly. All this, however, I only discovered afterwards. So, without anticipating, I will narrate the facts exactly as they occurred to me.

When we mounted the gangway of the *Jumna* at Suez, and began the process of frizzling down the Red Sea, I noted on deck almost at once an odd-looking young man of twenty-two or thereabouts, with a curious faint pea-green complexion. He was the wishy-washiest young man I ever beheld in my life; an achromatic study: in spite of the delicate pea-greeniness of his skin, all the colouring matter of the body seemed somehow to have faded out of him. Perhaps he had been bleached. As he leant over the taffrail, gazing down with open mouth and vacant stare at the water, I took a good long look at him. He interested me much—because he was so exceptionally uninteresting; a pallid, anæmic, indefinite hobbledehoy, with a high, narrow forehead, and sketchy features. He had watery, restless eyes of an insipid light blue; thin, yellow hair, almost white in its paleness; and twitching hands that played nervously all the time with a shadowy moustache. This shadowy moustache seemed to absorb as a rule the best part of his attention; it was so sparse and so blanched that he felt it continually— to assure himself, no doubt, of the reality of its existence. I need hardly add that he wore an eye-glass.

He was an aristocrat, I felt sure; Eton and Christ Church: no ordinary person could have been quite so flavourless. Imbecility like his is only to be attained as the result of long and judicious selection.

He went on gazing in a vacant way at the water below, an ineffectual patrician smile playing feebly round the corners of his mouth meanwhile. Then he turned and stared at me as I lay back in my deck-chair. For a minute he looked me over as if I were a horse for sale. When he had finished inspecting me, he beckoned to somebody at the far end of the quarter-deck.

The somebody sidled up with a deferential air which confirmed my belief in the pea-green young man's aristocratic origin. It was such deference as the British flunkey pays only to blue blood; for he has gradations of flunkeydom. He is respectful to wealth; polite to acquired rank; but servile only to hereditary nobility. Indeed, you can make a rough guess at the social status of the person he addresses by observing which one of his twenty-seven nicely graduated manners he adopts in addressing him.

The pea-green young man glanced over in my direction, and murmured something to the satellite, whose back was turned towards me. I felt sure, from his attitude, he was asking whether I was the person he suspected me to be. The satellite nodded assent, whereat the pea-green young man, screwing up his face to fix his eye-glass, stared harder than ever. He must be heir to a peerage, I felt convinced; nobody short of that rank would consider himself entitled to stare with such frank unconcern at an unknown lady.

Presently it further occurred to me that the satellite's back seemed strangely familiar. 'I have seen that man somewhere, Elsie,' I whispered, putting aside the wisps of hair that blew about my face.

'So have I, dear,' Elsie answered, with a slight shudder. And I was instinctively aware that I too disliked him.

As Elsie spoke, the man turned, and strolled slowly past us, with that ineffable insolence which is the other side of the flunkey's insufferable self-abasement. He cast a glance at us as he went by, a withering glance of brazen effrontery. We knew him now, of course; it was that variable star, our old acquaintance, Mr. Higginson, the courier.

He was here as himself this time; no longer the count or the mysterious faith-healer. The diplomat hid his rays under the garb of the man-servant.

'Depend upon it, Elsie,' I cried, clutching her arm with a vague sense of fear, 'this man means mischief. There is danger ahead. When a creature of Higginson's sort, who has risen to be a count and a fashionable physician, descends again to be a courier, you may rest assured it is because he has something to gain by it. He has some deep scheme afloat. And *we* are part of it.'

'His master looks weak enough and silly enough for anything,' Elsie answered, eyeing the suspected lordling. 'I should think he is just the sort of man such a wily rogue would naturally fasten upon.'

'When a wily rogue gets hold of a weak fool, who is also dishonest,' I said, 'the two together may make a formidable combination. But never mind. We're forewarned. I think I shall be even with him.'

That evening, at dinner in the saloon, the pea-green young man strolled in with a jaunty air and took his seat next to us. The Red Sea, by the way, was kinder than the Mediterranean: it allowed us to dine from the very first evening. Cards had been laid on the plates to mark our places. I glanced at my neighbour's. It bore the inscription, 'Viscount Southminster.'

That was the name of Lord Kynaston's eldest son—Lady Georgina's nephew; Harold Tillington's cousin! So *this* was the man who might possibly inherit Mr. Marmaduke Ashurst's money! I remembered now how often and how fervently Lady Georgina had said, 'Kynaston's sons are all fools.' If the rest came up to sample, I was inclined to agree with her.

It also flashed across me that Lord Southminster might have heard through Higginson of our meeting with Mr. Marmaduke Ashurst at Florence, and of my acquaintance with Harold Tillington at Schlangenbad and Lungern. With a woman's instinct, I jumped at the fact that the pea-green young man had taken passage by this boat, on purpose to baffle both me and Harold.

Thinking it over, it seemed to me, too, that he might have various possible points of view on the matter. He might desire, for example, that Harold should marry me, under the impression that his marriage with a penniless outsider would annoy his uncle; for the pea-green young man doubtless thought that I was still to Mr. Ashurst just that dreadful adventuress. If so, his obvious cue would be to promote a good understanding between Harold and myself, in order to make us marry, so that the urbane old gentleman might then disinherit his favourite nephew, and make a new will in Lord Southminster's interest. Or, again, the pea-green young man might, on the contrary, be aware that Mr. Ashurst and I had got on admirably together when we met at Florence; in which case his aim would naturally be to find out something that might set the rich uncle against me. Yet once more, he might merely have heard that I had drawn up Uncle Marmaduke's will at the office, and he might desire to worm the contents of it out of me. Whichever was his design, I resolved to be upon my guard in every word I said to him, and leave no door open to any trickery either way. For of one thing I felt sure, that the colourless young man had torn himself away from the mud-honey of Piccadilly for this voyage to India only because he had heard there was a chance of meeting me.

That was a politic move, whoever planned it—himself or Higginson; for a week on board ship with a person or persons is the very best chance of getting thrown in with them; whether they like it or lump it, they can't easily avoid you.

It was while I was pondering these things in my mind, and resolving with myself not to give myself away, that the young man with the pea-green face lounged in and dropped into the next seat to me. He was dressed (amongst other things) in a dinner jacket and a white tie; for myself, I detest such fopperies on board ship; they seem to me out of place; they conflict with the infinite possibilities of the situation. One stands too near the realities of things. Evening dress and *mal-de-mer* sort ill together.

As my neighbour sat down, he turned to me with an inane smile which occupied all his face. 'Good evening,' he said, in a baronial drawl. 'Miss Cayley, I gathah? I asked the skippah's leave to sit next yah. We ought to be friends—rathah. I think yah know my poor deah old aunt, Lady Georgina Fawley.'

I bowed a somewhat freezing bow. 'Lady Georgina is one of my dearest friends,' I answered.

'No, really? Poor deah old Georgey! Got somebody to stick up for her at last, has she? Now that's what I call chivalrous of yah. Magnanimous, isn't it? I like to see people stick up for their friends. And it must be a novelty for Georgey. For between you and me, a moah cantankerous, spiteful, acidulated, old cough-drop than the poor deah soul it 'ud be difficult to hit upon.'

'Lady Georgina has brains,' I answered; 'and they enable her to recognise a fool when she sees him. I will admit that she does not suffer fools gladly.'

He turned to me with a sudden sharp look in the depths of the lack-lustre eyes. Already it began to strike me that, though the pea-green young man was inane, he had his due proportion of a certain insidious practical cunning. 'That's true,' he answered, measuring me. 'And according to her, almost everybody's a fool—especially her relations. There's a fine knack of sweeping generalisation about deah, skinny old Georgey. The few people she reahlly likes are all archangels; the rest are blithering idiots; there's no middle course with her.'

I held my peace frigidly.

'She thinks me a very special and peculiah fool,' he went on, crumbling his bread.

'Lady Georgina,' I answered, 'is a person of exceptional discrimination. I would almost always accept her judgment on anyone as practically final.'

He laid down his soup-spoon, fondled the imperceptible moustache with his tapering fingers, and then broke once more into a cheerful expanse of smile which reminded me of nothing so much as of the village idiot. It spread over his face as the splash from a stone spreads over a millpond. 'Now that's a nice cheerful sort of thing to say to a fellah,' he ejaculated, fixing his eye-glass in his eye, with a few fierce contortions of his facial muscles. 'That's encouraging, don't yah know, as the foundation of an acquaintance. Makes a good cornah-stone. Calculated to place things at once upon what yah call a friendly basis. Georgey said you had a pretty wit; I see now why she admiahed it. Birds of a feathah: very wise old proverb.'

I reflected that, after all, this young man had nothing overt against him, beyond a fishy blue eye and an inane expression; so, feeling that I had perhaps gone a little too far, I continued after a minute, 'And your uncle, how is he?'

'Marmy?' he inquired, with another elephantine smile; and then I perceived it was a form of humour with him (or rather, a cheap substitute) to speak of his elder relations by their abbreviated Christian names, without any prefix. 'Marmy's doing very well, thank yah; as well as could be expected. In fact, bettah. Habakkuk on the brain: it's carrying him off at last. He has Bright's disease very bad—drank port, don't yah know—and won't trouble this wicked world much longah with his presence. It will be a happy release—especially for his nephews.'

I was really grieved, for I had grown to like the urbane old gentleman, as I had grown to like the cantankerous old lady. In spite of his fussiness and his Stock Exchange views on the interpretation of Scripture, his genuine kindliness and his real liking for me had softened my heart to him; and my face must have shown my distress, for the pea-green young man added quickly with an afterthought: 'But *you* needn't be afraid, yah know. It's all right for Harold Tillington. You ought to know that as well as anyone—and bettah: for it was you who drew up his will for him at Florence.'

I flushed crimson, I believe. Then he knew all about me! 'I was not asking on Mr. Tillington's account,' I answered. 'I asked because I have a personal feeling of friendship for your uncle, Mr. Ashurst.'

His hand strayed up to the straggling yellow hairs on his upper lip once more, and he smiled again, this time with a curious undercurrent of foolish craftiness. 'That's a good one,' he answered. 'Georgey told me you were original. Marmy's a millionaire, and many people love millionaires for their money. But to love Marmy for himself—I do call that originality! Why, weight for age, he's acknowledged to be the most portentous old boah in London society!'

'I like Mr. Ashurst because he has a kind heart and some genuine instincts,' I answered. 'He has not allowed all human feeling to be replaced by a cheap mask of Pall Mall cynicism.'

'Oh, I say; how's that for preaching? Don't you manage to give it hot to a fellah, neithah! And at sight, too, without the usual three days of grace. Have some of my champagne? I'm a forgiving creachah.'

'No, thank you. I prefer this hock.'

'Your friend, then?' And he motioned the steward to pass the bottle.

To my great disgust, Elsie held out her glass. I was annoyed at that. It showed she had missed the drift of our conversation, and was therefore lacking in feminine intuition. I should be sorry if I had allowed the higher mathematics to kill out in me the most distinctively womanly faculty.

From that first day forth, however, in spite of this beginning, Lord Southminster almost persecuted me with his persistent attentions. He did all a man could possibly do to please me. I could not make out precisely what he was driving at; but I saw he had some artful game of his own to play, and that he was playing it subtly. I also saw that, vapid as he was, his vapidity did not prevent him from being worldly wise with the wisdom of the self-seeking man of the world, who utterly distrusts and disbelieves in all the higher emotions of humanity. He harped so often on this string that on our second day out, as we lolled on deck in the heat, I had to rebuke him sharply. He had been sneering for some hours. 'There are two kinds of silly simplicity, Lord Southminster,' I said, at last. 'One kind is the silly simplicity of the rustic who trusts everybody; the other kind is the silly simplicity of the Pall Mall clubman who trusts nobody. It is just as foolish and just as one-sided to overlook the good as to overlook the evil in humanity. If you trust everyone, you are likely to be taken in; but if you trust no one, you put yourself at a serious practical disadvantage, besides losing half the joy of living.'

'Then you think me a fool, like Georgey?' he broke out.

'I should never be rude enough to say so,' I answered, fanning myself.

'Well, you're what I call a first-rate companion for a voyage down the Red Sea,' he put in, gazing abstractedly at the awnings. 'Such a lovely, freezing mixture! A fellah doesn't need ices when *you're* on tap. I recommend you as a refrigeratah.'

'I am glad,' I answered demurely, 'if I have secured your approbation in that humble capacity. I am sure I have tried hard for it.'

Yet nothing that I could say seemed to put the man down. In spite of rebuffs, he was assiduous in running down the companion-ladder for my parasol or my smelling-bottle; he fetched me chairs; he stayed me with cushions; he offered to lend me books; he pestered me to drink his wine; and he kept Elsie in champagne, which she annoyed me by accepting. Poor dear Elsie clearly failed to understand the creature. 'He's so kind and polite, Brownie, isn't he?' she would observe in her simple fashion. 'Do you know, I think he's taken quite a fancy to you! And he'll be an earl by-and-by. I call it romantic. How lovely it would seem, dear, to see you a countess!'

'Elsie,' I said severely, with one hand on her arm, 'you are a dear little soul, and I am very fond of you; but if you think I could

sell myself for a coronet to a pasty-faced young man with a pea-
green complexion and glassy blue eyes—I can only say, my child,
you have misread my character. He isn't a man: he's a lump of
putty!'

I think Elsie was quite shocked that I should apply these terms
to a courtesy lord, the eldest son of a peer. Nature had endowed
her with the profound British belief that peers should be spoken of
in choice and peculiar language. 'If a peer's a fool,' Lady Georgina
said once to me, 'people think you should say his temperament
does not fit him for the conduct of affairs; if he's a roué or a drunk-
ard, they think you should say he has unfortunate weaknesses.'

What most of all convinced me, however, that the wishy-
washy young man with the pea-green complexion must be playing
some stealthy game, was the demeanour and mental attitude of
Mr. Higginson, his courier. After the first day, Higginson appeared
to be politeness and deference itself to us. He behaved to us both,
almost as if we belonged to the titled classes. He treated us with the
second best of his twenty-seven graduated manners. He fetched
and carried for us with a courtly grace which recalled that distinguished diplomat, the Comte de Laroche-sur-Loiret, at the station
at Malines with Lady Georgina. It is true, at his politest moments,
I often caught the undercurrent of a wicked twinkle in his eye,
and felt sure he was doing it all with some profound motive. But
his external demeanour was everything that one could desire from
a well-trained man-servant; I could hardly believe it was the same
man who had growled to me at Florence, 'I shall be even with you
yet,' as he left our office.

'Do you know, Brownie,' Elsie mused once, 'I really begin
to think we must have misjudged Higginson. He's so extremely
polite. Perhaps, after all, he is really a count, who has been exiled
and impoverished for his political opinions.'

I smiled and held my tongue. Silence costs nothing. But Mr.
Higginson's political opinions, I felt sure, were of that simple com-
munistic sort which the law in its blunt way calls fraudulent. They
consisted in a belief that all was his which he could lay his hands
on.

'Higginson's a splendid fellow for his place, yah know, Miss
Cayley,' Lord Southminster said to me one evening as we were

approaching Aden. 'What I like about him is, he's so doosid intelligent.'

'Extremely so,' I answered. Then the devil entered into me again. 'He had the doosid intelligence even to take in Lady Georgina.'

'Yaas; that's just it, don't you know. Georgey told me that story. Screamingly funny, wasn't it? And I said to myself at once, "Higginson's the man for me. I want a courier with jolly lots of brains and no blooming scruples. I'll entice this chap away from Marmy." And I did. I outbid Marmy. Oh, yaas, he's a first-rate fellah, Higginson. What *I* want is a man who will do what he's told, and ask no beastly unpleasant questions. Higginson's that man. He's as sharp as a ferret.'

'And as dishonest as they make them.'

He opened his hands with a gesture of unconcern. 'All the bettah for my purpose. See how frank I am, Miss Cayley. I tell the truth. The truth is very rare. You ought to respect me for it.'

'It depends somewhat upon the *kind* of truth,' I answered, with a random shot. 'I don't respect a man, for instance, for confessing to a forgery.'

He winced. Not for months after did I know how a stone thrown at a venture had chanced to hit the spot, and had vastly enhanced his opinion of my cleverness.

'You have heard about Dr. Fortescue-Langley too, I suppose?' I went on.

'Oh, yaas. Wasn't it real jam? He did the doctor-trick on a lady in Switzerland. And the way he has come it ovah deah simple old Marmy! He played Marmy with Ezekiel! Not so dusty, was it? He's too lovely for anything!'

'He's an edged tool,' I said.

'Yaas; that's why I use him.'

'And edged tools may cut the user's fingers.'

'Not mine,' he answered, taking out a cigarette. 'Oh deah no. He can't turn against *me*. He wouldn't dare to. Yah see, I have the fellah entirely in my powah. I know all his little games, and I can expose him any day. But it suits me to keep him. I don't mind telling yah, since I respect your intellect, that he and I are engaged in pulling off a big *coup* togethah. If it were not for that, I wouldn't be

heah. Yah don't catch me going away so fah from Newmarket and
the Empire for nothing.'

'I judged as much,' I answered. And then I was silent.

But I wondered to myself why the neutral-tinted young man
should be so communicative to an obviously hostile stranger.

For the next few days it amused me to see how hard our lordling
tried to suit his conversation to myself and Elsie. He was absurdly
anxious to humour us. Just at first, it is true, he had discussed the
subjects that lay nearest to his own heart. He was an ardent votary
of the noble quadruped; and he loved the turf—whose sward, we
judged, he trod mainly at Tattersall's. He spoke to us with erudi-
tion on 'two-year-old form,' and gave us several 'safe things' for the
spring handicaps. The Oaks he considered 'a moral' for Clorinda.
He also retailed certain choice anecdotes about ladies whose
Christian names were chiefly Tottie and Flo, and whose honoured
surnames have escaped my memory. Most of them flourished, I
recollect, at the Frivolity Music Hall. But when he learned that our
interest in the noble quadruped was scarcely more than tepid, and
that we had never even visited 'the Friv.,' as he affectionately called
it, he did his best in turn to acquire our subjects. He had heard us
talk about Florence, for example, and he gathered from our talk
that we loved its art treasures. So he set himself to work to be
studiously artistic. It was a beautiful study in human ineptitude.
'Ah, yaas,' he murmured, turning up the pale blue eyes ecstatically
towards the mast-head. 'Chawming place, Florence! I dote on the
pickchahs. I know them all by heart. I assuah yah, I've spent houahs
and houahs feeding my soul in the galleries.'

'And what particular painter does your soul most feed upon?' I
asked bluntly, with a smile.

The question staggered him. I could see him hunting through
the vacant chambers of his brain for a Florentine painter. Then a
faint light gleamed in the leaden eyes, and he fingered the straw-
coloured moustache with that nervous hand till he almost put a
visible point upon it. 'Ah, Raphael?' he said, tentatively, with an
inquiring air, yet beaming at his success. 'Don't you think so?
Splendid artist, Raphael!'

'And a very safe guess,' I answered, leading him on. 'You can't
go far wrong in mentioning Raphael, can you? But after him?'

He dived into the recesses of his memory again, peered about him for a minute or two, and brought back nothing. 'I can't remembah the othah fellahs' names,' he went on; 'they're all so much alike; all in *elli*, don't yah know; but I recollect at the time they impressed me awfully.'

'No doubt,' I answered.

He tried to look through me, and failed. Then he plunged, like the noble sportsman that he was, on a second fetch of memory. 'Ah—and Michael Angelo,' he went on, quite proud of his treasure-trove. 'Sweet things, Michael Angelo's!'

'Very sweet,' I admitted. 'So simple; so touching; so tender; so domestic!'

I thought Elsie would explode; but she kept her countenance. The pea-green young man gazed at me uneasily. He had half an idea by this time that I was making game of him.

However, he fished up a name once more, and clutched at it. 'Savonarola, too,' he adventured. 'I adore Savonarola. His pick-chahs are beautiful.'

'And so rare!' Elsie murmured.

'Then there is Fra Diavolo?' I suggested, going one better. 'How do you like Fra Diavolo?'

He seemed to have heard the name before, but still he hesitated. 'Ah—what did he paint?' he asked, with growing caution.

I stuffed him valiantly. 'Those charming angels, you know,' I answered. 'With the roses and the glories!'

'Oh, yaas; I recollect. All askew, aren't they? like this! I remembah them very well. But——' a doubt flitted across his brain, 'wasn't his name Fra Angelico?'

'His brother,' I replied, casting truth to the winds. 'They worked together, you must have heard. One did the saints; the other did the opposite. Division of labour, don't you see; Fra Angelico, Fra Diavolo.'

He fingered his cigarette with a dubious hand, and wriggled his eye-glass tighter. 'Yaas, beautiful; beautiful! But——' growing suspicious apace, 'wasn't Fra Diavolo also a composah?'

'Of course,' I assented. 'In his off time, he composed. Those early Italians—so versatile, you see; so versatile!'

He had his doubts, but he suppressed them.

'And Torricelli,' I went on, with a side glance at Elsie, who was choking by this time. 'And Chianti, and Frittura, and Cinquevalli, and Giulio Romano.'

His distrust increased. 'Now you're trying to make me commit myself,' he drawled out. 'I remembah Torricelli—he's the fellah who used to paint all his women crooked. But Chianti's a wine; I've often drunk it; and Romano's—well, every fellah knows Romano's is a restaurant near the Gaiety Theatre.'

'Besides,' I continued, in a drawl like his own, 'there are Risotto, and Gnocchi, and Vermicelli, and Anchovy—all famous paintahs, and all of whom I don't doubt you admiah.'

Elsie exploded at last. But he took no offence. He smiled inanely, as if he rather enjoyed it. 'Look heah, you know,' he said, with his crafty smile; 'that's one too much. I'm not taking any. You think yourselves very clevah for kidding me with paintahs who are really macaroni and cheese and claret; yet if I were to tell you the Lejah was run at Ascot, or the Cesarewitch at Doncastah, why, you'd be no wisah. When it comes to art, I don't have a look in; but I could tell you a thing or two about starting prices.'

And I was forced to admit that there he had reason.

Still, I think he realised that he had better avoid the subject of art in future, as we avoided the noble quadruped. He saw his limitations.

Not till the last evening before we reached Bombay did I really understand the nature of my neighbour's project. That evening, as it chanced, Elsie had a headache and went below early. I stopped with her till she dozed off; then I slipped up on deck once more for a breath of fresh air, before retiring for the night to the hot and stuffy cabins. It was an exquisite evening. The moon rode in the pale green sky of the tropics. A strange light still lingered on the western horizon. The stifling heat of the Red Sea had given way long since to the refreshing coolness of the Indian Ocean. I strolled a while on the quarter-deck, and sat down at last near the stern. Next moment, I was aware of somebody creeping up to me.

'Look heah, Miss Cayley,' a voice broke in; 'I'm in luck at last! I've been waiting, oh, evah so long, for this opportunity.'

I turned and faced him. 'Have you, indeed?' I answered. 'Well, I have *not*, Lord Southminster.'

I tried to rise, but he motioned me back to my chair. There were ladies on deck, and to avoid being noticed I sank into my seat again.

'I want to speak to you,' he went on, in a voice that (for him) was almost impressive. 'Half a mo, Miss Cayley. I want to say—this last night—you misunderstand me.'

'On the contrary,' I answered, 'the trouble is—that I understand you perfectly.'

'No, yah don't. Look heah.' He bent forward quite romantically. 'I'm going to be perfectly frank. Of course yah know that when I came on board this ship I came—to checkmate yah.'

'Of course,' I replied. 'Why else should you and Higginson have bothered to come here?'

He rubbed his hands together. 'That's just it. You're always clevah. You hit it first shot. But there's wheah the point comes in. At first, I only thought of how we could circumvent yah. I treated yah as the enemy. Now, it's all the othah way. Miss Cayley, you're the cleverest woman I evah met in this world; you extort my admiration!'

I could not repress a smile. I didn't know how it was, but I could see I possessed some mysterious attraction for the Ashurst family. I was fatal to Ashursts. Lady Georgina, Harold Tillington, the Honourable Marmaduke, Lord Southminster—different types as they were, all succumbed to me without one blow.

'You flatter me,' I answered, coldly.

'No, I don't,' he cried, flashing his cuffs and gazing affectionately at his sleeve-links. ''Pon my soul, I assuah yah, I mean it. I can't tell you how much I admiah yah. I admiah your intellect. Every day I have seen yah, I feel it moah and moah. Why, you're the only person who has evah out-flanked my fellah, Higginson. As a rule I don't think much of women. I've been through several London seasons, and lots of 'em have tried their level best to catch me; the cleverest mammas have been aftah me for their Ethels. But I wasn't so easily caught; I dodged the Ethels. With you, it's different. I feel'—he paused—'you're a woman a fellah might be really proud of.'

'You are too kind,' I answered, in my refrigerator voice.

'Well, will you take me?' he asked, trying to seize my hand. 'Miss Cayley, if you will, you will make me unspeakably happy.'

It was a great effort—for him—and I was sorry to crush it.
'I regret,' I said, 'that I am compelled to deny you unspeakable
happiness.'

'Oh, but you don't catch on. You mistake. Let me explain.
You're backing the othah man. Now, I happen to know about that,
and I assuah you, it's an error. Take my word for it, you're staking
your money on the wrong fellah.'

'I do not understand you,' I replied, drawing away from his
approach. 'And what is more, I may add, you could never understand me.'

'Yaas, but I do. I understand perfectly. I can see where you go
wrong. You drew up Marmy's will; and you think Marmy has
left all he's worth to Harold Tillington; so you're putting every
penny you've got on Harold. Well, that's mere moonshine. Harold
may think it's all right; but it's not all right. There's many a slip
'twixt the cup and the Probate Court. Listen heah, Miss Cayley:
Higginson and I are a jolly sight sharpah than your friend Harold.
Harold's what they call a clevah fellah in society, and I'm what they
call a fool; but I know bettah than Harold which side of my bread's
buttahed.'

'I don't doubt it,' I answered.

'Well, I have managed this business. I don't mind telling you
now, I had a telegram from Marmy's valet when we touched at
Aden; and poor old Marmy's sinking. Habakkuk's been too much
for him. Sixteen stone going under. Why am I not with him?
yah may ask. Because, when a man of Marmy's temperament is
dying, it's safah to be away from him. There's plenty of time for
Marmy to altah his will yet—and there are othah contingencies.
Still, Harold's quite out of it. You take my word for it; if you back
Harold, you back a man who's not going to get anything; while if
you back me, you back the winnah, with a coronet into the bargain.' And he smiled fatuously.

I looked at him with a look that would have made a wiser man
wince. But it fell flat on Lord Southminster. 'Do you know why
I do not rise and go down to my cabin at once?' I said, slowly.
'Because, if I did, somebody as I passed might see my burning
cheeks—cheeks flushed with shame at your insulting proposal—
and might guess that you had asked me, and that I had refused

you. And I should shrink from the disgrace of anyone's knowing that you had put such a humiliation upon me. You have been frank with me—after your kind, Lord Southminster; frank with the frankness of a low and purely commercial nature. I will be frank with you in turn. You are right in supposing that I love Harold Tillington—a man whose name I hate to mention in your presence. But you are wrong in supposing that the disposition of Mr. Marmaduke Ashurst's money has or can have anything to do with the feelings I entertain towards him. I would marry him all the sooner if he were poor and penniless. You cannot *understand* that state of mind, of course; but you must be content to *accept* it. And I would not marry *you* if there were no other man left in the world to marry. I should as soon think of marrying a lump of dough.' I faced him all crimson. 'Is *that* plain enough? Do you see now that I really mean it?'

He gazed at me with a curious look, and twirled what he considered his moustache once more, quite airily. The man was imperturbable—a pachydermatous imbecile. 'You're all wrong, yah know,' he said, after a long pause, during which he had regarded me through his eye-glass as if I were a specimen of some rare new species. 'You're all wrong, and yah won't believe me. But I tell yah, I know what I'm talking about. You think it's quite safe about Marmy's money—that he's left it to Harold, because you drew the will up. I assuah you that will's not worth the paper it's written on. You fancy Harold's a hot favourite: he's a rank outsidah. I give you a chance, and you won't take it. I want yah because you're a remarkable woman. Most of the Ethels cry when they're trying to make a fellah propose to 'em; and I don't like 'em damp: but *you* have some go about yah. You insist upon backing the wrong man. But you'll find your mistake out yet.' A bright idea struck him. 'I say—why don't you hedge? Leave it open till Marmy's gone, and then marry the winnah?'

It was hopeless trying to make this clod understand. His brain was not built with the right cells for understanding me. 'Lord Southminster,' I said, turning upon him and clasping my hands, 'I will not go away while you stop here. But you have some spark enough of a gentleman in your composition, I hope, not to inflict your company any longer upon a woman who does not desire it.

I ask you to leave me here alone. When you have gone, and I have had time to recover from your degrading offer, I may perhaps feel able to go down to my cabin.'

He stared at me with open blue eyes—those watery blue eyes. 'Oh, just as you like,' he answered. 'I wanted to do you a good turn, because you're the only woman I evah really admiahed—to say admiah, don't you know; not trotted round like the Ethels: but you won't allow me. I'll go if you wish it; though I tell you again, you're backing the wrong man, and soonah or latah you'll discover it. I don't mind laying you six to four against him. Howevah, I'll do one thing for yah: I'll leave this offah always open. I'm not likely to marry any othah woman—not good enough, is it?—and if evah you find out you're mistaken about Harold Tillington, remembah, honour bright, I shall be ready at any time to renew my offah.'

By this time, I was at boiling-point. I could not find words to answer him. I waved him away angrily with one hand. He raised his hat with quite a jaunty air and strolled off forward, puffing his cigarette. I don't think he even knew the disgust with which he inspired me.

I sat some hours with the cool air playing about my burning cheeks before I mustered up courage to rise and go down below again.

CHAPTER IX

THE ADVENTURE OF THE MAGNIFICENT MAHARAJAH

OUR arrival at Bombay was a triumphal entry. We were received like royalty. Indeed, to tell the truth, Elsie and I were beginning to get just a leetle bit spoiled. It struck us now that our casual connection with the Ashurst family in its various branches had succeeded in saddling us, like the Lady of Burleigh, 'with the burden of an honour unto which we were not born.' We were everywhere treated as persons of importance; and, oh dear, by dint of such treatment we began to feel at last almost as if we had been raised in the purple. I felt that when we got back to England we should turn up our noses at plain bread and butter.

Yes, life has been kind to me. Have your researches into English literature ever chanced to lead you into reading Horace Walpole, I wonder? That polite trifler is fond of a word which he coined himself—'Serendipity.' It derives from the name of a certain happy Indian Prince Serendip, whom he unearthed (or invented) in some obscure Oriental story; a prince for whom the fairies or the genii always managed to make everything pleasant. It implies the faculty, which few of us possess, of finding whatever we want turn up accidentally at the exact right moment. Well, I believe I must have been born with serendipity in my mouth, in place of the proverbial silver spoon, for, wherever I go, all things seem to come out exactly right for me.

The *Jumna*, for example, had hardly heaved to in Bombay Harbour when we noticed on the quay a very distinguished-looking Oriental potentate, in a large, white turban with a particularly big diamond stuck ostentatiously in its front. He stalked on board with a martial air, as soon as we stopped, and made inquiries from our captain after someone he expected. The captain received him with that odd mixture of respect for rank and wealth, combined with true British contempt for the inferior black man, which is universal among his class in their dealings with native Indian nobility. The Oriental potentate, however, who was accompanied by a gorgeous

suite like that of the Wise Men in Italian pictures, seemed satisfied
with his information, and moved over with his stately glide in our
direction. Elsie and I were standing near the gangway among our
rugs and bundles, in the hopeless helplessness of disembarkation.
He approached us respectfully, and, bowing with extended hands
and a deferential air, asked, in excellent English, 'May I venture to
inquire which of you two ladies is Miss Lois Cayley?'

'*I* am,' I replied, my breath taken away by this unexpected greet-
ing. 'May I venture to inquire in return how you came to know I
was arriving by this steamer?'

He held out his hand, with a courteous inclination. 'I am the
Maharajah of Moozuffernuggar,' he answered in an impressive
tone, as if everybody knew of the Maharajah of Moozuffernuggar
as familiarly as they knew of the Duke of Cambridge.
'Moozuffernuggar in Rajputana—*not* the one in the Doab. You
must have heard my name from Mr. Harold Tillington.'

I had not; but I dissembled, so as to salve his pride. 'Mr.
Tillington's friends are *our* friends,' I answered, sententiously.

'And Mr. Tillington's friends are *my* friends,' the Maharajah
retorted, with a low bow to Elsie. 'This is no doubt Miss Petheridge.
I have heard of your expected arrival, as you will guess, from
Tillington. He and I were at Oxford together; I am a Merton man.
It was Tillington who first taught me all I know of cricket. He took
me to stop at his father's place in Dumfriesshire. I owe much to his
friendship; and when he wrote me that friends of his were arriving by
the *Jumna*, why, I made haste to run down to Bombay to greet them.'

The episode was one of those topsy-turvy mixtures of all places
and ages which only this jumbled century of ours has witnessed; it
impressed me deeply. Here was this Indian prince, a feudal Rajput
chief, living practically among his vassals in the Middle Ages when
at home in India; yet he said, 'I am a Merton man,' as Harold himself might have said it; and he talked about cricket as naturally as
Lord Southminster talked about the noble quadruped. The oddest
part of it all was, we alone felt the incongruity; to the Maharajah,
the change from Moozuffernuggar to Oxford and from Oxford
back again to Moozuffernuggar seemed perfectly natural. They
were but two alternative phases in a modern Indian gentleman's
education and experience.

Still, what were we to do with him? If Harold had presented me with a white elephant I could hardly have been more embarrassed than I was at the apparition of this urbane and magnificent Hindoo prince. He was young; he was handsome; he was slim, for a rajah; he wore European costume, save for the huge white turban with its obtrusive diamond; and he spoke English much better than a great many Englishmen. Yet what place could he fill in my life and Elsie's? For once, I felt almost angry with Harold. Why couldn't he have allowed us to go quietly through India, two simple unofficial journalistic pilgrims, in our native obscurity?

His Highness of Moozuffernuggar, however, had his own views on this question. With a courteous wave of one dusky hand, he motioned us gracefully into somebody else's deck chairs, and then sat down on another beside us, while the gorgeous suite stood by in respectful silence—unctuous gentlemen in pink-and-gold brocade—forming a court all round us. Elsie and I, unaccustomed to be so observed, grew conscious of our hands, our skirts, our postures. But the Maharajah posed himself with perfect unconcern, like one well used to the fierce light of royalty. 'I have come,' he said, with simple dignity, 'to superintend the preparations for your reception.'

'Gracious heavens!' I exclaimed. 'Our reception, Maharajah? I think you misunderstand. We are two ordinary English ladies of the proletariat, accustomed to the level plain of professional society. We expect no reception.'

He bowed again, with stately Eastern deference. 'Friends of Tillington's,' he said, shortly, 'are persons of distinction. Besides, I have heard of you from Lady Georgina Fawley.'

'Lady Georgina is too good,' I answered, though inwardly I raged against her. Why couldn't she leave us alone, to feed in peace on dak-bungalow chicken, instead of sending this regal-mannered heathen to bother us?

'So I have come down to Bombay to make sure that you are met in the style that befits your importance in society,' he went on, waving his suite away with one careless hand, for he saw it fussed us. 'I mentioned you to His Honour the Acting-Governor, who had not heard you were coming. His Honour's aide-de-camp will follow shortly with an invitation to Government House while you remain in Bombay—which will not be many days, I don't doubt, for there is nothing in this city of plague to stop for. Later on, during your progress up country, I do myself the honour to hope that you will stay as my guests for as long as you choose at Moozuffernuggar.'

My first impulse was to answer: 'Impossible, Maharajah; we couldn't dream of accepting your kind invitation.' But on second thoughts, I remembered my duty to my proprietor. Journalism first: inclination afterwards! My letter from Egypt on the rescue of the Englishwoman who escaped from Khartoum had brought me great *éclat* as a special correspondent, and the *Daily Telephone* now billed my name in big letters on its placards, so Mr. Elworthy wrote me. Here was another noble chance; must I not strive to rise to it? Two English ladies at a native court in Rajputana!—that ought to afford scope for some rattling journalism!

'It is extremely kind of you,' I said, hesitating, 'and it would give us great pleasure, were it feasible, to accept your friendly offer. But—English ideas, you know, Prince! Two unprotected women! I hardly see how we could come alone to Moozuffernuggar, unchaperoned.'

The Maharajah's face lighted up; he was evidently flattered that we should even thus dubiously entertain his proposal. 'Oh, I've thought about that, too,' he answered, growing more colloquial in tone. 'I've been some days in Bombay, making inquiries and preparations. You see, you had not informed the authorities of your intended visit, so that you were travelling *incognito*—or should it be *incognita?*—and if Tillington hadn't written to let me know your movements, you might have arrived at this port without anybody's knowing it, and have been compelled to take refuge in an hotel on landing.' He spoke as if we had been accustomed all our lives long to be received with red cloth by the Mayor and Corporation, and presented with illuminated addresses and the freedom of the city in a gold snuff-box. 'But I have seen to all that. The Acting-Governor's aide-de-camp will be down before long, and I have arranged that if you consent a little later to honour my humble roof in Rajputana with your august presence, Major Balmossie and his wife will accompany you and chaperon you. I have lived in England: of course I understand that two English ladies of your rank and position cannot travel alone—as if you were Americans. But Mrs. Balmossie is a nice little soul, of unblemished character'—that sweet touch charmed me—'received at Government House'—he had learned the respect due to Mrs. Grundy—'so that if you will accept my invitation, you may rest assured that everything will be done with the utmost regard to the—the unaccountable prejudices of Europeans.'

His thoughtfulness took me aback. I thanked him warmly. He unbent at my thanks. 'And I am obliged to you in return,' he said. 'It gives me real pleasure to be able, through you, to repay Harold Tillington part of the debt I owe him. He was so good to me at Oxford. Miss Cayley, you are new to India, and therefore—as yet—no doubt unprejudiced. You treat a native gentleman, I see, like a human being. I hope you will not stop long enough in our country to get over that stage—as happens to most of your countrymen and countrywomen. In England, a man like myself is an Indian prince; in India, to ninety-nine out of a hundred Europeans, he is just "a damned nigger."'

I smiled sympathetically. 'I think,' I said, venturing under these circumstances on a harmless little swear-word—of course, in quotation marks—'you may trust me never to reach "damn-nigger" point.'

'So I believe,' he answered, 'if you are a friend of Harold Tillington's. Ebony or ivory, he never forgot we were two men together.'

Five minutes later, when the Maharajah had gone to inquire about our luggage, Lord Southminster strolled up. 'Oh, I say, Miss Cayley,' he burst out, 'I'm off now; ta-ta; but remembah, that offah's always open. By the way, who's your black friend? I couldn't help laughing at the airs the fellah gave himself. To see a niggah sitting theah, with his suite all round him, waving his hands and sunning his rings, and behaving for all the world as if he were a gentleman; it's reahly too ridiculous. Harold Tillington picked up with a fellah like that at Oxford—doosid good cricketer too; wondah if this is the same one.'

'Good-bye, Lord Southminster,' I said, quietly, with a stiff little bow. 'Remember, on your side, that your "offer" was rejected once for all last night. Yes, the Indian prince is Harold Tillington's friend, the Maharajah of Moozuffernuggar—whose ancestors were princes while ours were dressed in woad and oak-leaves. But you were right about one thing; *he* behaves—like a gentleman.'

'Oh, I say,' the pea-green young man ejaculated, drawing back; 'that's anothah in the eye for me. You're a good 'un at facers. You gave me one for a welcome, and you give me one now for a parting shot. Nevah mind, though, I can wait; you're backing the wrong fellah—but you're not the Ethels, and you're well worth waiting for.' He waved his hand. 'So-long! See yah again in London.'

And he retired, with that fatuous smile still absorbing his features.

Our three days in Bombay were uneventful; we merely waited to get rid of the roll of the ship, which continued to haunt us for hours after we landed—the floor of our bedrooms having acquired an ugly trick of rising in long undulations, as if Bombay were suffering from chronic earthquake. We made the acquaintance of His Honour the Acting Governor, and His Honour's consort. We were also introduced to Mrs. Balmossie, the lady who was to chaperon us to Moozuffernuggar. Her husband was a soldierly Scotchman from Forfarshire, but she herself was English—a flighty little body with a perpetual giggle. She giggled so much over the idea of the Maharajah's inviting us to his palace that I wondered why on earth she accepted his invitation. At this she seemed surprised. 'Why, it's one of the jolliest places in Rajputana,' she answered, with a bland Simla smile; '*so* picturesque—he, he, he—and *so* delightful. Simpkin flows like water—Simpkin's baboo English for champagne, you know—he, he, he; and though of course the Maharajah's only a native like the rest of them—he, he, he—still, he's been educated at Oxford, and has mixed with Europeans, and he knows how to make one—he, he, he—well, thoroughly comfortable.'

'But what shall we eat?' I asked. 'Rice, ghee, and chupatties?'

'Oh dear no—he, he, he—Europe food, every bit of it. Foie gras, and York ham, and wine *ad lib.* His hospitality's massive. If it weren't for that, of course, one wouldn't dream of going there. But Archie hopes some day to be made Resident, don't you know; and it will do him no harm—he, he, he—with the Foreign Office, to have cultivated friendly relations beforehand with His Highness of Moozuffernuggar. These natives—he, he, he—so absurdly sensitive!'

For myself, the Maharajah interested me, and I rather liked him. Besides, he was Harold's friend, and that was in itself sufficient recommendation. So I determined to push straight into the heart of native India first, and only afterwards to do the regulation tourist round of Agra and Delhi, the Taj and the mosques, Benares and Allahabad, leaving the English and Calcutta for the tail-end of my journey. It was better journalism. As I thought that thought, I began to fear that Mr. Elworthy was right after all, and that I was a born journalist.

On the day fixed for our leaving Bombay, whom should I meet but Lord Southminster—with the Maharajah—at the railway station!

He lounged up to me with that eternal smile still vaguely pervading his empty features. 'Well, we shall have a jolly party, I gathah,' he said. 'They tell me this niggah is famous for his tigahs.'

I gazed at him, positively taken aback. 'You don't mean to tell me,' I cried, 'you actually propose to accept the Maharajah's hospitality?'

His smile absorbed him. 'Yaas,' he answered, twirling his yellow moustache, and gazing across at the unconscious prince, who was engaged in overlooking the arrangements for our saloon carriage. 'The black fellah discovahed I was a cousin of Harold's, so he came to call upon me at the club, of which some Johnnies heah made me an honorary membah. He's offahed me the run of his place while I'm in Indiah, and, of course, I've accepted. Eccentric sort of chap; can't make him out myself: says anyone connected with Harold Tillington is always deah to him. Rum start, isn't it?'

'He is a mere Oriental,' I answered, 'unused to the ways of civilised life. He cherishes the superannuated virtue of gratitude.'

'Yaas; no doubt—so I'm coming along with you.'

I drew back, horrified. 'Now? While I am there? After what I told you last week on the steamer?'

'Oh, that's all right. I bear yah no malice. If I want any fun, of course I must go while *you're* at Moozuffernuggar.'

'Why so?'

'Yah see, this black boundah means to get up some big things at
his place in your honah; and one naturally goes to stop with anyone
who has big things to offah. Hang it all, what does it mattah who a
fellah is if he can give yah good shooting? It's shooting, don't yah
know, that keeps society in England togethah!'

'And therefore you propose to stop in the same house with
me!' I exclaimed, 'in spite of what I have told you! Well, Lord
Southminster, I should have thought there were limits which even
your taste——'

He cut me short with an inane grin. 'There you make your
blooming little erraw,' he answered airily. 'I told yah, I keep my
offah still open; and, hang it all, I don't mean to lose sight of yah
in a hurry. Some other fellah might come along and pick you up
when I wasn't looking; and I don't want to miss yah. In point of
fact, I don't mind telling yah, I back myself still for a couple of
thou' soonah or latah to marry yah. It's dogged as does it; faint
heart, they say, nevah won fair lady!'

If it had not been that I could not bear to disappoint my Indian
prince, I think, when I heard this, I should have turned back then
and there at the station.

The journey up country was uneventful, but dusty. The Mofussil
appears to consist mainly of dust; indeed, I can now recall nothing
of it but one pervading white cloud, which has blotted from my
memory all its other components. The dust clung to my hair after
many washings, and was never really beaten out of my travelling
clothes; I believe part of it thus went round the world with me to
England. When at last we reached Moozuffernuggar, after two
days' and a night's hard travelling, we were met by a crowd of
local grandees, who looked as if they had spent the greater part
of their lives in brushing back their whiskers, and we drove up at
once, in European carriages, to the Maharajah's palace. The look
of it astonished me. It was a strange and rambling old Hindoo
hill-fort, high perched on a scarped crag, like Edinburgh Castle,
and accessible only on one side, up a gigantic staircase, guarded
on either hand by huge sculptured elephants cut in the living
sandstone. Below clustered the town, an intricate mass of tangled
alleys. I had never seen anything so picturesque or so dirty in my
life; as for Elsie, she was divided between admiration for its beauty

and terror at the big-whiskered and white-turbaned attendants. 'What sort of rooms shall we have?' I whispered to our moral guarantee, Mrs. Balmossie. 'Oh, beautiful, dear,' the little lady smirked back. 'Furnished throughout—he, he, he—by Liberty. The Maharajah wants to do honour to his European guests—he, he, he—he fancies, poor man, he's quite European. That's what comes of sending these creatures to Oxford! So he's had suites of rooms furnished for any white visitors who may chance to come his way. Ridiculous, isn't it? *And champagne*—oh, gallons of it! He's quite proud of his rooms—he, he, he—he's always asking people to come and occupy them; he thinks he's done them up in the best style of decoration.'

He had reason, for they were as tasteful as they were dainty and comfortable. And I could not for the life of me make out why his hospitable inclination should be voted 'ridiculous.' But Mrs. Balmossie appeared to find all natives alike a huge joke together. She never even spoke of them without a condescending smile of distant compassion. Indeed, most Anglo-Indians seem first to do their best to Anglicise the Hindoo, and then to laugh at him for aping the Englishman.

After we had been three days at the palace and had spent hours in the wonderful temples and ruins, the Maharajah announced with considerable pride at breakfast one morning that he had got up a tiger-hunt in our special honour.

Lord Southminster rubbed his hands.

'Ha, that's right, Maharaj,' he said, briskly. 'I do love big game. To tell yah the truth, old man, that's just what I came heah for.'

'You do me too much honour,' the Hindoo answered, with quiet sarcasm. 'My town and palace may have little to offer that is worth your attention; but I am glad that my big game, at least, has been lucky enough to attract you.'

The remark was thrown away on the pea-green young man. He had described his host to me as 'a black boundah.' Out of his own mouth I condemned him—he supplied the very word—he was himself nothing more than a born bounder.

During the next few days, the preparations for the tiger-hunt occupied all the Maharajah's energies. 'You know, Miss Cayley,' he said to me, as we stood upon the big stairs, looking down on the

Hindoo city, 'a tiger-hunt is not a thing to be got up lightly. Our
people themselves don't like killing a tiger. They reverence it too
much. They're afraid its spirit might haunt them afterwards and
bring them bad luck. That's one of our superstitions.'

'You do not share it yourself, then?' I asked.

He drew himself up and opened his palms, with a twinkling of
pendant emeralds. 'I am royal,' he answered, with naïve dignity,
'and the tiger is a royal beast. Kings know the ways of kings. If
a king kills what is kingly, it owes him no grudge for it. But if a
common man or a low-caste man were to kill a tiger—who can say
what might happen?'

I saw he was not himself quite free from the superstition.

'Our peasants,' he went on, fixing me with his great black eyes,
'won't even mention the tiger by name, for fear of offending him;
they believe him to be the dwelling-place of a powerful spirit. If
they wish to speak of him, they say "the great beast," or "my lord,
the striped one." Some think the spirit is immortal, except at the
hands of a king. But they have no objection to see him destroyed
by others. They will even point out his whereabouts, and rejoice
over his death; for it relieves the village of a serious enemy, and
they believe the spirit will only haunt the huts of those who actually kill him.'

'Then you know where each tiger lives?' I asked.

'As well as your gamekeepers in England know which covert
may be drawn for foxes. Yes; 'tis a royal sport, and we keep it for
Maharajahs. I myself never hunt a tiger till some European visitor
of distinction comes to Moozuffernuggar, that I may show him
good sport. This tiger we shall hunt to-morrow, for example, he
is a bad old hand. He has carried off the buffaloes of my villagers
over yonder for years and years, and of late he has also become a
man-eater. He once ate a whole family at a meal—a man, his wife,
and his three children. The people at Janwargurh have been pester-
ing me for weeks to come and shoot him; and each week he has
eaten somebody—a child or a woman; the last was yesterday—but
I waited till you came, because I thought it would be something to
show you that you would not be likely to see elsewhere.'

'And you let the poor people go on being eaten, that we might
enjoy this sport!' I cried.

He shrugged his shoulders, and opened his palms. 'They were villagers, you know—ryots: mere tillers of the soil—poor naked peasants. I have thousands of them to spare. If a tiger eats ten of them, they only say, "It was written upon their foreheads." One woman more or less—who would notice her at Moozuffernuggar?'

Then I perceived that the Maharajah was a gentleman, but still a barbarian.

The eventful morning arrived at last, and we started, all agog, for the jungle where the tiger was known to live. Elsie excused herself. She remarked to me the night before, as I brushed her back hair for her, that she had 'half a mind' not to go. 'My dear,' I answered, giving the brush a good dash, 'for a higher mathematician, that phrase lacks accuracy. If you were to say "seven-eighths of a mind" it would be nearer the mark. In point of fact, if you ask my opinion, your inclination to go is a vanishing quantity.'

She admitted the impeachment with an accusing blush. 'You're quite right, Brownie; to tell you the truth, I'm afraid of it.'

'So am I, dear; horribly afraid. Between ourselves, I'm in a deadly funk of it. But "the brave man is not he that feels no fear"; and I believe the same principle applies almost equally to the brave woman. I mean "that fear to subdue" as far as I am able. The Maharajah says I shall be the first girl who has ever gone tiger-hunting. I'm frightened out of my life. I never held a gun in my born days before. But, Elsie, recollect, this is *splendid* journalism! I intend to go through with it.'

'You offer yourself on the altar, Brownie.'

'I do, dear; I propose to die in the cause. I expect my proprietor to carve on my tomb, "Sacred to the memory of the martyr of journalism. She was killed, in the act of taking shorthand notes, by a Bengal tiger."'

We started at early dawn, a motley mixture. My short bicycling skirt did beautifully for tiger-hunting. There was a vast company of native swells, nawabs and ranas, in gorgeous costumes, whose precise names and titles I do not pretend to remember; there were also Major Balmossie, Lord Southminster, the Maharajah, and myself—all mounted on gaily-caparisoned elephants. We had likewise, on foot, a miserable crowd of wretched beaters, with dirty white loin-cloths. We were all very brave, of course—demonstratively brave—and we talked a great deal at the start about the exhilaration given by 'the spice of danger.' But it somehow struck me that the poor beaters on foot had the majority of the danger and extremely little of the exhilaration. Each of us great folk was mounted on his own elephant, which carried a light basket-work howdah in two compartments: the front one intended for the noble sportsman, the back one for a servant with extra guns and ammunition. I pretended to like it, but I fear I trembled vis-ibly. Our mahouts sat on the elephants' necks, each armed with a pointed goad, to whose admonition the huge beasts answered like clock-work. A born journalist always pretends to know everything beforehand, so I speak carelessly of the 'mahout,' as if he were a familiar acquaintance. But I don't mind telling you aside, in confi-dence, that I had only just learnt the word that morning.

The Maharajah protested at first against my taking part in the actual hunt, but I think his protest was merely formal. In his heart of hearts I believe he was proud that the first lady tiger-hunter should have joined his party.

Dusty and shadeless, the road from Moozuffernuggar fares straight across the plain towards the crumbling mountains. Behind, in the heat mist, the castle and palace on their steeply-scarped crag, with the squalid town that clustered at their feet, reminded me once more most strangely of Edinburgh, where I used to spend my vacations from Girton. But the pitiless sun dif-fered greatly from the grey haar of the northern metropolis. It warmed into intense white the little temples of the wayside, and beat on our heads with tropical garishness.

I am bound to admit also that tiger hunting is not quite all it is cracked up to be. In my fancy I had pictured the gallant and blood-thirsty beast rushing out upon us full pelt from some grass-grown nullah at the first sniff of our presence, and fiercely attacking both men and elephants. Instead of that, I will confess the whole truth: frightened as at least one of us was of the tiger, the tiger was still more desperately frightened of his human assailants. I could see clearly that, so far from rushing out of his own accord to attack us, his one desire was to be let alone. He was horribly afraid; he skulked in the jungle like a wary old fox in a trusty spinney. There was no nullah (whatever a nullah may be), there was only a waste of dusty cane-brake. We encircled the tall grass patch where he lurked, forming a big round with a ring-fence of elephants. The beaters on foot, advancing, half naked, with a caution with which I could fully sympathise, endeavoured by loud shouts and gesticulations to rouse the royal beast to a sense of his position. Not a bit of it; the royal beast declined to be drawn; he preferred retirement. The Maharajah, whose elephant was stationed next to mine, even apologised for the resolute cowardice with which he clung to his ignoble lurking-place.

The beaters drew in: the elephants, raising their trunks in air and sniffing suspicion, moved slowly inward. We had girt him round now with a perfect ring, through which he could not possibly break without attacking somebody. The Maharajah kept a fixed eye on my personal safety. But still the royal animal crouched and skulked, and still the black beaters shrieked, howled, and gesticulated. At last, among the tall perpendicular lights and shadows of the big grasses and bamboos, I seemed to see something move— something striped like the stems, yet passing slowly, slowly, slowly between them. It moved in a stealthy undulating line. No one could believe till he saw it how the bright flame-coloured bands of vivid orange-yellow on the monster's flanks, and the interspersed black stripes, could fade away and harmonise, in their native surroundings, with the lights and shades of the upright jungle. It was a marvel of mimicry. 'Look there!' I cried to the Maharajah, pointing one eager hand. 'What is that thing there, moving?'

He stared where I pointed. 'By Jove,' he cried, raising his rifle with a sportsman's quickness, 'you have spotted him first! The tiger!'

The terrified beast stole slowly and cautiously through the tall grasses, his lithe, silken side gliding in and out snakewise, and only his fierce eyes burning bright with gleaming flashes between the gloom of the jungle. Once I had seen him, I could follow with ease his sinuous path among the tangled bamboos, a waving line of beauty in perpetual motion. The Maharajah followed him too, with his keen eyes, and pointed his rifle hastily. But, quick as he was, Lord Southminster was before him. I had half expected to find the pea-green young man turn coward at the last moment; but in that I was mistaken: I will do him the justice to say, whatever else he was, he was a born sportsman. The gleam of joy in his leaden eye when he caught sight of the tiger, the flush of excitement on his pasty face, the eagerness of his alert attitude, were things to see and remember. That moment almost ennobled him. In sight of danger, the best instincts of the savage seemed to revive within him. In civilised life he was a poor creature; face to face with a wild beast he became a mighty shikari. Perhaps that was why he was so fond of big-game shooting. He may have felt it raised him in the scale of being.

He lifted his rifle and fired. He was a cool shot, and he wounded the beast upon its left shoulder. I could see the great crimson stream gush out all at once across the shapely sides, staining the flame-coloured stripes and reddening the black shadows. The tiger drew back, gave a low, fierce growl, and then crouched among the jungle. I saw he was going to leap; he bent his huge backbone into a strong downward curve, took in a deep breath, and stood at bay, glaring at us. Which elephant would he attack? That was what he was now debating. Next moment, with a frightful R'-r'-r'-r', he had straightened out his muscles, and, like a bolt from a bow, had launched his huge bulk forward.

I never saw his charge. I never knew he had leapt upon me. I only felt my elephant rock from side to side like a ship in a storm. He was trumpeting, shaking, roaring with rage and pain, for the tiger was on his flanks, its claws buried deep in the skin of his forehead. I could not keep my seat; I felt myself tossed about in the frail howdah like a pill in a pill-box. The elephant, in a death grapple, was trying to shake off his ghastly enemy. For a minute or two, I was conscious of nothing save this swinging move-ment. Then, opening my eyes for a second, I saw the tiger, in all his terrible beauty, clinging to the elephant's head by the claws of his forepaws, and struggling for a foothold on its trunk with his mighty hind legs, in a wounded agony of despair and vengeance. He would sell his life dear; he would have one or other of us.

Lord Southminster raised his rifle again; but the Maharajah shouted aloud in an angry voice: 'Don't fire! Don't fire! You will kill the lady! You can't aim at him like that. The beast is rocking so that no one can say where a shot will take effect. Down with your gun, sir, instantly!'

My mahout, unable to keep his seat with the rocking, now dropped off his cushion among the scrub below. He could speak a few words of English. 'Shoot, Mem Sahib, shoot!' he cried, flinging his hands up. But I was tossed to and fro, from side to side, with my rifle under my arm. It was impossible to aim. Yet in sheer terror I tried to draw the trigger. I failed; but somehow I caught my rifle against the side of my cage. Something snapped in it somewhere. It went off unexpectedly, without my aiming or firing. I shut my eyes. When I opened them again, I saw a swimming picture of the great sullen beast, loosing his hold on the elephant. I saw his brindled face; I saw his white tusks. But his gleaming pupils burned bright no longer. His jaw was full towards me: I had shot him between the eyes. He fell, slowly, with blood streaming from his nostrils, and his tongue lolling out. His muscles relaxed; his huge limbs grew limp. In a minute, he lay stretched at full length on the ground, with his head on one side, a grand, terrible picture.

My mahout flung up his hands in wonder and amazement. 'My father!' he cried aloud. 'Truly, the Mem Sahib is a great shikari!'

The Maharajah stretched across to me. 'That was a wonderful shot!' he exclaimed. 'I could never have believed a woman could show such nerve and coolness.'

Nerve and coolness, indeed! I was trembling all over like an Italian greyhound, every limb a jelly; and I had not even fired: the rifle went off of itself without me. I am innocent of having ever endangered the life of a haycock. But once more I dissembled. 'Yes, it *was* a difficult shot,' I said jauntily, as if I rather liked tiger-hunting. 'I didn't think I'd hit him.' Still the effect of my speech was somewhat marred, I fear, by the tears that in spite of me rolled down my cheek silently.

''Pon honah, I nevah saw a finah piece of shooting in my life,' Lord Southminster drawled out. Then he added aside, in an undertone, 'Makes a fellow moah determined to annex her than evah!'

I sat in my howdah, half dazed. I hardly heard what they were saying. My heart danced like the elephant. Then it stood still within me. I was only aware of a feeling of faintness. Luckily for my reputation as a mighty sportswoman, however, I just managed to keep up, and did not actually faint, as I was more than half inclined to do.

Next followed the native pæan. The beaters crowded round the fallen beast in a chorus of congratulation. Many of the villagers also ran out, with prayers and ejaculations, to swell our triumph. It was all like a dream. They hustled round me and salaamed to me. A woman had shot him! Wonderful! A babel of voices resounded in my ears. I was aware that pure accident had elevated me into a heroine.

'Put the beast on a pad elephant,' the Maharajah called out.

The beaters tied ropes round his body and raised him with difficulty.

The Maharajah's face grew stern. 'Where are the whiskers?' he asked, fiercely, in his own tongue, which Major Balmossie interpreted for me.

The beaters and the villagers, bowing low and expanding their hands, made profuse expressions of ignorance and innocence. But the fact was patent—the grand face had been mangled. While they had crowded in a dense group round the fallen carcass, somebody had cut off the lips and whiskers and secreted them.

'They have ruined the skin!' the Maharajah cried out in angry tones. 'I intended it for the lady. I shall have them all searched, and the man who has done this thing——'

He broke off, and looked around him. His silence was more terrible by far than the fiercest threat. I saw him now the Oriental despot. All the natives drew back, awestruck.

'The voice of a king is the voice of a great god,' my mahout murmured, in a solemn whisper. Then nobody else said anything.

'Why do they want the whiskers?' I asked, just to set things straight again. 'They seem to have been in a precious hurry to take them!'

The Maharajah's brow cleared. He turned to me once more with his European manner. 'A tiger's body has wonderful power after his death,' he answered. 'His fangs and his claws are very potent charms. His heart gives courage. Whoever eats of it will never know fear. His liver preserves against death and pestilence. But the highest virtue of all exists in his whiskers. They are mighty talismans. Chopped up in food, they act as a slow poison, which no doctor can detect, no antidote guard against. They are also a sovereign remedy against magic or the evil eye. And administered to women, they make an irresistible philtre, a puissant love-potion. They secure you the heart of whoever drinks them.'

'I'd give a couple of monkeys for those whiskahs,' Lord Southminster murmured, half unnoticed.

We began to move again. 'We'll go on to where we know there is another tiger,' the Maharajah said, lightly, as if tigers were partridges. 'Miss Cayley, you will come with us?'

I rested on my laurels. (I was quivering still from head to foot.) 'No, thank you, Maharajah,' as unconcernedly as I could; 'I've had quite enough sport for my first day's tiger-hunting. I think I'll go back now, and write a newspaper account of this little adventure.'

'You have had luck,' he put in. 'Not everyone kills a tiger his first day out. This will make good reading.'

'I wouldn't have missed it for a hundred pounds,' I answered.

'Then try another.'

'I wouldn't try another for a thousand,' I cried fervently.

That evening, at the palace, I was the heroine of the day. They toasted me in a bumper of Heidsieck's dry monopole. The men made speeches. Everybody talked gushingly of my splendid courage and my steadiness of hand. It was a brilliant shot, under such difficult circumstances. For myself, I said nothing. I pretended to look modest. I dared not confess the truth—that I never fired at all. And from that day to this I have never confessed it, till I write it down now in these confiding memoirs.

One episode cast a gloom over my ill-deserved triumph. In the course of the evening, a telegram arrived for the pea-green young man by a white-turbaned messenger. He read it, and crumpled it up carelessly in his hand. I looked inquiry. 'Yaas,' he answered, nodding. 'You're quite right. It's that! Pooah old Marmy has gone, aftah all! Ezekiel and Habakkuk have carried off his sixteen stone at last! And I don't mind telling yah now—though it was a neah thing—it's *I* who am the winnah!'

CHAPTER X

THE ADVENTURE OF THE CROSS-EYED Q.C.

THE 'cold weather,' as it is humorously called, was now drawing to a close, and the young ladies in sailor hats and cambric blouses, who flock to India each autumn for the annual marriage-market, were beginning to resign themselves to a return to England—unless, of course, they had succeeded in 'catching.' So I realised that I must hurry on to Delhi and Agra, if I was not to be intercepted by the intolerable summer.

When we started from Moozuffernuggar for Delhi and the East, Lord Southminster was starting for Bombay and Europe. This surprised me not a little, for he had confided to my unsympathetic ear a few nights earlier, in the Maharajah's billiard-room, that he was 'stony broke,' and must wait at Moozuffernuggar for lack of funds 'till the oof-bird laid' at his banker's in England. His conversation enlarged my vocabulary, at any rate.

'So you've managed to get away?' I exclaimed, as he dawdled up to me at the hot and dusty station.

'Yaas,' he drawled, fixing his eye-glass, and lighting a cigarette. 'I've—p'f—managed to get away. Maharaj seems to have thought—p'f—it would be cheapah in the end to pay me out than to keep me.'

'You don't mean to say he offered to lend you money?' I cried.

'No; not exactly that: I offahed to borrow it.'

'From the man you call a nigger?'

His smile spread broader over his face than ever. 'Well, we borrow from the Jews, yah know,' he said pleasantly, 'so why the jooce shouldn't we borrow from the heathen, also? Spoiling the Egyptians, don't yah see?—the same as we used to read about in the Scripchah when we were innocent kiddies. Like marriage, quite. You borrow in haste—and repay at leisure.'

He strolled off and took his seat. I was glad to get rid of him at the main line junction.

In accordance with my usual merciful custom, I spare you the details of our visit to Agra, Muttra, Benares. At Calcutta, Elsie left me. Her health was now quite restored, dear little soul—I felt I had done that one good thing in life if no other—and she could no longer withstand the higher mathematics, which were beckoning her to London with invisible fingers. For myself, having so far accomplished my original design of going round the world with twopence in my pocket, I could not bear to draw back at half the circuit; and Mr. Elworthy having willingly consented to my return by Singapore and Yokohama, I set out alone on my homeward journey.

Harold wrote me from London that all was going well. He had found the will which I drew up at Florence in his uncle's escritoire, and everything was left to him; but he trusted, in spite of this untoward circumstance, long absence might have altered my determination. 'Dear Lois,' he wrote, 'I *expect* you to come back to England and marry me!'

I was brief, but categorical. Nothing, meanwhile, had altered my resolve. I did not wish to be considered mercenary. While he was rich and honoured, I could never take him. If, some day, fortune frowned—but, there—let us not forestall the feet of calamity: let us await contingencies.

Still, I was heavy in heart. If only it had been otherwise! To say the truth, I should be thrown away on a millionaire; but just think what a splendid managing wife a girl like me would have made for a penniless pauper!

At Yokohama, however, while I dawdled in curiosity shops, a telegram from Harold startled me into seriousness. My chance at last! I knew what it meant; that villain Higginson!

'Come home at once. I want your evidence to clear my character. Southminster opposes the will as a forgery. He has a strong case; the experts are with him.'

Forgery! That was clever. I never thought of that. I suspected them of trying to forge a will of their own; but to upset the real one—to throw the burden of suspicion on Harold's shoulders—how much subtler and craftier!

I saw at a glance it gave them every advantage. In the first place, it put Harold virtually in the place of the accused, and compelled him to defend instead of attacking—an attitude which prejudices people against one from the outset. Then, again, it implied positive criminality on his part, and so allowed Lord Southminster to assume the air of injured innocence. The eldest son of the eldest brother unjustly set aside by the scheming machinations of an unscrupulous cousin! Primogeniture, the ingrained English love for keeping up the dignity of a noble family, the prejudice in favour of the direct male line as against the female—all were astutely utilised in Lord Southminster's interest. But worst of all, it was *I* who had type-written the will—I, a friend of Harold's, a woman whom Lord Southminster would doubtless try to exhibit as his *fiancée*. I saw at once how much like conspiracy it looked: Harold and I had agreed together to concoct a false document, and Harold had forged his uncle's signature to it. Could a British jury doubt when a Lord declared it?

Fortunately, I was just in time to catch the Canadian steamer from Japan to Vancouver. But, oh, the endless breadth of that broad Pacific! How time seemed to lag, as each day one rose in the morning, in the midst of space; blue sky overhead; behind one, the hard horizon; in front of one, the hard horizon; and nothing else visible: then steamed on all day, to arrive at night, where?—why, in the midst of space; starry sky overhead; behind one, the dim horizon; in front of one, the dim horizon; and nothing else visible. The Nile was child's play to it.

Day after day we steamed, and night after night were still where we began—in the centre of the sea, no farther from our starting-point, no nearer to our goal, yet for ever steaming. It was endlessly wearisome; who could say what might be happening meanwhile in England?

At last, after months, as it seemed, of this slow torture, we reached Vancouver. There, in the raw new town, a telegram awaited me. 'Glad to hear you are coming. Make all haste. You may be just in time to arrive for the trial.'

Just in time! I would not waste a moment. I caught the first train on the Canadian Pacific, and travelled straight through, day and night, to Montreal and Quebec, without one hour's interval.

I cannot describe to you that journey across a continent I had never before seen. It was endless and hopeless. I only know that we crawled up the Rocky Mountains and the Selkirk Range, over spider-like viaducts, with interminable effort, and that the prairies were just the broad Pacific over again. They rolled on for ever. But we did reach Quebec—in time we reached it; and we caught by an hour the first liner to Liverpool.

At Prince's Landing-stage another telegram awaited me. 'Come on at once. Case now proceeding. Harold is in court. We need your evidence.—GEORGINA FAWLEY.'

I might still be in time to vindicate Harold's character.

At Euston, to my surprise, I was met not only by my dear cantankerous old lady, but also by my friend, the magnificent Maharajah, dressed this time in a frock-coat and silk hat of Bond Street glossiness.

'What has brought you to England?' I asked, astonished. 'The Jubilee?'

He smiled, and showed his two fine rows of white teeth. 'That, nominally. In reality, the cricket season (I play for Berks). But most of all, to see dear Tillington safe through this trouble.'

'He's a brick!' Lady Georgina cried with enthusiasm. 'A regular brick, my dear Lois! His carriage is waiting outside to take you up to my house. He has stood by Harold—well, like a Christian!'

'Or a Hindu,' the Maharajah corrected, smiling.

'And how have you been all this time, dear Lady Georgina?' I asked, hardly daring to inquire about what was nearest to my soul—Harold.

The cantankerous old lady knitted her brows in a familiar fashion. 'Oh, my dear, don't ask: I haven't known a happy hour since you left me in Switzerland. Lois, I shall never be happy again without you! It would pay me to give you a retaining fee of a thousand a year—honour bright, it would, I assure you. What I've suffered from the Gretchens since you've been in the East has only been equalled by what I've suffered from the Mary Annes and the Célestines. Not a hair left on my scalp; not one hair, I declare to you. They've made my head into a *tabula rasa* for the various restorers. George R. Sims and Mrs. S. A. Allen are going to fight it out between them. My dear, I wish *you* could take my maid's place; I've always said——'

I finished the speech for her. 'A lady can do better whatever she turns her hand to than any of these hussies.'

She nodded. 'And why? Because her hands *are* hands; while as
for the Gretchens and the Mary Annes, "paws" is the only word
one can honestly apply to them. Then, on top of it all comes
this trouble about Harold. So distressing, isn't it? You see, at the
point which the matter has reached, it's simply impossible to save
Harold's reputation without wrecking Southminster's. Pretty position that for a respectable family! The Ashursts hitherto have been
quite respectable: a co-respondent or two, perhaps, but never anything serious. Now, either Southminster sends Harold to prison,
or Harold sends Southminster. There's a nice sort of dilemma! I
always knew Kynaston's boys were born fools; but to find they're
born knaves, too, is hard on an old woman in her hairless dotage.
However, *you've* come, my child, and *you'll* soon set things right.
You're the one person on earth I can trust in this matter.'

Harold go to prison! My head reeled at the thought. I staggered out into the open air, and took my seat mechanically in the
Maharajah's carriage. All London swam before me. After so many
months' absence, the polychromatic decorations of our English
streets, looming up through the smoke, seemed both strange and
familiar. I drove through the first half mile with a vague consciousness that Lipton's tea is the perfection of cocoa and matchless
for the complexion, but that it dyes all colours, and won't wash
clothes.

After a while, however, I woke up to the full terror of the situation. 'Where are you taking me?' I inquired.

'To my house, dear,' Lady Georgina answered, looking anxiously at me; for my face was bloodless.

'No, that won't do,' I answered. 'My cue must be now to
keep myself as aloof as possible from Harold and Harold's back-
ers. I must put up at an hotel. It will sound so much better in
cross-examination.'

'She's quite right,' the Maharajah broke in, with sudden conviction. 'One must block every ball with these nasty swift bowlers.'

'Where's Harold?' I asked, after another pause. 'Why didn't he
come to meet me?'

'My dear, how could he? He's under examination. A cross-eyed
Q.C. with an odious leer. Southminster's chosen the biggest bully
at the Bar to support his contention.'

'Drive to some hotel in the Jermyn Street district,' I cried to the Maharajah's coachman. 'That will be handy for the law courts.' He touched his hat and turned. In a sort of dickey behind sat two gorgeous-turbaned Rajput servants.

That evening Harold came round to visit me at my rooms. I could see he was much agitated. Things had gone very badly. Lady Georgina was there; she had stopped to dine with me, dear old thing, lest I should feel lonely and give way; so had Elsie Petheridge. Mr. Elworthy sent a telegram of welcome from Devonshire. I knew at least that my friends were rallying round me in this hour of trial. The kind Maharajah himself would have come too, if I had allowed him, but I thought it inexpedient. They explained everything to me. Harold had propounded Mr. Ashurst's will—the one I drew up at Florence—and had asked for probate. Lord Southminster intervened and opposed the grant of probate on the ground that the signatures were forgeries. He propounded instead another will, drawn some twenty years earlier, when they were both children, duly executed at the time, and undoubtedly genuine; in it, testator left everything without reserve to the eldest son of his eldest brother, Lord Kynaston.

'Marmy didn't know in those days that Kynaston's sons would all grow up fools,' Lady Georgina said tartly. 'Besides which, that was before the poor dear soul took to plunging on the Stock Exchange and made his money. He had nothing to leave, then, but his best silk hat and a few paltry hundreds. Afterwards, when he'd feathered his nest in soap and cocoa, he discovered that Bertie— that's Lord Southminster—was a first-class idiot. Marmy never liked Southminster, nor Southminster Marmy. For after all, with all his faults, Marmy *was* a gentleman; while Bertie—well, my dear, we needn't put a name to it. So he altered his will, as you know, when he saw the sort of man Southminster turned out, and left practically everything he possessed to Harold.'

'Who are the witnesses to the will?' I asked.

'There's the trouble. Who do you think? Why, Higginson's sister, who was Marmy's *masseuse*, and a waiter—Franz Markheim—at the hotel at Florence, who's dead, they say—or, at least, not forthcoming.'

'And Higginson's sister forswears her signature,' Harold added gloomily; 'while the experts are, most of them, dead against the genuineness of my uncle's.'

'That's clever,' I said, leaning back, and taking it in slowly. 'Higginson's sister! How well they've worked it! They couldn't prevent Mr. Ashurst from making his will, but they managed to supply their own tainted witnesses! If it had been Higginson himself, now, he'd have had to be cross-examined; and in cross-examination, of course, we could have shaken his credit, by bringing up the episodes of the Count de Laroche-sur-Loiret and Dr. Fortescue-Langley. But his sister! What's she like? Have you anything against her?'

'My dear,' Lady Georgina cried, 'there the rogue has bested us. Isn't it just like him? What do you suppose he has done? Why, provided himself with a sister of tried respectability and blameless character.'

'And she denies that it is her handwriting?' I asked.

'Declares on her Bible oath she never signed the document!'

I was fairly puzzled. It was a stupendously clever dodge. Higginson must have trained up his sister for forty years in the ways of wickedness, yet held her in reserve for this supreme moment.

'And where is Higginson?' I asked.

Lady Georgina broke into a hysterical laugh. 'Where is he, my dear? That's the question. With consummate strategy, the wretch has disappeared into space at the last moment.'

'That's artful again,' I said. 'His presence could only damage their case. I can see, of course, Lord Southminster has no need of him.'

'Southminster's the wiliest fool that ever lived,' Harold broke out bitterly. 'Under that mask of imbecility, he's a fox for trickiness.'

I bit my lip. 'Well, if you succeed in evading him,' I said, 'you will have cleared your character. And if you don't—then, Harold, our time will have come; you will have your longed-for chance of trying me.'

'That won't do me much good,' he answered, 'if I have to wait fourteen years for you—at Portland.'

Next morning, in court, I heard Harold's cross-examination. He described exactly where he had found the contested will in his uncle's escritoire. The cross-eyed Q.C, a heavy man with bloated features and a bulbous nose, begged him, with one fat uplifted fore-finger, to be very careful. How did he know where to look for it?

'Because I knew the house well: I knew where my uncle was likely to keep his valuables.'

'Oh, indeed; not because you had put it there?'

The court rang with laughter. My face grew crimson.

After an hour or two of fencing, Harold was dismissed. He stood down, baffled. Counsel recalled Lord Southminster.

The pea-green young man, stepping briskly up, gazed about him, open-mouthed, with a vacant stare. The look of cunning on his face was carefully suppressed. He wore, on the contrary, an air of injured innocence combined with an eye-glass.

'You did not put this will in the drawer where Mr. Tillington found it, did you?' counsel asked.

The pea-green young man laughed. 'No, I certainly didn't put it theah. My cousin Harold was man in possession. He took jolly good care I didn't come neah the premises.'

'Do you think you could forge a will if you tried?

Lord Southminster laughed. 'No, I don't,' he answered, with a well-assumed naïveté. 'That's just the difference between us, don't yah know. I'm what they call a fool, and my cousin Harold's a pre-cious clevah fellah.'

There was another loud laugh.

'That's not evidence,' the judge observed, severely.

It was not. But it told far more than much that was. It told strongly against Harold.

'Besides,' Lord Southminster continued, with engaging frank-ness, 'if I forged a will at all, I'd take jolly good care to forge it in my own favah.'

My turn came next. Our counsel handed me the incriminated will. 'Did you draw up this document?' he asked.

I looked at it closely. The paper bore our Florentine water-mark, and was written with a Spread-Eagle. 'I type-wrote it,' I answered, gazing at it with care to make sure I recognised it.

Our counsel's business was to uphold the will, not to cast asper-sions upon it. He was evidently annoyed at my close examination. 'You have no doubts about it?' he said, trying to prompt me.

I hesitated. 'No, no doubts,' I answered, turning over the sheet and inspecting it still closer. 'I type-wrote it at Florence.'

'Do you recognise that signature as Mr. Marmaduke Ashurst's?' he went on.

I stared at it. Was it his? It was like it, certainly. Yet that *k*? and those *s*'s? I almost wondered.

Counsel was obviously annoyed at my hesitation. He thought I was playing into the enemy's hands. 'Is it his, or is it not?' he inquired again, testily.

'It is his,' I answered. Yet I own I was troubled.

He asked many questions about the circumstances of the interview when I took down the will. I answered them all. But I vaguely felt he and I were at cross-purposes. I grew almost as uncomfortable under his gaze as if he had been examining me in the interest of the other side. He managed to fluster me. As a witness for Harold, I was a grotesque failure.

Then the cross-eyed Q.C, rising and shaking his huge bulk, began to cross-examine me. 'Where did you type-write this thing, do you say?' he said, pointing to it contemptuously.

'In my office at Florence.'

'Yes, I understand; you had an office at Florence—after you gave up retailing bicycles on the public roads; and you had a partner, I think—a Miss Petherick, or Petherton, or Pennyfarthing, or something?'

'Miss Petheridge,' I corrected, while the court tittered.

'Ah, Petheridge, you call it! Well, now, answer this question carefully. Did your Miss Petheridge hear Mr. Ashurst dictate the terms of his last will and testament?'

'No,' I answered. 'The interview was of a strictly confidential character. Mr. Ashurst took me aside into the back room at our office.'

'Oh, he took you aside? Confidential? Well, *now* we're getting at it. And did anybody but yourself see or hear any part whatsoever of this precious document?'

'Certainly not,' I replied. 'It was a private matter.'

'Private! oh, very! Nobody else saw it. Did Mr. Ashurst take it away from the office in person?'

'No; he sent his courier for it.'

'His courier? The man Higginson?'

'Yes; but I refused to give it to Higginson. I took it myself that night to the hotel where Mr. Ashurst was stopping.'

'Ah! You took it yourself. So the only other person who knows anything at first hand about the existence of the alleged will is this person Higginson?'

'Miss Petheridge knows,' I said, flushing. 'At the time, I told her of it.'

'Oh, *you* told her. Well, that doesn't help us much. If what you are swearing isn't true—remember, you are on your oath—what you told Miss Petherick or Petheridge or Pennyfarthing, "at the time," can hardly be regarded as corroborative evidence. Your word then and your word now are just equally valuable—or equally worthless. The only person who knows beside yourself is Higginson. Now, I ask you, *where* is Higginson? *Are* you going to produce him?'

The wicked cunning of it struck me dumb. They were keeping him away, and then using his absence to cast doubts on my veracity. 'Stop!' I cried, taken aback, 'Higginson is well known to be a rogue, and he is keeping away lest he may damage your side. I know nothing of Higginson.'

'Yes, I'm coming to that in good time. Don't be afraid that we're going to pass over Higginson. You admit this man is a man of bad character. Now, what do you know of him?'

I told the stories of the Count and of Dr. Fortescue-Langley.

The cross-eyed cross-examiner leant across towards me and leered. 'And this is the man,' he exclaimed, with a triumphant air, 'whose sister you pretended you had got to sign this precious document of yours?'

'Whom Mr. Ashurst got to sign it,' I answered, red-hot. 'It is not *my* document.'

'And you have heard that she swears it is not her signature at all?'

'So they tell me. She is Higginson's sister. For all I know, she may be prepared to swear, or to forswear, anything.'

'Don't cast doubt upon our witnesses without cause! Miss Higginson is an eminently respectable woman. You gave this document to Mr. Ashurst, you say. There your knowledge of it ends. A signature is placed on it which is not his, as our experts testify. It purports to be witnessed by a Swiss waiter, who is not forthcoming, and who is asserted to be dead, as well as by a nurse who denies her signature. And the only other person who knows of its existence before Mr. Tillington "discovers" it in his uncle's desk is—the missing man Higginson. Is that, or is it not, the truth of the matter?'

'I suppose so,' I said, baffled.

'Well, now, as to this man Higginson. He first appears upon the scene, so far as you are concerned, on the day when you travelled from London to Schlangenbad?'

'That is so,' I answered.

'And he nearly succeeded then in stealing Lady Georgina Fawley's jewel-case?'

'He nearly took it, but I saved it.' And I explained the circumstance.

The cross-eyed Q.C. held his fat sides with his hands, looking incredulously at me, and smiled. His vast width of waistcoat shook with silent merriment. 'You are a very clever young lady,' he murmured. 'You can explain away anything. But don't you think it just as likely that it was a plot between you two, and that owing to some mistake the plot came off unsuccessful?'

'I do not,' I cried, crimson. 'I never saw the Count before that morning.'

He tried another tack. 'Still, wherever you went, this man Higginson—the only other person, you admit, who knows about the previous existence of the will—turned up simultaneously. He was always turning up—at the same place that you did. He turned up at Lucerne, as a faith-healer, didn't he?'

'If you will allow me to explain,' I cried, biting my lip.

He bowed, all blandness. 'Oh, certainly,' he murmured. 'Explain away everything!'

I explained, but of course he had discounted and damaged my explanation.

He made no comment. 'And then,' he went on, with his hands on his hips, and his obtrusive rotundity, 'he turned up at Florence, as courier to Mr. Ashurst, at the very date when this so-called will was being concocted?'

'He was at Florence when Mr. Ashurst dictated it to me,' I
answered, growing desperate.

'You admit he was in Florence. Good! Once more he turned up
in India with my client, Lord Southminster, upon whose youth and
inexperience he had managed to impose himself. And he carried
him off, did he not, by one of these strange coincidences to which
you are peculiarly liable, on the very same steamer on which *you*
happened to be travelling?'

'Lord Southminster told me he took Higginson with him
because a rogue suited his book,' I answered, warmly.

'Will you swear his lordship didn't say "*the* rogue suited his
book"—which is quite another thing?' the Q.C. asked blandly.

'I will swear he did not,' I replied. 'I have correctly reported
him.'

'Then I congratulate you, young lady, on your excellent memory.
My lud, will you allow me later to recall Lord Southminster to testify on this point?'

The judge nodded.

'Now, once more, as to your relations with the various mem-
bers of the Ashurst family. You introduced yourself to Lady
Georgina Fawley, I believe, quite casually, on a seat in Kensington
Gardens?'

'That is true,' I answered.

'You had never seen her before?'

'Never.'

'And you promptly offered to go with her as her lady's maid to
Schlangenbad in Germany?'

'In place of her lady's maid, for one week,' I answered.

'Ah; a delicate distinction! "In place of her lady's maid." You
are a lady, I believe; an officer's daughter, you told us; educated at
Girton?'

'So I have said already,' I replied, crimson.

'And you stick to it? By all means. Tell—the truth—and stick
to it. It's always safest. Now, don't you think it was rather an odd
thing for an officer's daughter to do—to run about Germany as
maid to a lady of title?'

I tried to explain once more; but the jury smiled. You can't
justify originality to a British jury. Why, they would send you to

prison at once for that alone, if they made the laws as well as dispensing them.

He passed on after a while to another topic. 'I think you have boasted more than once in society that when you first met Lady Georgina Fawley you had twopence in your pocket to go round the world with?'

'I had,' I answered—'and I went round the world with it.'

'Exactly. I'm getting there in time. With it—and other things. A few months later, more or less, you were touring up the Nile in your steam dahabeeah, and in the lap of luxury; you were taking saloon-carriages on Indian railways, weren't you?'

I explained again. 'The dahabeeah was in the service of the *Daily Telephone*,' I answered. 'I became a journalist.'

He cross-questioned me about that. 'Then I am to understand,' he said at last, leaning forward with all his waistcoat, 'that you sprang yourself upon Mr. Elworthy at sight, pretty much as you sprang yourself upon Lady Georgina Fawley?'

'We arranged matters quickly,' I admitted. The dexterous wretch was making my strongest points all tell against me.

'H'm! Well, he was a man: and you will admit, I suppose,' fingering his smooth fat chin, 'that you are a lady of—what is the stock phrase the reporters use?—considerable personal attractions?'

'My Lord,' I said, turning to the Bench, 'I appeal to you. Has he the right to compel me to answer that question?'

The judge bowed slightly. 'The question requires no answer,' he said, with a quiet emphasis. I burned bright scarlet.

'Well, my lud, I defer to your ruling,' the cross-eyed cross-examiner continued, radiant. 'I go on to another point. When in India, I believe, you stopped for some time as a guest in the house of a native Maharajah.'

'Is that matter relevant?' the judge asked, sharply.

'My lud,' the Q.C. said, in his blandest voice, 'I am striving to suggest to the jury that this lady—the only person who ever beheld this so-called will till Mr. Harold Tillington—described in its terms as "Younger of Gledcliffe," whatever that may be—produced it out of his uncle's desk—I am striving to suggest that this lady is—my duty to my client compels me to say—an adventuress.'

He had uttered the word. I felt my character had not a leg left to stand upon before a British jury.

'I went there with my friend, Miss Petheridge——' I began.

'Oh, Miss Petheridge once more—you hunt in couples?'

'Accompanied and chaperoned by a married lady, the wife of a Major Balmossie, on the Bombay Staff Corps.'

'That was certainly prudent. One ought to be chaperoned. Can you produce the lady?'

'How is it possible?' I cried. 'Mrs. Balmossie is in India.'

'Yes; but the Maharajah, I understand, is in London?'

'That is true,' I answered.

'And he came to meet you on your arrival yesterday.'

'With Lady Georgina Fawley,' I cried, taken off my guard.

'Do you not consider it curious,' he asked, 'that these Higginsons and these Maharajahs should happen to follow you so closely round the world?—should happen to turn up wherever you do?'

'He came to be present at this trial,' I exclaimed.

'And so did you. I believe he met you at Euston last night, and drove you to your hotel in his private carriage.'

'With Lady Georgina Fawley,' I answered, once more.

'And Lady Georgina is on Mr. Tillington's side, I fancy? Ah yes, I thought so. And Mr. Tillington also called to see you; and likewise Miss Petherick—I beg your pardon, Petheridge. We must be strictly accurate—where Miss Petheridge is concerned. And, in fact, you had quite a little family party.'

'My friends were glad to see me back again,' I murmured.

He sprang a fresh innuendo. 'But Mr. Tillington did not resent your visit to this gallant Maharajah?'

'Certainly not,' I cried, bridling. 'Why should he?'

'Oh, we're getting to that too. Now answer me this carefully. We want to find out what interest you might have, supposing a will were forged, on either side, in arranging its terms. We want to find out just who would benefit by it. Please reply to this question, yes or no, without prevarication. Are you or are you not conditionally engaged to Mr. Harold Tillington?'

'If I might explain——' I began, quivering.

He sneered. 'You have a genius for explaining, we are aware. Answer me first, yes or no; we will qualify afterward.'

I glanced appealingly at the judge. He was adamant. 'Answer as counsel directs you, witness,' he said, sternly.

'Yes, I am,' I faltered. 'But——'

'Excuse me one moment. You promised to marry him conditionally upon the result of Mr. Ashurst's testamentary dispositions?'

'I did,' I answered; 'but——'

My explanation was drowned in roars of laughter, in which the judge joined, in spite of himself. When the mirth in court had subsided a little, I went on: 'I told Mr. Tillington I would only marry him in case he was poor and without expectations. If he inherited Mr. Marmaduke Ashurst's money, I could never be his wife.' I said it proudly.

The cross-eyed Q.C. drew himself up and let his rotundity take care of itself. 'Do you take me,' he inquired, 'for one of Her Majesty's horse-marines?'

There was another roar of laughter—feebly suppressed by a judicial frown—and I slank away, annihilated.

'You can go,' my persecutor said. 'I think we have got—well, everything we wanted from you. You promised to marry him, if all went ill! That is a delicate feminine way of putting it. Women like these equivocations. They relieve one from the onus of speaking frankly.'

I stood down from the box, feeling, for the first time in my life, conscious of having scored an ignominious failure.

Our counsel did not care to re-examine me; I recognised that it would be useless. The hateful Q.C. had put all my history in such an odious light that explanation could only make matters worse— it must savour of apology. The jury could never understand my point of view. It could never be made to see that there are adventuresses and adventuresses.

Then came the final speeches on either side. Harold's advocate said the best he could in favour of the will our party propounded; but his best was bad; and what galled me most was this—I could see he himself did not believe in its genuineness. His speech amounted to little more than a perfunctory attempt to put the most favourable face on a probable forgery.

As for the cross-eyed Q.C., he rose to reply with humorous confidence. Swaying his big body to and fro, he crumpled our will and our case in his fat fingers like so much flimsy tissue-paper. Mr. Ashurst had made a disposition of his property twenty years ago—the right disposition, the natural disposition; he had left the bulk of it as childless English gentlemen have ever been wont to leave their wealth—to the eldest son of the eldest son of his family. The Honourable Marmaduke Courtney Ashurst, the testator, was the scion of a great house, which recent agricultural changes, he regretted to say, had relatively impoverished; he had come to the succour of that great house, as such a scion should, with his property acquired by honest industry elsewhere. It was fitting and reasonable that Mr. Ashurst should wish to see the Kynaston peerage regain, in the person of the amiable and accomplished young nobleman whom he had the honour to represent, some portion of its ancient dignity and splendour.

But jealousy and greed intervened. (Here he frowned at Harold.) Mr. Harold Tillington, the son of one of Mr. Ashurst's married sisters, cast longing eyes, as he had tried to suggest to them, on his cousin Lord Southminster's natural heritage. The result, he feared, was an unnatural intrigue. Mr. Harold Tillington formed the acquaintance of a young lady—should we say young lady? (he withered me with his glance)—well, yes, a lady, indeed, by birth and education, but an adventuress by choice—a lady who, brought up in a respectable, though not (he must admit) a distinguished sphere, had lowered herself by accepting the position of a lady's maid, and had trafficked in patent American cycles on the public high-roads of Germany and Switzerland. This clever and designing woman (he would grant her ability—he would grant her good looks) had fascinated Mr. Tillington—that was the theory he ventured to lay before the jury to-day; and the jury would see for themselves that whatever else the young lady might be, she had distinctly a certain outer gift of fascination. It was for them to decide whether Miss Lois Cayley had or had not suggested to Mr. Harold Tillington the design of substituting a forged will for Mr. Marmaduke Ashurst's undeniable testament. He would point out to them her singular connection with the missing man Higginson, whom the young lady herself described as a rogue, and from whom she had done her very best to dissociate herself in this court—but ineffectually. Wherever Miss Cayley went, the man Higginson went independently. Such frequent recurrences, such apt juxtapositions, could hardly be set down to mere accidental coincidence.

He went on to insinuate that Higginson and I had concocted the disputed will between us; that we had passed it on to our fellow-conspirator, Harold; and that Harold had forged his uncle's signature to it, and had appended those of the two supposed witnesses. But who, now, were these witnesses? One, Franz Markheim, was dead or missing; dead men tell no tales: the other was obviously suggested by Higginson. It was his own sister. Perhaps he forged her name to the document. Doubtless he thought that family feeling would induce her, when it came to the pinch, to accept and endorse her brother's lie; nay, he might even have been foolish enough to suppose that this cock-and-bull will would not be disputed. If so, he and his master had reckoned without Lord Southminster, a gentleman who concealed beneath the careless exterior of a man of fashion the solid intelligence of a man of affairs, and the hard head of a man not to be lightly cheated in matters of business.

The alleged will had thus not a leg to stand upon. It was 'type-written' (save the mark!) 'from dictation' at Florence, by whom? By the lady who had most to gain from its success—the lady who was to be transformed from a shady adventuress, tossed about between Irish doctors and Hindu Maharajahs, into the lawful wife of a wealthy diplomatist of noble family, on one condition only—if this pretended will could be satisfactorily established. The signatures were forgeries, as shown by the expert evidence, and also by the oath of the one surviving witness.

The will left all the estate—practically—to Mr. Harold Tillington, and five hundred pounds to whom?—why, to the accomplice Higginson. The minor bequests the Q.C. regarded as ingenious inventions, pure play of fancy, 'intended to give artistic verisimilitude,' as Pooh-Bah says in the opera, 'to an otherwise bald and unconvincing narrative.' The fads, it was true, were known fads of Mr. Ashurst's; but what sort of fads? Bimetallism? Anglo-Israel? No, braces and shoe-horns—clearly the kind that would best be known to a courier like Higginson, the sole begetter, he believed, of this nefarious conspiracy.

The cross-eyed Q.C., lifting his fat right hand in solemn adjuration, called upon the jury confidently to set aside this ridiculous fabrication, and declare for a will of undoubted genuineness, a will drawn up in London by a firm of eminent solicitors, and preserved ever since by the testator's bankers. It would then be for his lordship to decide whether in the public interest he should recommend the Crown to prosecute on a charge of forgery the clumsy fabricator of this preposterous document.

The judge summed up—strongly in favour of Lord Southminster's will. If the jury believed the experts and Miss Higginson, one verdict alone was possible. The jury retired for three minutes only. It was a foregone conclusion. They found for Lord Southminster. The judge, looking grave, concurred in their finding. A most proper verdict. And he considered it would be the duty of the Public Prosecutor to pursue Mr. Harold Tillington on the charge of forgery.

I reeled where I sat. Then I looked round for Harold.

He had slipped from the court, unseen, during counsel's address, some minutes earlier!

That distressed me more than anything else on that dreadful day. I wished he had stood up in his place like a man to face this vile and cruel conspiracy.

I walked out slowly, supported by Lady Georgina, who was as white as a ghost herself, but very straight and scornful. I always knew Southminster was a fool,' she said aloud; 'I always knew he was a sneak; but I did not know till now he was also a particularly bad type of criminal.'

On the steps of the court, the pea-green young man met us. His air was jaunty. 'Well, I was right, yah see,' he said, smiling and withdrawing his cigarette. 'You backed the wrong fellah! I told you I'd win. I won't say moah now; this is not the time or place to recur to that subject; but, by-and-by, you'll come round; you'll think bettah of it still; you'll back the winnah!'

I wished I were a man, that I might have the pleasure of kicking him.

We drove back to my hotel and waited for Harold. To my

horror and alarm, he never came near us. I might almost have doubted him—if he had not been Harold.

I waited and waited. He did not come at all. He sent no word, no message. And all that evening we heard the newsboys shouting at the top of their voice in the street, 'Extra Speshul! the Ashurst Will Kise; Sensational Developments! Mysterious Disappearance of Mr. 'Arold Tillington.'

CHAPTER XI

THE ADVENTURE OF THE ORIENTAL ATTENDANT

I DID not sleep that night. Next morning, I rose very early from a restless bed with a dry, hot mouth, and a general feeling that the solid earth had failed beneath me.

Still no news from Harold! It was cruel, I thought. My faith almost flagged. He was a man and should be brave. How could he run away and hide himself at such a time? Even if I set my own anxiety aside, just think to what serious misapprehension it laid him open!

I sent out for the morning papers. They were full of Harold. Rumours, rumours, rumours! Mr. Tillington had deliberately chosen to put himself in the wrong by disappearing mysteriously at the last moment. He had only himself to blame if the worst interpretation were put upon his action. But the police were on his track; Scotland Yard had 'a clue': it was confidently expected an arrest would be made before evening at latest. As to details, authorities differed. The officials of the Great Western Railway at Paddington were convinced that Mr. Tillington had started, alone and undisguised, by the night express for Exeter. The South-Eastern inspectors at Charing Cross, on the other hand, were equally certain that he had slipped away with a false beard, in company with his 'accomplice' Higginson, by the 8.15 P.M. to Paris. Everybody took it for granted, however, that he had left London.

Conjecture played with various ultimate destinations—Spain, Morocco, Sicily, the Argentine. In Italy, said the *Chronicle*, he might lurk for a while—he spoke Italian fluently, and could manage to put up at tiny *osterie* in out-of-the-way places seldom visited by Englishmen. He might try Albania, said the *Morning Post*, airing its exclusive 'society' information: he had often hunted there, and might in turn be hunted. He would probably attempt to slink away to some remote spot in the Carpathians or the Balkans, said the *Daily News*, quite proud of its geography. Still, wherever he went, leaden-footed justice in this age, said the *Times*, must surely over-

take him. The day of universal extradition had dawned; we had
no more Alsatias: even the Argentine itself gives up its rogues—at
last; not an asylum for crime remains in Europe, not a refuge in
Asia, Africa, America, Australia, or the Pacific Islands.

I noted with a shudder of horror that all the papers alike took
his guilt as certain. In spite of a few decent pretences at not pre-
judging an untried cause, they treated him already as the detected
criminal, the fugitive from justice. I sat in my little sitting-room
at the hotel in Jermyn Street, a limp rag, looking idly out of the
window with swimming eyes, and waiting for Lady Georgina. It
was early, too early, but—oh, why didn't she come! Unless *somebody* soon sympathised with me, my heart would break under this
load of loneliness!

Presently, as I looked out on the sloppy morning street, I was
vaguely aware through the mist that floated before my dry eyes
(for tears were denied me) of a very grand carriage driving up
to the doorway—the porch with the four wooden Ionic pillars. I
took no heed of it. I was too heart-sick for observation. My life
was wrecked, and Harold's with it. Yet, dimly through the mist,
I became conscious after a while that the carriage was that of an
Indian prince; I could see the black faces, the white turbans, the
gold brocades of the attendants in the dickey. Then it came home
to me with a pang that this was the Maharajah.

It was kindly meant; yet after all that had been insinuated in
court the day before, I was by no means overpleased that his dusky
Highness should come to call upon me. Walls have eyes and ears.
Reporters were hanging about all over London, eager to distin-
guish themselves by successful eavesdropping. They would note,
with brisk innuendoes after their kind, how 'the Maharajah of
Moozuffernuggar called early in the day on Miss Lois Cayley, with
whom he remained for at least half an hour in close consultation.'
I had half a mind to send down a message that I could not see him.
My face still burned with the undeserved shame of the cross-eyed
Q.C.'s unspeakable suggestions.

Before I could make my mind up, however, I saw to my surprise
that the Maharajah did not propose to come in himself. He leaned
back in his place with his lordly Eastern air, and waited, looking
down on the gapers in the street, while one of the two gorgeous

attendants in the dickey descended obsequiously to receive his orders. The man was dressed as usual in rich Oriental stuffs, and wore his full white turban swathed in folds round his head. I could not see his features. He bent forward respectfully with Oriental suppleness to take his Highness's orders. Then, receiving a card and bowing low, he entered the porch with the wooden Ionic pillars, and disappeared within, while the Maharajah folded his hands and seemed to resign himself to a temporary Nirvana.

A minute later, a knock sounded on my door. 'Come in!' I said, faintly; and the messenger entered.

I turned and faced him. The blood rushed to my cheek. 'Harold!' I cried, darting forward. My joy overcame me. He folded me in his arms. I allowed him, unreproved. For the first time he kissed me. I did not shrink from it.

Then I stood away a little and gazed at him. Even at that crucial moment of doubt and fear, I could not help noticing how admirably he made up as a handsome young Rajput. Three years earlier, at Schlangenbad, I remembered, he had struck me as strangely Oriental-looking: he had the features of a high-born Indian gentleman, without the complexion. His large, poetical eyes, his regular, oval face, his even teeth, his mouth and moustache, all vaguely recalled the highest type of the Eastern temperament. Now, he had blackened his face and hands with some permanent stain—Indian ink, I learned later—and the resemblance to a Rajput chief was positively startling. In his gold brocade and ample white turban, no passer-by, I felt sure, would ever have dreamt of doubting him.

'Then you knew me at once?' he said, holding my face between his hands. 'That's bad, darling! I flattered myself I had transformed my face into the complete Indian.'

'Love has sharp eyes,' I answered. 'It can see through brick walls. But the disguise is perfect. No one else would detect you.'

'Love is blind, I thought.'

'Not where it ought to see. There, it pierces everything. I knew you instantly, Harold. But all London, I am sure, would pass you by, unknown. You are absolute Orient.'

'That's well; for all London is looking for me,' he answered, bitterly. 'The streets bristle with detectives. Southminster's knaveries

have won the day. So I have tried this disguise. Otherwise, I should
have been arrested the moment the jury brought in their verdict.'

'And why were you not?' I asked, drawing back. 'Oh, Harold,
I trust you; but why did you disappear and make all the world
believe you admitted yourself guilty?'

He opened his arms. 'Can't you guess?' he cried, holding them
out to me.

I nestled in them once more; but I answered through my
tears—I had found tears now—'No Harold; it baffles me.'

'You remember what you promised me?' he murmured, leaning over me and clasping me. 'If ever I were poor, friendless,
hunted—you would marry me. Now the opportunity has come
when we can both prove ourselves. To-day, except you and dear
Georgey, I haven't a friend in the world. Everyone else has turned
against me. Southminster holds the field. I am a suspected forger;
in a very few days I shall doubtless be a convicted felon. Unjustly, as
you know; yet still—we must face it—a convicted felon. So I have
come to claim you. I have come to ask you now, in this moment of
despair, will you keep your promise?'

I lifted my face to his. He bent over it trembling. I whispered
the words in his ear. 'Yes, Harold, I will keep it. I have always loved
you. And now I will marry you.'

'I knew you would!' he cried, and pressed me to his bosom.

We sat for some minutes, holding each other's hands, and
saying nothing; we were too full of thought for words. Then, suddenly, Harold roused himself. 'We must make haste, darling,' he
cried. 'We are keeping Partab outside, and every minute is precious, every minute's delay dangerous. We ought to go down at
once. Partab's carriage is waiting at the door for us.'

'Go down?' I exclaimed, clinging to him. 'How? Why? I don't
understand. What is your programme?'

'Ah, I forgot I hadn't explained to you! Listen here, dearest—
quick; I can waste no words over it. I said just now I had no friends
in the world but you and Georgey. That's not true, for dear old
Partab has stuck to me nobly. When all my English friends fell
away, the Rajput was true to me. He arranged all this; it was his
own idea; he foresaw what was coming. He urged me yesterday,
just before the verdict (when he saw my acquaintances beginning

to look askance), to slip quietly out of court, and make my way by unobtrusive roads to his house in Curzon Street. There, he darkened my face like his, and converted me to Hinduism. I don't suppose the disguise will serve me for more than a day or two; but it will last long enough for us to get safely away to Scotland.'

'Scotland?' I murmured. 'Then you mean to try a Scotch marriage?'

'It is the only thing possible. We must be married to-day, and in England, of course, we cannot do it. We would have to be called in church, or else to procure a license, either of which would involve disclosure of my identity. Besides, even the license would keep us waiting about for a day or two. In Scotland, on the other hand, we can be married at once. Partab's carriage is below, to take you to King's Cross. He is staunch as steel, dear fellow. Do you consent to go with me?'

My faculty for promptly making up such mind as I possess stood me once more in good stead. 'Implicitly,' I answered. 'Dear Harold, this calamity has its happy side—for without it, much as I love you, I could never have brought myself to marry you!'

'One moment,' he cried. 'Before you go, recollect, this step is irrevocable. You will marry a man who may be torn from you this evening, and from whom fourteen years of prison may separate you.'

'I know it,' I cried, through my tears. 'But—I shall be showing my confidence in you, my love for you.'

He kissed me once more, fervently. 'This makes amends for all,' he cried. 'Lois, to have won such a woman as you, I would go through it all a thousand times over. It was for this, and for this alone, that I hid myself last night. I wanted to give you the chance of showing me how much, how truly you loved me.'

'And after we are married?' I asked, trembling.

'I shall give myself up at once to the police in Edinburgh.'

I clung to him wistfully. My heart half urged me to urge him to escape. But I knew that was wrong. 'Give yourself up, then,' I said, sobbing. 'It is a brave man's place. You must stand your trial; and, come what will, I will strive to bear it with you.'

'I knew you would,' he cried. 'I was not mistaken in you.'

We embraced again, just once. It was little enough after those years of waiting.

'Now come!' he cried. 'Let us go.'

I drew back. 'Not with you, dearest,' I whispered. 'Not in the Maharajah's carriage. You must start by yourself. I will follow you at once, to King's Cross, in a hansom.'

He saw I was right. It would avoid suspicion, and it would prevent more scandal. He withdrew without a word. 'We meet,' I said, 'at ten, at King's Cross Station.'

I did not even wait to wash the tears from my eyes. All red as they were, I put on my hat and my little brown travelling jacket. I don't think I so much as glanced once at the glass. The seconds were precious. I saw the Maharajah drive away, with Harold in the dickey, arms crossed, imperturbable, Orientally silent. He looked the very counterpart of the Rajput by his side. Then I descended the stairs and walked out boldly. As I passed through the hall, the servants and the visitors stared at me and whispered. They spoke with nods and liftings of the eyebrows. I was aware that that morning I had achieved notoriety.

At Piccadilly Circus, I jumped of a sudden into a passing hansom. 'King's Cross!' I cried, as I mounted the step. 'Drive quick! I have no time to spare.' And, as the man drove off, I saw, by a convulsive dart of someone across the road, that I had given the slip to a disappointed reporter.

At the station I took a first-class ticket for Edinburgh. On the platform, the Maharajah and his attendants were waiting. He lifted his hat to me, though otherwise he took no overt notice. But I saw his keen eyes follow me down the train. Harold, in his Oriental dress, pretended not to observe me. One or two porters, and a few curious travellers, cast inquiring eyes on the Eastern prince, and made remarks about him to one another. 'That's the chap as was up yesterday in the Ashurst will kise!' said one lounger to his neighbour. But nobody seemed to look at Harold; his subordinate position secured him from curiosity. The Maharajah had always two Eastern servants, gorgeously dressed, in attendance; he had been a well-known figure in London society, and at Lord's and the Oval, for two or three seasons.

'Bloomin' fine cricketer!' one porter observed to his mate as he passed.

'Yuss; not so dusty for a nigger,' the other man replied. 'Fustrite bowler; but, Lord, he can't 'old a candle to good old Ranji.'

As for myself, nobody seemed to recognise me. I set this fact down to the fortunate circumstance that the evening papers had published rough wood-cuts which professed to be my portrait, and which naturally led the public to look out for a brazen-faced, raw-boned, hard-featured termagant.

I took my seat in a ladies' compartment by myself. As the train was about to start, Harold strolled up as if casually for a moment. 'You think it better so?' he queried, without moving his lips or seeming to look at me.

'Decidedly,' I answered. 'Go back to Partab. Don't come near me again till we get to Edinburgh. It is dangerous still. The police may at any moment hear we have started and stop us half-way; and now that we have once committed ourselves to this plan it would be fatal to be interrupted before we have got married.'

'You are right,' he cried; 'Lois, you are always right, somehow.'

I wished I could think so myself; but 'twas with serious misgivings that I felt the train roll out of the station.

Oh, that long journey north, alone, in a ladies' compartment—with the feeling that Harold was so near, yet so unapproachable: it was an endless agony. *He* had the Maharajah, who loved and admired him, to keep him from brooding; but I, left alone, and confined with my own fears, conjured up before my eyes every possible misfortune that Heaven could send us. I saw clearly now that if we failed in our purpose this journey would be taken by everyone for a flight, and would deepen the suspicion under which we both laboured. It would make me still more obviously a conspirator with Harold.

Whatever happened, we must strain every nerve to reach Scotland in safety, and then to get married, in order that Harold might immediately surrender himself.

At York, I noticed with a thrill of terror that a man in plain clothes, with the obtrusively unobtrusive air of a detective, looked carefully though casually into every carriage. I felt sure he was a spy, because of his marked outer jauntiness of demeanour, which hardly masked an underlying hang-dog expression of scrutiny. When he reached my place, he took a long, careless stare at me—a seemingly careless stare, which was yet brimful of the keenest observation. Then he paced slowly along the line of carriages, with a glance at each, till he arrived just opposite the Maharajah's compartment. There he stared hard once more. The Maharajah descended; so did Harold and the Hindu attendant, who was dressed just like him. The man I took for a detective indulged in a frank, long gaze at the unconscious Indian prince, but cast only a hasty eye on the two apparent followers. That touch of revelation relieved my mind a little. I felt convinced the police were watching the Maharajah and myself, as suspicious persons connected with the case; but they had not yet guessed that Harold had disguised himself as one of the two invariable Rajput servants.

We steamed on northward. At Newcastle, the same detective strolled, with his hands in his pockets, along the train once more, and puffed a cigar with the nonchalant air of a sporting gentleman. But I was certain now, from the studious unconcern he was anxious to exhibit, that he must be a spy upon us. He overdid his mood of careless observation. It was too obvious an assumption. Precisely the same thing happened again when we pulled up at Berwick. I knew now that we were watched. It would be impossible for us to get married at Edinburgh if we were thus closely pursued. There was but one chance open; we must leave the train abruptly at the first Scotch stopping station.

The detective knew we were booked through for Edinburgh. So much I could tell, because I saw him make inquiries of the ticket examiner at York, and again at Berwick, and because the ticket-examiner thereupon entered a mental note of the fact as he punched my ticket each time: 'Oh, Edinburgh, miss? All right'; and then stared at me suspiciously. I could tell he had heard of the Ashurst will case. He also lingered long about the Maharajah's compartment, and then went back to confer with the detective. Thus, putting two and two together, as a woman will, I came to the conclusion that the spy did not expect us to leave the train before we reached Edinburgh. That told in our favour. Most men trust much to just such vague expectations. They form a theory, and then neglect the adverse chances. You can only get the better of a skilled detective by taking him thus, psychologically and humanly.

By this time, I confess, I felt almost like a criminal. Never in my life had danger loomed so near—not even when we returned with the Arabs from the oasis. For then we feared for our lives alone; now, we feared for our honour.

I drew a card from my case before we left Berwick station, and scribbled a few hasty words on it in German. 'We are watched. A detective! If we run through to Edinburgh, we shall doubtless be arrested or at least impeded. This train will stop at Dunbar for one minute. Just before it leaves again, get out as quietly as you can—at the last moment. I will also get out and join you. Let Partab go on; it will excite less attention. The scheme I suggest is the only safe plan. If you agree, as soon as we have well started from Berwick, shake your handkerchief unobtrusively out of your carriage window.'

I beckoned a porter noiselessly without one word. The detective was now strolling along the fore-part of the train, with his back turned towards me, peering as he went into all the windows. I gave the porter a shilling. 'Take this to a black gentleman in the next carriage but one,' I said, in a confidential whisper. The porter touched his hat, nodded, smiled, and took it.

Would Harold see the necessity for acting on my advice?—I wondered. I gazed out along the train as soon as we had got well clear of Berwick. A minute—two minutes—three minutes passed; and still no handkerchief. I began to despair. He was debating, no doubt. If he refused, all was lost, and we were disgraced for ever.

At last, after long waiting, as I stared still along the whizzing line, with the smoke in my eyes, and the dust half blinding me, I saw, to my intense relief, a handkerchief flutter. It fluttered once, not markedly, then a black hand withdrew it. Only just in time, for even as it disappeared, the detective's head thrust itself out of a farther window. He was not looking for anything in particular, as far as I could tell—just observing the signals. But it gave me a strange thrill to think even now we were so nearly defeated.

My next trouble was—would the train draw up at Dunbar? The 10 A.M. from King's Cross is not set down to stop there in Bradshaw, for no passengers are booked to or from the station by the day express; but I remembered from of old when I lived at Edinburgh, that it used always to wait about a minute for some engine-driver's purpose. This doubt filled me with fresh fear;

did it draw up there still?—they have accelerated the service so much of late years, and abolished so many old accustomed stoppages. I counted the familiar stations with my breath held back. They seemed so much farther apart than usual. Reston—Grant's House—Cockburnspath—Innerwick.

The next was Dunbar. If we rolled past *that*, then all was lost. We could never get married. I trembled and hugged myself.

The engine screamed. Did that mean she was running through? Oh, how I wished I had learned the interpretation of the signals!

Then gradually, gently, we began to slow. Were we slowing to pass the station only? No; with a jolt she drew up. My heart gave a bound as I read the word 'Dunbar' on the station notice-board.

I rose and waited, with my fingers on the door. Happily it had one of those new-fashioned slip-latches which open from inside. No need to betray myself prematurely to the detective by a hand displayed on the outer handle. I glanced out at him cautiously. His head was thrust through his window, and his sloping shoulders revealed the spy, but he was looking the other way—observing the signals, doubtless, to discover why we stopped at a place not mentioned in Bradshaw.

Harold's face just showed from another window close by. Too soon or too late might either of them be fatal. He glanced inquiry at me. I nodded back, 'Now!' The train gave its first jerk, a faint backward jerk, indicative of the nascent intention of starting. As it braced itself to go on, I jumped out; so did Harold. We faced one another on the platform without a word. 'Stand away, there,' the station-master cried, in an angry voice. The guard waved his green flag. The detective, still absorbed on the signals, never once looked back. One second later, we were safe at Dunbar, and he was speeding away by the express for Edinburgh.

It gave us a breathing space of about an hour.

For half a minute I could not speak. My heart was in my mouth. I hardly even dared to look at Harold. Then the station-master stalked up to us with a threatening manner. 'You can't get out here,' he said, crustily, in a gruff Scotch voice. 'This train is not timed to set down before Edinburgh.'

'We *have* got out,' I answered, taking it upon me to speak for my fellow-culprit, the Hindu—as he was to all seeming. 'The logic of facts is with us. We were booked through to Edinburgh, but we wanted to stop at Dunbar; and as the train happened to pull up, we thought we needn't waste time by going on all that way and then coming back again.'

'Ye should have changed at Berwick,' the station-master said, still gruffly, 'and come on by the slow train.' I could see his careful Scotch soul was vexed (incidentally) at our extravagance in paying the extra fare to Edinburgh and back again.

In spite of agitation, I managed to summon up one of my sweetest smiles—a smile that ere now had melted the hearts of rickshaw coolies and of French *douaniers*. He thawed before it visibly. 'Time was important to us,' I said—oh, he guessed not how important; 'and besides, you know, it is so good for the company!'

'That's true,' he answered, mollified. He could not tilt against the interests of the North British shareholders. 'But how about yer luggage? It'll have gone on to Edinburgh, I'm thinking.'

'We *have* no luggage,' I answered boldly.

He stared at us both, puckered his brow a moment, and then burst out laughing. 'Oh, ay, I see,' he answered, with a comic air of amusement. 'Well, well, it's none of *my* business, no doubt, and I will not interfere with ye; though why a lady like you——' He glanced curiously at Harold.

I saw he had guessed right, and thought it best to throw myself unreservedly on his mercy. Time was indeed important. I glanced at the station clock. It was not very far from the stroke of six, and we must manage to get married before the detective could miss us at Edinburgh, where he was due at 6.30.

So I smiled once more that heart-softening smile. 'We have each our own fancies,' I said, blushing—and, indeed (such is the pride of race among women), I felt myself blush at the bare idea that I was marrying a black man, in spite of our good Maharajah's kindness. 'He is a gentleman, and a man of education and culture.' I thought that recommendation ought to tell with a Scotchman. 'We are in sore straits now, but our case is a just one. Can you tell me who in this place is most likely to sympathise—most likely to marry us?'

He looked at me—and surrendered at discretion. 'I should think anybody would marry ye who saw yer pretty face and heard yer sweet voice,' he answered. 'But, perhaps ye'd better present yerself to Mr. Schoolcraft, the U.P. minister at Little Kirkton. He was aye soft-hearted.'

'How far from here?' I asked.

'About two miles,' he answered.

'Can we get a trap?'

'Oh, ay, there's machines always waiting at the station.'

We interviewed a 'machine,' and drove out to Little Kirkton. There, we told our tale in the fewest words possible to the obliging and good-natured U.P. minister. He looked, as the station-master had said, 'soft-hearted'; but he dashed our hopes to the ground at once by telling us candidly that unless we had had our residence in Scotland for twenty-one days immediately preceding the marriage, it would not be legal. 'If you were Scotch,' he added, 'I could go through the ceremony at once, of course; and then you could apply to the sheriff to-night for leave to register the marriage in proper form afterward; but as one of you is English, and the other I judge'—he smiled and glanced towards Harold—'an Indian-born subject of Her Majesty, it would be impossible for me to do it: the ceremony would be invalid, under Lord Brougham's Act, without previous residence.'

This was a terrible blow. I looked away appealingly. 'Harold,' I cried in despair, 'do you think we could manage to hide ourselves safely anywhere in Scotland for twenty-one days?'

His face fell. 'How could I escape notice? All the world is hunting for me. And then the scandal! No matter where you stopped—however far from me—no, Lois darling, I could never expose you to it.'

The minister glanced from one to the other of us, puzzled. 'Harold?' he said, turning over the word on his tongue. 'Harold? That doesn't sound like an Indian name, does it? And——' he hesitated, 'you speak wonderful English!'

I saw the safest plan was to make a clean breast of it. He looked the sort of man one could trust on an emergency. 'You have heard of the Ashurst will case?' I said, blurting it out suddenly.

'I have seen something about it in the newspapers; yes. But it did not interest me: I have not followed it.'

I told him the whole truth; the case against us—the facts as we knew them. Then I added, slowly, 'This is Mr. Harold Tillington, whom they accuse of forgery. Does he look like a forger? I want to marry him before he is tried. It is the only way by which I can prove my implicit trust in him. As soon as we are married, he will give himself up at once to the police—if you wish it, before your eyes. But married we must be. *Can't* you manage it somehow?' My pleading voice touched him. 'Harold Tillington?' he murmured. 'I know of his forbears. Lady Guinevere Tillington's son, is it not? Then you must be Younger of Gledcliffe.' For Scotland is a village: everyone in it seems to have heard of every other.

'What does he mean?' I asked. 'Younger of Gledcliffe?' I remembered now that the phrase had occurred in Mr. Ashurst's will, though I never understood it.

'A Scotch fashion,' Harold answered. 'The heir to a laird is called Younger of so-and-so. My father has a small estate of that name in Dumfriesshire; a *very* small estate: I was born and brought up there.'

'Then you are a Scotchman?' the minister asked.

'Yes,' Harold answered frankly: 'by remote descent. 'We are trebly of the female line at Gledcliffe; still, I am no doubt more or less Scotch by domicile.'

'Younger of Gledcliffe! Oh, yes, that ought certainly to be quite sufficient for our purpose. Do you live there?'

'I have been living there lately. I always live there when I'm in Britain. It is my only home. I belong to the diplomatic service.'

'But then—the lady?'

'She is unmitigatedly English,' Harold admitted, in a gloomy voice.

'Not quite,' I answered. 'I lived four years in Edinburgh. And I spent my holidays there while I was at Girton. I keep my boxes still at my old rooms in Maitland Street.'

'Oh, that will do,' the minister answered, quite relieved; for it was clear that our anxiety and the touch of romance in our tale had enlisted him in our favour. 'Indeed, now I come to think of it, it suffices for the Act if one only of the parties is domiciled in Scotland. And as Mr. Tillington lives habitually at Gledcliffe, that settles the question. Still, I can do nothing save marry you now by religious service in the presence of my servants—which constitutes what we call an ecclesiastical marriage—it becomes legal if afterwards registered; and then you must apply to the sheriff for a warrant to register it. But I will do what I can; later on, if you like, you can be re-married by the rites of your own Church in England.'

'Are you quite sure our Scotch domicile is good enough in law?' Harold asked, still doubtful.

'I can turn it up, if you wish. I have a legal hand-book. Before Lord Brougham's Act, no formalities were necessary. But the Act was passed to prevent Gretna Green marriages. The usual phrase is that such a marriage does not hold good unless one or other of the parties either has had his or her usual residence in Scotland, or else has lived there for twenty-one days immediately preceding the date of the marriage. If you like, I will wait to consult the authorities.'

'No, thank you,' I cried. 'There is no time to lose. Marry us first, and look it up afterwards. "One or other" will do, it seems. Mr. Tillington is Scotch enough, I am sure; he has no address in Britain but Gledcliffe: we will rest our claim upon that. Even if the marriage turns out invalid, we only remain where we were. This is a preliminary ceremony to prove good faith, and to bind us to one another. We can satisfy the law, if need be, when we return to England.'

The minister called in his wife and servants, and explained to them briefly. He exhorted us and prayed. We gave our solemn consent in legal form before two witnesses. Then he pronounced us duly married. In a quarter of an hour more, we had made declaration to that effect before the sheriff, the witnesses accompanying us, and were formally affirmed to be man and wife before the law of Great Britain. I asked if it would hold in England as well.

'You couldn't be firmer married,' the sheriff said, with decision, 'by the Archbishop of Canterbury in Westminster Abbey.'

Harold turned to the minister. 'Will you send for the police?' he said, calmly. 'I wish to inform them that I am the man for whom they are looking in the Ashurst will case.'

Our own cabman went to fetch them. It was a terrible moment. But Harold sat in the sheriff's study and waited, as if nothing unusual were happening. He talked freely but quietly. Never in my life had I felt so proud of him.

At last the police came, much inflated with the dignity of

so great a capture, and took down our statement. 'Do you give yourself in charge on a confession of forgery?' the superintendent asked, as Harold ended.

'Certainly not,' Harold answered. 'I have not committed forgery. But I do not wish to skulk or hide myself. I understand a warrant is out against me in London. I have come to Scotland, hurriedly, for the sake of getting married, not to escape apprehension. I am here, openly, under my own name. I tell you the facts; 'tis for you to decide; if you choose, you can arrest me.'

The superintendent conferred for some time in another room with the sheriff. Then he returned to the study. 'Very well, sir,' he said, in a respectful tone, 'I arrest you.'

So that was the beginning of our married life. More than ever, I felt sure I could trust in Harold.

The police decided, after hearing by telegram from London, that we must go up at once by the night express, which they stopped for the purpose. They were forced to divide us. I took the sleeping-car; Harold travelled with two constables in an ordinary carriage. Strange to say, notwithstanding all this, so great was our relief from the tension of our flight, that we both slept soundly.

Next morning we arrived in London, Harold guarded. The police had arranged that the case should come up at Bow Street that afternoon. It was not an ideal honeymoon, and yet, I was somehow happy.

At King's Cross, they took him away from me. Still, I hardly cried. All the way up in the train, whenever I was awake, an idea had been haunting me—a possible clue to this trickery of Lord Southminster's. Petty details cropped up and fell into their places. I began to unravel it all now. I had an inkling of a plan to set Harold right again.

The will we had proved——but I must not anticipate.

When we parted, Harold kissed me on the forehead, and murmured rather sadly, 'Now, I suppose it's all up. Lois, I must go. These rogues have been too much for us.'

'Not a bit of it,' I answered, new hope growing stronger and stronger within me. 'I see a way out. I have found a clue. I believe, dear Harold, the right will still be vindicated.'

And red-eyed as I was, I jumped into a hansom, and called to the cabman to drive at once to Lady Georgina's.

CHAPTER XII

THE ADVENTURE OF THE UNPROFESSIONAL DETECTIVE

'Is Lady Georgina at home?' The discreet man-servant in sober black clothes eyed me suspiciously. 'No, miss,' he answered. 'That is to say—no, ma'am. Her ladyship is still at Mr. Marmaduke Ashurst's—the late Mr. Marmaduke Ashurst, I mean—in Park Lane North. You know the number, ma'am?'

'Yes, I know it,' I replied, with a gasp; for this was indeed a triumph. My one fear had been lest Lord Southminster should already have taken possession—why, you will see hereafter; and it relieved me to learn that Lady Georgina was still at hand to guard my husband's interests. She had been living at the house, practically, since her brother's death. I drove round with all speed, and flung myself into my dear old lady's arms.

'Kiss me,' I cried, flushed. 'I am your niece!' But she knew it already, for our movements had been fully reported by this time (with picturesque additions) in the morning papers. Imagination, ill-developed in the English race, seems to concentrate itself in the lower order of journalists.

She kissed me on both cheeks with unwonted tenderness. 'Lois,' she cried, with tears in her eyes, 'you're a brick!' It was not exactly poetical at such a moment, but from her it meant more than much gushing phraseology.

'And you're here in possession!' I murmured.

The Cantankerous Old Lady nodded. She was in her element, I must admit. She dearly loved a row—above all, a family row; but to be in the thick of a family row, and to feel herself in the right, with the law against her—that was joy such as Lady Georgina had seldom before experienced. 'Yes, dear,' she burst out volubly, 'I'm in possession, thank Heaven. And what's more, they won't oust me without a legal process. I've been here, off and on, you know, ever since poor dear Marmy died, looking after things for Harold; and I shall look after them still, till Bertie Southminster succeeds in ejecting me, which won't be easy. Oh, I've held the fort by main force, I can tell you; held it like a Trojan. Bertie's in a precious great hurry to move in, I can see; but I won't allow him. He's been down here this morning, fatuously blustering, and trying to carry the post by storm, with a couple of policemen.'

'Policemen!' I cried. 'To turn you out?'

'Yes, my dear, policemen: but (the Lord be praised) I was too much for him. There are legal formalities to fulfil yet; and I won't budge an inch, Lois, not one inch, my dear, till he's fulfilled every one of them. Mark my words, child, that boy's up to some devilry.'

'He is,' I answered.

'Yes, he wouldn't be in such a rampaging hurry to get in—being as lazy as he's empty-headed—takes after Gwendoline in that—if he hadn't some excellent reason for wishing to take possession: and depend upon it, the reason is that he wants to get hold of something or other that's Harold's. But he sha'n't if I can help it; and, thank my stars, I'm a dour woman to reckon with. If he comes, he comes over my old bones, child. I've been overhauling everything of Marmy's, I can tell you, to checkmate the boy if I can; but I've found nothing yet, and till I've satisfied myself on that point, I'll hold the fort still, if I have to barricade that pasty-faced scoundrel of a nephew of mine out by piling the furniture against the front door—I will, as sure as my name's Georgina Fawley!'

'I know you will, dear,' I assented, kissing her, 'and so I shall venture to leave you, while I go out to institute another little enquiry.'

'What enquiry?'

I shook my head. 'It's only a surmise,' I said, hesitating. 'I'll tell you about it later. I've had time to think while I've been coming back in the train, and I've thought of many things. Mount guard till I return, and mind you don't let Lord Southminster have access to anything.'

'I'll shoot him first, dear.' And I believe she meant it.

I drove on in the same cab to Harold's solicitor. There I laid my fresh doubts at once before him. He rubbed his bony hands. 'You've hit it!' he cried, charmed. 'My dear madam, you've hit it! I never did like that will. I never did like the signatures, the witnesses, the look of it. But what could I do? Mr. Tillington propounded it. Of course it wasn't my business to go dead against my own client.'

'Then you doubted Harold's honour, Mr. Hayes?' I cried, flushing.

'Never!' he answered. 'Never! I felt sure there must be some mistake somewhere, but not any trickery on—your husband's part. Now, *you* supply the right clue. We must look into this, immediately.'

He hurried round with me at once in the same cab to the court. The incriminated will had been 'impounded,' as they call it; but, under certain restrictions, and subject to the closest surveillance, I was allowed to examine it with my husband's solicitor, before the eyes of the authorities. I looked at it long with the naked eye and also with a small pocket lens. The paper, as I had noted before, was the same kind of foolscap as that which I had been in the habit of using at my office in Florence; and the type-writing—was it mine? The longer I looked at it, the more I doubted it.

After a careful examination I turned round to our solicitor. 'Mr. Hayes,' I said, firmly, having arrived at my conclusion, 'this is *not* the document I type-wrote at Florence.'

'How do you know?' he asked. 'A different machine? Some small peculiarity in the shape of the letters?'

'No, the rogue who typed this will was too cunning for that. He didn't allow himself to be foiled by such a scholar's mate. It is written with a Spread Eagle, the same sort of machine precisely as my own. I know the type perfectly. But——' I hesitated.

'But what?'

'Well, it is difficult to explain. There is character in type-writing, just as there is in handwriting, only, of course, not quite so much of it. Every operator is liable to his own peculiar tricks and blunders. If I had some of my own type-written manuscript here to show you, I could soon make that evident.'

'I can easily believe it. Individuality runs through all we do, however seemingly mechanical. But are the points of a sort that you could make clear in court to the satisfaction of a jury?'

'I think so. Look here, for example. Certain letters get habitually mixed up in typewriting; *c* and *v* stand next one another on the keyboard of the machine, and the person who typed this draft sometimes strikes a *c* instead of a *v*, or *vice versâ*. I never do that. The letters I tend to confuse are *s* and *w*, or else *e* and *r*, which also come very near one another in the arbitrary arrangement. Besides, when I type-wrote the original of this will, I made no errors at all; I took such very great pains about it.'

'And this person did make errors?'

'Yes; struck the wrong letter first, and then corrected it often by striking another rather hard on top of it. See, this was a *v* to begin with, and he turned it into a *c*. Besides, the hand that wrote this will is heavier than mine: it comes down *thump, thump, thump*, while mine glides lightly. And the hyphens are used with a space between them, and the character of the punctuation is not exactly as I make it.'

'Still,' Mr. Hayes objected, 'we have nothing but your word. I'm afraid, in such a case, we could never induce a jury to accept your unsupported evidence.'

'I don't want them to accept it,' I answered. 'I am looking this up for my own satisfaction. I want to know, first, who wrote this will. And of one thing I am quite clear: it is *not* the document I drew up for Mr. Ashurst. Just look at that *x*. The *x* alone is conclusive. My type-writer had the upper right-hand stroke of the small *x* badly formed, or broken, while this one is perfect. I remember it well, because I used always to improve all my lower-case *x*'s with a pen when I re-read and corrected. I see their dodge clearly now. It is a most diabolical conspiracy. Instead of forging a will in Lord Southminster's favour, they have substituted a forgery for the real will, and then managed to make my poor Harold prove it.'

'In that case, no doubt, they have destroyed the real one, the original,' Mr. Hayes put in.

'I don't think so,' I answered, after a moment's deliberation. 'From what I know of Mr. Ashurst, I don't believe it is likely he would have left his will about carelessly anywhere. He was a secretive man, fond of mysteries and mystifications. He would be sure to conceal it. Besides, Lady Georgina and Harold have been taking care of everything in the house ever since he died.'

'But,' Mr. Hayes objected, 'the forger of this document, supposing it to be forged, must have had access to the original, since you say the terms of the two are identical; only the signatures are forgeries. And if he saw and copied it, why might he not also have destroyed it?'

A light flashed across me all at once. 'The forger *did* see the original,' I cried, 'but not the fair copy. I have it all now! I detect their trick! It comes back to me vividly! When I had finished typing the copy at Florence from my first rough draft, which I had taken down on the machine before Mr. Ashurst's eyes, I remember now that I threw the original into the waste-paper basket. It must have been there that evening when Higginson called and asked for the will to take it back to Mr. Ashurst. He called for it, no doubt, hoping to open the packet before he delivered it and make a copy of the document for this very purpose. But I refused to let him have it. Before he saw me, however, he had been left by himself for ten minutes in the office; for I remember coming out to him and finding him there alone; and during that ten minutes, being what he is, you may be sure he fished out the rough draft and appropriated it!'

'That is more than likely,' my solicitor nodded. 'You are tracking him to his lair. We shall have him in our power.'

I grew more and more excited as the whole cunning plot unravelled itself mentally step by step before me. 'He must then have gone to Lord Southminster,' I went on, 'and told him of the legacy he expected from Mr. Ashurst. It was five hundred pounds—a mere trifle to Higginson, who plays for thousands. So he must have offered to arrange matters for Lord Southminster if Southminster would consent to make good that sum and a great deal more to him. That odious little cad told me himself on the *Jumna* they were engaged in pulling off "a big *coup*" between them. He thought then I would marry him, and that he would so secure my connivance in his plans; but who would marry such a piece of moist clay? Besides, I could never have taken anyone but Harold.' Then another clue came home to me. 'Mr. Hayes,' I cried, jumping at it, 'Higginson, who forged this will, never saw the real document itself at all; he saw only the draft; for Mr. Ashurst altered one word *viva voce* in the original at the last moment, and I made a pencil note of it on my cuff at the time: and see, it isn't here, though I inserted it in the final clean copy of the will—the word 'especially.' It grows upon me more and more each minute that the real instrument is hidden somewhere in Mr. Ashurst's house—Harold's house—our house; and that *because* it is there Lord Southminster is so indecently anxious to oust his aunt and take instant possession.'

'In that case,' Mr. Hayes remarked, 'we had better go back to Lady Georgina without one minute's delay, and, while she still holds the house, institute a thorough search for it.'

No sooner said than done. We jumped again into our cab and started. As we drove back, Mr. Hayes asked me where I thought we were most likely to find it.

'In a secret drawer in Mr. Ashurst's desk,' I answered, by a flash of instinct, without a second's hesitation.

'How do you know there's a secret drawer?'

'I don't know it. I infer it from my general knowledge of Mr. Ashurst's character. He loved secret drawers, ciphers, cryptograms, mystery-mongering.'

'But it was in that desk that your husband found the forged document,' the lawyer objected.

Once more I had a flash of inspiration or intuition. 'Because White, Mr. Ashurst's valet, had it in readiness in his possession,' I answered, 'and hid it there, in the most obvious and unconcealed place he could find, as soon as the breath was out of his master's body. I remember now Lord Southminster gave himself away to some extent in that matter. The hateful little creature isn't really clever enough, for all his cunning,—and with Higginson to back him,—to mix himself up in such tricks as forgery. He told me at Aden he had had a telegram from 'Marmy's valet,' to report progress; and he received another, the night Mr. Ashurst died, at Moozuffernuggar. Depend upon it, White was more or less in this plot; Higginson left him the forged will when they started for India; and, as soon as Mr. Ashurst died, White hid it where Harold was bound to find it.'

'If so,' Mr. Hayes answered, 'that's well; we have something to go upon. The more of them, the better. There is safety in numbers—for the honest folk. I never knew three rogues hold long together, especially when threatened with a criminal prosecution. Their confederacy breaks down before the chance of punishment. Each tries to screen himself by betraying the others.'

'Higginson was the soul of the plot,' I went on. 'Of that you may be sure. He's a wily old fox, but we'll run him to earth yet. The more I think of it, the more I feel sure, from what I know of Mr. Ashurst's character, he would never have put that will in so exposed a place as the one where Harold says he found it.'

We drew up at the door of the disputed house just in time for the siege. Mr. Hayes and I walked in. We found Lady Georgina face to face with Lord Southminster. The opposing forces were still at the stage of preliminaries of warfare.

'Look heah,' the pea-green young man was observing, in his drawling voice, as we entered; 'it's no use your talking, deah Georgey. This house is mine, and I won't have you meddling with it.'

'This house is not yours, you odious little scamp,' his aunt retorted, raising her shrill voice some notes higher than usual; 'and while I can hold a stick you shall not come inside it.'

'Very well, then; you drive me to hostilities, don't yah know. I'm sorry to show disrespect to your grey hairs—if any—but I shall be obliged to call in the police to eject yah.'

'Call them in if you like,' I answered, interposing between them. 'Go out and get them! Mr. Hayes, while he's gone, send for a carpenter to break open the back of Mr. Ashurst's escritoire.'

'A carpentah?' he cried, turning several degrees whiter than his pasty wont. 'What for? A carpentah?'

I spoke distinctly. 'Because we have reason to believe Mr. Ashurst's real will is concealed in this house in a secret drawer, and because the keys were in the possession of White, whom we believe to be your accomplice in this shallow conspiracy.'

He gasped and looked alarmed. 'No, you don't,' he cried, stepping briskly forward. 'You don't, I tell yah! Break open Marmy's desk! Why, hang it all, it's my property.'

'We shall see about that after we've broken it open,' I answered grimly. 'Here, this screw-driver will do. The back's not strong. Now, your help, Mr. Hayes—one, two, three; we can prise it apart between us.'

Lord Southminster rushed up and tried to prevent us. But Lady Georgina, seizing both wrists, held him tight as in a vice with her dear skinny old hands. He writhed and struggled all in vain: he could not escape her. 'I've often spanked you, Bertie,' she cried, 'and if you attempt to interfere, I'll spank you again; that's the long and the short of it!'

He broke from her and rushed out, to call the police, I believe, and prevent our desecration of pooah Marmy's property.

Inside the first shell were several locked drawers, and two or three open ones, out of one of which Harold had fished the false will. Instinct taught me somehow that the central drawer on the left-hand side was the compartment behind which lay the secret receptacle. I prised it apart and peered about inside it. Presently I saw a slip-panel, which I touched with one finger. The pigeon-hole flew open and disclosed a narrow slit. I clutched at something—the will! Ho, victory! the will! I raised it aloft with a wild shout. Not a doubt of it! The real, the genuine document!

We turned it over and read it. It was my own fair copy, written at Florence, and bearing all the small marks of authenticity about it which I had pointed out to Mr. Hayes as wanting to the forged and impounded document. Fortunately, Lady Georgina and four of the servants had stood by throughout this scene, and had watched our demeanour, as well as Lord Southminster's.

We turned next to the signatures. The principal one was clearly Mr. Ashurst's—I knew it at once—his legible fat hand, 'Marmaduke Courtney Ashurst.' And then the witnesses? They fairly took our breath away.

'Why, Higginson's sister isn't one of them at all,' Mr. Hayes cried, astonished.

A flush of remorse came over me. I saw it all now. I had misjudged that poor woman! She had the misfortune to be a rogue's sister, but, as Harold had said, was herself a most respectable and blameless person. Higginson must have forged her name to the document; that was all; and she had naturally sworn that she never signed it. He knew her honesty. It was a master-stroke of rascality.

'The other one isn't here, either,' I exclaimed, growing more puzzled. 'The waiter at the hotel! Why, that's another forgery! Higginson must have waited till the man was safely dead, and then used him similarly. It was all very clever. Now, who are these people who really witnessed it?'

'The first one,' Mr. Hayes said, examining the handwriting, 'is Sir Roger Bland, the Dorsetshire baronet: he's dead, poor fellow; but he was at Florence at the time, and I can answer for his signature. He was a client of mine, and died at Mentone. The second is Captain Richards, of the Mounted Police: he's living still, but he's away in South Africa.'

'Then they risked his turning up?'

'If they knew who the real witnesses were at all—which is doubtful. You see, as you say, they may have seen the rough draft only.'

'Higginson would know,' I answered. 'He was with Mr. Ashurst at Florence at the time, and he would take good care to keep a watch upon his movements. In my belief, it was he who suggested this whole plot to Lord Southminster.'

'Of course it was,' Lady Georgina put in. 'That's absolutely certain. Bertie's a rogue as well as a fool: but he's too great a fool to invent a clever roguery, and too great a knave not to join in it foolishly when anybody else takes the pains to invent it.'

'And it *was* a clever roguery,' Mr. Hayes interposed. 'An ordinary rascal would have forged a later will in Lord Southminster's favour and run the risk of detection; Higginson had the acuteness to forge a will exactly like the real one, and to let your husband bear the burden of the forgery. It was as sagacious as it was ruthless.'

'The next point,' I said, 'will be for us to prove it.'

At that moment the bell rang, and one of the house-servants—all puzzled by this conflict of interests—came in with a telegram, which he handed me on a salver. I broke it open, without glancing at the envelope. Its contents baffled me: 'My address is Hotel Bristol, Paris; name as usual. Send me a thousand pounds on account at once. I can't afford to wait. No shillyshallying.'

The message was unsigned. For a moment, I couldn't imagine who sent it, or what it was driving at.

Then I took up the envelope. 'Viscount Southminster, 24 Park Lane North, London.'

My heart gave a jump. I saw in a second that chance, or Providence, had delivered the conspirators into my hands that day. The telegram was from Higginson! I had opened it by accident.

It was obvious what had happened. Lord Southminster must have written to him on the result of the trial, and told him he meant to take possession of his uncle's house immediately. Higginson had acted on that hint, and addressed his telegram where he thought it likely Lord Southminster would receive it earliest. I had opened it in error, and that, too, was fortunate, for even in dealing with such a pack of scoundrels, it would never have occurred to me to violate

somebody else's correspondence had I not thought it was addressed
to me. But having arrived at the truth thus unintentionally, I had,
of course, no scruples about making full use of my information.

I showed the despatch at once to Lady Georgina and Mr.
Hayes. They recognised its importance. 'What next?' I inquired.
'Time presses. At half-past three Harold comes up for examination
at Bow Street.'

Mr. Hayes was ready with an apt expedient. 'Ring the bell for
Mr. Ashurst's valet,' he said, quietly. 'The moment has now arrived
when we can begin to set these conspirators by the ears. As soon
as they learn that we know all, they will be eager to inform upon
one another.'

I rang the bell. 'Send up White,' I said. 'We wish to speak to
him.'

The valet stole up, self-accused, a timid, servile creature, rubbing his hands nervously, and suspecting mischief. He was a rat
in trouble. He had thin brown hair, neatly brushed and plastered
down, so as to make it still thinner, and his face was the average
narrow cunning face of the dishonest man-servant. It had an
ounce of wile in it to a pound or two of servility. He seemed just
the sort of rogue meanly to join in an underhand conspiracy, and
then meanly to back out of it. You could read at a glance that his
principle in life was to save his own bacon.

He advanced, fumbling his hands all the time, and smiling
and fawning. 'You wished to see me, sir?' he murmured, in a dep-
recatory voice, looking sideways at Lady Georgina and me, but
addressing the lawyer.

'Yes, White, I wished to see you. I have a question to ask you.
Who put the forged will in Mr. Ashurst's desk? Was it you, or some
other person?'

The question terrified him. He changed colour and gasped. But
he rubbed his hands harder than ever and affected a sickly smile.
'Oh, sir, how should *I* know, sir? *I* had nothing to do with it. I suppose—it was Mr. Tillington.'

Our lawyer pounced upon him like a hawk on a titmouse.
'Don't prevaricate with me, sir,' he said, sternly. 'If you do, it may
be worse for you. This case has assumed quite another aspect. It
is you and your associates who will be placed in the dock, not Mr.

Tillington. You had better speak the truth; it is your one chance, I warn you. Lie to me, and instead of calling you as a witness for our case, I shall include you in the indictment.'

White looked down uneasily at his shoes, and cowered. 'Oh, sir, I don't understand you.'

'Yes you do. You understand me, and you know I mean it. Wriggling is useless; we intend to prosecute. We have unravelled this vile plot. We know the whole truth. Higginson and Lord Southminster forged a will between them——'

'Oh, sir, *not* Lord Southminster! His lordship, I'm sure——'

Mr. Hayes's keen eye had noted the subtle shade of distinction and admission. But he said nothing openly. 'Well, then, Higginson forged, and Lord Southminster accepted, a false will, which purported to be Mr. Marmaduke Ashurst's. Now, follow me clearly. That will could not have been put into the escritoire during Mr. Ashurst's life, for there would have been risk of his discovering it. It must, therefore, have been put there afterward. The moment he was dead, you, or somebody else with your consent and connivance, slipped it into the escritoire; and you afterwards showed Mr. Tillington the place where you had set it or seen it set, leading him to believe it was Mr. Ashurst's will, and so involved him in all this trouble. Note that that was a felonious act. We accuse you of felony. Do you mean to confess, and give evidence on our behalf, or will you force me to send for a policeman to arrest you?'

The cur hesitated still. 'Oh, sir,' drawing back, and fumbling his hands on his breast, 'you don't mean it.'

Mr. Hayes was prompt. 'Hesslegrave, go for a policeman.'

That curt sentence brought the rogue on his marrow-bones at once. He clasped his hands and debated inwardly. 'If I tell you all I know,' he said, at last, looking about him with an air of abject terror, as if he thought Lord Southminster or Higginson would hear him, 'will you promise not to prosecute me?' His tone became insinuating. 'For a hundred pounds I could find the real will for you. You'd better close with me. To-day is the last chance. As soon as his lordship comes in, he'll hunt it up and destroy it.'

I flourished it before him, and pointed with one hand to the broken desk, which he had not yet observed in his craven agitation.

'We do not need your aid,' I answered. 'We have found the will, ourselves. Thanks to Lady Georgina, it is safe till this minute.'

'And to me,' he put in, cringing, and trying after his kind to curry favour with the winners at the last moment. 'It's all *my* doing, my lady! I wouldn't destroy it. His lordship offered me a hundred pounds more to break open the back of the desk at night, while your ladyship was asleep, and burn the thing quietly. But I told him he might do his own dirty work if he wanted it done. It wasn't good enough while your ladyship was here in possession. Besides, I wanted the right will preserved, for I thought things might turn up so; and I wouldn't stand by and see a gentleman like Mr. Tillington, as has always behaved well to me, deprived of his inheritance.'

'Which is why you conspired with Lord Southminster to rob him of it, and to send him to prison for Higginson's crime,' I interposed calmly.

'Then you confess you put the forged will there?' Mr. Hayes said, getting to business.

White looked about him helplessly. He missed his headpiece, the instigator of the plot. 'Well, it was like this, my lady,' he began, turning to Lady Georgina, and wriggling to gain time. 'You see, his lordship and Mr. Higginson——' he twirled his thumbs and tried to invent something plausible.

Lady Georgina swooped. 'No rigmarole!' she said, sharply. 'Do you confess you put it there or do you not—reptile?' Her vehemence startled him.

'Yes, I confess I put it there,' he said at last, blinking. 'As soon as the breath was out of Mr. Ashurst's body I put it there.' He began to whimper. 'I'm a poor man with a wife and family, sir,' he went on, 'though in Mr. Ashurst's time I always kep' that quiet; and his lordship offered to pay me well for the job; and when you're paid well for a job yourself, sir——'

Mr. Hayes waved him off with one imperious hand. 'Sit down in the corner there, man, and don't move or utter another word,' he said, sternly, 'until I order you. You will be in time still for me to produce at Bow Street.'

Just at that moment, Lord Southminster swaggered back, accompanied by a couple of unwilling policemen. 'Oh, I say,' he cried, bursting in and staring around him, jubilant. 'Look heah, Georgey, *are* you going quietly, or must I ask these coppahs to evict you?' He was wreathed in smiles now, and had evidently been fortifying himself with brandies and soda.

Lady Georgina rose in her wrath. 'Yes, I'll go if you wish it, Bertie,' she answered, with calm irony. 'I'll leave the house as soon as you like—for the present—till we come back again with Harold and *his* policemen to evict you. This house is Harold's. Your game is played, boy.' She spoke slowly. 'We have found the other will— we have discovered Higginson's present address in Paris—and we know from White how he and you arranged this little conspiracy.'

She rapped out each clause in this last accusing sentence with deliberate effect, like so many pistol-shots. Each bullet hit home. The pea-green young man, drawing back and staring, stroked his shadowy moustache with feeble fingers in undisguised astonishment. Then he dropped into a chair and fixed his gaze blankly on Lady Georgina. 'Well, this is a fair knock-out,' he ejaculated, fatuously disconcerted. 'I wish Higginson was heah. I really don't quite know what to do without him. That fellah had squared it all up so neatly, don't yah know, that I thought there couldn't be any sort of hitch in the proceedings.'

'You reckoned without Lois,' Lady Georgina said, calmly.

'Ah, Miss Cayley—that's true. I mean, Mrs. Tillington. Yaas, yaas, I know, she's a doosid clevah person—for a woman—now isn't she?'

It was impossible to take this flabby creature seriously, even as a criminal. Lady Georgina's lips relaxed. 'Doosid clever,' she admitted, looking at me almost tenderly.

'But not quite so clevah, don't yah know, as Higginson!'

'There you make your blooming little erraw,' Mr. Hayes burst in, adopting one of Lord Southminster's favourite witticisms—the sort of witticism that improves, like poetry, by frequent repetition. 'Policemen, you may go into the next room and wait; this is a family affair; we have no immediate need of you.'

'Oh, certainly,' Lord Southminster echoed, much relieved. 'Very propah sentiment! Most undesirable that the constables should mix themselves up in a family mattah like this. Not the place for inferiahs!'

'Then why introduce them?' Lady Georgina burst out, turning on him.

He smiled his fatuous smile. 'That's just what I say,' he answered. 'Why the jooce introduce them? But don't snap my head off!'

The policemen withdrew respectfully, glad to be relieved of this unpleasant business, where they could gain no credit, and might possibly involve themselves in a charge of assault. Lord Southminster rose with a benevolent grin, and looked about him pleasantly. The brandies and soda had endowed him with irrepressible cheerfulness.

'Well?' Lady Georgina muttered.

'Well, I think I'll leave now, Georgey. You've trumped my ace, yah know. Nasty trick of White to go and round on a fellah. I don't like the turn this business is taking. Seems to me, the only way I have left to get out of it is—to turn Queen's evidence.'

Lady Georgina planted herself firmly against the door. 'Bertie,' she cried, 'no, you don't—not till we've got what we want out of you!'

He gazed at her blandly. His face broke once more into an imbecile smile. 'You were always a rough 'un, Georgey. Your hand did sting! Well, what do you want now? We've each played our cards, and you needn't cut up rusty over it—especially when you're winning! Hang it all, I wish I had Higginson heah to tackle you!'

'If you go to see the Treasury people, or the Solicitor-General, or the Public Prosecutor, or whoever else it may be,' Lady Georgina said, stoutly, 'Mr. Hayes must go with you. We've trumped your ace, as you say, and we mean to take advantage of it. And then you must trundle yourself down to Bow Street afterwards, confess the whole truth, and set Harold at liberty.'

'Oh, I say now, Georgey! The whole truth! the whole blooming truth! That's really what I call humiliating a fellah!'

'If you don't, we arrest you this minute—fourteen years' imprisonment!'

'Fourteen yeahs?' He wiped his forehead. 'Oh, I say! How doosid uncomfortable! I was nevah much good at doing anything by the sweat of my brow. I ought to have lived in the Garden of Eden. Georgey, you're hard on a chap when he's down on his luck.

It would be confounded cruel to send me to fourteen yeahs at Portland.'

'You would have sent my husband to it,' I broke in, angrily, confronting him.

'What? You too, Miss Cayley?—I mean Mrs. Tillington. Don't look at me like that. Tigahs aren't in it.'

His jauntiness disarmed us. However wicked he might be, one felt it would be ridiculous to imprison this schoolboy. A sound flogging and a month's deprivation of wine and cigarettes was the obvious punishment designed for him by nature.

'You must go down to the police-court and confess this whole conspiracy,' Lady Georgina went on after a pause, as sternly as she was able. 'I prefer, if we can, to save the family—even you, Bertie. But I can't any longer save the family honour—I can only save Harold's. You must help me to do that; and then, you must give me your solemn promise—in writing—to leave England for ever, and go to live in South Africa.'

He stroked the invisible moustache more nervously than before. That penalty came home to him. 'What, leave England for evah? Newmarket—Ascot—the club—the music-halls!'

'Or fourteen years' imprisonment!'

'Georgey, you spank as hard as evah!'

'Decide at once, or we arrest you!'

He glanced about him feebly. I could see he was longing for his lost confederate. 'Well, I'll go,' he said at last, sobering down; 'and your solicitaw can trot round with me. I'll do all that you wish, though I call it most unfriendly. Hang it all, fourteen yeahs would be so beastly unpleasant!'

We drove forthwith to the proper authorities, who, on hearing the facts, at once arranged to accept Lord Southminster and White as Queen's evidence, neither being the actual forger. We also telegraphed to Paris to have Higginson arrested, Lord Southminster giving us up his assumed name with the utmost cheerfulness, and without one moment's compunction. Mr. Hayes was quite right: each conspirator was only too ready to save himself by betraying his fellows. Then we drove on to Bow Street (Lord Southminster consoling himself with a cigarette on the way), just in time for Harold's case, which was to be taken, by special arrangement, at 3.30.

A very few minutes sufficed to turn the tables completely on the conspirators. Harold was discharged, and a warrant was issued for the arrest of Higginson, the actual forger. He had drawn up the false will and signed it with Mr. Ashurst's name, after which he had presented it for Lord Southminster's approval. The pea-green young man told his tale with engaging frankness. 'Bertie's a simple Simon,' Lady Georgina commented to me; 'but he's also a rogue; and Higginson saw his way to make excellent capital of him in both capacities—first use him as a catspaw, and then blackmail him.'

On the steps of the police-court, as we emerged triumphantly, Lord Southminster met us—still radiant as ever. He seemed wholly unaware of the depths of his iniquity: a fresh dose of brandy had restored his composure. 'Look heah,' he said, 'Harold, your wife has bested me! Jolly good thing for you that you managed to get hold of such a clevah woman! If you hadn't, deah boy, you'd have found yourself in Queeah Street! But I say, Lois—I call yah Lois because you're my cousin now, yah know—you were backing the wrong man aftah all, as I told yah. For if you'd backed *me*, all this wouldn't have come out; you'd have got the tin and been a countess as well, aftah the governah's dead and gone, don't yah see. You'd have landed the double event. So you'd have pulled off a bettah thing for yourself in the end, as I said, if you'd laid your bottom dollah on me for winnah!'

Higginson is now doing fourteen years at Portland; Harold and I are happy in the sweetest place in Gloucestershire; and Lord Southminster, blissfully unaware of the contempt with which the rest of the world regards him, is shooting big game among his 'boys' in South Africa. Indeed, he bears so little malice that he sent us a present of a trophy of horns for our hall last winter.

THE END

Printed in the United Kingdom
by Lightning Source UK Ltd.
134038UK00001B/66/P